P9-DVT-423

THE
HOUSE
ON
SUGARBUSH
ROAD

Méira Cook

ENFIELD
&WIZENTY

Enfield & Wizenty
(an imprint of Great Plains Publications)
345-955 Portage Avenue
Winnipeg, MB R3G OP9
www.greatplains.mb.ca

Great Plains Publications gratefully acknowledges the financial support provided for its publishing program by the Government of Canada through the Canada Book Fund; the Canada Council for the Arts; the Province of Manitoba through the Book Publishing Tax Credit and the Book Publisher Marketing Assistance Program; and the Manitoba Arts Council.

Design & Typography by Relish New Brand Experience Inc.
Printed in Canada by Friesens
First Edition

LIBRARY AND ARCHIVES CANADA CATALOGUING IN PUBLICATION

Cook, Méira, 1964-
    The house on Sugarbush Road / Méira Cook.

Issued also in electronic formats.
ISBN 978-1-926531-30-4

    I. Title.

PS8555.O567H69 2012   C813'.54   C2012-903581-5

FSC
www.fsc.org

MIX
Paper from
responsible sources
FSC® C016245

ENVIRONMENTAL BENEFITS STATEMENT

Great Plains Publications saved the following resources by printing the pages of this book on chlorine free paper made with 100% post-consumer waste.

TREES	WATER	ENERGY	SOLID WASTE	GREENHOUSE GASES
9	4,088	3	259	907
FULLY GROWN	GALLONS	MILLION BTUs	POUNDS	POUNDS

Environmental impact estimates were made using the Environmental Paper Network Paper Calculator. For more information visit www.papercalculator.org.

To Mark

THE HOUSE OF BEAUTY MAPULE

Isaac Mapule
Deceased

Beauty Mapule

Hosiah Mopede
Second husband

Gcina Mopede

Givvie Mopede
Murdered

Dhlamina Mopede
Beauty's stepdaughter

Unmentionable Woman,
"that skaberash"
Deserted

Lucky Mapule

Siemela Mapule
née iMofutsi
Second wife

Rothman

A boy, name of Luther

A girl, name of Louisa

THE HOUSE OF DU PLESSIS

Ouma du Plessis — Groot Oupa du Plessis

Lourens "Meneer" du Plessis

Magda Moffert
née du Plessis

Johannes Moffert

Ilse du Plessis
née Marais

Benjamin du Plessis

3 daughters, 3 sons-in-law,
many grandchildren

1

GIVEN

Whenever she grew angry thinking of Lucky's neglect, Beauty Mapule reminded herself that he was her boy, her first-born, her lucky charm. Only she wished he would send money for Rothman now and again. No, she wasn't angry but she was sad through to her bones even though she must hide this sadness from the world. Always and wherever she was, even here in this late-night winter kitchen, Beauty dragged her sad anger around her as if it was a goose down quilt, pulling it across her shoulders and over her head, blocking out the world in soft hisses and drifting feathers. Yes, anger was always soft like this, a punch in the stomach with no strength behind it. A kiss on the lips from someone who was about to leave you.

Mostly Beauty wore herself out with the anger that curved her spine into the bridge between yesterday and tomorrow. But today, *tcha*, today she was too tired. Why always this sadness soft as marrow inside the bones of her anger? Nights when she couldn't sleep, in the cross-hatching of bird sounds before dawn, Beauty knew that it was because the child's ghost wouldn't come to her. Why did Givvie, her love-one, her daughter, the ghost she longed for with all her heart remain locked on the other side?

Nightly, Beauty turned her thoughts to milk in an effort to draw Givvie out of hiding and into the garden, across the threshold and up the stairs. But to her shame, her daughter remained hidden. There was nothing she could offer that Givvie wanted enough to cross over for. Not love, not pity nourishing as a saucer of milk. Not her mother's grief or tears and not the blood-recognition of one who'd held her baby head cupped in the palm of her hand and who missed her more every day that she was gone.

The plain truth of it was that neither of her natural children came to call anymore. Not Lucky whose fancy wife Siemela was heavy again and who didn't approve of her mother-in-law being an ousie, a domestic. And not Givvie who had died too far from home to find her way back, perhaps, and all the milk in the world, all the honey in the voice and love in the heart could not coax her.

Once, on her way home to visit Mamma Thlali and Rothman, Beauty had glimpsed, from the window of the rural bus, a woman with a plastic bucket struggling along a sand road. Of course there were many such women, such roads, such buckets—first empty then filled with water, with cow's milk, goat's—but for a moment before the bus passed this one, engulfing her in a billow of dust, the fatigue of the two women, walker and onlooker, seemed briefly to coincide. Same road she must take every day, imagined Beauty, and then another day, and then another. At the end of her life, a day a day a day.

Beauty understood such weariness better than most. The long road, the empty bucket.

You called her Given, that was the first mistake, Mamma Thlali said the day Beauty came from identifying the body.

Mamma Thlali, said Beauty, I do not wish to hear from you on this matter.

Call a child Given, said Mamma Thlali, expect her to be Taken.

Then Beauty's anger boiled over and she grasped the handle of the saucepan and threw the cooking oil at Mamma Thlali. It was fortunate that neither woman had thought to light the Primus all day and the oil was cool but Mamma Thlali shrieked as if scalded and shortly after fell silent or perhaps Beauty had merely ceased to hear. Dhlamina Mopede, Beauty's stepdaughter from Hosiah, put her arms around Beauty but she scarcely felt her. At this time a great darkness fell over Beauty and she neither noticed the men who congregated to consult in the shade nor heard the women who came to grieve with her and console her. For days Beauty squatted on the dirt floor of the shanty in Hammanskraal, rocking backwards and forwards in the dark. Days.

Time passed as slowly as a cloud picking over the uneven stubble of the veld grasses. Outside, the sky was a hard-edged, thick blue. The sky was an upturned plastic bowl trapping the shantytown. Tick tick tick, the landscape contracted beneath this sky, tick tick tick, like a tin roof expanding in the midday sun, like the rattle of sparrow claws on gravel. All day Beauty crouched watching a flinching square of light fall through the window, inch down the wall, across the floor and up the opposite wall.

Then it was night.

During the day she counted dust motes, the summer geckos clinging to the heat inside the roof, pinpoints of light shining through empty nail holes in the corrugated iron of Mamma Thlali's walls. Colours of the earth: red dust of Hammanskraal. Black loam of summer gardens, grey clay of winter gardens. Ochre fallow of the veld. Ochre fallow picked out in smoking charcoal stubble. Cool green lucerne fields from the train window, chrome yellow of mustard seed and canola from the rural bus. Red blood against red earth. One dry as dust, one wet as leaking life. How one sank into the other leaving a darkening trail.

All this counting gave Beauty an appetite for precision until, one day, she tried to count the soft pulses at her wrist only to discover that they had disappeared.

The police wouldn't return the bodies. It was during the worst of the Emergency and any funeral was likely to provoke what Sergeant Viljoen—clearing the thorns from his throat, *gragh-gragh*—was sorry to call a Political Incident. Mamma Thlali went to wait with the other mothers and daughters, sisters and wives, outside the police compound in the greasy rain. Beauty remained in the rocking darkness, feeling for her lost pulse without anxiety or hopefulness.

In the end it was Ilse who came to find her. Well, Meneer actually but Ilse sent him.

Meneer arrived one day in his black Mercedes with the diplomatic plates dusty from the road and the effort of the incline. When the driver halted, the car was immediately surrounded by children who'd never seen a Mercedes close up, let alone a white man. From her squatting doorway Beauty watched as the driver, a Xhosa with tribal scars incised upon his cheekbones, scrambled to assist his master from the car but Meneer was already picking his way around scrawny chickens, garbage, children. A goat, udders hanging too far down. Flies, their wings, their choral buzz that was the sound of that exact hour of the morning and the veld and the angle of the sun, the glare.

Meneer picked his way past shanties of sheet metal or rusty corrugated iron, their tin roofs held down by rocks and tires, a full-grown pumpkin or two. Meneer wore a black suit same colour as the car, same shine. Hunching a little as if to say *excuse me, excuse me,* Meneer paused to ask a woman for directions then followed her pointing finger to the shack where Beauty huddled in the dark, one hand to her wrist.

Meneer in his suit the colour of the Mercedes, his tie, in his top pocket a hanky little-bit creased, not like when Beauty managed the ironing. At his wrists heavy gold protea studs pinning the cuffs together. On his feet the shoes were polished so hard that Beauty winced from the glare. All this Beauty noticed, all at once—suit, tie, hanky, the gold points at his wrists, bright shoes—all this she noticed and the darkness, one-two-three, was gone. Stooping to enter the shack Meneer crouched on his haunches opposite her. *Ahem-hem.*

Meneer was at his ease despite the stench of refuse from the village dump, the stink of windborne sewage from open-air latrines, the children jostling in the doorway with their wide crusty eyes and streaming nostrils.

Ilse and I, Meneer took her arm, we want to help.

Fifteen were killed altogether, he continued since Beauty remained silent. How was Givvie involved in all this trouble?

Beauty tried to speak, tried, but only a small cracked sound—*caw-caw*—emerged from her throat. A crow choking on dead flesh at the side of the road. Mamma Thlali hastened to stand beside her but the Mamma only knew a little Afrikaans, no English. In what words she could muster Mamma Thlali tried to explain:

The child was caught in the middle. She was walking home from the Retief School. The other children, also, they were walking home.

Also. Suddenly the pass-breakers and the police were in the middle of the road. The children caught fright, they tried to run through the stones and the bullets.

Outside, a woman's pitched voice could be heard raised in ululation. Other voices joined in until the air was thick with communal mourning. Meneer looked at Beauty, her bowed head. He wanted to say he was sorry; he wanted to ease her pain, to tell her that the Good Lord, that the Lord—*Ag, hemel!* Meneer spread his hands, palms open.

Tell me what I can do to help.

Beauty opened her mouth.

Caw, came out. *Caw-Caw.*

So Mamma Thlali must tell Meneer the story. How Sergeant Viljoen was saying that all the bodies had to be buried together, the one on top of the other, in the municipal plot. How there was to be no funeral, no rites, no prayers. How the mothers could not get permission to wash the bodies or to watch over them, to consign the young ones to the care of the ancestors.

In her agitation Mamma Thlali pulled at the copper wire she'd threaded through her ear holes, yanking until she drew blood, the blood trickling down warm and quick into her collar. And as she spoke she counted off the articles of dismissal on her fingers: how the mothers could neither get permission to wash the little bodies, nor to watch over them, nor even to will the dear ones to the watchfulness of their ancestors.

Meneer listened and nodded, clicked his pen and wrote in his notebook, *yes-yes, and the Sergeant says this interment will be when?* After he had written a letter to himself in this very notebook, Meneer asked Mamma Thlali to come to the morgue with him. Then Meneer clicked his fingers and the Xhosa who was leaning against the car so the children wouldn't come too close, hurried over to load Mamma Thlali into the back seat.

Then only Beauty was left at her threshold with the pariah dogs that nobody owned panting out their thirst in the shade that moved so swiftly over the course of a morning that the dogs seemed always to be scrambling after the broken bits of shadow thrown down by acacia and fever trees. On such a day even the wind seemed to pant, each breath stale and fusty, stinking of dung and mould and waste. Dust and dust and dust.

All afternoon, Beauty wandered amongst the specters of the recent dead, those who had died with the violent instruments of their various deaths fresh upon them. Those burnt by fire or drowned in water. Crash victims wearing bent fenders as crowns, broken metal and shattered glass about their twisted bodies; spies and those thought to be spies, traitors and those deemed traitorous bearing necklaces of tire, pendants of flame, trailing thick black smoke in their wakes. Suicides holding their ropes, their rifles, their poison; the murdered with their gaping wounds, their broken bones, their gaping, broken hearts.

But of those children forever running, forever falling, as they faded into the forever vanishing distance — of those children, there was neither sight nor sound.

Much later that evening the travellers returned, a fresh layer of red dust coating the Mercedes. Beauty heard the rough hitch of tires on the dirt road long before the headlights swung through the valley and into the shantytown. When the motor halted Mamma Thlali climbed out breathing heavily. She looked tired, as if she had been breaking the law all day with her bare hands. Meneer was also weary, his eyes hollow and sunk in their sockets. This Beauty noticed and also the little vein in his cheek that jumped when he blinked.

Meneer told the Xhosa driver to *hekelemanzi* and together the two men lifted a wooden coffin out of the car. Here, said Meneer, handing the other one a shovel and he showed him where he must make haste to dig. That night Meneer and the driver, name of Gili Zikalala, together with Mamma Thlali and Dhlamina, watching, and Beauty, helping, dug a grave for the coffin in the veld behind the hut. When the moon lay swollen above the eastern horizon they lowered the small coffin into the grave and, taking turns with the shovel but Beauty first, covered it over with earth. Just before the first shovelful of red dirt fell, *ko ko ko*, onto the bare pine Meneer signed Gili Zikalala he must pull off his driver's cap. Taking his Bible from the car, Meneer stood at the raw grave and read The Lord is My Shepherd and Mamma Thlali sang Hallelujah Hallelujah He Will Come. But Beauty neither sang nor prayed nor even did she clear her throat to say Amen when Meneer had commenced walking with the Lord through the Valley of the Shadow of Death.

When the little grave was covered over with earth, when Beauty on her hands and knees had patted the earth closed, when the Xhosa had cleaned the shovel and backed away, then Mamma Thlali cleared her throat.

Thank you, she said to Meneer and she cupped both hands together in front of her as she said this and bowed her head to indicate that a true service had been done her family. For in this way, with cupped hands and a bowed head, a child thanks an adult for some great favour out of her reach. Mamma Thlali who was even then an old woman and learned in the ancestral ways, wished to show Meneer that before him she was a grateful child.

Then Mamma Thlali turned to Beauty and in the Zulu language of her mother's people said, We have covered the sleeping child with blankets for the night.

And she said, The time for mourning is over because the child is asleep, *sinjalo thina maZulu.* We Zulus are like that.

Goodnight my mother.

Stay safe, my child.

After that Beauty felt eased and she allowed Meneer to help her up off her knees.

Much later they would commemorate the child and all the fallen with a funeral wake sponsored by Meneer in which an ox was slaughtered and roasted on the spit. Mutton and beetroot was served and samp and beans, roasted mielies, pumpkin, and ginger beer. And although lager was offered no one got drunk and there was much somber wiping of eyes amongst the men, frank weeping and ululating amongst the women, when an elder asked the people to remember all who had been murdered but especially the children, these children who would be present at all gatherings and so they must make a place for them at their tables always. But this feast in which Beauty would sit straight-backed and silent with Mamma Thlali to her right, this feast was still to come.

Goodnight my mother.

Stay safe, my child.

But the child wasn't asleep she was dead and Mamma Thlali and Dhlamina and Rothman were alive and needed to eat and even if she, Beauty, was neither hungry nor even truly alive anymore she was the only one able to feed them. So when the black Mercedes turned around in the dust that night and made its way hesitantly down the dark roads towards the beaded highway far below, Beauty was sitting in the back seat, her doek tied neatly, her hands silent in her lap. Inside the car the engine meshed easily with the gears, the tires rolled smoothly over tarmac. From where Beauty sat she could see the rolls at the back of the Xhosa's head, smooth and thick. Meneer turned around to ask if she had remembered to bring everything she required and she nodded, clutching her handbag.

No, she had left nothing behind.

Ah, but she'd left someone behind that day. Not Givvie who was dead and at peace, perhaps, but too shocked by those days in the cold mortuary to ever come back. Not Mamma Thlali or Dhlamina or Rothman (the one too old, the others too young to leave home) but herself, Beauty, the woman who had knelt in the dark all those days and who knelt there still no matter how quickly or how silently they sped away from her in the big ministerial Mercedes with the diplomatic plates.

And where were they going by means of such silent, air-conditioned speed? Only another couple of hours, said Meneer, turning his head to reassure Beauty that she mustn't worry, they would soon be in the city.

Never in her life had Beauty travelled so swiftly. Whenever she visited Mamma Thlali on the land it took a day by train and then there was the rural bus after that. Now she could barely catch sight of the dry grasses and trees, the leached rocks of the land around Hammanskraal glimpsed between power lines that stretched out into the distance, dipping and rising with the road. Hwhap! went the telephone poles that seemed to fall like skittles in the Mercedes' tailwind — hwhap, hwhap, hwhap.

To accustom herself to the momentum her life had gathered and to turn her thoughts away from her child that they had planted between the mielie stalks, Beauty imagined instead the room she would soon enter without knocking, her own bedroom in the servant's quarters behind the house on Sugarbush Road. Ilse had given her a key to this room that she kept in the coin compartment of her worn purse inside the large all-purpose handbag which reposed, ungainly and stuffed to capacity, between her feet on the humming, carpeted floor of the Mercedes that was purring its way southwards to the city.

Closing her eyes, lowering her aching head to the leather headrest, Beauty tried to picture the room that she would shortly enter by way of this very key whose outline against the plastic of her coin purse was as familiar as the iron bed hoisted on bricks to guard against the tokoloshe, maybe he would come, and the cockroaches and ants and mole crickets, for sure they would come. Beneath the bed was a cardboard suitcase and a zinc bath scuffed with rust spots and the bed itself was shoved up against the wall, right up. In addition, Beauty had hung a Basuto blanket around the outside of the bed on a shower rail that stretched from one wall to the other. Such an arrangement afforded a small measure of privacy and protected the sleeper from various bad dreams and evil spirits winging their way through the dark suburban night. Her bedside table was a tomato crate overturned and covered with a length of hand-stitched cloth.

Closing her eyes, Beauty tried to remember what was placed on this table. A Sotho Bible book-marked with the yellowed strip of paper upon which, long ago, Hosiah Mopede had written the poem that began *She walks in Beauty like the Night Something-Something*. Yes, this Bible and a plastic flashlight, a handful of thick, fluted kitchen candles and a box of matches. The shiny alarm clock that Meneer had given her so she could wake up early to make tea for everyone and sweep out the kitchen. On wire hangers in the wardrobe hung her neatly ironed overalls, pink and peach, matching doeks stuffed into the apron pockets. Also a hand-embroidered ceremonial robe, white with luxurious blue borders and a gold badge embossed with her name, pinned to a rectangle of green, to remind her of the days when she'd danced in the veld on Thursday afternoons with Hosiah Mopede, first preacher of Zion Church of Christ.

Last month the new gardener, Agremon, had put up a corner shelf for her and on this shelf she stored her supplies: packages of maize meal, stacked tins of Star Pilchards, spills of salt, tins of condensed milk that she collected for Givvie. Used to. On the wall a calendar from the Zoo Lake butchery, pictures torn from the fashion magazines that Ilse threw out. A snapshot of a woman standing in front of a shack with her arm around a little girl. The woman had a blurred smile on her face and the little girl's bare feet drummed in the dust, rubbing the veld bald.

2

THE HOUSE ON SUGARBUSH ROAD

From his second storey bedroom in the house on Sugarbush Road Benjamin du Plessis looked up at the hazy sky. Behind his eyes he felt the tight sunrise of a growing tension headache. Balancing his spectacles on top of his head he massaged the flesh between his eyes, yawning to ease his temples.

Far above the roofs of the suburbs an arterial road arrowed off into the middle distance where the gleam of car metal and windshield flashed light. In the garden below him a couple of hadedas broke from the mangy winter pelt, huffing themselves clumsily, raucously, skywards. Startled, Benjamin retreated indoors, yawning, to gulp the cup of black coffee that Beauty had dumped on his night stand. Today she'd even managed to spill most of it. Half in the cup, half in the saucer. A reproach in the form of wry mouthfuls of spite and muddy grounds.

Benjamin gazed at the little puddle of coffee that was already warping the pages of the medical article he'd been reading and thought that perhaps this was Beauty's way of mourning. Shame, she missed his mother as who did not. Ilse du Plessis, the glamorous, the charming Ilse had died two years ago but there was no one—no one in the whole city, he sometimes thought—who'd forgotten her winsome ways. Wherever he went, whenever he introduced himself, someone or other would say, *Not Ilse's boy, are you?* Oh of course they would recall his father, Lourens du Plessis whom everyone had called Meneer and who had been a politician and always in the news, but it was on the subject of Ilse that their eyes would sparkle and their tongues quicken. *Do you remember when she...and that frock she wore, my Lord!* And someone would always interrupt at this point: *You won't remember me, of course, my boy, but I knew you when you were this high!*

It was strange, Benjamin sometimes thought, that his father who had been a man of such painstakingly good intentions was so often overlooked. But, finally, an elder statesman, he'd been a mere handshake from the honours he so richly deserved and the seat in Mandela's new government was his for the taking. For a day or two, a week perhaps, he'd seemed to be on the verge of enjoying the fruits of a lifetime of earnest labour and not even his political opponents could begrudge him his just reward. And then it was all over; a motor vehicle collision on the way to a gala event, both du Plessis, Meneer and Ilse, killed on impact although the driver of the other vehicle had survived to repent his hangover in peace. *Humba Khale!* The newspaper headlines cried out on the day of his father's funeral, *Go in Peace Old Comrade!* And the outpouring of grief was sincere and sustained but the fact remained that whenever he introduced himself someone would be sure to exclaim, *Not Ilse's boy, are you?* And then, as likely as not, would come the reminiscences of the parties, the wonderful galas and luncheons and receptions at that beautiful old house on Sugarbush Road. *You might not remember, my boy, you were only this high after all, but an old house in Parktown North. Beautiful oak door, high ceilings, and a garden made for afternoon cricket. What? You don't say?*

He could hardly credit it himself, of course, so it didn't surprise him that others were astonished to hear that he still lived in the house on Sugarbush Road although it would be more accurate to say that he'd come back. Come home again. He'd received news of the accident while overseas enjoying a medical residency with no immediate plans to return, perhaps ever. But return he did, helter skelter, to a country in mourning and his old room in the old house on the same old street. Railway train curtains at the windows, his ham radio in pieces on the window sill. Beauty presiding and his grief-stricken Ouma barely able to stand upright at the graves of the son and daughter-in-law she'd lived with for years and who should never have preceded her into the dark hereafter.

Well what could he do? He'd come home, of course. And two years later here he was still, the reluctant master of the house on Sugarbush

Road caught between a past so radiant it illuminated the present and a future he couldn't even begin to imagine. But somebody had to look after Ouma, didn't they, he rationalized to himself and he could hardly put Beauty out on the street. She'd worked for his family for some thirty years, after all, and she hadn't always been such an old battleaxe with her scowls and her carps and her early morning burnt offerings of caffeine and slopped malice.

Benjamin sighed, drank off his coffee, now cold, and rooted about in his cupboard for his running shoes. He never felt like jogging, never, so he forced a sort of false bonhomie, whistling as he climbed into his sweats, humming as he tied his runners, then took the stairs two, *three* at a time. He stopped by the front door and, with an expertise born of practice, began to manipulate the security key pad that would allow him to exit the house within two minutes, a feat not easily accomplished given the gleaming array of hardware — Yale locks, safety chains, brackets and latches and bolts — that encrusted the once smooth surface of the vast oak door. His mission successfully accomplished with — check — thirty-five seconds to spare, one last superhuman test of strength remained: attempting a wind-gulping sprint down the driveway before the electronic gates of the house on Sugarbush Road clanged shut on their rollers and Dr. Benjamin du Plessis, consulting physician in Internal Medicine and … ah, what the hell. A man in a tracksuit who couldn't scale a pair of metal fence posts was a sorry sight no matter his professional credentials. The alternative was to haul ass back to the house and begin again, humiliated and out of breath.

So Benjamin reached deep, drew a little something extra into his lungs; lurched forward.

Dry and crackling, hair on end with static effort, Benjamin squeezed through the gates with *yes!* a whole second more than half a second to spare. Doubled over and heaved sincerely. Slowly the world righted itself, the sky resumed its proper place in the universe, the sun broke reluctantly through cloud cover.

Stretching impatiently before casting preparation to the winds, Benjamin hunkered off at the hobbled gait that he fondly thought of as his opening gambit. The night had coaxed a fragile frost; every step rang a thin tinkle upon icy lawns. Breathe, breathe, Benjamin reminded himself. His angular, awkward body jerking and stalling, Benjamin persevered.

Oolah! Anya! a neighbour along Mebos Avenue suddenly called her dogs to heel, her voice sounding metallic on the thin morning air. *Oolah,* called the woman, *Anya, kom hierso!* Dobermans and Alsatians bounded up to fences and security gates, to houses bundled up in razor wire and walls topped with curving spikes. Haunches sprung, ears pricked, the dogs barked furiously their necks rippling in waves of anger until it was clear that the stranger was just passing by. Somewhere in the distance a car alarm sounded, a pair of hadedas passed raucously overhead. Stumbling, gasping, Benjamin ran.

When the wind was from the east as it was today it carried the stink of sulphur from industry, the fertilizer factories and gasworks on the outskirts of the city. On his way to supervising his rural outreach clinics Benjamin would pass these factories with their by-products of dog meat and poultry grains. The smell of sulphur and weariness about summed it up; he'd barely slept last night between urgent calls from the hospital. Now his head felt abused and top heavy, jammed with anxieties.

The barking of dogs thinned suddenly. Benjamin lengthened his stride to accelerate into the Zoo Lake road. There was the smell of decaying mud and reeds and then he was skirting the water with its sullen metallic gleam, its sleepy winter geese. Old newspapers and bulging plastic bags, discarded bus tickets, tires, broken bottles and cigarette butts littered the lake. And every week it was more difficult to ignore the mess of human habitation encroaching from the squatter camp on the northern shore. Already Benjamin could make out the cardboard boxes where the squatters slept, rotting wooden boards, rusty corrugated iron, bricks lifted from construction sites. A slow lasso of smoke hung unevenly on the winter air and the cry of a hungry baby spiked steeply in the distance.

On his second lap the winter geese woke abruptly into shrillness, picking at the paper cups and sandwich wrappers at his feet. Over the years their droppings had cut into the paving stones in acidic layers. Suddenly a figure hunched in a trench coat materialized on the path before him, lurching forward, and Benjamin's blood thinned. In recent months two more bodies—"horribly mutilated"—the newspapers reported, had been recovered in the vicinity of the Zoo Lake. Visitors should be warned, instructed these same papers, to remain on the footpaths, avoid isolated spots. The trench coat whirred into focus propelled apparently by a stick figure too puny to assert his presence except in the mechanical forward progression of the coat which Benjamin now noticed was of majestic proportions.

Shuffle-shuffle.

Morning, mouthed Benjamin.

Collar lowered to reveal a mouth crimped by cold. *Molo.*

Chapped hands, fingers. Wind-chapped lips.

As Benjamin passed the coat and its homeless occupant he remembered his Ouma's often repeated admonitions to *lock* the house and *lock* the car, boykie, whatever you do.

Might as well remain inside, Benjamin thought, behind bars, behind razor wire, eyes wide open all night long. Not being afraid in this city that mined fear as it had once mined gold demanded so many wearisome acts of self-deception that it was easy to see why folks simply gave up, disappeared behind fences or into the vast neon advertisement, the crackling white noise that was America.

No one even walks in this city anymore! his Ouma had exclaimed one day. Instead, the middle classes drove to shopping malls, to office complexes, to stately pleasure domes where they nudged their Jeeps and SUVs and luxury vehicles up to guarded entrances then fled into buildings, fumbling at cell phones and remote control alarms. Ah Johannesburg! old Markham would often rhapsodize.

Johannesburg, Johannesburg—there were more women raped in this city than anywhere else in the world, in the *planet* even! More children abducted, more virgins despoiled, more fatal road accidents, higher casualties, less medical staff, and the highest rate of qualified paramedical attrition in the world! But for all his cynicism Markham, senior surgical resident and staff consultant at the Gen remained, like Benjamin, at his state-funded post, too weary from his days of surgery and shift, intake and rounds, to leave. And all about them the city writhed and coiled. Hijackers toting guns and knives, housebreakers wielding bolt-cutters and hacksaws, muggers and carjackers and common car thieves with crowbar in one hand and what his Ouma had once described as a *very* hot wire in the other.

Smash and grab affairs the newspapers reported with monosyllabic dash, hit-and-run jobs, *skiet-en-donner* shoot outs. *Ja*, scolded Ouma, rape-and-murder, torture-and-kill, why-not and what-have-you, *tcha*. As for the migrant population of childish young thugs who roved the streets in hasty midnight packs—these were the children wet-nursed on hunger and crime and scavenging. Driving home late at night Benjamin would catch darting shadows in the backward drift of his headlights, dense and insubstantial as smoke.

But, in truth, Benjamin knew that this was neither a city of fear nor of desire but a city of lapses, of finely calibrated amnesias. First the buildings came down, the lean-tos and shacks and makeshift clinker homes. Next the shantytowns and the squatter camps were dismantled, the informal settlements and even the state-subsidized housing schemes. Then the people themselves began to disappear. No one knew where they'd disappeared to because the ones who returned had forgotten everything except their names which they held out in cupped hands as a beggar holds a tin can. Finally the names began to disappear, street names changing rapidly, in the blink of an eye. One day you woke up and found yourself living on Victory Avenue, Heroes Drive, Liberation Row. It was a city, suddenly, of abrupt victories and enormous losses.

Five years ago a woman had been brought into the Gen during Benjamin's trauma shift, her left shin crushed. A bulldozer, the Associated Press photographer who'd found her had explained. Although the tibia was irreparable, the wound hopelessly infected, the woman had laughed ceaselessly as Benjamin examined her and, almost continuously, for the twenty-four hours she'd remained in Intensive Care following the operation in which her leg was amputated.

Does anyone know why? asked Benjamin finally exasperated. The nurses shrugged.

Two days later the photographer returned. He showed Benjamin a grainy photograph of a woman hiding her face in her apron as a bulldozer careened into the front of her home. The number eleven, hand painted on the collapsed front wall, was just visible. The woman appeared to be weeping but in fact she was laughing, the photographer explained. He'd found her sitting on a rock beside her dismantled house, her shin exposed to the ragged bone, laughing uproariously.

The woman's laughter was a fine needle under the taut skin of the hospital ward.

Benjamin showed her the photograph.

Eleven years! she pointed, laughing.

Laughing, hitting her thigh with the flat of her palm. Eleven years exactly we've been living in this house!

Benjamin ran, sweated, huffed, stumbled. Benjamin ran.

Beauty hovered on the threshold balancing a tea tray in one hand. The room with the rose wallpaper seemed to swell slightly behind drapes already closed against the pale afternoon with its moth wings and powdered face. *Ah suka*, Beauty remembered how Mamma Thlali had sighed the last time she visited. *All my fatigue*, said Mamma Thlali pulling at her ear lobe, *lies buried beneath this earth*.

The darkness drained the roses from the walls, the faces caught behind glass in the picture frames on the dresser. Ouma looked half asleep, she was leaning away from the small halo of light under the bedside lamp and her eyes were in shadow but her hands, usually clawed into prayer by arthritis, were limp for once, faithless.

Ko ko ko! Time for the tea and toast, Mama.

Although Beauty called her Ouma sometimes and sometimes Madam, she was always *Mama* at the end of a sentence. It gave them both the illusion of familiarity without the indignity that familiarity breeds.

Put it down on the table, Beauty. I'll have a sip just now.

She didn't move into the light so Beauty knew that she was weeping again. *Hai* Mama, enough with the tears already! But Beauty remembered that the tears begun so long ago were nowhere near their end, nowhere near, and that Ouma would be in her grave, her mouth filled with earth before they ceased and even then. The oak outside the window bent to catch a hoopoe in its branches and the *hoop-hoop* of the bird's panic threw pulses like heartbeats into the room.

It was still light outside, only four o'clock on a midwinter's day. Ouma's room faced the wide stoep that looked out onto the veld beyond which Beauty could hear the rumble of the Zoo Lake road, cars zippering the streets open and closed. A cold wind chivvied leaves and cigarette butts and newspapers through the gutters. Thin washes of sunlight opened in squares on the wide floor planks as Beauty threw back the curtains. How she hated dark rooms and besides the darkness was bad for Ouma, turned her pale and wrinkled like something scuttling from under what your foot turned over in the veld. Not to say that she wasn't pale and wrinkled already, but in the respectable way of old women rather than in the skelm way of insects with their sideways dart and leap. But everyone knew that dark rooms, rooms shaded by drapes in the middle of the day, rooms that blocked even the meagre sunlight of late June, everyone knew that these rooms trained the eye for the eternal darkness, as Hosiah would have said, once had said, but long ago and before he too had disappeared into that very darkness with all the rest.

Ouma's hands were red and hot-looking even when they were cold to the touch, with ropey knots at the knuckles. Beauty settled herself on the old leather riempie stool beside the bed and began to rub Ouma's hands between her own. *Chafing*, Dr. Geldenhys had explained, chafing them into warmth. She remembered those hands from when they were strong and agile from grasping at life and when the rings they wore made circles in the shadows of rooms following the progress of a lit cigarette. Ouma still flashed her rings: the antique diamond solitaire that Groot Oupa had given her when they were married, the spray of rubies when Lourens was born.

A good ruby darkens with age, Beauty. Becomes rarer and more valuable, Ouma once told her. Like virtue.

Her laughter had been as deep as the rubies would be many years later for, true enough, the rubies had indeed darkened with age. Where they'd once appeared tacky, almost wet, they were old blood now, dried and clotted.

They'll have to come off, Dr. Geldenhys had explained, pointing out how the gold bands were digging into Ouma's fingers.

She must go down to de Koening Jewellers and have the rings cut off, he told Beauty. Won't hurt at all, he reassured, thinking perhaps that she was like other women, that she cared more about pain than memory, and that it would be a relief to have the dratted things off.

But Beauty knew that Ouma would never have the rings removed, never, because they reminded her that she was alive; Ouma du Plessis still alive at eighty-five.

Pelo kwa teng ke phuti, Mamma Thlali would often say. Although nobody knew exactly how old Mamma Thlali was, Beauty thought that she was probably the same age as Ouma. Same age but in much better health; strong in body, stout of spirit. *Pelo kwa teng ke phuti.* The heart is a springing buck, a *duiker.* And it was true, was it not? Because here was Ouma and even with her wrinkles and her crooked hands, inside was the heart of a young jumping somebody.

And *stubborn*, you wouldn't believe!

Beauty tried to pour tea from the fat brown pot, smooth honey over toast but Ouma, who never did what was good for her, as Beauty very well knew, pushed her cup away, said she wanted to be alone. *Humba wena,* was Beauty nothing but a handkerchief for some old white woman to crush in her hands?

Hoop-hoop from the winter garden, the hopeless call of the hoopoe caught in its cage of branches, reminded Beauty that it was late in the season, late in the afternoon, and just plain *too late*, she sometimes thought. Besides, she must peel potatoes for supper while out in the veld the Chinaman waited with his fahfee game. She'd dreamed of magic pennies last night which meant lucky numbers today, money in the pocket, which please God she needed to build her house, the little house to shelter Mamma Thlali if she was still alive, Rothman if he was still at school, and her own, her old bones when the time came to drag them out of this diseased city. As she would say to the children when they were young, all the children—those dead and those misplaced—as she would sing, *wee wee wee*. All the way home.

Beauty kicked the bed roughly and only mostly by mistake on her way out and the dog that had been hiding underneath skittered out and gave her a cringing look before burying his head between his forepaws. She was glad to leave Ouma alone, cross old woman let her sit there forever. But Ouma called her back, she was always calling Beauty these days, disguising the request as a favour since both women knew that obedience was the river that had run dry between them; do this and do that only the bedrock against which habit grated like stones.

Now Ouma cleared her throat.

Kom skinder 'n bietjie, she said struggling to sit upright, bracing against pain, the sadness of late afternoon, the cry of the hoopoe and the light draining from the sky. Come talk to me a while.

Well, thought Beauty, and what now? But she came back to sit on the riempie stool.

Have you had any luck with the fahfee lately? asked Ouma who took a great interest in games of chance.

No, Ouma. Not for two weeks now. No one from this block has won even five rand from the Chinaman.

Well, he's cheating you, the bugger. That's plain as the nose on your face, girl. Wake up and smell the ... the ...

Ouma faltered. Now what did the buggers drink? She'd known a Chinaman once but he'd drunk tea same as everyone else. Morosely she pulled at her bottom lip.

But Beauty didn't think he was cheating, more's the pity. No, Ouma, she said, sometimes the luck is all on one side. And that in itself is bad luck. Now no one wants to bet with the Chinaman and he says he's losing money because of ill will.

Ha! snorted Ouma, serves him right. Serves him right, the old faker.

She grinned suddenly showing all her teeth as was her way. Did you hear my grandson galumphing his way out of here this morning, Beauty? Thought he wasn't going to make it. I was lying here by myself and I thought, I bet you anything the alarm goes off before he gets out of the gate but no, he made it. Only just, though. Only just. *Ag*, his father was such an athlete: cricket and rugby and water polo— anything with a ball and any sort of ball at all. And then this one comes along, the apple that fell far from the tree as they say. Ha!

Ouma had a good sort of laugh, Beauty had to grant her that, hearty and full-blooded. It made a person want to join her in her merriment and for a moment the two women sat back and laughed at the thought of poor Benjamin and his early morning sprint from the house just seconds in advance of that pesky burglar alarm.

Presently Ouma said, *ag*, do you remember when ... and then she was off on one of her remembrances of Benjamin when he was a little boy and not at all the great clumsy lout that he was today and Beauty stopped listening. She just stopped her ears to that old woman droning on in the twilight. And why? Because of memory, which she'd come first to distrust then to dislike and more recently to hate with a passion.

So many were gone, disappeared, vanished into the shadows that Beauty thought of the city as a memory-eater. Stay too long and the memories fall out of the head as teeth fall out of the mouth after a long illness. Whenever Beauty saw a woman with gaps in her smile because of these missing teeth she thought of the children who'd disappeared, *pfft-pfft* like that, out of the air. One minute they were kicking up dust in the street or squatting in the four o'clock shade, the next a neighbour came running to say that Lucas or Sipile or Sixpence was being dragged away by township boys chanting *Impimpi! Impimpi!* Or the *Abasocongi*, the neck-wringers grabbed these little ones, these dear orphans. All night the smell of burning rubber and something worse that didn't have a name but all the people recognized the smell. A smell that fattened over time.

In the morning the whole western township stunk of the abattoir.

It wasn't the only manner in which the children were snatched, one by one, then three and four and five at a time so that mothers dreamed of a hollow-throated tokoloshe beating his cow-hide drum as all the children fell into rank behind him. But it wasn't the tokoloshe, Beauty knew, who pulled up to the curb in a police van, who thrust out his hairy arms, drawing the children into the barricaded darkness. And it wasn't the tokoloshe who whispered terrible things into the tilted ears of informers, whose eyes behind the visors of his riot gear were blank and tearless. No, Beauty had seen Mister Tokoloshe leaving the city long ago, tail between his legs and limping from a blow to the flanks. Something uglier, more evil-smelling and destructive had taken his place.

Some nights Beauty dreamed of a land where all the lost children would be returned to their mothers. Those children who'd followed the tokoloshe into the coldness of the memory graves where the mothers couldn't follow. One by one, the mothers would gather. Each mother with a remnant clasped in her hand: a piece of cloth, a few lines of scripture found beneath a pillow that hadn't been slept upon, a wad of chewing gum. Buttons, a knuckle bone. The mothers would step forward one by one, one by one, one by one. The mothers would hand over these relics worn thin with grief.

Some nights Beauty dreamed of the huge brass cash register behind which the tokoloshe sat farting and picking the green onions from his teeth. Each time a mother appeared before him he stretched out one scaly hand to palm her offering as if it was a claim slip, a receipt. Pompously, with the drool of enterprise wet upon his chin he entered the numbers into his enormous till, rat-a-tat-tat. *Ping!*

After one of these tokoloshe dreams Beauty stayed away from the Chinaman for days. Days. No luck to be hoarded into a little heap of sugar and tobacco, no numbers to tally. Even number 7 which was the number of the skelm, the sly one, was unsafe to bet upon in these circumstances.

As for Beauty who even though she was given this very name at birth was only once called beautiful and that was in the poem Hosiah

Mopede, first preacher of the Church of Zion in the Veld, wrote for her about walking beautiful in the night something-something. A good thing he wrote it down because, *ai kona*, it was hard to hold the memories in her head. Everything in the right order like the deck of solitaire she sometimes spread for Ouma. And the city, this memory-eater place that wouldn't allow her to sit quietly, hands in her lap, eyes closed. No, instead she must always be thinking and planning: How to build the house, her little house. Who must she speak to about buying cheap building supplies? How must she explain to Mamma Thlali that they must move soon and so forth and so on etcetera as Meneer used to dictate to his secretary in the old days, those days she would return to if she could because those were the days when her Givvie (her own) was warm in her arms and snug in the bed they shared together.

Ouma was still going on about the old days without any sign of coming to an end. Rather than listen to her which at these times she tried to do as little of as possible, Beauty began once more to try to recapture the sound of her daughter's voice which had for so long now eluded her. And why? Was memory like the Chinaman's numbers? If so then forgetfulness was a run of very bad luck indeed; such a number and then another burying remembrance as Givvie had left little by little and her voice was the first thing to disappear. Or was it rather that the dead carried their voices with them when they followed the swallows to that place where there was only singing? Singing and hosannas and psalms of praise to anoint the son of God, as Hosiah had once explained. But Givvie's voice had been reedy, Beauty thought, grass and water. A thin voice like a blade of grass stretched taut between two fingers. Even that day when Ilse was away and she, Beauty, had run upstairs to dial the phone because of all the rumours. *Send someone to call Givvie*, she'd told Sipho at the Post Office. *I'll phone back in an hour.*

Imagining the tiny Post Office at Hammanskraal exchange to steady her nerves: a flyblown map of the region divided into postal districts, last year's Scenic Moments calendar provided by *Die Vriend* newspaper services. Also: a yellowed poster brittle with age entitled Birds of Southern Africa, advertisements for the Jubilee Commemorative stamp series that no one had taken down for fifty years, Sipho's prized collection of Beautiful Girls lovingly torn from *Bona* Magazine, old flypapers dropping dusty insects. And Givvie, waiting, hopping impatiently on one foot, the other.

Hau mama, her own, her Givvie run all the way.

Take care, nunkula, little one, Beauty managed before she heard a key in the lock.

Ilse's key in the lock, her footsteps in the hall. *Tock-ck tock-ck,* high heels on polished wood, as Beauty slammed the phone on Givvie who was still laughing at her mother's fright.

Afterwards it turned out Ilse didn't mind, wouldn't have noticed that Beauty dialled the telephone. But how was she to know? All the other madams hated their girls to get cheeky, wouldn't allow trunk calls, locked the phone up tight. Like Juffrou Terheyden, Rosie's madam, or Mrs. Jacobs who wound a rubber band around the rotary dial and Sisi just took it off when she wanted to use the phone and put it back after and foolish Mrs. Jacobs didn't understand why her phone bill was so high. Screamed bloody murder at the Baas, *Who you phoning, jou donner? Who you talking to behind my back?*

Served him right, thought Beauty, for what he was making Sisi do out back by the servant's quarters, *siestog.*

Goodnight my mother.

Stay safe, my child. Yes, even in your dreams.

Ouma, who had talked herself into something of a standstill now, bestirred herself sleepily.

Ahem-ahem, Beauty.

Yes, Mama.

You remember Madam Magda's coming to visit tomorrow?

Yes, Mama.

What do you like better, Beauty?

What Mama?

Do you like dogs or cats better, Beauty? If you must choose?

Hau. Tcha, Mama! What kind of nonsense?

Always this nonsense accompanied the memories, but always. Now Beauty must sit here, say she liked one thing over another, such and such over this and that when, in truth, she hated both. Ouma roused herself once more and began to grow querulous over her daughter's fondness for cats.

You know how many cats she has by now, Beauty? That one?

Three-four, Mama?

Five, Beauty. Five cats. Five Persians I'd trade like that, like *that*, for one wet mongrel, *jy weet?* Wouldn't give up my Eli-brak for all the damn hoity-toit cats in the world, hnh?

But Mama, why do you want to talk? Sleep now.

Ouma nodded sleepily, her head slumped forward on her chest and she began to make little popping sounds with her mouth. Po po po.

The dog, that Eli-bag-of-bones, rose as if at the mention of his name and shook himself out. Dander spun off into the stale air. Shake shake. Old jersey, old moth-eaten nonsense! With one impatient scooping-up foot Beauty ousted the dog from the room, helping herself to a slice of toast so as to sweeten irritation and because she liked to watch honey curling off the knife. Honey the colour of memory. All the photographs in the room of long ago dead people were honey-coloured with age. *Sepia,* Ouma had once told her. Yes, honey seeping into photographs, turning the faces sweet with grief.

As Beauty ate her bread and honey she thought suddenly that it didn't matter whether Ilse had allowed her to telephone Givvie or not, it only mattered that she, Beauty Mapule, had slammed her daughter in half that day. Yes, and that was why she laughed to herself when the other maids widened their eyes to say *such* a good madam, that one — she didn't mind Beauty using the household pots to cook her mieliepap, the everyday dishes to eat off, she even gave Beauty a ceramic mug for her tea. Not expecting her to use the tin cups reserved for kitchen girls everywhere, the cups that sat on the bottom shelf of all the cupboards in the neighbourhood, maybe all the cupboards of all the houses in all the white suburbs of the city, there beside the mouse traps and the cleaning fluid.

And even if Ilse didn't lock up the sugar and tea leaves like Juffrou Terheyden or mark the level of the brandy like Mrs. Bowen or buy the servant's meat from the "horse meat" butcher like Mrs. Goldberg (the family ate kosher-only, she'd once explained to Mary-my-Girl, from Liebermann's Kosher Butchery and there's no such thing as horse meat anyway, my girl, not in the *sub*urbs), even if she didn't notice when the phone was warm from use, didn't see when the cream was skimmed, the honey diminished (spooned into screw top jars to take home to Mamma Thlali and Dhlamina and Givvie) and the oil siphoned off, even if she failed to catch Beauty's quick-thief hands busy beneath her apron, pocketing a bunch of grapes, a handful of litchis, even if Ilse never flinched when Beauty required time off to go home, advances on her wages or extra mieliemeal, Beauty didn't need Mamma Thlali to warn her that one couldn't count upon the abundance of the fountain ahead.

Sedibana pele ga se ikanngwe. That was her mother-in-law's favourite piece of advice in those days. Always delivered with a raised finger, a well-aimed *thwack* of tobacco. Make provision in life, Mamma Thlali would caution, do not trust to find a store of food, a place to rest or a drinking fountain along the journey.

It was dark outside. The window panes threw back reflections of the room and of the two women defenseless in the small circle of lamplight. Beauty caught a glimpse of the white doek wound about her head like a spirit, like the thoughts she kept to herself. Well, six-thirty, time to cut the inside from the outside. Beauty drew the remaining curtains, careful not to rattle their brass rings then snapped on the powerful outdoor lights so that no one could peer into the house. Behind the security fence, the remote-control gates, the barred windows and barricaded doors, the house on Sugarbush Road hunkered in the shadows thrown by floodlights set in pairs along the driveway where soon Benjamin would roar up in his silver car whose shine was a testament to the industry of Agremon, car-washer.

Inside Ouma's room, in the warmth of the lamplight, roses were blooming in the wallpaper. A rainbow shimmered on the surface of the cold tea, wavered and broke up. Sticky toast, capsules for old age, for illness, for pain, a bag of water-lumpy ice. Eli with his sly dog's glance sidled into the room averting his eyes from Beauty. Cringe and lunge, cringe and lunge, haunches lowered he beggared his way around the room to his mistress' side. Tilted his narrow fox terrier's head so that the maroon vault of his jaw was suddenly exposed. *Ag, jirre man,* Beauty was disgusted but Ouma woke and settled her palm on the runway between his ears before dropping off to sleep again, her mouth slack.

Frowning and clicking her tongue, Beauty hustled into the kitchen to peel potatoes for supper.

Cold, the kitchen was always cold this time of night. She knew every inch of the kitchen by touch, had rubbed her fingertips smooth on its surfaces but coldness was what greeted her when she entered. Well, that was the way of rooms that didn't belong to you. Beyond the kitchen with its hissing fluorescent lights, its humming refrigerator, beyond the hiss and hum of electrical circuits working to pull warmth and light into the room, Beauty heard water running in the servant's quarters. The kitchen was adjacent to the servant's rooms out back where already she could hear Agremon, Ouma's part-time gardener and her own some-time lover, running water in the cement bathroom.

Well, not adjacent really, just nearby. Near enough to hear drains gurgling or to smell meat cooking on the hot plate, but still outside. And near enough, once, for Ilse to hear Beauty's cries for help that time the tsotsi climbed over the wall and ambushed her in her room. Meneer called the police and they came and quickly too because of who he was, but not before the tsotsi made Beauty into a *skaberash* that day, a whore. And not before her heart turned soft and flyblown as what he called her when he pinned her to the wall breathing rotten fruit into her face.

Soft guava soft guava ssofff—tt—hnn-nnn-ngg…

Afterwards, Meneer clicked his tongue at the sight of the broken glass that Beauty had lined along the top of the garden wall. The glass from smashed milk bottles was partially wedged into new cement and there was blood streaking the name Nels Dairy where the tsotsi had cut his hand when he hoisted himself over. But broken glass was no—what was the word the Sergeant had used—no de*terr*ent. Next day the builders came to string great loops of razor wire across the top of the wall and over the back gate too, which thank the Lord looked to be working so far. But still, Beauty was glad of Agremon anyway. Because he was quiet and left her alone with her memories, because he was another warm body with his smell of garden sweat and fifty-cent pipe tobacco and a de*terr*ent, if ever there was one, against bad dreams.

As she so often did these days Beauty allowed her mind to range over her expenses while doing a rapid tally of projected costs and hoped-for income. So much for monthly groceries to take home to Mamma Thlali and Rothman, so much for the radio from Freedman Electronics that Rothman wanted. Perhaps such a gift would mollify him, transform him into the good boy, the loving grandson that she longed for, instead of the dropout, the tsotsi, he was rapidly becoming. For what road could he take without attending school, what could he become—a hawker, a squatter, a pusher, a pimp? A township clever? A beggar or a burglar? Or worst of all a domestic like his ouma. Piss-poor and working for peanuts. Beauty winced.

So much for spare change to play the Chinaman's game because that wasn't spending, *nè*, on account of how she might one day win the kitty. And not five rand fifty here and there, just enough to keep her coming back for more, but really truly win, with enough money —after the groceries, the radio for Rothman, a winter coat for Mamma Thlali—suf*fic*ient money for the little house she planned to build to shelter what was left of her family when she could no longer bend her stiff neck beneath the yoke, ox that she was. A house, yes, and perhaps a couple of bantams for eggs and a goat for the milk. Ah, but what use was plotting so far into the future? *Lenao ga le na nko.* The foot cannot smell where it is going.

Beauty stamped her feet to warm them, shut the kitchen curtains, heated oil as she heard Benjamin's car churning up the driveway. He always wanted his supper as soon as he came home from the hospital, that greedy so and so. Bee-*eep*, the alarm flashed red then green as he huffed the garage door on its rollers. From the kitchen Beauty heard the car wind down, settling on its chassis, engine humming long after he'd turned off the ignition.

Evening, Beauty. Found the paper caught in the razor wire again. That delivery boy must throw like this, hey, *over* the shoulder. Tell him if you see him, won't you?

Demonstrating, Benjamin slid his briefcase and a torn copy of the evening *Star* across the kitchen table, smiled, and bounded up the stairs to his room where Beauty knew he'd strip quickly, tossing his clothes into the laundry hamper, then step into the shower where hot water would pour steadily for five and a half minutes exactly before ending on a gurgle. Beauty itched with disapproval, the hair under her doek prickling. Why always this to-do with the shower? Why always such quantities of water bubbling in the upstairs geyser, sluicing through pipes, gurgling in the outside drains? Did that one think hot water fell from the skies? And all that noise and nuisance and expense to produce, five and a half minutes later, the same man, very same, hair sleeked back, face glowing with heat!

As soon as Beauty heard the upstairs shower open to full throttle she turned over Benjamin's briefcase, unzipped briskly then searched in the compartment where he kept his parking change. Dexterously she palmed a five rand coin then replaced the briefcase just so.

He'd never notice, he hadn't yet.

And *if* he noticed, what then? Would he believe that the good Beauty was stealing from him?

Thirty years she's been with me, she once heard Ilse tell someone. I'd trust her with my life.

Beauty had never stolen from Ilse, never. Not money and not hot water. Well, hardly ever.

Not like that somebody upstairs, that so and so, piece of nonsense. He must be full of dirt inside to want to be so clean on the outside.

When Beauty had first come to work for Ilse and Lourens du Plessis in the house on Sugarbush Road Ilse had pushed a bundle into

Beauty's arms and said in that careless way of hers, Meet Benjamin, see that he doesn't get into any mischief! Oh, and, and try to love him—that would be good too.

And she had. The first certainly and the second, the second also, for who doesn't learn to love what one has care of and Beauty wasn't immune to love. Far from it. She had Givvie with her in those days and the little boy doted on Givvie. Beauty remembered how the children would play together in the garden taking turns to push each other from the tire swing that hung over the sturdiest arm of the plum tree. All afternoon—Benjamin, legs short of the ground, Givvie's just long enough—the children would swing from the tree, hair shooting up, a jumble of elbow, knee, and nape against blue sky.

In truth, she'd never stopped loving the little boy, that little boy whom she'd held and rocked to sleep. Whose food she had cooked and whose sheets she had washed. No, she loved him still but the man he'd become and whose food she still cooked and sheets she still washed she did not love, no quite the opposite. It was a riddle but one she did not care to solve except through spite and such small daily acts of belligerence as lay within her scope.

Shrugging now, clearing her throat of the accumulated phlegm of disgust, Beauty spat into her cooking oil. *Phphttzz-tz-z*, hot enough to fry the chips, hnh?

By the time Benjamin came down, Friday night's fish had been limply warmed over and the chips were rising to the top of the oil. Beauty lifted them into a brown paper bag with a slotted spoon. Then she waited for him to shake his newspaper open before she began jerking the bag with a tremendous crackling and so on, up and down and side to side, because she knew he hated the noise. Hated it. Could tell by his hands tightening across the paper that he wished she would just get that oily racket over with before he came down, could tell by his left foot tapping beneath the tablecloth. But he never chastised her because he was—and she always laughed to herself when she remembered this word—a lib-er-al, *nè*? A white man who'd voted for Mandela in the last election, a man who didn't believe that blacks were inferior. But look at the standard of education, she once heard him telling his mother, the quality of living. *Tcha, tcha.*

Sorry, sorry. I was just now cooking the Master's supper.

That's okay, Beauty. No problem, but—

—*but call me Ben, okay? Yebo,* the boarder bled like a liberal, just like. Bled for the blacks, the poor, the sick, the dying. There was so much pain and so much pity in his heart but Beauty was sick of washing the blood from his clothes. One day, truly, he would bleed to death, that one. But meanwhile he was just fine, thank you very much, even with all the blood loss and meanwhile he still gave Beauty his socks and underwear to wash, his shirts to iron. Meanwhile he still expected her to clean his bathroom, vacuum his bedroom, ask Agremon to wash his car on Saturday afternoons. And although he paid her handsomely, some would say *over*paid her because of his bad conscience, and Beauty made sure to hold her hand to the small of her back when she climbed the stairs to his room—*hau! phew! yoh yoh yoh!*—such money, Beauty knew, was also bloody.

How's that grandson of yours, Beauty? he asked her once. Now he was always wanting to know about Rothman, how old and what standard in school.

See that he stays in school, Beauty. Must stay in school until matric. Otherwise no joy, no money, no respect.

Humba humba, Beauty yelled at him at these times but always in her head. She herself had left Thaba'Nchu Primary before she was even old enough to bleed.

Thichara ona ke ya rona, the children would chant in unison.

This is our teacher.
E tswa kwa sekolong sa Thaba'Nchu.
He comes from Thaba'Nchu School.

But Beauty had taken the fifty rand that Benjamin had given her, folding the money carefully beneath the strap of her brassiere.

For Rothman, you must buy school books for him, Benjamin had instructed, speaking slowly because she was a fool, a *mampara,* a *pampoen* who'd never even matriculated.

E tlile go ruta, e tlile go ruta, the children chanted in those far away days.

He has come to teach, he has come to teach.
E tlile go ruta lefoko la Modimo.
He has come to teach the word of God.

But in the end it was good that she told Benjamin about Rothman because now he must lend her money whenever she confided one of her hard luck tales in the voice and the manner she reserved especially for him.

Rothman he is needing a coat, Musta, for the winter. Rothman he say the school she is wanting the students they must buy new uniforms, Musta.

And Benjamin always said, For sure, Beauty. And he gave her money, whatever she asked for but she was careful not to ask for too much. For sure, Beauty, and he never minded, at least never reminded what she owed. Not like Ilse who'd kept a separate column for Beauty's borrowings in the accounts binder where she'd marked every payday. Still, this grown-up Benjamin was a man, a *liberal*, and she knew enough, she wasn't born under a stone, to mistrust him. As the saying went, *meno masweu polaa a tshega.*

Why is it you say white teeth may kill? Beauty asked Mamma Thlali the first time she was admonished with this proverb. All of us, we all have white teeth; even the black man has white teeth. Mamma Thlali split her lips with a grin before explaining that all teeth were white because all smiles might conceal the plots that deceived. *Yebo,* white as teeth, that was how Beauty would think of Benjamin in future, with his bleeding heart and his trembling hands and his white teeth that gnawed on the bottom of his lip whenever she distressed him in these small kitchen ways.

Yes, Beauty possessed these white teeth, very same, and she understood all about the killing laughter that turned full grown men to simpletons. Laughter that drew malice to a head, laughter that concentrated the poison in the hearts of men. Kind laughter that calmed and appeased and lulled only to break into wickedness, spiteful jesting when least expected.

Anything you want, Musta? Beauty enquired after she'd angled his heaped plate before him, poured a glass of milk, swept the crumbs from around his feet with her dustpan (actually getting down on her knees because she knew it humiliated him more than her). Benjamin hated, *hated* her to call him Musta.

Call me Ben, Beauty, *please*, he'd tell her over and over. I'm not your Master.

In her life, her whole life, Beauty had never called anyone Master for real but only for spite. Even Lourens du Plessis was always Meneer to her, to everyone who knew him: the businessmen who phoned — is Meneer there, *meisie?* — and even the women in long dresses who came to the house in those days, sweeping across the polished ox-blood stoep and through the front door where he'd be waiting with a white rose in his lapel and his hands outstretched, *Welcome, Welcome!* And they would say, *Meneer, such a treat to see you in the pink! Meneer, what splendid weather you've arranged for our garden party! Meneer, alles is altyd so fantasties hierby!* Meneer this and Meneer that.

Benjamin was looking at her now with dog's eyes. Smiling through his white teeth.

All right, Musta, said Beauty.

What did they take? asked Ouma, offering her daughter an aniseed rusk to dip in her coffee.

They t-took Fiela, they took Fiela and now all the cats are d-dead.

Magda began to sob, harshly at first, as if her tear ducts had rusted shut. Indeed it seemed to Ouma that her tears were very slightly tinged with copper sulfate for they deposited faint rust marks on her cheeks like the water from disused pipes. Ouma put her arms around her daughter.

There there, she murmured. But Magda was inconsolable.

Away for a month, not even, visiting her daughter and her new grandchild in America she'd returned to a burgled flat from which her latest maid — lazy, tardy, but until now satisfyingly corporeal — had disappeared. Worst of all, the Persians she'd bred from kittens, lavishing upon them all the affection of her widowed heart, all the bounty of her well-stocked cupboards were dead, all of them, starved to death in the wake of her maid's defection.

Ag, the smell, the flies! Magda sobbed.

Ouma held her daughter's hands and waited for the tears to dry. As always, a faint scent of the pear drops Magda loved, the naphthalene in which she impregnated her clothes, wafted from her. Ouma closed her eyes and recalled how her daughter had once bustled about her large suburban kitchen, peering squint-eyed down the spout of a jug or banging the sides of a mixing bowl with a wooden spoon. As neat and quick as the cats she bred.

Magda, who'd been a perfect martyr to her husband's sour tartar of a mother, the redoubtable Mrs. Moffert—nobody would have dreamt of calling her by her first name—had remained buoyant throughout her trying marriage. At holidays and family dinners Magda would ladle fragrant chicken curry and brinjals, steaming rice, straight from the stove onto crested dinner plates, darting from living room to kitchen, her skin, as now, very lightly sweated so that even in the harsh dryness, the dust of winter, she appeared moist, wistful, limpid. Strange to think that this woman with her tendency to melt and fizzle like sherbet should have shared a childhood with Lourens because the two were as different as chalk and cheese. A large Tretchikoff painting of a mother and child, huge oily tears seeping from blue-veined lids, had once hung over the buffet in Magda's dining room where she was prone to serving her little teas: scones, anchovy toast, balls of chilled butter, a dish of grated sweetmilk cheese.

Kitsch! Lourens used to tease his sister good-naturedly but Ouma noticed that he always took care to seat himself with his back to the weeping pair.

Magda and her *boet*, as she'd called him in the way of children; they were a pair of cherries forking off the same stalk. For they'd been allies for most of their lives, Magda and Lourens, growing up in the shadow of the formidable Groot Oupa, a Voortrekker type who believed himself to be under siege from any number of ferocious enemies. The English! The Blacks! The Commies!

As die jakkals kom dan is alles verby! Groot Oupa's favourite homily was always uttered with one finger pointing towards the mountains through which the scavengers of the Bokhof river estuary once prowled. When the jackals come then all is lost! Along the perimeter of the family farm he'd planted warning trees, trees with harmful names to frighten away marauders: pain tree, fever tree, camelthorn, quiver tree, sickle tree, and pin oak. But, in truth, the region had been free of jackals for centuries.

Remembering her husband now, Ouma drew so deeply on her cigarette that the insides of her cheeks burned.

The woman sitting before her, her tear ducts straining to empty their grief, this woman had once been young, fresh-faced, *openhartig*. Open hearted, open handed, and sincere as self-pity. Even the colours she'd worn were straightforward, simple — powder blue to match her eyes, blush pink her cheeks. But in later years she'd had the good sense to put herself into the hands of a series of fashion advisers, a string of manicured young women in the very best stores. Young women who knew about corsetry, hosiery, *maquillage*, as Magda had once described her search for a particular shade of rouge. Yes, *rouge* not blusher for her daughter wasn't one to forsake the vocabulary of a lifetime.

Today she was wearing a burgundy suit from Jaeger and it suited her generous lines. In all else Magda resisted nothing so strenuously as change, Ouma reflected (the tears showed no inclination to slow, the sobs to cease), resisting change not because she'd suffered a surfeit but rather the opposite: she had begun as she meant to go on. She'd been a matronly baby and a somewhat nose-heavy toddler and had developed over the years into a handsome woman but always with a touch of the dowager about her. Perhaps this instinctive elderliness had made it easier for her when she'd consented to move in with her husband's miserable mother, thought Ouma. *Ag*, but she herself had always disliked the exacting Mrs. Moffert whose unpunctual death had finally set her daughter free to live her own life although she apparently chose to do so from her late mother-in-law's apartment.

Now Magda gulped and bent her great frosted blonde head so that Ouma could gaze into the precise waves of her weekly coiffure that resembled a golden rosette won for honours in the field of dressage. A chrysanthemum drooping upon its thick stalk.

Sterkte, murmured Ouma patting her knee. Strength.

Behind French windows the lawn looked thirsty. Ouma wondered if she should ask Agremon to water what was left of the grass before it curled up and blew away entirely. *Ag*, this winter drought! Once again the churches were filling with farmers praying for rain. As if in response to her mother's sideways glance, Magda's tears gave way to a flow of words.

…and I wrote out all the instructions, you know me…liver in the fridge and even a little broth and all their milk. Dr. Mehring, he said it must have taken about five days but they'd already have gone into a, a coma by then. My little cats, my kittens! *Hemel*, you wouldn't *believe* the stink—

Magda began to weep.

What about Fiela? asked Ouma.

It was merely something to say since both women knew that Fiela had disappeared in the same way that the television and the video recorder, the Moffert family silverware and Turkish carpets and Magda's winter fur had disappeared, real fox fur with gold buttons.

She's welcome to the coat, wept Magda, her and those tsotsis. Don't think I don't know. But she promised, hand on heart she *promised* to feed the cats, my Marie Antoinette and my Elizabeth Regina and Jackie O and my sweet Princess Grace, *ag juffie!* All these months she's worked for me, her royal highness, Queen Fiela Radebe, almost a year now and has she bought a bite of food, a stitch of clothing in all this time? Every three months on the dot I must buy for her two new overalls with matching doeks—not green, Madam, because this is an unlucky colour if you don't mind! That's what she tells me, and what do I do but find her the peach, the pink, the yellow instead.

Naturally. And all in good cotton, of course, not polyester like the cheap Madams buy.

Yes, and you know what Mrs. Moffert was like, the way she carried on. But I turned a blind eye. I said to myself as long as she's kind to my Persians what does it matter if she burns the meat and goes through my drawers and steals my perfume? What does it matter if she answers the door to perfect strangers and takes eggs and sugar and teabags from the cupboard? Did I care that she broke every plate of my good wedding china by the end of six months? Did I give it a second thought that she brought in the evening paper late every night, crumpled to hell and gone? I thought to myself so long as she helps with the cats she can help herself to the butter and the good rye bread when she thinks I'm not looking. When aren't I looking? A widow has to see everything.

Hunching her shoulders Magda began to weep again, her face in her hands. Old age had come upon her more or less silently, her mother now noticed, on fastidious little crow's feet. She patted her daughter's back, poured tea, but was hard pressed to find any comfort in her predicament. Apart from her mantelpiece cluttered with wedding groups and baby pictures, the odd graduate peering rakishly from beneath a tilted mortar board, and the trips overseas to visit scattered daughters and grandchildren, the sons-in-law who barely tolerated her, Magda led a lonely life. And always with the radio playing in the background. "Doctor on Call" Monday nights where, with many a solemn shake of the head, she was able to confirm her deeply held hyperchondriasis and "Lawyer on the Air" on Tuesdays from which she emerged with a sense of nicely judged labour disputive-ness despite the fact, Ouma knew, that Magda Moffert neé du Plessis had never worked a day in her life. Wednesdays was "Investment Portfolio," one of her daughter's weekly highlights, second only to "Pet Advice" with Doctor Piet Pieterse which consumed Thursday evenings in a pleasant blur of chitchat with like-minded pet owners most of whom seemed to breed Rottweilers and Ridgebacks these days, but still, an animal was an animal as far as Magda was concerned, a companion in life.

Shame. By Friday her daughter was always in a jolly mood, buoyant, merry, jauntily convinced that she was going to triumph over the weekly Lotto sweepstakes, not as a matter of luck so much as of right. After all, Magda Madeleine Petrus Moffert *deserved* to win the national lottery. No one else was so deserving; it was about *time* that something good happened to her. But by Saturday it was all over and she was impecunious again, at least in her own estimation, and there was nothing to look forward to except a selection of golden oldies and community announcements on Radio Highveld's easy listening station until Monday night rolled around again and the good physician resumed the air waves.

And now, of course, I have to find someone else! Magda, who had quieted a little, began to wail again at the enormity of this task.

But who will I find now? Who can I trust? These days it's all through word of mouth and you know how these girls stick together.

Well what about Beauty, Ouma offered. Perhaps she knows someone.

Ja-nee, ek is moeg. Moeg! Magda stooped to scratch the deep cleft between Eli's ears. The animal writhed, pushing himself ecstatically beneath her hand.

Tired, you hear? The whole country is going to the dogs.

Hearing this last word and believing himself to be addressed, Eli threw back his head and howled obligingly.

Quiet, hush, you foolish brak! Ouma shooed him away.

Yes, to the dogs, Magda continued. Mark my words the animals are always the first ones to suffer. Like rats leaving the city because of that piper, you remember? Some piper of somewhere or other. And after the rats who's next? The children, that's who. And the children, they've already left, not so? Immigration, hah! This country's number one export, *jy weet*. Our kids, our children.

Shoo! Voetsak! Ouma addressed herself ostensibly to Eli who was still snuffling in eager agreement.

Outside, the day was gray and jowly but rain still hadn't fallen and Agremon had left the hose on for the garden's weekly hour of rationing.

Now the characteristic *sss-nick ssnick* of water rotating through sprinkler heads could be heard from garden to garden, the sight of water arcing across lawns then drifting off-course with the wind. It was that time of afternoon when women called to one another from opposite sides of the street, careless of who heard them. A sprinkling of raindrops fell and Agremon ran out to turn off the hose.

Magda clucked approvingly.

Not like one of those monkeys in overalls who turn on the hose at the first sign of rain. I had one once, you wouldn't believe! Remember Halftime? He used to stand there staring into the distance like he's waiting for the coming of the Lord, no less. Then the rain starts but does he turn off the tap and maybe save his madam a little bit of water? A laying hen would have more sense, I tell you. Now they're busy running the country, making the *big* decisions. Not whether to water the roses and in what kind of rainstorm, but health care and pensions and cricket concessions and whatnot.

Somewhat cheered by her invective, Magda began gathering up her car coat and keys, her handbag. Stretching, yawning hugely, she began her usual voluminous preparations for departure. At the door she embraced Ouma closely, stepped back then hugged her again.

We must think of the children, she murmured dabbing at her eyes with a crumpled handkerchief extracted from her watch strap.

When she'd gone the exhaustion Ouma always felt after one of her daughter's visits overwhelmed her. As she lay on her bed, fully dressed but limp, she listened to the wind that rose and, in its tug and drift, seemed to break up Magda's sentences, her words scattering like so much dust. After a while even the last word — *children* — dispersed on the wind and Ouma slept.

3
EMERGENCY ROOMS

The holiday death toll, always an astonishing figure, had quadrupled that year. An automobile or minibus taxi seemed to crash every hour, then every half hour. It was enough for a driver merely to slew his eyes from the road for a moment for carnage to result. Accident victims were brought into the hospital in relays. First all the beds were filled, the stretchers and gurneys, then the food trolleys, the cleaners' wagons, even a wheelbarrow from a nearby building site. Men and women, children with steering wheels poking from their chests, piled silently in corridors all that month. The smell of burning flesh was a horror and then an habituation. Benjamin sutured, removed glass, iron fragments, ball bearings from tender flesh. Benjamin cut into skin, set limbs, draw-stringed flesh. Benjamin staunched wounds with one hand, pronounced death with the other. Two fingers drawn across the eyes had become a hieroglyph for death. *Nothing we can do here, nurse, who's next?*

One shift, after thirty straight hours working trauma, his theatre gown a butcher's apron, Benjamin sketched this sign twenty-three times on twenty-three cooling temples.

How many today, Doctor? asked the undertaker at midday.

Twenty-*five*, corrected Sister. The doctor has counted too low. Benjamin began to shake so badly that Sister Nongena drew him into the sluice room, her cool hand sliding across his forehead.

No man, *humba wena*, she grumbled, you're too hot. Come back after you drink something. Or, no, she corrected herself taking his juddering pulse. Come back tomorrow.

Markham and his team had already taken over the next shift and Benjamin was still shaking, the world jumping up and down before his eyes. Fatigue. Or something. He grabbed a clean shirt and drove into town where the streets were burning hot and the gutters were slippery with fruit skins, a pear leaking pulp, impossibly overripe bananas. On blankets spread in the filthy street women were selling plates of burning tomatoes and avocados that seemed to ripen as he watched. Benjamin stumbled past makeshift tables cluttered with shoes and cheap gaudy toys, loose toffees and squares of Chappies bubblegum and crocheted blankets and slabs of butter piled high and curding in the midday sun.

He swayed suddenly, nudging a man who was clutching a bunch of earpieces. The sunglasses to which they were attached swung heedlessly this way and that. In his other hand the vendor held a spread of cards. *Sorry, sorry*—Benjamin tried to gain purchase on the cracked pavement but the man merely grunted, his head turned to take in the game of poker at his feet, players kneeling on the pavement or squatting on bales of newspaper.

All about him layabouts, merchants, beggars, street poets, and entrepreneurs hustled for the same square of shadowless pavement on this blazing midday. Hawkers and dealers, vendors and lenders and sellers of dreams, bookies, pawnbrokers, and punters jostled for space while taxis snarled at a nearby terminus and a scrap metal dealer with a supermarket trolley full of junk—hubcaps, fenders, a stash of ball bearings and was that a manhole cover?—rumbled towards him. Swee-*swee*, the trolley made its shrill splay-wheeled way towards Benjamin, passed him, and was immediately swallowed into the swift mercantile life of the central business district where nothing was too small to be sold. Along these ragged back alleys where hawkers were offering "extra-special prices"—*for you Mama, rock bottom!*—one could purchase loose cigarettes, a couple of aspirin, three beers from a six pack, individual tea bags, or a spill of dagga in a paper twist.

Sir, sir we have what you need! clamoured the hawkers. Double what you want at half the price!

Above the heads of crooning vendors and hurrying pedestrians and darting children, lingerie flapped on wire hangers. Shirts, still wrapped in their cocoons of thin, dry cleaning plastic, swayed above the street knocking light into the eyes of passersby. With the flat of his hand Benjamin tried to shade his eyes, rake away the hair on his forehead, but he only succeeded in jostling an ousie adroitly balanced between vast shopping bags.

Tcha. Suka wena, man.

Sorry, Mama. 'Scuse please.

His brain felt addled, over-easy and a little runny. Should wear a hat in this heat. Should.

Gingerly, stepping over water trickling in greasy streams through the gutters, Benjamin made his way past an alley of shops preceded by shadowy awnings that beckoned the passerby with the promise of darkness and quiet. He found himself in a general store fitted with a multitude of shelves, all manner of dry goods stacked against the walls. Battered tins of Koo peaches and pears. Dusty Jungle Oats and Joko tea, a dented tin of Milo leaning up against seeping packets of Impala Mieliemeal, bundles of kitchen candles in torn wax wrapping giving way to string bags of oranges glowing like lamps in the dim store. The women at the door were busy arguing over the price of goods and fingering tinny-looking saucepans but they parted ranks for Benjamin.

Salaam Aleikem. The storekeeper in his crocheted skullcap hurried forward. How can I help the young gentleman?

A Coke. Bottled water. Something cold.

Ah, apologies, no license to sell cold drinks. Sir, perhaps I may interest you in a pair of embroidered slippers, finest quality, a packet of Emporium tea, a cure for stomach-and-headache?

The storekeeper gestured to a window display of patent cures. Remedies for kidney disease, sluggishness of the bowels or liver, heart failure, stomach sickness, lung congestion, bone and blood and muscle pain. A bright vial, obligingly labelled Tokoloshe Prevention, was wedged between dusty boxes of skin lightening creams and hair relaxants. Benjamin touched the tube of cloudy liquid, What's in here?

But something about him had evidently failed to please the storekeeper who cut short his inquiry with a brisk hand.

Out please. The gentleman must leave. Nothing good enough for him here. If the young gentleman does not require a cure for the stomach-and-headache combined he must depart already. Now-now. Please sir, who does not suffer from pain neither in the stomach nor in the head, *lucky* sir, you are being asked, sir, to leave.

Giggling, chortling, hissing, once again the women parted ranks, though minimally, and Benjamin was squeezed from between their combined bulks.

Outside the heat was a jawbone, Benjamin caught between cracking pavement and the sky's hard palate. A blunt sun hammered. On Diagonal Street where the glass Stock Exchange building flashed and burned Benjamin stumbled along behind milling stockbrokers and investment bankers in search of lunch. Vendors were stationed all along the street selling curries, roasted mielies, pumpkin slices, pap and stew. On open air grills heaps of boerewors steamed, looking slightly raw like coils of intestines even when cooked. The mingled smells of savory mince and spices and burnt coffee splattered up like frying oil. When had he last eaten?

Two beef samosas. Keep the change.

No beef, want chicken?

Behind the vendor a stunted tree grew. Its leaves had long since fallen, been lost, abandoned, stolen. The tree sprouted in the narrow wind tunnel between steel-framed buildings. Plastic bags that had been discarded by hawkers or dropped in the gutter by passersby ballooned from its branches. The branches of the tree snagged at the plastic bags and the wind, sliding between steel and glass buildings, filled each bag until it crackled.

Want chicken, mister? Mister?

The curry vendor tapped Benjamin smartly on the wrist leaving a moist fingerprint. Benjamin stared at the small whorl of sweat on his wrist, looked up into the damply impatient eyes of his lover.

All right, chicken.

Mustapha Kunju, parents deceased. Some relative—an aunt?—out by Umhlanga. No one else, it seemed, owed him any allegiance. He had well-cut eyes and lean hard cowboy hips. He wore a navy T-shirt and jeans but looked cool as if the skin beneath the thin cotton was mint-flavoured. When he talked about money, the cost of living, he rubbed his thumb briskly across his fingertips as if he was feeling a length of cloth.

Benjamin had met Mustapha on Diagonal Street on a day very much like this one, just as long, just as hot. The Stock Exchange building had flashed and burned in a terrible light. It had been so hot that week that the people drank beer all day long, with every meal. Few bothered to foam the beer into a glass but simply tilted their heads back and poured. People drank to quench their fierce thirsts, to tamp down the dust in their throats. The people were like matchsticks that year, they bumped heads and flared in the streets. Benjamin had been working double, triple, shifts at the hospital. Bodies were brought in, their heads still smoking.

What can I get you, Mister, he'd asked that first day.

Benjamin had a thirst like Tantalus, he'd sluiced bottled water down his throat, drained a Lion in one foamy swallow. The more he'd drunk the thirstier he became, his armpits hummed, his stomach plummeted as if he were falling. Mustapha wiped the back of his neck with a napkin. Here every day, he allowed finally, between eleven and five.

Here, he'd said, hitching a thumb under his brow and rubbing wearily. Six days a week, *ja*.

Benjamin looked back once but Mustapha was serving a customer. Behind him the stunted tree bent into the wind, its plastic bags rustling with the names of chain stores and clothing manufacturers. *Ackermans*, crackled the tree, *Foschini Fashions, Pick'n Pay, Hyperama Superstore*.

He'd met Mustapha a year ago, the boy working so hard it seemed his thin brown wrists would be whittled to nothing, would snap like the branches of a winter tree. Every evening Mustapha would wheel his barrow to the depot, clean and scour the metal trays, grill frame, heat racks. When he'd disinfected and soaked the steel warming pans and scrubbed his ladles and tongs, the spatula and skimmer, when every last turner and strainer and draining spoon was shining then he'd run a slow chamois over every inch of his twin gas cannisters. Done. Mustapha was a demon for hygiene.

No one ever got sick eating off my cart, he told Benjamin that first night. Excepting heartburn.

Then home to Undine Flats in Yeoville where Benjamin would watch Mustapha's nimble fingers fold vegetable and chicken samosas into neat triangles, whip up savory batches of lamb curry and green mango chutney, working far into the night until all the televisions in all the windows across the way had flickered out, one by one, and the sick baby in the next door flat had swallowed its wind and the shrieking woman in the room above their heads had either been beaten to death or passed out cold, who knew what went on in this place. Mustapha was going to leave Undine Flats as soon as he could, all he needed was the cash.

Up at first light, cycling through Newtown to the depot with his careful packages of food, his homemade atjar, his gas cooker. All day in the sun if he was lucky—the wind and rain if he wasn't—purveying hot curry to fat businessmen, jowly stockbrokers. Making change in his head, breaking a twenty, handing out packages of relish, plastic forks, napkins for greasy chins. Want chicken, Mister, want beef? When the police came around Mustapha had a folded fifty ready to hand. When the food inspector came calling, a representative from the City Health Department, the chairman of the Small Businesses Assistance Committee, when each of these illustrious busybodies with their clipboards and their drumming fingers came to poke assorted noses into Mustapha's steaming pots he must send them away with a couple of bills to thicken their wallets. A man from the Entrepreneurial Association, another and much larger one from something called Vendors Security Union, a rather doubtful representative from Central Business District's long defunct Chamber of Commerce, the list went on. Bribery went down easy as jelly, was expected, necessary, but acquiring a license was near to impossible. Mustapha was too young, it transpired, to manage a business in the city centre but how else was he to make a living, he asked Benjamin, his eyes ardent, dark as wet stone. How else was he to live?

Nee wat, bugger this, bokkie, he'd shrug. *Moenie* worry about me, okay?

When Mustapha was in a good mood Benjamin was his bokkie, his sweetie, his lovey, but more often these days Benjamin was merely boy wallah, a nickname that roamed somewhere between endearment and spite depending upon any number of variables, from the rate of samosa consumption to the success of his latest specialty which this week was *kerrie vetkoek,* a delicate fruit curry in fried bread concoction and luckily a hit with the lunch crowd, thank you very much, *dankie.*

Jur-ruh! Boy wallah, you mustn't think you can just pitch up here every day, Mustapha would exclaim on those rare lunch hours, public holidays or early closing Saturdays, when Benjamin would discover him idling between street vendors who were doing a brisk trade in porridge and tripe or pumpkin roasted on braziers, his own fragrant snacks ignored in favour of mutton and beans or the stringy gluey mess of goat's meat stew that was the staple of the Delicious Africa Takeaway Café. At other times he'd chafe at being watched by Benjamin as he grated ginger and garlic into hot ghee, adding saffron, turmeric, and fenugreek at calculated intervals, for the secret to Indian spices was freshness, naturally. Freshness and chronology. As his Auntie Sallah would nod approvingly, *making up a mosaic for the tongue and taste buds, na?* In the dim kitchen of the old flat in Yeoville little natural light penetrated save for that cast by the piercing wisdom of Mustapha's redoubtable Auntie Sallah who could always be relied upon for gastronomic enlightenment.

If you add all the spices hurly-burly, na, then how can the tongue know if it's tasting madras or mud? When he quoted his auntie, Mustapha's voice unconsciously acquired the rushing lilt of south India, of Kerala and of the coastal people from whom he was but two generations removed.

It was the Yeoville flat that offered the first clue towards understanding Mustapha. Or rather it was Yeoville itself, that run-down neighbourhood on the edges of the downtown district, a habitation that was unique to its inhabitants and yet to an onlooker, perhaps, no different to any other down-at-heel suburb. Ah, the Yeovillites, a people unto themselves; to Benjamin it often seemed as if they were blown solely by the winds of good and ill fortune. All kinds of people lived there, revolving in separate worlds, apparently unaffected by their neighbours. On Saturdays religious Jews walked to synagogue, bouncing on the balls of their feet, oblivious of the buskers and panhandlers crowding the streets. Students and artists, pensioners, marketers, Jehovah's Witnesses dispensing copies of *The Watchtower* and Salvation Army box-rattlers going about their business, stepping around addicts queuing up at the early morning methadone clinic and making a swift detour around blank-eyed Sarafina at the corner of Rockey with her shopping trolley full of scavenged refuse.

In recent years there had been a perceptible downturn in the fortunes of the neighbourhood. Balconies blowsy with washing tumbled overhead and everywhere broken windows were replaced with flapping plastic or cardboard backing. Nowadays when Benjamin glanced over Mustapha's balcony at the strips of ragged grass between outbuildings he often glimpsed a couple of bedraggled bantams scratching in the dirt or the shit-encrusted haunches of the old goat pastured in the communal yard of a neighbouring low-rise.

But when football teams won or lost, when politicians were elected or deposed, when jubilation or outrage ran high, the Yeovillites came into their own, hurling bottles from balconies, tossing rotten fruit through windows, setting illegal firecrackers in doorways. Raging, running through the streets, confiding their joy or despair to the winds. Yet, come morning, the chaos of the night would be followed by great gentleness, neighbourliness even, as children would gather in the streets to collect the debris of the night before and with skilled and peaceful fingers bend coat hangers and tin cans into wire cars to roll through the gutters on their bottle cap wheels.

Nee wat, bugger this! Mustapha would grumble about the noise, the dirt—*die hele gemors*—the whole bloody mess. But what could one do, how could one prosper in this city where so many obstacles stood in the way of a boy's progress?

Méira Cook

Mustapha, whose skin reflected, returned, the sun's light. Mustapha who seemed always to be enveloped in a shimmer of nerves, a sheen of perspiration that ran clear and odourless as a child's sweat. Buying a business, he informed his boy wallah, even just a couple of takeaway wagons, was beyond his means. *Well* beyond. There was the value of mobile stove and fixtures plus goodwill not to mention all the bribery, the graft ... His voice trailed off wistfully, *ooh gonna*.

Gently, tactfully, his fingers encircling a thin wrist, Benjamin would break in at this point wondering aloud if perhaps Mustapha would allow him, ahem-ahem, to as*sist*.

Could even set you up in the catering business, he offered. Make the food yourself, get some curry boys to do the selling.

Why, what'll you get out of it? the boy demanded but without anger. For it was clear that Benjamin had fallen in love and Mustapha seemed to sense that the other man's fall signaled his own ascent.

Mustapha whose eyes were fiery as vindaloo but whose breath was sweet and subtle as apricot atchar.

Ah, well.

Mr. So-and-So any better? asked Ouma with a great wink.

Benjamin was telling his Ouma all about his day, the patients and their visitors, the nurses ticking down shiny hospital corridors in pairs. All Benjamin's patients were Mr. So-and-So's of one sort or another, a concession to confidentiality and the pleasing fiction that disease could be mocked, waylaid by humour.

Sighing, Benjamin raked the hair off his forehead and examined his scrubbed-looking nails. Shrug, hnh, looks like kidney failure. Then he went on to describe the choked hospital ward, his patient looped in tubes and catheters, the family gathering to stare silently at a urine bag, waiting all afternoon for a thin trickle of yellow hope.

Lighting a cigarette abruptly, the way he did each time he was preparing to give up smoking for good, Benjamin gazed over Ouma's head at a couple of Skotnes woodcuts. His father had been an art collector and evidence of his fondness for Preller and Boonzaier hung about the walls in pleasantly inexact patterns of light on shadow.

Hmm-mm, he murmured shaking his head gently at the inevitability of kidney failure.

Ag, ja, Ouma agreed amiably. It was at times like these that she enjoyed her grandson most, his tired woodwindy voice that brought the outside world into the dim rooms of her ever more limited world. The high airy rooms that had once been the centre of so many parties had grown quiet over the years. But Benjamin was immersed in his story, intent.

Only last week he'd admitted a patient, a benzene drunk, half beaten to death. Mr. Wilson, the nurses called him for some reason best known to themselves. The man could barely speak, let alone remember his name. Thighs raw with urine, stinking to high heaven, gangrenous and infected, he'd had to have three—excuse me, *four*—fingers amputated. *And* the small toes on both feet. So much internal damage he'd never be able to draw a full breath again. Lucky though, one of the lucky ones.

But here's the funny thing, he went on. Soon as he starts recovering, Mr. Wilson, who still hasn't said a word to anyone, you understand, he begins to count his rosary. But naturally he doesn't have a string of beads. So he counts, this is crazy, he starts to count on the stumps of his fingers and toes.

A Catholic! Ouma exclaimed who was Calvinist to the core. Ha!

Picked it up from Catholic Mission School, Nurse Tsitsi reckons. Now it's all he remembers. So how d'you like that? Quite a to-do.

Yes, a to-do, Ouma agreed, lulled by her grandson's presence. She drew strength from him at these times and quite forgot her irritation at his ways. The thump of his footsteps on the stairs, his nervous hands, his failure to live up to the robust example of his manly Papa.

Come here, boykie, she said putting her arms around his neck. For a while the two rocked backwards and forwards in the gathering dusk.

Earlier, Beauty had gone about the house locking up, drawing curtains and blinds, checking doors and setting the alarm before padding off to her room in her down-at-heel slippers. Now the house seemed to hum with the concealed electricity of vigilance. It was a warm evening but Ouma was glad of the comfort of her old angora shawl, the wool smelling faintly of perfume and cigarette smoke and fortitude. From her easy chair she could see into the floodlit garden where moths flashed like electrical pulses and bats flitted in the shadows.

Benjamin—ah, how tired he looked—slumped across from her in the deep leather armchair that Lourens had once favoured, perhaps because it offered an unimpeded view of his beloved Boonzaiers and their rich oily colours. But whether her grandson was examining these with any evidence of delight Ouma couldn't judge for the circle of lamplight ended abruptly after it had picked out his wide mouth and high-bridged rather bony nose and his eyes remained in darkness until he leaned forward when she suddenly noticed how weary they were. A nerve twanged at his temple and he slurred the ends of his words, his voice reminding Ouma of a musical instrument in need of tuning.

… same old madness, Benjamin was saying, apparently in reply to something (what was it, now?) she'd asked.

To cover her confusion at having lost the thread of the conversation Ouma clicked her silver lighter to the tip of one of her satin filters and drew deeply. She thought for a moment, pulling all the while at her lower lip, then decided on a topic of a general enough nature to convince her grandson that she had been listening and not dreaming.

Ag, people are all the same! she countered. But how can we ever know what goes on in another person's head? Take Beauty, for instance. She comes to me the other day, comes to me out of the blue. Says Mandela wants all the people to live in houses. Where's *her* house? she wants to know. Beauty, I told her, you live in a house right now. If this is her house, she says, then she's getting rid of all the flowers. *Right now.* And she grabs the vase of roses by my bed and before I can say *mampara* she's off to the kitchen and that's that for the rest of the afternoon.

Benjamin was intrigued. What's she got against roses?

That's what I asked her the next day. Beauty, I said to her, what does our president have against flowers? No, it's not all flowers, she says. Good, I tell her, because it can't be that he hates proteas on account of they're the national flower, *jy weet*, and I myself have seen pictures of the huge vases of strilitzea and gladioli at Tuynhuis. *Hau* Madam, she says, it's got nothing to do with President Mandela but she herself, she can't stand the smell of roses in this house. It's very unlucky, she tells me. For two weeks now she's lost against the Chinaman and no one's heard from the boss man at Thandile Construction so it looks like that's her deposit down the drain. Oh, and her grandson—she has the good grace to hang her head—her grandson wants to buy a radio. *Wragtig*! Yes, she tells me that he's decided he must become a disc jockey, if you *don't* mind, and that will make his fortune and also it will provide for his Ouma in her old age.

A disc jockey! Benjamin whistled. Well but he's still at school isn't he? The grandson.

Beauty, I said, you must stop listening to that boy *straight away*. No Madam, she tells me, at first she also thought the grandson was just making trouble but already he's explained to her how much money he'll be making. Wrote down the number on a piece of paper, no less. Such a number as took her breath away, evidently, not to mention her *brain*, because now she wants me to loan her a couple of thousand to start him off then he can buy the clothes and the fancy shoes and the what-have-you so the radio will hire him to disc jockey their music. And if I lend you the money, Beauty, I asked, will you stop throwing out all my roses? But I felt bad when I saw her face. Listen Beauty, I said, this is a very serious matter, you must tell your grandson he must pull himself together and knock these tsotsi ideas out of his head. Let him rather concentrate on school, I said. If he works hard and matriculates in a couple of years then we'll talk about where to send him next.

Benjamin sighed. I've tried to talk to her about Rothman but—

Ag, what can you say? I'm prepared to put five thousand rand into a Nedbank savings account for him, for Rothman, I told her. Compound interest and what have you. When he matriculates he can come for the money pro*vid*ed he's got a better plan how to use it. Trade school, perhaps, or an apprenticeship with a motor mechanic. And maybe, also, he can ask his Ouma not to stamp about the house complaining of the smell of this, the smell of that.

So that was what all the stamping was about last night. Sounds like you made quite an impression on her, Ouma.

Poor Beauty. She's very superstitious, you know. Very. Now she's got it into her head that this terrible smell is turning her luck sour. I can't smell any roses, I told her. Next thing you know, boom-bang, she's got all the ground floor windows open. Airing out the place, she tells me. Do you want us to be burgled? I asked her. Do you want us to be slaughtered in our beds?

Ah, so *you're* the foot?

Ha! the famous foot that can't smell where it's going. She's told you about this foot, has she?

Benjamin laughed. Doesn't tell me a thing. No, but yesterday she comes storming into the kitchen. Muttering that the effing foot can't smell again. No idea what she's on about. Still don't know what she means.

Ag, what does anything mean, boykie? A kick in the behind, probably. Shame, poor Beauty. She hasn't had an easy life, you know.

This was certainly true and Benjamin was forced to concede that many feet, whether able to smell or not, had obstructed the path of the luckless Beauty. Grandfather in the hall struck ten and Benjamin yawned helplessly. Eli, hearing Grandfather, shuffled to his feet. Rummaging about busily, nose in haunches, he circled until, unaccountably satisfied, he settled down once again in the same position. There, nose against the warm, nubby comfort of Ouma's shins, he peered up at Benjamin, yawning.

Ah-aah. Benjamin felt the cartilage at the sides of his own jaw contract in sympathy. Giving in to the impulse, he yawned until his cheeks cracked and his eyes watered. How long since he'd had a good night's sleep? Dog years, as the saying went. Bloody *seven* nights on call for every one night of sleep in which his body raced in vain to catch up with a week's worth of deprivation. He was suddenly so exhausted that he couldn't imagine climbing the stairs to his room.

But you're exhausted, my boykie, Ouma was chiding warmly. *Moeg in murg en been.* Bone-marrow weary as my mother used to say.

The hand she held out was heavy with stones in their old-fashioned settings. It trembled slightly but noticeably as it just touched him on the cheek then brushed clumsily at the hair clumped on his forehead.

Nag, my seun, she leaned forward to breathe him in, rocking a little in her chair. Let me sit here a bit longer, boykie.

But Benjamin put an arm around her and drew her gently upright, Come on Ouma, let's get you off to bed, old girl. Careful now.

She was tired and she leaned heavily into him so that by the time they reached her room Benjamin was winded. But Ouma, who had drawn strength from her grandson's youth and vigour, was wide awake again and it was another half hour at least before he could get her settled and comfortable in her bed.

Come here, boykie, she said at the last, drawing him down for a resounding goodnight kiss. Whatever anyone said, the du Plessis had always been a family that loved to kiss one another and old Ouma most of all. Gazing down at her now, half asleep on her propped pillows, Benjamin felt tenderness stir in him once again. Well perhaps it was no hardship to remain in the house a little while longer. Just until his Ouma...and then perhaps—. Fumbling at the light switch Benjamin turned and made his weary way upstairs.

The dog came skidding into the kitchen where Beauty was rinsing dishes, her hands drifting in warm water. Barked three short yips, *kri kri kri,* to say he needed to be let out. Switching off the alarm, Beauty unlocked the kitchen door sighing heavily and managing to catch him a sharp blow on the flank as he trotted out looking reproachfully over his shoulder at her. His left eye was cast into relief by the black patch that fell over one side of his narrow face. Such a *mampara,* that one, such a mongrel! First he wanted to be inside, now he must go out.

Méira Cook

Was she the servant of this four-legged piece of nonsense? Such a life he led, always falling with his bum in the butter. A lucky somebody just to be born into this world without a harness.

Beauty hated dogs, all dogs, but this one especially was her brown-and-white, black-eyed worst.

How many dogs in this city? Agremon asked once, coming home hoarse from shouting *Humba, humba wena!* at the de Wets' twin Rottweilers.

The dogs in this city are raised on dark meat. They are hungry for the black man's flesh, he explained to Beauty.

When the white man first came to Egoli he looked around and saw free men and wild dogs. The men and the dogs lived together but not in the same hut, not in the same room. One outside, one inside, that's how it was then. Ha ha, said the white man to himself, I'll tame the dogs and the blacks together. So he turned the black man out into the cold so we must live always in the servant's quarters at the back of the house.

But the dogs, these he welcomed indoors. From then on all the dogs slept on the beds of white women. *Yebo*, the dogs ate in the kitchens and were fattened on meat and warm milk.

Ai kona, Beauty chastised him, enough with the blah-blah, why do you want to make up such bloody nonsense, such rubbish stories?

But secretly she agreed with him only what was the use of complaining? Was the world cured by complaint? Were the hands, the back, eased by storytelling?

How many dogs in this city? Agremon repeated. As many dogs as there are people. No, more...

Tcha, where was that animal now? Beauty ventured outside where the air stunk like polony kept too long at the back of the fridge. The night swarmed with stars cracking and snapping in the cold air. Beauty pushed her hands deep into her apron pockets, fingering a hand-rolled cigarette, waiting for the bloody dog to do his business. From inside the house she heard the snap of Benjamin's voice cutting off the ringing telephone in mid-thread. *Yes, okay. Right away,* he promised. Must be the hospital, must be. Carefully she toed off a slipper even though it was too cold, took aim and hurled it into a suspicious bush. Yelping, skittering, cringing, the dog retreated indoors.

Ag, sies. Sies!

One two, one two. Call-me-Ben thumping down the stairs on his way out.

Thanks for supper, Beauty, de*lici*ous. See you soon, okay.

The car cleared its throat, garage doors hawking sharply on their rollers and he was gone. His headlights swung across the windows pinning her momentarily against the stove. Outside the darkness heaved and settled, thickening above the trees and the loose rectangle of the veld. Beauty watched the Audi sliding towards the highway thickly coated in neon, towards cars that neither swerved nor slowed.

Towards rocks, perhaps, and shattered glass, she hoped.

She was glad he'd gone, leaving her the kitchen to tidy, the supper dishes to wash, the floor to sweep and mop. But she was glad he'd finally left the house. Still, at times, Beauty wished people would stop coming in and going out in this manner — men and dogs — always moving, no one satisfied with their lot in life. *Mona morula o mona o le mongwe*, as Mamma Thlali had reminded her many times after Isaac died and Beauty seemed to be wandering from his memory in her grief. The one who sucks a marula fruit sucks only from that one tree. Perhaps she was getting old but Beauty wished that people would just stay put. Come home, lock up the door, take off their coat and shoes and settle down for the night with the sweet but homely taste of the marula fruit on the tongue. Maybe smoke a cigarette, maybe take a pinch of snuff. Everything dry and warm inside no matter what madness and fright were going on outside.

Actually, though, thought Beauty as she drained the greasy water from the kitchen sink, Benjamin was kind to Agremon in his careless but generous fashion, paying him well, not noticing, once, that he'd paid him twice in one week, not insisting he plant scrappy flower beds with marigold borders but only that he rake leaves in the autumn, water the lawn in summer, and clear dog shit all year round. The full acreage was unusually large for a city plot and was made up of two double stands knocked together and overgrown with fruit trees: peach, plum, apricot, fig, and mulberry. It was all Agremon could do to keep up with the pruning, the picking, and the composting not to mention the fruit that ripened all through the summer months and that he must gather in buckets and baskets for Ouma so that she must always have something to give to this one and that one.

Here Magda, *liefie*, Ouma would urge, pressing boxes full, mounded with late summer fruit upon her daughter.

For *konfyt, nè. Ag,* Agremon, take Madam Magda's boxes down to the car. Please, *jong.*

Or she would herself haul litre jars of apricots to Romi Salon to give to her hairdresser who Ouma said liked to make chutney, this hairdresser, this receiver of free produce fresh from the trees, *tcha.* For this one six figs for breakfast, for that one a bushel of plums to make jam, the next a basket of peaches with the sun still warm on their flesh and that flesh so tender as almost to take the finger marks of the good Agremon whose labour did not quite grow free as fruit from the trees but almost. Yea verily, as the Bible was so fond of remarking.

Yea verily must woman bear child and man must draw his living from the land each by the sweat of their brow and their back and so forth, forever and ever amen. Twice a week, at dusk, Beauty sold bags of fruit to the neighbourhood domestics. The fruit, gathered daily in the morning with the dew still wet (and Ouma asleep, of course, although who was she to mind, was there not enough, *more* than enough to go around?) lasted well into the evening and, when wrapped in newspaper then rolled snugly in innocent-looking plastic bags, could be merchandized cheaply but for a smart profit. All summer a steady stream of visitors would make their way to the servant's quarters out back departing with their bundles of plums and peaches, their apricots, a handful of almonds or a couple of hairy figs to be split against the thumb.

But that was in the summer, of course. Winter held no such bounty, promised little in the way of market gardens or, to put it another way, the means by which nothing very much might be converted into something profitable. But one day Agremon returned early from a gardening job. Wet streaks stained his trousers and he shuffled as he walked, one hand pressed against his stomach. *Ai kona*! What was this? When Beauty hustled him into their shared room, in her alarm scolding him for soiling his street clothes, Agremon hastily pulled a knotted handkerchief from the front of his trousers. Grimed with soil, the handkerchief was wringing wet and when carefully unknotted was shown to contain a small spindly plant drawn up by its thread-like roots.

To grow behind the compost, Agremon informed her proudly. But Beauty didn't recognize his green prize for although clearly a wild plant it resembled neither the roadside cosmos nor the khakibos she was so used to seeing in the veld. It was only when Agremon placed his forefinger against his thumb, slit his eyelids and pretended to inhale deeply that Beauty understood. Now the little dagga plant was growing nicely in the sunny spot she'd selected for it behind the compost heap and already Beauty had set her mind to cultivating a lucrative cash crop whose illegal status would add considerably to its value. Hah, might even light up a smoke herself once in a while. Might even.

As for Agremon, nobody could say he needed to relax. That man was born without agitation, Beauty figured. Not a sharp bone in his body or a sharp word in his head. He was even playful on the subject of Ouma, calling her Madam to her face but Pick-Up in private because of how she was always telling him—pick-*up* the lawnmower, Agremon, instead of *rolling* it over the quarry tile. Which he only did because the lawnmower was heavy and he was getting old and not at all because he was a lazy somebody. But to be fair, Ouma never called him the garden boy or her live-in, she never yelled across the veld—Aaa-*gree-EEE*-mon—when she saw him dawdling with his half-loaf and gravy on the days he worked for her. And she didn't begrudge the piecework he did for the neighbours. But best of all Ouma didn't care that he was sharing Beauty's room in the servant's quarters behind the kitchen. Although why should she care but you never knew, other madams did.

Other madams didn't let their kitchen girls share a room with any-one, not even their own children who had to be packed up and sent home as soon as they were on the dry teat. As soon as the milk cooled on their lips and wherever home was which was usually a tin shanty in the town-ships or a lean-to out in the homelands. And if you were lucky there was a grandmother or an aunt to teach them their chores, the family way and the tribal way. Other madams didn't let their girls have babies even, although how could you put a stop to such a thing? You couldn't, not really, but these other madams hated when their girls fell pregnant because of how it slowed them in their housework and hated even more when the ousies left to give birth and they'd have to hire temporary help.

Eyes squinched, mouths pursed, these madams watched their fat-tening maids as if to say — *See? You see what I have to put up with?* Or, *Can you believe the cheek?* And so on.

Of course, some women were lucky. They lost their jobs but they kept their babies. Such as Tuesday Dube who lived in Soweto with her babies and worked in a crèche and threaded Zulu beadwork for tourists at night and didn't get much sleep. And the babies weren't as fat as they could have been on account of how Tuesday's milk had dried up what with hard work and worry, but the babies, bless their hearts, were alive, thriving.

Yes, some women were lucky and Beauty, too, was lucky, no ques-tion. When Beauty first came to work for the du Plessis she already had Lucky who was living with Mamma Thlali in the country. Lucky by name and by nature, as it turned out, and as his father made certain it should be so. For Isaac Mapule, already dying, had taken the trouble to travel back from where the swallows themselves do not return, all the while cupping his son's name carefully in his big miner's hands: Lucky. Lucky Mapule.

Sometimes Lucas, always lucky.

When Lucky had completed his standard eight at the Missionary School there by Hammanskraal, the Father said he would help him to get a place at a technikon in the city. At this time Beauty thought she would have no more children but later, praise God, she was given two daughters by Hosiah Mopede, first preacher of the Church of Zion in the Veld: one inherited, one natural. The dog came cringing into the kitchen and swung her a wide berth. Fixing Beauty with his urine-coloured eyes he flopped into a corner. The scrabble of his yellow claws on the quarry tile squinched her eyes in disgust. Beauty began to sweep out the kitchen but her thoughts remained elsewhere.

Mama, when did you become grey? Lucky exclaimed the first time he came to visit his mother after a year had passed. He was already a highbuck by then; he wore a cut stone on his pinkie finger which he flashed at his mother, the son whose bottom she had wiped all those years ago although in truth the years seemed to pass like a summer thunderstorm. Flash, flash, and the next day the earth was still parched to the touch. There was no imprint when you walked upon it.

Mama, when did you become grey?

Five years ago, my son, she could have replied. But some words were like doors, like faces, like books. They too could be slammed shut.

That was the year Lucky came to visit Mamma Thlali. His Ouma who'd brought him up and what did he bring her for Christmas, that one? Not a blanket for warmth or a new kettle, for the old one—and this Beauty had reminded him, this repeatedly—the old kettle was peeling in layers of rust which imparted to the evening tea an iron-like flavour, a bitter corrosive odour. Neither did he bring a paraffin stove nor even a footstool so that the old lady could take the weight off her swollen ankles at night. No, none of these gifts, uh-*uh*.

Look, Ouma, her grandson had said, her firstborn, her Lucky boy. Look what I have for you. Special treat!

That was when he gave her the book entitled "Recent Employees of Metro Johannesburg Postal Service, Year 1986/7." In this book, page 56, was a picture of "Lacky Mapelu" grinning like a split melon, and also some writing to say who he was, where he came from, who his people were. (Father; South Sotho, Mine Manager, Deceased. Mother; Sotho and Zulu, Home-Maker.)

Hnn? Mine Manager? *Managed* to die young is all, Beauty scolded her son.

And who is this new — lowering her voice, slitting her eyes — home-making somebody, hmm?

Means what you do, Mama, replied the boy, not meeting her eye. Means keeping the house clean, a housekeeper, em … domestic worker, explained the boy she'd carried for nine months in her womb and then another twelve months safety-pinned to her back in a blanket while she scrubbed floors and toilets and white babies' backsides in order to keep him, her lucky Lucky boy, fat and happy.

Home-Maker, *Ha!*

Although what this boy who was so ashamed that his mother was a servant, an ousie, what this boy daydreamed was also correct. For how many homes had Beauty not already made in the secret rooms of her mind where a woman — even a maid, even a kitchen girl — may dream of her own house, made and built and paid for.

But still, Beauty couldn't resist pulling the highbuck's smartly tailored leg one last time. My son, she began, it seems that your father was a Mine Manager and yet his slow-witted family didn't even know it. More fool they. And then again your mother was a Home-Maker but little suspected her own worth. You, however, son of both these very important people, it seems you, too, are not who you claim. And she thumped the catalogue meaningfully, her forefinger picking out the mangled caption beneath "Mr. Lacky Mapelu's" split-melon grin.

Shoo-weh! gasped Lucky the full horror of this, his first appearance in picture and print, overwhelming him for once.

Meanwhile there was Mamma Thlali, very solemn, turning the pages. Admiring the smile of her lucky grandson and fingering, with one strong, work-harried forefinger, the words printed beneath his photograph. For surely she could not read them, surely not. And only then did it dawn on that ungrateful rubbish, that sharper-than-a-serpent's-tooth — as Hosiah would have preached — how he had shamed her, his grandmother, only then.

Hah, Ouma, he stumbled. *'Skies*, sorry-sorry. But she was too swift for him.

The House on Sugarbush Road

Sit down, my son. She drew him to her. And she did not say, My eyes are dim and clouded today. She did not say, My spectacles are cracked. She did not say, The light is fading too fast from the sky. She did not pretend she could or could not read.

Thus did she draw the shame from him as from a boil.

Sit down, my son, she gestured, and tell me rather the story. And then she remained quite silent for the rest of the visit, silent the better to listen as some children would do well to heed. But Lucky was relieved and relief bubbled up in him like froth to the head of a glassful of beer and he told stories and then more stories. About his job at the Post Office, his responsibilities, his ambitions, in short, his intention to jump like a springbok from strength to strength. All afternoon as the sun set behind the little patch of corn, melons, and beans, the three good pumpkin plants, Mamma Thlali listened patiently, only the knucklebones pushed through her earlobes clicking gently, as Lucky told of his boss, Mr. P.E.L. iMofutsi, and how proud this gentleman was of his newest employee. How frequently he was heard to say that he couldn't ask for a better worker. No, not even from a son.

Ha, the years seemed to pass so quickly, Beauty reflected, returning to herself with a thump. She'd been born with ghost belief, all her people were. The people from her mother's side, that is, because her father's clan were forbidden to talk about the spirit world; it was a mystery and must remain with the key in the lock. But when Beauty married her first husband, Isaac Mapule, she took his faith in the Methodist Church and the aunts and uncles, the grandmothers who had always flickered at the corners of her eyes when she was a child, these dear ones left her. But then Isaac died from the mine dust and already she was eight months heavy. When their son came she didn't know what to name him. Mamma Thlali wanted to call the child Vukile which means Arisen, for the dawn that broke at the moment of his birth, or Pulane, for the rains that soaked this very dawn but Beauty, who always obeyed her mother-in-law, Beauty said to Mamma Thlali, let us wait.

Why do you want to wait, exclaimed Mamma Thlali appalled. You want the child to die without baptizing? Then what name will you put on the cross?

Mamma Thlali, said Beauty, let us wait.

That night Isaac came to her in her sleep and he spoke in the old gentle voice before the coal dust had turned his words to stone.

Lucky, he told her. Name the child Lucky. We are lucky to have him and luck shall be his lot in life.

When Beauty awoke she put the hungry infant to her breast and said, *Eat Lucky, eat my Lucky boy.*

Next day the rains ceased and the heat, so recently assuaged, began to rouse itself again within the walls of the corrugated iron shack. Mamma Thlali, who was Isaac's mother, in fact, and not her own, Mamma Thlali took down the amulets and charms she had purchased from her Sangoma, the cross and the Book, the beeswax candles that the Sisters had given her, and she swaddled the baby in blankets. Beauty found a safety pin and fastened the blankets around her shoulders and together the two women walked across the veld to the Roman Catholic Mission, to Frere Church, where the Reverend Ndlovu made the sign of the cross with holy water on the forehead of Lucky Mapule, baptismal name Lucas, clan name Makgothi. But his mother always called him Lucky for the good luck that such a name would bring and for the trouble her husband had taken to come all the way home from so far away, carrying this name in the palm of his hand.

But, of course, these days Lucky Mapule worked somewhere in the city centre and Beauty hardly ever saw him anymore.

Lucky was a new kind of black man, a Civil Servant he called himself. He wore white shirts to work and a striped tie, and he lived in a rented flat in one of the old grey areas near Joubert Park. Once the Whites-Only had lived there but later, during the Emergency, these whites had fled one by one then in couples and families and finally in whole city blocks until no one was left. Maybe a pensioner here and there, a shut-in, perhaps, bleary eyes peering down at the street from between dirt-stiffened lace curtains. And those on the fringes of society with nothing to lose and nowhere else to go. Your suicides, Lucky would say clucking dismissively, your pushers, your hookers, your squatters, your pimps. But Lucky, true to his name, had found himself a nice flat where he lived with his new family which didn't, unfortunately, include his oldest son, Rothman, by his first wife, on account of what Lucky called Rothman's *in*-so-lence—even pronouncing the word like a white man. And he had arranged a good life for himself and his young family with his important job at the Post Office Customs Branch and his fat new wife.

Indeed, Siemela iMofutsi, eldest daughter of Mr. P.E.L iMofutsi, senior postal employee and Lucky's esteemed boss, was herself as plump and rosy and potentially milk-yielding as the glossiest and fat-test-rumped of the two hundred heifers that her father had demanded as part of her bridal dowry. A stout man with a cross-hatched forehead, Lucky's prospective father-in-law had enclosed Beauty's hand in his own two vast hands the first time they'd met. And laughed uproariously when she referred to him, in the traditional manner, as Mr. P.E.L. iMofutsi—*My dear, even those who don't know me for long call me Peli for short!*—a joke she'd suspected of being habitual.

And without further ado this great *mbongolo*, as she was to report later to Mamma Thlali, this imbecile, this *fool*, began to address her—the mother of his son-in-law and a woman deserving of the traditional seemliness accorded an elder—not by her last name and her title as was respectable, as was fitting, but merely by her given, unearned name: as Beauty.

By name and by nature, my dear!

Followed by a double wink and a rude squeeze upon whatever he could grab, that ill-bred *mampara*. *Yoh weh!* exclaimed Mamma Thlali in apparent consternation as she fiddled with the eagle feather she'd pulled through her right ear in order to conceal, perhaps, a sly grin at her daughter-in-law's expense.

With such an oiled tongue for a father-in-law and such a great big shiny girl for a wife, Lucky seemed set to fulfill all that his name betokened when Isaac Mapule had first brought it back, this name precious as water, in his cupped hands from so far away and so long ago.

Yes indeed, this boy, this first son, did indeed think of himself as a lucky man, he'd once told Beauty. He still visited his mother in those days although it took two buses to get to Sugarbush Road from Joubert Park and he only got weekends off when the buses ran once every two, three hours. Yes, my son, said Beauty, you are blessed. And she cooked putu with sour milk for his supper. Because his wife, Beauty knew, was a fashionable somebody, a real Mrs. So-and-So, and surely she wouldn't trouble to cook mieliemeal but instead would merely purchase white bread in plastic bags from the Greek Caffy.

Lucky, Beauty thought to herself but did not say, because you had the good fortune to be born to a mother who devoted herself to the scrubbing of white people's dirt so that her son could learn to read and write.

This is our teacher, this is our teacher, the children of Thaba'Nchu Primary had chanted in long-ago unison. *This is our teacher, he comes from Thaba'Nchu School.*

And it was this reading and writing that had suited Lucky for his job at the Post Office Customs Branch, weekends off *and* public holidays. So one of them was lucky, at least. But naturally Beauty didn't mention *who* was the lucky one and in the end she was glad of this because after that time when she made tomato-onion gravy for the putu and opened a tin of Star Pilchards so he could have a snack before he went back to stand by the Putco bus stop, after that time her son stopped visiting.

True, he sent word through his stepsister, Dhlamina, to say that he was doing well, they were all doing well. True, he phoned the house on Sugarbush Road to say she must wish him well, he was a father again. Once, twice, he sent money to buy Ouma a Christmas present. Something for the cold, Ma, he wrote, maybe a heater. *Tcha*, she clicked her tongue in disgust, and where must they plug this, this *wonderful* heater? Had he failed to recollect, her son who'd grown strong against the warmth of her broad back, had he forgotten, this blessed child whose feet had never touched the ground until he was in his second year, that there was not the slightest spark of electric light on either side of the street upon which his Ouma lived nor in any corner or cranny of Mamma Thlali's small tin shanty?

Only the gutter of candles and the smoky flame of the paraffin fire. Which, Mamma Thlali was in the habit of remarking, was sufficient since not all the darkness in the world could extinguish the light from a single candle. Not all the darkness in the world. This Mamma Thlali often extolled but Beauty thought otherwise. Particularly when her son sent postal orders instructing his mother to buy impossible gifts for Ouma making it clear that the boy recalled neither his candle-dim infancy nor his grandmother's bright wisdom. *Yebo.*

Tcha, thought Beauty. But was it possible that inside she was also glad? Glad that her son was so far from want that he had entirely forgotten poverty. The cold that had clutched at his little feet when he was young and that the smoky paraffin stove could never altogether burn away.

And what about my grandchildren? Beauty asked him once.

Ahem-hem, said Lucky, in order to first clear his throat of lies. Ahem-*hem.*

So, said Beauty, when are these fine children, the boy who looks like you and his sister, when are they coming to visit their Ouma?

Soon, he told her. Soon, Ma.

But by this soon, Beauty knew, her son didn't mean next week or next month or the day before Christmas. This soon meant never and never was because the children mustn't see their Ouma in her doek and apron; they mustn't see her on her knees scrubbing floors or polishing the banisters. Clapping her hands together for every morsel that came her way as a sign of gratitude according to the old way.

He has come to teach, he has come to teach, chanted the long ago children of Thaba'Nchu Primary in Beauty's head.

He has come to teach the word of God.

Why don't you come visit us instead, Ma? Lucky had asked.

Ahem-hem, he coughed, breathing impatiently down the receiver, a very busy man, very. Ahem-*hem*.

Beauty had clicked her tongue wearily into the mouthpiece. Far away the sweet clear voices of unlettered children rose and fell, rose and fell.

He has come to teach, he has come to teach
He has come to teach the word of God.

Don't pull out the knife! shouted the triage Sister when the man first walked in.

It keeps the blood from making a big mess, she added helpfully.

For some reason the tall skinny fellow who'd just strolled into Emergency with a knife ratcheted in his upper arm reminded Benjamin of someone. He couldn't quite think who though. The man barely stumbled though he was badly wounded, cocky, a township smart-face, as they said around here.

Hey, Pantsula Joe!

Shuu! Madoda, *shuu*!

Yerrr-rr-a!

Everywhere the man's entrance was greeted with exclamations of mock horror and thrilled rapture for surely his strut, his gaze, even the cut of his wide-lapelled suit was homage to those big spenders, lovers of booze and women and jazz, rebels who lived dangerously and carried a big knife.

Which in this case was buried almost to the hilt in the man's upper arm.

Cheers, comrades! With his other arm the man managed a sweeping wave to the room before spiraling slowly down to one knee where he was caught and eased to the ground by a passing orderly. Then the nurse's station seemed to go rigid with sirens and alarms calling out different coloured codes as the dying passengers of a highway collision were rushed in and the air turned coldly forensic.

Much later, hours and hours later, when Benjamin finally got to his stalwart patient he found the man asleep on a makeshift stretcher in the hospital corridor. With his eyes closed the fugitive resemblance that Benjamin had noticed was even stronger but again he couldn't place it. The man smelled of beer and sour mash and was wholly pissed off to be roused. Tabo, his name was. A last name beginning with a hum and ending on a lullaby—Mphalala , no *Sha*balala. The flesh around the tourniquet was livid and the knife had to be grappled out during which procedure the patient failed to endear himself to his medical team by passing mercifully from consciousness but instead bucked and jerked, cursing and imploring his maker but finally, the Demerol beginning to flood his system, he regained his expansive sense of humour.

Hey, madoda, he called peering over at an adjoining gurney. *Madoda!* he pitched his bass louder when the patient, from whom wafted the saturated odours of urine and benzene, failed to respond. Hey, man, what you in for?

Just you leave our Mr. Wilson alone, okay? scolded Nurse Tsitsi. What you want bother this old man for, hmm?

No bother, just asking thanks. With his free hand Tabo rubbed his ears since he could no longer believe them.

Don't thank me, Nurse Tsitsi snapped. After all I'm not the doctor.

Momentarily chastened, Tabo was able to rouse himself. *O itlhokomele, monna*. Take care of yourself, man, he called benignly as Nurse Tsitsi huffed the benzene drunk from view with a rattle of skimpy curtains along their steel railings. Preoccupied with sutures and staples Benjamin heard Sister ask the patient how come he walks into Emergency with a panga stuck in his arm.

Don't ask me, Sisi, Tabo grinned. I'm the lucky one. Now someone gives me *ponsella* when I'm not even looking.

This sort of comment always earned the approving laughter of the nurses who clustered about charmed by the unexpected humour of one of their few conscious patients, the man's verbal shrug and parry.

Besides, mocked Tabo, pretending to quote a proverb, he who is set upon by five dogs, no *six*, has little power to resist.

So, scoffed the nurse, now it's six dogs. *Yoh yoh yoh!* In another hour it will be a pack of wild dogs, then a lion or two. Perhaps by the end of the night there'll be four lions and a jackal in bed with you!

Yebo, Sisi, and maybe if I'm lucky also a nice fat nurse to share my dreams.

Hau, *skelm*! Now I *know* it was a woman who stabbed you because you cheeked her. Huh!

During this spirited exchange, the patient bracing good-naturedly against the pull of the surgical thread and Nurse Nofomela slapping the side of her head with an incredulous palm, Benjamin had brightened, his spirits lifting. Such moments of optimism were few enough. Most days stretched unbearably thin between shifts, surgery, intake, *staff* meetings for fuckssake. Daily rounds with interns and sniping senior residents, monthly research updates, initiatives, policy changes, and strategic planning sessions. Reports to the outgoing Chief of Internal Medicine, a scrofulous fellow with little enthusiasm for anything except the boundless replication of the pink triplicate form.

S'truth man! Markham had collared him only yesterday after a meeting to discuss hospital strategy in the face of the upcoming general strike that was threatening to take place at the end of the year.

S'truth man! yelled Markham clutching at his head. Are they all *befok in die kop*? Playing silly buggers with themselves, making demands left, right and centre but at the end of the day, *jong*, at the end of the day—. Markham would always break off at this point for it was clear that his own end would arrive sooner than any other end and truly what was a man to do, what *could* one man do, even a doctor…

But Markham was a good doctor. At month's end or during the dry season and again, during the rains, anytime when the moon was full and the skelms were out, whenever that is, the patients in Emergency were six deep and the nurses had put out a "drop everything" alert, he could be found taking double shifts on trauma. Where his pal, Dr. du Plessis joined him if he could get someone to cover at the free AIDS clinic in town. In this manner Benjamin spent his days gazing into the insides of things: mouths and ears and open wounds, shocked wide open eyes.

The city was exhausted, metallic-tasting, its inhabitants sickening, dying. It was as if a giant thermometer had broken under enormous pressure and mercury was spilling across the land, hither and yon. Whatever it touched was contaminated forever. Lately rumours that AIDS could be cured by raping a virgin had been circulating through the townships. Now young girls were being brought in from rural outreach clinics with terrible lesions. Children, infants. There were more every day; pubescent girls hunched over torn vaginas, children with herpes growing in their tender pink mouths. Benjamin no longer felt outrage but he welcomed the static in the winter air because it alerted him to human contact.

Hey, madoda, Tabo called as Benjamin began to suture his patient's final ligature drawing the stitches in, tight and close, and trying not to breathe in too deeply the smell of beer-infused sweat. Hey, madoda! he called again. What do you think of sweet Africa now?

Tabo had been on the verge of sleep, his words mumbled and drowsy and when he finished he fell asleep, really asleep, and Benjamin thought, of course, Kippie Nkonyane. That was who Tabo reminded him of, Kippie Nkonyane who was also tall and arrogant and apt to seek out trouble. Kippie Nkonyane.

His heart gave a terrible hurt lurch the way it always did when he remembered Kippie whom he'd first met at an Action Rights meeting in the basement of the old Varsity Student Union Building, Benjamin listening to the soaring rhetoric of the leaders of various banned groups, their exhortations to action.

Simunye! We are One!
Phambili ngo Mandela! Forward with Mandela!
Amandla! Amandla! Amandla!

In the dim basement offices telephones rang, a fax curled in upon itself, photocopy machines flashed out their subversive messages. Raised fists, raised spirits, high hopes.
Amandla! Yoweh! Phambili!

From where he stood somewhere near the back of the crowd, breathing in the fug of closely packed bodies and spiking adrenalin, Benjamin heard a corrosive mutter.

Ja, bra, an' who you gone bribe in heaven, hey? Gone suck off a fuckin' Archangel?

Shocked, more than, Benjamin swivelled to take in a lanky bloke with a frazzled look partly achieved by his shock of skinny dreads which corkscrewed off in all directions, a style that Benjamin would come to recognize as approximating the creative disarray of its owner's thoughts. Kippie Nkonyane. Tall, wiry, electric with nerves, his nails bitten down to the quick, the whites of his eyes always slightly reddened by the giff he smoked to calm the demon inside. *Being as how I am mos fucked, my bra,* he'd allow, inhaling, turning over in bed to roll another joint, best Durban poison scored off a truck just rolled in from the coast.

How d'you like your men?

Way I like my dagga, hey. Strong and long-bloody-lasting.

It was a joke between them, their first.

Before that though—the jokes and what came after, the shared marijuana and what came before—there was that moment in the basement of the Student Union when Benjamin turned in some consternation to confront a belligerent Kippie, pissed off, as he would take pains to explain—he was a great one for explanations, was Kippie—not so much by the message as at the messenger. Full with his own ear-brag, that one, *sies*! was his chief objection to the painful sincerity of that year's president of the Student Democratic Council. While the illegal assembly in their underground bunker chanted the words to *Nkosi Sikelel' iAfrika,* that beautiful banned hymn to a teetering country, Kippie expanded a little on his theme.

No, but it's all a lotta bloody nonsense, *bongani* my bra. Res-o-lutions towards a peaceful con-sti-tution leading to the next great rev-o-lution. Pah! Because Africa, *jy weet,* nothing changes. One fuckin' fascist after another and it's all so much fizzle on the tongue thanks for fat-bloody-nothing. Fuckin' sherbet. Aspirin in a can of beer. *Ja* sweet, *ja* Africa.

Stoned and eloquent, Kippie Nkonyane held forth. Somewhere in one of the shabby offices with the hand-drawn faces of banned African leaders peeling off the walls and the lists of the disappeared and the numbers of the dead typed up and tacked to notice boards, a telephone rang, cut off abruptly. *Kom ons gaan blow*, winked Kippie, grasping Benjamin by the arm and the two blew out into the slur of a late winter afternoon, Kippie skidding through traffic, pulling Benjamin in his wake. In an unacknowledged "grey" area of the city where blacks were lawfully prevented from renting flats but did, in the condemned block in which Kippie illegally shared student digs with a hazardous number of itinerant renters — in a room, on a bed — Benjamin discovered his own version of sweet sweet Africa.

Meanwhile, under the new Emergency Laws newspapers were being censored. In protest some of the liberal dailies began to include blanked out words and paragraphs, even entire columns, in their press runs. A nation could measure its ignorance by way of these wordless spaces.

Poetic, *nè*? Met-a-phorical, scoffed Kippie, drawing out the syllables as he did when especially moved to scorn.

In the illegal flat on Juta Street Benjamin's real education commenced. Late at night men with crackling eyes congregated in the unheated rooms arguing and remonstrating in a blast of languages: Zulu, Xhosa, English, Sotho. They seldom bothered to notice Benjamin but in the early hours of the morning, the strangers bunking down where they could or disappearing like smoke into the night, Kippie would whisper hoarsely in his ear until the rattle of dustbins in alleyways presaged the dawn. It seemed that people were dying in the townships, more and more every day. Children were being shot by riot squads, armed police, security forces. Men and women were disappearing, quietly and without emphasis, all over the city. And truth had been silenced, abruptly cut off.

For some reason Benjamin was reminded of the telephone that had stopped ringing that day at the Action Rights meeting, truth silent as a disconnected phone balanced on a trestle table off an empty office below the Student Union Building. Truth with its interrupted dial tone and stuttered ring. *Poetic, nè?* as Kippie would've mocked, had every right to mock for by this time Kippie Nkonyane had himself disappeared; Benjamin had no idea where. Gone home, gone missing, gone to the devil. If his friends knew they weren't telling, their always incipient distrust of Benjamin resurfacing with his lover's defection.

Might've been detained, might have.

Nah. Who'd want old Kippie? Even the boers got better things to do.

Zat so, hey? What you know, madoda. Huh!

Yebo man, maybe he's jolled off to Swaziland. Best weed on the continent, eh. Fuckin' smokes the brain.

Won't need it anyway, heard he's been hauled off on the *tjoek-tjoekietrein*. Pandas grabbed him off the street. Find whatever brain he's got left on the pavement outside John Vorster Square the day he falls out the window. *Ja*, twenty-first floor special, my bra.

This was the signal for the chorus, the inevitable black comedy chorus that the friends of Kippie Nkonyane sang to his lover as he stood in their midst, defenceless, bewildered, and only dimly anticipating the grief to come. *Piece of soap*, they chanted, *piece of soap, piece of soap, piece of soap...*

And in the bright lights of the examination room Benjamin heard the words still. They seemed to measure the distance between the boy he had been and the man he'd become. *Dr. du Plessis, Dr. du Plessis*, someone was paging, *Pick up line one*. The man called Tabo Shabalala suddenly stirred in his sleep and mumbled something. Nurse Tsitsi smiled as if she'd finally received the answer to a question but Benjamin was not so lucky and the answer which had for so long eluded him, eluded him still.

Ouma was sitting and smoking in a deck chair under the syringa, her face turned towards the sun, her silver cigarette lighter bundled in her lap. Although it was winter the tree hadn't yet lost its leaves and they zipped the light open and closed around her.

Oolah! Anya! The neighbour was calling her dogs again, her voice shuttling up and down on the wind. *Ag jirre, kom hierso*, she called pitching her voice so that it could be heard between the thump of shovels hitting dull winter earth as the workmen who were building her retaining wall began their morning's labour. With her foot Ouma nudged at Eli who stirred briefly before stretching his legs then settling again with a heartfelt sigh.

Pick rattle tock.

Shaya, *shaya*! One of the workers flapped a stray horsefly from his brow.

Shadows slanted across the morning stubble. With the hours they would shorten, inch by inch, until noon when tired, thirsty, trickling with sweat, each man would stand full on his shadow, a dark halo looped overhead.

All summer kikuyu grew thickly between cracked slasto, beneath the outdoor tap, but the winter grass was straggly and the earth between the spokes of dry kikuyu was dull and red. A thin ray of winter sunlight slanted through the trees and pinged off the fishpond. For a moment Ouma imagined that the pond was full of water, brimful of fish, the stone fountain splashing and its urn centrepiece permanently damp as it once had been, and overgrown with mosses and lichen. But it was the figment of a moment. The treacherous sun had merely flashed off the wire mesh that covered the empty pond. There were no fish, no falling water, no echo of clinking glasses and party laughter tumbling over into this present moment. *Such nonsense!* thought Ouma, catching herself up. For the fish had died oh so many years ago, the pond long been drained and the fountain disconnected. Only the stone urn remained, blanched and cracked, propped up by sheets of rusty chicken wire.

Yet sometimes—and despite the nostalgia for which she never failed to scold herself—Ouma still thought that she could hear the sound of the guests as they'd thronged through the old house, their exclamations and shouts, the high-pitched collision of ice cubes in briefly empty glasses. And, after all, it was the same old house. The same old oak trim with its beefy grain like good marbled meat. The same oak front door darkening with age and the same oak banisters trailing carved

Méira Cook

grape leaves through the slats of the newel post. Once women had swayed through the rooms in their dancing shoes and their powdered shoulders and men, their shirt fronts stiff with starch, had steered them about to the beat of a swing band whose leader had worn a signet ring that flashed at his finger on the downbeat. Yes, what one remembered!

In those days, Ouma now recalled, the front door always stood ajar and the French windows were always flung open to the garden so that life seemed to be a constant jumble of inside and outside. Children and dogs tracking muddy prints across quarry tile while workmen and caterers and servants passed in and out. And the house on Sugarbush Road, in turn, had raised its voice to the wind: the music of gramophone records and radio melodies, her son baritone-ing *Nessum Dorma* in the shower and her daughter-in-law's high heels echoing through the rooms.

Ouma tentatively straightened her aching fingers. It was the arthritis again, the arthritis to which she was *a martyr*, according to her daughter, but the fact of the matter was that she was often in pain and her fingers had already begun to grow askew, their joints shrunken as if all the moisture had been sucked from them. A sudden image of Lourens sucking the marrow from his soup bones flashed into her mind. *Ag*, how he'd loved his food, her boy, but the old food, the childhood food best of all. Oxtail soup with knucklebones, hot Malay curry with Durban spices. His mother's famous cathedral-shaped Madeira cake and her lamingtons dipped in dark Bourneville cocoa and rolled in desiccated coconut. Well, Ilse had been a terrible cook, comically so, and if Ouma could make herself useful in the kitchen during one of her visits then why stand on ceremony?

So, boiled mutton—*real* mutton that is, none of your lamb chops or God forbid tough old sheep stew—served with homemade chutney, pumpkin and corn fritters on the side. And for lunch the next day, fatty mutton sandwiches, *heaven!* Heaven between two slices of bread and a slick of grease on the chin to prove it.

For a moment Ouma's remembrances were interrupted by Eli who shifted and settled, one mongrelish ear tossed inside out over the high

The House on Sugarbush Road

arch of his skull. Ouma sighed and lit another cigarette watching as a couple of hadedas squawked across the lawn. When they reached the shade of the fountain they bundled themselves raggedly, hopelessly, into the air, at the last possible moment gaining purchase on the wind. Their shrieks cut off abruptly as they disappeared from view.

With the silence that fell in their wake the exaggerated pick-rattle-tock of the workers resounded through the garden. Ash built to a peak then toppled from her cigarette. Without glancing to see where it had fallen Ouma brushed her shoulders impatiently, waving away the dog who was trying to nuzzle the drift of leaves between her feet. Something caught her eye and she looked up to see Beauty dragging her morning shadow across the lawn. Beauty was twisting her hands in her apron so Ouma knew that mischief was afoot and she turned her face away pretending not to witness her progress until the other woman was almost upon her, clearing her throat for attention in the accusatory way that Ouma had come to know so well. *Tcha*, what did she want *now*. But then Ouma suddenly remembered her promise to Magda and called out:

Beauty, tell me do you have a girl for Mrs. Magda? Someone who can begin immediately, straight away?

Beauty thought for a moment, her head cocked to one side.

But what happened to Mrs. Magda's girl?

Never you mind, my girl. Least said soonest mended. What about that stepdaughter of yours, where's she working now?

Beauty shrugged. It was possible that Dhlamina was in need of a job, she often was. And just as often, she was not. Dhlamina was a law unto herself, she'd seldom needed Beauty's help when she was growing up and she had never required her advice now that she was grown. Well, all right, she would ask. But a more pressing need had arisen.

Mama, she cleared her throat. What about the old couch that you told Agremon to put under the verandah?

What about the sofa, Beauty?

For storage.

Yes?

If Mama doesn't want it anymore then can Beauty take it away, the *so*fa?

Of course, Beauty, surely. Ouma was relieved.

But where will you put it? It's too big for your room, hey. Much too.

Beauty cleared her throat gustily as if to say I'm glad you asked.

Mama, I must talk to you about the house, now.

What house is this, Beauty?

I've told Mama already about the house I'm planning to build. There in Hammanskraal.

And I've told Beauty many times, *many* times, that such a house cannot be built.

Ouma scattered ash for emphasis but Beauty stood firm, even advancing a step to demonstrate that this time she would not be waylaid.

Here is what my mother-in-law says, began Beauty launching into her carefully prepared recital.

She says we squatters are like crows in a mielie field and the farmer does not like us to eat his ripe mielies or even to sleep amongst the dead stooks. He chases us with scarecrows and guns, with dogs and with the law. We take off only to alight on the next field or the next. It only remains to see which one grows weary, the farmer or the crows.

In fact Mamma Thlali had said no such thing being given neither to flights of fancy nor to self pity but Beauty was proud of her way with words and immediately set about describing hunger which gnawed like the million-mouthed appetite of a swarm of locusts settling as one upon a maize field. Carried away, Beauty continued to explain this locust vision to Ouma but Ouma interrupted her as if she had a train to catch, a cake to bake. A fire to kindle or a fire to extinguish.

But you are not a squatter, Beauty. And neither is your mother-in-law. Didn't Master Lourens already give you a loan you must pay the municipality for the land? That was two years ago last September, and since then has anyone ever asked Beauty to repay the loan?

Beauty looked at Ouma. She was brushing at the shoulders of her shawl as if Beauty's problems were ash, were so much smoke and ash that they could be flicked out of the air with a wave of the hand. So Beauty began again, patiently, to explain why she needed the house. Her mother-in-law was growing older, more infirm, struggling daily with her patch of corn, melon, beans, and three good pumpkin plants. And did the Mama know, hadn't Beauty already explained that the tin roof had blown away again in the seasonal rains? It wasn't enough merely to shore up the foundations of the old shanty again and again, replacing leaks with clay from the river and spreading dried dung on the floor, for even though Mamma Thlali still appreciated the traditional ways, the earth around Hammanskraal had grown sour, the grazing scant, and everyone knew that a hungry woman, an elderly woman, was more susceptible to the elements.

Then there was Rothman. Surely Ouma agreed that the poor boy needed a house, a home mind you, not a tin lean-to, stolen sheet iron held down with rocks for a roof. Maybe a tire or two for a lightning conductor. No, assuredly, her grandson deserved to grow up in a house with brick walls, taps that could be turned on and off, a front door that opened wide to welcome visitors, yes, but that could be locked up smartly against the skelms of the night, also.

All this Beauty tried to explain but she was hampered by the Ouma's bad opinion of Rothman which was unjust because the boy was never given half, no, not even a *quarter*, of a chance. His mother was a Xhosa and everyone knows a Xhosa will steal a teacup from under your nose. And in the end she'd stolen much worse than a teacup, abandoning her son to flee to the city with her shoes in her hand like the skaberash she was, *tcha*. Even Mamma Thlali whom Beauty considered to be a model of kind feeling had nothing good to say about Rothman's mother who was as wicked as she was beautiful. Indeed, as Mamma Thlali took pains to make clear, the first attribute was often a result of the second insofar as a woman with no discernable mark upon her body might harbour the secret marks of jealousy and resentment in her heart. When such a woman committed some wickedness—and this when she was heavy—the child must pay the consequences. Sometimes the defect was as plain as a harelip or a club foot, sometimes months must pass—years, a decade—before the mother's sin rose to the surface of the child's life but rise it would, rise it must, as surely as oil in water.

Beauty realized that she had fallen into an agitated silence so she corkscrewed her hands into the pockets of her apron. The other woman was sitting behind her smoke and her sunglasses in the shade of the syringa so Beauty couldn't see how her words had worked upon her except that there was so much ash on the ground it looked as if Ouma had burned herself out.

What do you want me to do Beauty? she asked eventually but in the manner of one who says I have washed my hands of this matter. In the manner of a mouth that closes, top lip on bottom lip, the argument grasped firmly between the teeth.

Last month my grandson gave you two thousand rand for the contractor. And what happened to this money?

The contractor says it's not enough, Mama. He says he will keep the money safe until I give him the rest.

Ag Beauty, what kind of a man is he, this contractor? Such nonsense!

No, Mama, he is an honest one, this time, said Beauty who certainly hoped he was but truly, how was she to know? Was she a worm that she could crawl into a man's skull to know what was going on in his brain?

Ouma tapped a column of ash from her cigarette wishing she could get rid of Beauty as easily. Gravely, she observed the ash fall and scatter in the spokes of the kikuyu at her feet. Beauty also watched the ash uncurl and, taking this for a sign, shuffled off towards the house.

Contemplating her retreating back Ouma knew that this wasn't the end of the matter, not nearly. And it was no use asking if Beauty had remembered to get a receipt, the money was gone like so much else Ouma had seen the du Plessis give her over the years: secondhand dresses and suits and winter jackets, new clothes for the children and grandchildren, funds to bail or to bury this one and that one, hundred rand notes every January to buy school books for that no-good grandson of hers, that Rothman. Money orders to keep the mother-in-law plump on maize meal and sour milk; cheques to buy new spectacles for Beauty, to pay for her gall-bladder operation, to warm her old age with woolen blankets and flannel underwear. Cash that had flowed in what seemed like an unbroken stream from Lourens' wallet to Beauty's pocket. And barely a thank you, seldom a by-your-leave, but that was to be expected, wasn't it, living in this greedy heartsick city.

An old woman burning away like a cheap cigarette. That's what they saw, even Beauty who should have known better, and all whites were wealthy, weren't they, all old women weak. So she should expect to be impor*tune*d on street corners and parking lots, at traffic lights and shopping centres and now here, *here* in her own garden. Please Madam this, and please Missus that, and will Mama only lend me, give me, buy me? An old woman, good only for the money she could still funnel into a pocket, a pair of cupped hands. Bonuses and Christmas boxes and elaborate pretend loans that saved face but fooled nobody.

So Beauty wanted a house, did she? And in what had she been living these past thirty years? And at whose expense? Ilse and Lourens had always treated her with respect, never scolded or maligned her, never shamed her as others shamed their servants. Why, when that daughter of hers was little she had lived with Beauty in her room behind the kitchen. Unheard of at the time! Ouma still remembered how Lourens would cut a thick wedge of watermelon for the child every night in summer, choose a couple of navel oranges or a ripe banana in winter.

Here, Beauty, for the little one, she must stay healthy.

Ah, but it was always summer in those days, thought Ouma. Givvie and Benjamin were always bounding about the garden where fruits seemed to grow so thickly upon the trees that they rained down with every footfall. Ouma had a sudden memory of a child's knee painted in mercurochrome reds and iodine blues topped with an open-pored sticking plaster. And Beauty's sway-backed walk as she followed behind the children, moving easily from haunch to haunch.

Not too fast *nunu!* Don't fall *gogga!*

To stop herself from weeping Ouma lit another cigarette. Blew in, blew out.

Ag, it was always the way when one began to remember one's children. Memory ambushed one and then the pain began again. Take her son, for example. Lourens had worked so hard and for so long, shame. All he'd done to further the cause, to — what was it? — to *ha*sten the revolution. And to what end? This cinder, this echo of herself thrown back each time Beauty opened her mouth. This sad old ghost woman centered in the other woman's eyes.

No-ja.

But her son had been a hero, had he not? It was clear to all who'd known him that his greatest satisfaction was in the struggle for other people's freedoms and this despite Groot Oupa's mockery and the disapprobation of his own people. *Soutpiel!* his father had always taunted him and the press had called him a *veraaier*, a turncoat, and worse but by the time he died he'd become a national treasure, a hero. As one headline mourned: "Go Well, Old Friend — *Humba Kahle!*" And it was clear that if he hadn't passed away when he did he would have received great honours in Mandela's new government.

Ah, well. *Humba Kahle*, old comrade. *Sakabona.*

It was no good, the tears were coming swiftly as they always did whenever Ouma thought of her son, of Lourens, whom she'd been so proud of although she had seldom understood his ways. To comfort herself she turned her thoughts to other people's children. That Rothman, for instance, was a skelm pure and simple. *Krom en skeef,* as her mother would have said, a crooked soul. Who knew why? But the fact remained that the boy was a bad seed who would never grow into the sturdy oak that would one day shelter his grandmother's old bones. No, Ouma recognized an outlaw, a good-for-nothing, a rubbish, an out-and-out piece of nonsense when she saw one. And she had no intention, *thank* you very much, as Magda would say, of financing his criminal schemes. *Baie dankie en totsiens*. Truly, the house that Beauty wished to build was nothing more than a pipe dream and for the life of her Ouma did not understand the other woman's fixation with putting down roots in the shifting red dust of Hammanskraal. Even Beauty, ingrate that she was, must realize that she lived in a perfectly good house. Water and electricity, light and air and space, proximity to shops and bus routes, all up to snuff. And if that wasn't luxury to a woman who'd just come in off the street one day then Ouma didn't know, she just did not know what the world had come to.

The first time Ouma laid eyes on Beauty, Beauty was wearing two dresses, a skirt, three blouses, and a couple of cardigans. All she possessed, in fact. It was the middle of summer and Beauty had come knocking on the front door of the house on Sugarbush Road. Lourens and Ilse had just moved in and Ouma was visiting to take care of young Benjamin who was still an infant at the time. An infant in arms, an infant with the croup to be precise, and Ouma had flung open the door at her wit's end. Well she'd never been good with babies, never. The first time Beauty laid eyes on Ouma, Ouma was balancing a squalling child on her hip, her poor head pounding in protest against the racket.

You have a maid, Madam? I need work.

The woman on the threshold was wearing all her clothes at once which density added to her girth, her gleaming brow, sweat, odour of toil, and surprisingly, her dignity. A pair of newly-whitened veldskoen hung from the belt about her waist. Balanced on her head was a careful bundle containing, Ouma later learned, all her worldly possessions along with a five pound bag of maize meal.

She had wide cheekbones and a sharply modeled chin lending a look of triangular austerity to her face. A strange parti-coloured skin, dark in areas in others patched by a too-liberal application of the harsh ammoniac skin-lightening creams that were popular when she was a girl. Up from the country she was searching for work, with nowhere to live, no money to buy food, no references and very little hope. The layers of her clothing rustled and slipped, *sha sha sha*, but when she saw the baby, when she spied Benjamin, her expression, carefully civil but downcast in all its lines, softened slightly but noticeably, at least to a grandmother's eyes, and she indicated with a gesture that she wished to take the infant from Ouma. What an odd figure she made standing there in the filtered leafy light from the street! A layered woman with a large bundle on her head and a smaller one in her arms.

Sha sha sha.

Beauty had rocked the baby in her arms, *tula-tula*. Gradually the squall ebbed and the child had fallen into an exhausted but honest-to-goodness sleep. Sitting in the garden under the syringa tree Ouma smiled at the memory.

Oolah! Anya! called her neighbour.

An Egyptian goose passed overhead on its great wings throwing the garden into brief shadow.

Oolah! Anya!

Ouma abruptly shifted her gaze from the past to the hard glitter of the garden, the metallic sheen on the fishpond, the sun thrown like a newly minted coin against the French windows. *Ping!* Enough, she thought as she struggled up out of her chair, scattering ash. It was time to wander indoors and out of the cold glare of winter.

4

THE CITY BUILT ON GOLD

W hy don't you visit us instead, Ma? repeated Lucky weakly.

So Beauty got dressed one Sunday morning in her smartest suit. The thin light of winter was brittle and cracked, very bright. Frost hung in the air like glass. Beauty took the number fifty-nine to Eloff Street and there she waited for the Putco bus to Hillbrow. Fifty, sixty minutes went by along with a bus "Not in Service, Thank You" that didn't even slow down as it approached the bus stop so that Beauty in her best outfit — navy skirt and jacket, maroon striped blouse, maroon doek, grey and dot scarf with the green felt and gold blazon of the Church of Zion badge pinned proudly to her breast — was soon drenched in gutter water.

An hour and then another hour and then half an hour again. When the correct bus finally came, the driver was full of agitation and he wouldn't give Beauty her change but motioned angrily towards the back of the bus, accelerating spitefully so that she lost her footing in the aisle, laddering her stockings and tearing her shin against a metal strut. A kind gentleman who was wrapped in a greatcoat against the cold got up to offer his seat because the bus was crowded with others who, like herself, had been waiting many hours for this bus with its tsotsi driver to pick them up and rattle them painfully towards their belated destinations.

When she got to Joubert Park Flats it was very late and the children were tired of waiting for their grandmother. Their names were Luther and Louisa.

What did you bring us, Ouma? asked the oldest, the boy.

But the children rolled up their noses at the putu she'd prepared the night before, letting it cool and wrapping it in tin foil the next morning.

Why on your day off you must still wear a doek? asked Siemela glancing at her mother-in-law's somber, gutter-bespattered clothes, her laddered stockings.

Siemela who was wearing a smart black hat trimmed in gold braid with shiny red cherries over the ear. Siemela who was wearing bright red stockings to match the cherries and a white blouse to set them off. Siemela who even though she only sat in her own living room in her own flat waiting for her mother-in-law's visit to begin — "*tcha*, when is she coming already, Lucas, I can't sit here all *day?*" — yet she held upon her lap a plush gold handbag in order to demonstrate how fashionable she was, how wealthy, this fat-rumped Siemela, second wife of Lucky Mapule, civil servant and post office employee, third level.

Look, Ma, gestured Lucky, and he turned his mother to face a glass dining room table surrounded by eight brassy chairs in pink velour slipcovers.

Not bad, eh? Sit now, pay later, *yebo*!

Very good quality, very expensive, added Siemela patting an over-stuffed cushion pinned by a large pink button in the centre.

Beauty noticed that the fabric strained against this plastic navel-like button as if the cushion — *scatter* pillow, Mama, Siemela corrected her — as if the cushion was a pregnant stomach creased by stretch marks.

Lucas, my husband, he says I deserve a little comfort in my old age! Siemela giggled prettily to show how far she was from this laughable and unlikely event, old age *iiiyoh*, impishly managing to shake her hat askew so that a couple of cherries dangled lustrously over her right eye.

Beauty gazed at Lucky who, while demonstrating the depth and comfort of one of his hire purchase chairs, was nevertheless looking a little sheepish. She gazed at the large glass table and at the eight pink and brass chairs. She gazed at Siemela who stared impudently back at her from between the lustre of her bright artificial cherries.

You must take care, my son. Where one soft fruit touches the skin of another in a basket of healthy fruit, all will eventually rot, she cautioned mildly. With a gentle hand she moved the cherries out of Siemela's eye.

HSsssssss ... Siemela's intake of breath was sharp and swift as butter burning in the pan. Butter turning brown and bubbling over. Butter, perhaps, shooting up to seek out the cook's tender flesh. Before she could say another word, however, the girl, who'd been listening to the grown-ups forlornly, pulled at her mother's arm.

Can we go play outside? she asked, Louisa, Beauty's granddaughter who wouldn't even try the putu.

Lucky started to say no, my girl, you must talk to your Ouma who came so far to visit but Siemela interrupted him: *yebo,* let the children go, why must they stay inside all day? Nothing for them to do here, *nothing*. Rather let them get fresh air by the park.

Later, while waiting for her second bus, Beauty took the food from her shopping bag. The wind blew leaves and cigarette butts through the gutters. Stink of coal fires, smoke, paraffin, exhaust fumes, exhaustion. The wind blew *tu tu tu* on the loose tin foil wrapping in her hand. Beauty stuffed the wrapped putu in a dustbin. From the corner of her eye she saw street children stirring in the shadows. Three, four darted to the dustbin, rummaging for the food that the stupid rich somebody had thrown away.

Humba, humba wena! Beauty shouted at the children. *Why must you eat this rotten food, hnh?*

But the children began to scream and shout.

Old woman, old woman! they taunted her, the taunt becoming the words to a song, the song chanted in unison with much clapping and stamping and spitting in the gutter, *pitoo!*

Old woman, old woman,
don't trip as you walk,
for you might stumble
and fall into your grave.

Anger gathered in her like a stomach spasm. Beauty grasped her shoe by the heel. Without aim, blindly, she heaved it into the night and the scattering children.

With Mustapha sitting beside him Benjamin was driving past the beggars plying their trade on Jan Smuts Avenue. The transparent beggars,
Mustapha called them. You must just learn to look through them, he
always told Benjamin. It was dusk and darkness seemed to rise from the
earth, a low winter sky thickening. At taxi ranks along the way commuters dawdled in weary queues, their bodies merging against bluegum and
eucalyptus so that it seemed as if bodies, trees, and earth were all composed of the same half-human half-mineral element. Benjamin shivered.

At traffic lights newspaper vendors held up their banners, headlines blurring then focusing again in approaching headlights. *Family of
15 Die in House Fire,* one of the vendors read aloud from *The Star,* his
face contorted into an expression of horror or compassion. The forced
smell of winter roses from flower stalls at the side of the road wafted
into the Audi. Benjamin drove swiftly past the broadsheets — *Girl (7)
Rape Ordeal; Rand Plunges Again! Alex Carnage: Pictures* — past the
beggars with their crutches and downcast eyes, their jingle pockets. At
every traffic intersection, every break in the road, the beggars held up
their handwritten signs — Pleese to Help, no Job, 3 to Fead, homles,
God Bles U. Cupped hands then *jingle, jingle.*

You must learn to look through them for chrissakes, lovey,
Mustapha always scolded whenever Benjamin rolled down his window and fumbled for change. This time the man who came forward
swiftly tucked his cap under his arm and accepted the money in the
traditional way with both palms cupped and a hasty bend of the knee,
thankyou-godbless. Usale kahle.

Tcha, an increasingly impatient Mustapha expostulated, intent
on jiggling the plastic dial of the car radio through static and white
noise and talk shows until he found a music station he could live with.
But when Benjamin glanced in the rearview mirror he saw the man
waving both hands above his head, stamping his feet on the ground.
Apparently demented with gratitude.

In truth it wasn't the beggars that Benjamin found impossible to
ignore so much as their grimy cardboard signs, misspelled and pathetic.
Where did they come from, these wayfarers, with their heartbroken

advertisements and pleas? Was there a street kiosk somewhere in the townships where a calligrapher sat scribbling? Tongue poking out, deliberately misspelling words, disfiguring letters, the better to invoke pity in the hearts of passing motorists? One by one, Benjamin imagined these professional beggars stepping forward to confide their woes to the scribe who'd commit them to ink, bossily advising on the price of unemployment, deformity, disease.

At yet another traffic light a man stepped forward, serenely holding up his sign —

UnemPloyed. 5 KIDs. One CanCEr.
One BraIN TumER, two AIDS.
One ReTard. WiFe HAS AnoreXia.
No Money No Food. God Bless Africa!

Catching Benjamin's eye, Mustapha grew defensive. Hey, a juba's got to sing for his supper, man. A juba's got to live.

A ray from the setting sun caught and, momentarily, held the outline of a minaret from one of the mosques out by Lenasia. Benjamin wanted to ask the boy what he was thinking but knew better. Nothing, wallah, Mustapha would have replied with some scorn. Stop making complications.

In the smoky winter evening men and women continued to wait patiently for their transport. As Benjamin watched, a minibus tacked across the road as if at the mercy of the wind, sliding to an abrupt halt just as the lights turned green, then revving officiously as they changed. This particular taxi had only one broken window and it was mended with cardboard rather than the usual scrap of flapping plastic but it lacked indicators and one brake light was smashed. As the van clipped a tight corner a man hastily stuck his hand out of the passenger window to execute an abbreviated scribble on the air. A hand signal that was indicative, no doubt, of sudden unrehearsed turns in the face of oncoming traffic. Benjamin flinched.

It had become commonplace to deride the taxi drivers for their mad antics, their death defying ways. They were deplored as road anarchists whose lawlessness put everyone at risk. The drivers along the Soweto highway and the old Potchefstroom Road were the worst but, as Ouma was inclined to point out, it was all much of a muchness. What does it matter where the taxi's going when it runs you over, my boykie!

Watch out for the Black Taxis, Ouma was fond of warning her grandson. They stop wherever they like, *sommer so*, middle of the street. Drunk, most of them, and no such thing as indicators, *tcha*.

Back in the silver Audi Benjamin swerved as a minibus taxi without working headlights swooped suddenly to the shoulder of the road where it idled aggressively while passengers climbed aboard. Somebody handed a string bag of oranges through the window before the vehicle revved off into the night that was cold and dark but in which, at least in the brief ride between highway and home, no rocks were thrown, no windshields shattered.

Ouma woke suddenly from a dream in which her son was alive and robust but unable, for some reason, to see her. She felt obscurely hurt by the dream as if Lourens had been deliberately ignoring her and she sat up briskly against her pillows and fumbled for her spectacles so as to bring the world back into focus. The room had been neatened as she slept and Beauty had cleared away the tray from the light supper she'd eaten earlier. But what had she eaten? Honey on toast, she recalled, and tea, of course. But it was no good. The sadness that the dream brought in its wake couldn't be kept at bay.

Shame Mama, Beauty had tried to comfort her in the days and weeks and months following the accident. My heart is sore.

Shame, Mama.

Ouma suddenly remembered an afternoon—how many years ago? She was visiting her son in the city only she'd been out for the afternoon and she was returning from God knows where but the front door was ajar because this was long ago and anyone was welcome to push open the door, dawdle in the parquet hall and exchange a friendly greeting with Grandfather before calling out *anyone home?*

Because in those days a mere latch key was thought sufficient to keep the world at bay. Hesitating in the hallway, all those years ago, Ouma heard children's voices coming from the garden. It was early summer, the plums were small and sour, the size of cherries. As if to hold down a corner of the windy lawn, somebody had piled a handful of rusks on a plate in the grass and there were also pink meringues, at once glutinous and crumbly. Across the garden two children ran towards Ouma—Beauty's girl, Givvie, and Benjamin. Hand in hand, joined at the wrist like gingerbread children, they galloped across the lawn.

Ag, they had been two of a kind, Ouma now recalled. Unprepossessing little beggars, the both of them. Suppers in the kitchen where the two would devour hard-boiled eggs softened with dabs of butter. Givvie solicitous and Benjamin worshipful. Perched on kitchen chairs, plates in their laps, a pair of long brown legs and a pair of short kicky legs dangled. Both pairs grass-nicked and dirty, swinging in time to the rise and fall of their voices. Ouma tried to recall these voices, their noisy chatter as the children pushed the soft yellow yolks into their mouths. Instead she remembered a gardener wearily sweeping the kitchen floor between their feet, rolling his eyes and occasionally cursing under his breath. Always Lourens had been terribly busy and Ilse had just come in from somewhere, was about to leave for somewhere else. She'd drift in on clouds of scent, one hand to her chignon, heels snapping on the slate. Goodbye my little love, *mon petit*. Kiss mummy gently, *gently*.

The Liberation Grill had recently opened but for how long it would remain so nobody knew. Like liberation itself it had been a long time coming but in a city in which restaurants opened and closed with the randomness of disgruntled oysters, an eating establishment had to showcase something rather more convincing than the accomplishment of good food to draw patrons to its stainless steel, attractively "raw" industrial-looking doors. For the Liberation Grill this something appeared to be the promise of revolution; freedom expressed through a subtle fusion of nouvelle cuisine and wittily disposed menu items. Steak Tutu and Rainbow Nation Trout! And for dessert might we recommend our famous Goodwill Chocolate Mousse? Triple layers of white, milk, and dark chocolate peacefully reconciled between buttery shortbread wafers. It all played to the tourist trade, of course, cheap sentiment with an undertone of irony for the initiated.

Now Benjamin watched Mus pout and huff as first one dish and then another caught his disdainful fancy. *So what?* he seemed to be asking himself. *Big deal. Big fat bloody deal.*

How had the lad graduated so rapidly, Benjamin wondered but not for the first time, from the urchin who'd never, he was willing to wager, entered a suburban restaurant and certainly not as a customer, to this increasingly hard to please epicure? This dining savant, this savage gourmet?

By the time the drinks arrived, Mustapha successfully quenching his delight at the bizarrely coloured cocktails, and the bruschetta been huffed away (not crisp enough), the floral arrangement suitably deplored (too stiff), Benjamin's stomach lining was hissing with irritation and the sting of hastily gulped alcohol. Blah blah blah, Mustapha's mouth opened and closed like a guppy, the twang and jerk of his touchingly overlarge Adam's apple failing, for once, to move Benjamin to tenderness. In fact, the only reason he remained sitting compliantly across the table from the boy, who at this moment was in a spirited discussion with the over-solicitous waiter about the ratio of ginger to garlic in Sweet Freedom Duck, was his new haircut and the resultant expanse of sleek brown neck visible above the raffishly splayed collar. Certainly Benjamin had failed, of late, to engage Mustapha in anything like the *esprit* he was even now exhibiting at the mere mention of orange zest.

Actually I met someone half interesting this week, Mustapha announced when the waiter at last departed.

Comes up to me on Diagonal. Wants to know am I Mr. Fa? And how is Mr. Fa? he asks. *Who?* I say. *Mr. Fa.* Oh, you want to speak to *Mus*tapha! I nearly died laughing.

Often Benjamin wasn't sure that he loved the boy but equally frequently a gush of tenderness washed away his irritation. Perhaps

I really do love him, thought Benjamin, gazing fondly at his lover's knobbly Adam's apple as it bobbed about in his throat. At least the things that once irritated now only amused and that, surely, was a sign of affection?

A seafood stew brimming with everything from lobster pincers to chicken wings was unveiled before them. Benjamin tried to imagine how the hapless chicken had made its way into the sea. Maybe the poor thing drowned, he mused, taking a wry forkful of Sisulu Seafood Stew and contemplating sending the whole mess of beak and claw back to the kitchen. *Un petit goût,* he imagined urging the seriously deluded chef. Just a taste, *c'est tout.*

Lips shiny with excitement and garlic butter, Mustapha chattered on.

Says he'll get me a permit for the corner of Sauer Street, near the Stock Exchange. This country you got to be black with a capital B, he says. Indian like me doesn't count. Anyway, this guy's what they call a real phanda, an operator. Wants to buy into the business, you know, Hurry-Curry Inc. That way *I* get the permit and he gets a share, well not a *big* share, but like a per*cen*tage of the profits. And *plus,* as an interested party he sends customers my way. Passengers and so forth. Says he knows some businessmen around there, they'll put in orders for takeout lunches, Christmas parties. Kind of thing.

Didn't believe him, at first. Told him I wasn't born yesterday and like that. He just looks at me, *ja china.* Then he scores me his business card. See you later, alligator.

Mustapha slid a rectangle of gold-coloured cardboard across the table. Sat back to catch his lover's reaction. Benjamin angled the card under the floating candles to make out the name. MADIBA MIIDA, TAXI MAN, was written above a single line in winsome italics: *Or What You Need.*

It was this last phrase that rankled Benjamin. That and the taxi man's preposterous name. What the hell did MADIBA MHDA, TAXI bloody MAN threaten in terms of danger, financial ruin, or just plain advantage taken-ness vis-à-vis the boy? It seemed one couldn't even let Mus out on the streets, these days, without supervision. Accepting gaudy business cards and promises and who knew what else from strangers. There he sat, a hundred and fifteen pounds soaking bloody wet with wrists you could snap between two fingers and it was no use offering advice. Advice and fifty cents would get you a phone call, maybe —*may*be—all things being equal which they never were in this city.

He had to be careful, but. Couldn't tell the boy to wise up. It would only provoke more flak, Benjamin knew. A hands on the hips, you're-not-the-boss-of-me stance that would last through dessert and halfway into next week. Look at him, though. Benjamin watched fondly as his lover slid a fork about the plate, his colour heightened by the red wine. Mustapha always ate well when he was excited, bless him. The rest of the time it was a sniff, a taste, and a shrug but give him a reason to forget food and it did Benjamin's heart good to watch him eat.

In the dark well of the restaurant, secured against the night, the patrons gave themselves over to the languour induced by rich sauces, thin washes of conversation transparent as consommé. Ice cubes collided against the sides of glasses, bright eyes flashed with secrets, gossip, confidences. A silk-lined fur slid off the back of a chair, scarves fluttered, elbows jostled, every now and then a waiter half-stumbled over a leg stretched recklessly between tables, *sorry sorry*. Mustapha grew expansive. Overflowing like a trifle, he absorbed wine and good cheer, giving off whiffs of creamy self-importance as he catalogued his business plans.

Question of roll over. No, or *turn* over, I mean. Orders per day, that's what I got to develop. Find a way to make more lunch hour portions at night, okay? But what's it to you, lovey, I'm not asking for *money!*

Only rent boys accepted cash from their rich lovers, Mustapha had informed Benjamin curtly from the start, such transactions being common knowledge in a city in which secrecy was the sieve that caught and failed to hold all manner of confidences.

As for Mustapha he never demanded, expected, so much as *asked* for money, *never*, often refusing cash when it was offered although he refused very little else; not expensive dinners or theatre tickets or gift-wrapped silk ties and designer cologne. Not the leather jacket he wore draped over his slim shoulders or casually looped from an index finger, and not the little ring of artfully bonded white and yellow gold that banded this same index finger. At an adjoining table a woman was feeding her lover spoonfuls of bitter fig sorbet, one hand cupped beneath his mouth. Mopping his lips she gazed upon him tenderly as if he was a large but agreeable infant. Mustapha winced, swiftly crossing his eyes for Benjamin's benefit.

Ah that old standby, derision.

The wince, the smirk, the gift of one of Mus's Special Faces! Against his better judgment Benjamin wondered if this relationship, the peripatetic love affair of Benjamin du Plessis and Mustapha Kunju, was destined to last. Still, in good conscience, he couldn't allow the boy to go ahead with this folly, striking deals with cocky taxi men in the business of procuring dreams and fantasies, the rectangular gold promise of *What You Need*.

Taking advantage of Mus's distraction Benjamin tried to slip the business card beneath the tablecloth with its gobs of sauce and winding bread crumb trail. But Mustapha was wise to him and snatched it back, sliding the taxi man's well-thumbed card into his wallet with those slender wincing fingers.

Her body was in the kitchen of the house on Sugarbush Road but her mind was remembering the pull of Meneer's great car returning her to the city after her daughter died. Beauty was recalling the swiftness of that journey, the swiftness of a life changing without warning. Abruptly, as if nothing had happened, as if a woman had merely sneezed then wiped her nose. Back from so far away, Beauty reflected once again that the best part of her had remained crouched on the floor of Mamma Thlali's shack in Hammanskraal whatever else she was doing which at the moment was rinsing the supper dishes. And she remembered how her life had been stolen from her and how she'd revenged herself by stealing everything she could back from life. But Lord — and now anger punched her softly in the stomach — from a distance it all looked the same. An old black woman like a ghost in the night, stealing away from her life.

History, ha! Mamma Thlali had scolded her, scolded her hard.

Mamma Thlali who in those days had been angry—righteous anger, hot and blazing—history, *ha*! Better wipe the past from your shoe, my daughter. Dog shit!

Yebo, dog shit, Beauty had agreed, swiping at Eli's puppy dog turds with a stick to knock them into the rockery so that Meneer didn't have to step too deeply into history when he came outside to feed his fish or what have you. But Lord how Mamma Thlali wearied her. That heavyset jaw, that head wagging from side to side between stretched lobes threaded with all kinds of odd talismans. Keys and spoons and beads, even stones from the riverbed. *Clang clang,* the noise of those crazy earrings punctuating her mother-in-law's grief.

Dog shit, *ja*! Beauty thought, wiping off her shoe on the grass. At that time Mamma Thlali was like a crazy Sangoma who spoke only in proverbs, in riddles, and so was likely to go hungry for her inability to request a piece of bread, to say please pass the meat, the salt. It was lucky that she had a daughter-in-law who got paid twice a month for knocking history out of sight at the end of a forked stick. And lucky, indeed, that this daughter-in-law was adept at wiping more than the stinking past from the heel of her shoe.

While Beauty was lost in her memories the dish water had grown cold, the dishes were scudding beneath a greasy scum of soapsuds. Fumbling to locate the plug, her hand wincing away from twining oddments, *sies!*, she sluiced hot water from the faucet over plates, cups, saucers, handfuls of crockery and Ouma's fat brown teapot. She filed the dishes in their draining slots and dumped the knives and forks in their caddies but the teapot required scouring with a bottle brush and as she scoured Beauty began to think about the house on Sugarbush Road, the house over which she'd rubbed herself thin with work and polish, this house with its wraparound verandah, shiny red stoep, the syringa behind and the tended gravel sweep in front, old Grandfather between display cases stocked with Meneer's medals, insignia, the memorabilia of twenty-four years in politics, and the dark oak banisters she must polish every month—even between the slats entwined with grape leaves—so that, over the years, the wood had taken on the deep brown glow of her back while her own skin had merely greyed and cracked with age. This house was not, had never been, her home.

True it was hers to sweep and clean, hers to rub into life every day between the warmth of her palms. It was hers to burnish by way of the bracing carbolic soap in dull green slabs that must be hewn into hand-sized pieces, usable portions to scrub the dishes and the pots, the walls and the floors, and yes, late at night, the weary body of Beauty Mapule, also. (Bloody *marvelous* stuff, Meneer would exclaim, admiring her handiwork. Nothing like pure carbolic soap, I tell you!) It was hers to smooth and fold, wiping surfaces over and over, bathroom tiles beaded with water, kitchen windows sweated with cooking smells and conversations, the floor with its skid marks from the lawnmower, running shoes, the cursed dog. In thirty-two years there wasn't a surface she hadn't rubbed until her fingertips had smoothed over, losing their whorls in the grain of imbuia and oak. One day they'd come to fingerprint her and her fingertips would be blank, thought Beauty. Then she would say to them: Go! Go, look for these precious fingerprints. Perhaps you'll find them on Grandfather who stands in the hall, ha-ha.

Even Beauty's late husband, Hosiah Mopede, Church of Zion, would lose his temper sometimes and thunder, Perhaps heaven too will have a kitchen door for all us kaffirs to queue behind!

In one of his rare angers, his forehead bunched and wrathful, he would pound one fist rhythmically into his palm: And we will stand before St. Peter like kitchen boys in broken-laced garden boots waiting for their bowls of pap and stew. For, lo, in my Father's heaven there are many mansions, are there not? And in every mansion there is a kitchen and at every kitchen door some poor black bastard is trying to sneak in and snatch a spoonful of sour porridge off the stove!

But his rages had been few and far between, Beauty reflected. Far more often he'd accepted his burden, the burden of his people to labour in the kitchens and gardens of the white suburbs. As for Me and My House We Will Serve the Lord, had been a favourite text, inevitably followed by an equally comforting quip: In the meantime we must be content to serve the blessed du Plessis (or the holy van Rensburgs or the hallowed ver Jaarsvelds or the sacred de Graafs).

She had long ago finished cleaning the teapot but even this small act filled her with contempt for the weak and milky tea that once Ilse and now Ouma preferred.

No sugar, and you must stir in the milk *afterwards*, Beauty, otherwise the tea will be scalded.

Scalded meant burnt. Burnt milk. Such nonsense tea, truly, it curdled Beauty's heart with contempt. Give her the African way of brewing tea any day. Good strong Rooibos or Joko or Five Roses tea, very strong, very. Three, four minutes to steep, then the teabag wrung out for all the goodness to dissolve in the radiant heat of a tin mug. Condensed milk and sugar added together. Brick red and thick and hot, scalding and sweet as the mercy of the Lord.

Just thinking about that strong brewed tea made Beauty long for a cup but she was too damn tired to even fill the kettle. Instead, fumbling in her apron pocket she found a hand-rolled cigarette. A couple of good long draws through the open window would settle the lungs, calm the mind. Afterwards she'd look in on Ouma who was, please God, asleep and not wanting to talk — *kom, Beauty, kan ons gaan 'n bietjie gesels? Mmm?* — and then she'd lock up for the night, slide in beside the blessed warmth of Agremon who wouldn't wake, couldn't, because Monday was his day at the de Wets and the de Wets possessed not one but two fierce Rottweilers and a garden about which they were most particular even in winter.

Smiling in anticipation of this unlooked-for pleasure, Beauty gentled a match from the box of kitchen matches and, without glancing down, struck it against the sandpaper strip on the side of the box. *Pppht.* Scowling, she flipped the used matchstick into the sink. Tried another, another.

Once more.

Awah! Always but *always.* Benjamin and his bloody matches! These days it seemed that whenever Beauty slid a match from the box of Lion Matches with its lone springbok bucking across the front cover, the matchstick was already used. Then she'd have to stand there with the rotten matchstick, its phosphorous tip as useless as a bent cigarette which she now also clutched in a hand grown stiff and unreasonable with anger. But if she still had a cigarette to light or — as had happened before and *how* many times? — a candle, the downstairs stove in the servant's quarters or Agremon's occasional pipe, then she'd have to search for another match and, finding that one used, another, and then another. *Tcha,* but why — *why* — did that man return the matches, those useless dead matches, to their box?

God in heaven, it was a black mystery to her what he meant by it but some dark witchcraft was intended, that was plain. Of *that* Beauty was certain.

Beauty rinsed the last of the sudsy water from the rim of the basin and the grouted edges of the sink. Wrung the dishcloth then her hands dry. A beam of sudden light from a car passing on the main road shafted the dim kitchen. Time to lock up and bed down. Be done. Time to be done.

She padded about the house fastening windows, locking doors, setting alarms. The big panelled oak door that Meneer had commissioned when the house was first built so that visitors could walk into the hall as if they were entering a church, this door had once been glossy and smooth. Beauty still polished the door every month or so with beeswax and furniture oil but now it was pocked with hardware, scarred with locks and chains and recessed peepholes. Beauty tested the Yale lock, the double latch, the Chubb, then drew the chain into its heavy slot.

The last thing she did every night, last thing of all, was wind Grandfather.

Ouma was lying still, a forearm hooked across her eyes, inert. But Beauty could tell she was asleep by the breath that rose and fell in her chest and the dog curled nose-to-haunches at the foot of her bed. As she watched, the dog turned around swiftly, his fur flashing blue static against the blanket.

Agremon was asleep by the time Beauty locked the kitchen door and picked her way across the backyard to her room. The smell of his supper, mieliepap and meat stew, hung heavily about the servant's quarters. He'd turned off the old ungainly stove that wobbled in the passageway but had neglected to rinse out the leftover pap. Now a dried-out husk of encrusted maize meal stuck to the sides of the enamel pot and would continue to do so until Beauty got round to levering off the mess with a blunt knife tomorrow or the day after. Some day, never.

At least Agremon seldom forgot to clean out the plastic dog dish which Beauty had for months now refused to touch. Scraping away the reeking, dried-up Epol with a stick, rinsing the sides with a blast from the hose. He even wiped away the drippings with a handful of grass or a bunch of leaves. He hardly ever forgot, no matter how weary he was, no matter how bone-sore the day had left him.

Inside the room, a pair of boots, their tongues lolling from gaping insoles, lay capsized beneath the bed. On the bedside table was an open tin of tobacco. Agremon slept restlessly with smoke on his breath and exhaustion sunk into the lines of his face. Beauty loosened her doek, splashed water on her face. With one hand clutching the cardigan about her shoulders she shrugged out of her overall and into her nylon nightie. The coldness of the concrete floor reached up through the rug, through the cracked soles of her slippers. She bent to turn on the heater, ignoring Ouma's voice that was always telling Beauty she mustn't fall asleep with the fire on, *nè*.

Yebo, Beauty would say to Ouma's face, but in these cold, hard, crackling highveld nights she had decided she would rather die of fire than of cold.

The electric heater with its two working bars imprinted itself on the darkness; cast a faint light, a faint warmth, transforming Beauty from a woman lost to herself, kneeling in a dark room, to a woman preparing to lay down beside her man. Agremon stirred, put his open hand on her breast.

Alive, the bars hummed, *not dead, not dead, not yet*.

A huge self-perfecting moon rose above the city. The moon rose high above the downtown core where newspapers and cigarette butts blew through the windy streets deserted at this late hour except for the dust-bin rummagers and the beggars, the lost children, the tsotsis, the scrap metal scavengers, the loose women. A night watchman in greatcoat and balaclava warmed himself beside a coal brazier, sneezing hugely between pinches of snuff.

Slowly the moon rose over the highway where smoke from a traffic collision was dispersing over mangled bodies and blazing vehicles, then it rose higher still, over the south western townships where children were composing celebration songs in their dreams, lifting their heroes on their shoulders, linking their arms and stamping their feet and singing—

N–e–l–s–o–n!
Ahona otshwanang leyena!
Hoof hoof left! Hoof hoof right!
There is nobody like him!

And from this height the moon shone down steadily on the high-veld, on dry riverbeds and water courses rattling their stones as if every paltry mouthful had already been sucked dry from the land. From this height too one could hear the peoples' prayers for rain wafting upwards, the clasp of hands lifted to an empty sky, the hoarse rasp of wheat shaken to ashes in the burning fields.

As the city's multitudinous sleepers turned over in their beds and the moon began its descent across the southern sky, something flickered down below. Something was slouching across the veld holding tight to its blue-black tongue with its hairy front paws. "Nothing will keep me away," it seemed to be saying, "nothing will keep me from your children."

The tokoloshe—for yes, it was he—that veld goblin turned and loped over the rim of the world. And darkness flew from the earth like a flock of birds.

5

THE LITTLE HOUSE OF BEAUTY MAPULE

S leek and glossy, with the well-formed, calcium rich bones of one
who has been raised on pap and milk, Dhlamina Mopede was presiding over the kitchen at 471 Wisteria Gardens, a happily content
domestic spirit. She was in her fifth month of pregnancy, the morning sickness that had plagued her a thing of the past and although
it was not in her nature to count her blessings, had she suddenly felt
the need to do so, the first of these would have been her new position
with Mrs. Magda. Dhlamina had never worked for a Madam before
and now she couldn't think why, given the force of her famous love
magnetism, this solution had never occurred to her.

Go ahead, Beauty had said when she'd told her about the job, but
that one is a real sourpuss. Don't say I didn't warn you, my daughter.

And it was true that Mrs. Magda wasn't exactly a joyous spirit but
what did Dhlamina care? One thing at least was certain, her cantan-
kerous employer was unlikely to fall in love with her and this indifference was a welcome change.

Tcha, Beauty would exclaim after one or another of her stepdaughter's employer's would fall prey to her redoubtable charms. What do
you want to cause such a fuss and a nonsense, my child?

But truly it was not Dhlamina's fault. Did she spice this one's food
with patent aphrodisiacs or spike that one's drink with home-distilled
love potions? No, assuredly not. For if other women might benefit
from a few drops of *Only You*, a squeeze of *Bobaby*, a splash of *Go
Kwalla*, Dhlamina Mopede had no need of any such artificial goads to
passion. The weather system that a person carries within herself and
that alerts the world to a sunny disposition or storm clouds ahead,
prevailing winds or a sudden drought of the heart was, in Dhlamina's

case, staunch and intemperate. She presented an unwavering magnetic north to all who came within her compass and most men were merely the iron filings that tossed and twitched in her wake.

But Dhlamina, it seemed, had finally found a solution to the love magnetism that had plagued her since adolescence. At this very moment, Mrs. Magda, undismayed by her new girl's charms was labouring over the daily crossword puzzle. Dhlamina beamed.

And she wants someone to cook too, Beauty had cautioned. So how are you going to manage that, my girl?

It was true that, apart from the takeaway stands and the vending kiosks she'd once fronted, Dhlamina had no real experience cooking. But she remained jaunty. In Mrs. Magda's kitchen, cookery books were piled on shelves, their glossy pages inflected with exclamations of sauce or wadded together with clarified butter and caramelized sugar. The largest of all these cookery books had toppled right off the shelf when she'd opened the kitchen cupboard; right off the shelf and into her waiting hands! It was a fat maroon book that was missing its slipcover but a firm hand in black ink had written directly on the inside cover, *Mrs. Moffert's Inquire Within*. Oho, thought Dhlamina, what have we here!

Mrs. Moffert's Inquire Within was written in a clipped old-fashioned style and there were few illustrations to aid the novice chef although the same hand that had signed the inside cover had appended various helpful hints and occasional reservations to some of the recipes. It was certainly not the most glamorous of the books piled haphazardly on the kitchen shelves but Dhlamina was a great believer in the felicities of chance and from the moment she'd felt the heft of *Mrs. Moffert* fall into her hands she knew she'd found her teacher. Humming now with the deep steady hum that was so much a part of her contentment that she no longer heard herself, Dhlamina bent to peer inside the oven where her homemade buttermilk rusks were drying overnight on a low heat. What a treat this would be for Mrs. Magda, Dhlamina thought, and for herself too for neither woman liked to dip stale Bokomo rusks, bought off the shelf, into their midmorning tea.

Next door, in the ornate dining room whose windows, fringed with potted plants, looked out onto a courtyard trained with the wisteria that would bloom in spring, Magda pondered her cryptic crossword.

"Plethoric River," she read aloud. "Eight letters." Her mouth formed the shape of the elusive word and she made small popping sounds with her lips.

Plethoric, plethoric...*po po po*.

Magda sneaked a glance at the straight clue.

Nineteen across, "perjorative battle," it says here. Plethoric, perjora — suddenly light dawned.

Sanguine, Dhlamina! Eight letters, Blood River, battle of. Plethoric, meaning to overflow, *ja*, like the rivers with the blood of the Zulus. Excellent.

Dhlamina chuckled. Must have given those Boers a big fright, Mrs. Magda. See all that Zulu blood.

Mmm.

But Dhlamina was well-launched on her subject and, ignoring Magda's distraction, she flung herself onto the chair beside her, her braids swaying from the cornrows that swirled across the crown of her head like graceful contour lines in a verdant field.

...because by Sibisi School they told us that the rivers overflowed with the blood of the Zulus so they must call the battle Blood River but me, I think they should have called it the Battle of the Big Surprise. The Battle of the Terrible Shock. *Awah!* Because that was the day the Boers learned that the Zulus bled the same colour as they did. Black skin, white skin, everyone bleeds red underneath!

Mrs. Magda had finally stopped scrabbling about amongst her cryptic clues and was paying attention so Dhlamina treated her to one of her legendary smiles, a smile that was itself a flowing river to which all the tributaries of her features—eyes, dimple, lips—contributed their fluent charm.

Ag! Magda was frequently startled by Dhalmina's outrageous observations but this time her maid's remarks had put her in mind of a story that, in her meandering way, she began to relate.

Reminds me of the time Ouma took me to John Orrs for tea. Eloff Street, long before your time, *meisie*, very smart it was in those days. And such a treat for a young girl, the dainties on their silver platters, the models in their evening gowns! Afterwards we'd always visit the ladies' room to adjust the corsets, *ag*, you know ... Hmm, I think I liked the powder room even more than the tea room—all those matrons on their upholstered stools powdering their noses in gilt-framed glass, ha! Sometimes Ouma had to nudge me in the ribs as if to say, Don't stare my girl, keep your eyes to yourself! Well, one day just as we're leaving, an ousie pushes past us, she wants to use the lavatory...

Magda trailed off. Too late it had occurred to her that her story might cause offense. Oh but really, if one wasn't even allowed one's memories ... She stared fixedly into the distance until Dhlamina, clicking her tongue impatiently, bustled off into the kitchen where loud music from the radio testified to her good-humoured pique. Left alone in that long ago afternoon Magda remembered how the powder room had fallen unnaturally silent at the ousie's entrance, the clatter of heels on tile, the chatter of voices, all stilled. It was her mother, of course, who'd stepped forward to tap the woman on her shoulder. Ouma had always worn her authority like brass buttons and epaulettes— a general going into battle! Head high, shoulders back, chin forward, right or wrong!

You can't come in here, my girl. Ouma had grasped the woman firmly by the arm. *Here is whites only. No, you must try and find a non-European lav down by the bus depot.*

All around the rose-hued room the women on their fringed stools had silently nodded their assent. One or two of the ladies rolled their eyes to themselves in their mirrors as if to say *cheeky monkey!* But others were stiff with outrage, their jaws rigid at this intrusion into the undefended harbour of white womanhood. Neither inclined to levity nor undue formality, Ouma had the bizarre situation firmly in control. Grasping the ousie by her shoulder she had succeeded in turning her about and was proceeding to hustle her from the cloakroom when the other woman suddenly jerked free. In one angry movement she bent and was suddenly hoisting Ouma's skirts, hiking up her petticoats and jabbing at the gusset of her formidable "two way."

Hey lady what's your fucken problem? We're all the same colour down there lady! Down there we're all the same colour!

Magda giggled suddenly. No, perhaps this story lost something to translation. Another time, another place. One in which women wore bust bodices and afternoon pearls and little girls accompanied their mothers into cloakrooms and shame was expunged with a layer of fine powder dabbed gently over the bridge of a shiny nose. Neither Magda nor her mother ever spoke of that afternoon again.

Magda was no closer to completing her crossword. She tapped her fingers on the shimmering surface of the mahogany dining table that had once belonged to her mother-in-law.

"Aged Breasts Depart," she read aloud. "Six letters." Once more her fingers tapped out the recalcitrant syllables but the clues remained stubbornly fixed on the page and the broadsheet folded before her remained as patchily blank as it had ever been. Magda allowed herself a surreptitious glance at the straight clue.

Seven down, "cling to, part from." Hmmm.

Tap tap tap.

The sun shining in through the windows was warm, perhaps too warm, and in its steady winter heat Magda grew lethargic and distracted. She patted her stiff blonde "set" but carefully refrained from glancing upwards to catch a glimpse of herself in the heavy bevelled looking glass that had once hung over her mother-in-law's sideboard. The thieves, led by the treacherous Fiela, had made off with the gilt-framed glass although the bulky Victorian sideboard remained as did the mahogany dining table and her treasured Tretchikoff mother-and-child oil, thank the Lord. What barbarians they were, Magda marvelled again, but then perhaps they'd been too busy plotting to kill her kittens to bother with one precious oil painting.

The old familiar lump rose in her throat and she began, as she had trained herself to do and with what anguish, to count her blessings.

There were the studio photographs on the mantelpiece that had remained intact despite the need to replace the odd piece of shattered glass and now wherever she looked her children and grandchildren smiled down upon her. The tsotsis had been greedy but oddly idiosyncratic so that many of Mrs. Moffert's more delicate treasures remained—a collection of Royal Doulton figurines, a couple of Staffordshire terriers, a Wedgwood teapot. Of course they'd been unsurprisingly thorough in divesting the apartment of the Moffert silver, the crested dinner service, the Turkish rugs and the television set, thought Magda sarcastically but she caught herself up quickly and returned to the thought of the Wedgwood teapot whose cool blue and cream cheeks turned tea time into a stately ceremony.

Yes, how often she remembered sitting before her mother-in-law at this very table as she counted silver forks and dessert spoons after a tea party. Placing each piece of heavy crested cutlery precisely in its narrow canteen. Or taking up her *petit-point*, arranging silks and cottons in well-bred rows on the occasional table, the characteristic curl of concentration like a charming asterisk between her brows. Writing precise and punctual thank you notes at her *escritoire*, pen and ink and blotting paper to hand. Blotting paper!

Poor Johannes! Magda spared a thought, as she sometimes did, for her husband who had passed away as he had lived, unemphatically. He'd been kindly and indulgent in providing her with the lifestyle she preferred and the daughters she craved but his mother stood astride his life like a colossus and she, too, had been expected to pay court. Patience, she'd reminded herself for years, for years! she can't last forever. Well she'll certainly die trying, the old fraud, Ouma would often mock in that way she had, throwing her head back and chortling to beat the band. The one thing Magda could say about her mother-in-law was that she was never vulgar, that she could certainly say.

When dear Johannes died—what was it? ten, no eleven years ago already—Magda found herself, rather to her surprise, invited, no en*treated*, to move in with old Mrs. Moffert. Two plucky widows together! And had the old girl not softened a little, had she not unbent ever so slightly towards her long-suffering daughter-in-law? Magda remembered her best from that time as a lofty presence dozing in the old wingback, her handsome profile set off by the guipure lace collar and good opal brooch she always wore on Sundays. And she had positively shuddered with tenderness for Elizabeth Regina, the first of the Persian kittens.

Magda sighed.

After Mrs. Moffert died Magda decided to remain on at Wisteria Gardens rather than construct for herself yet another version of a possible life. Besides she'd grown to like the home she had shared with her mother-in-law, the antiques and bric-a-brac, the archipelagos of comfort and indulgence they had created for themselves amongst the scatter pillows and shaded lamps and nesting tables of the cavernous old-fashioned apartment. And, once old Mrs. Moffert was respectably buried and decently mourned she glowed, positively *glowed* in the forgiving light of recollection. She had been a true lady, a gentlewoman, an aristocrat to the core. Not like her own mother whom honesty impelled her to admit could sometimes err on the side of vulgarity.

How Ouma would have laughed to see Dhlamina bustling about Mrs. Moffert's staid flat in her gaudy finery, Magda thought, but times had changed and the world had moved on, even her little world had moved on and bore no relation at all, she sometimes thought, to the one that had preceded it when she was a newly married woman with a young family and friends of her own. She suddenly thought of her bosom friend in those days, Patrice Verhoeffen with the homely freckled face of a bantam egg and a young family just like her own. They'd lost contact when Patrice moved to the coast but only yesterday someone at the hairdresser mentioned that she'd come back to the city. Give her a call, urged Ouma. Well, perhaps. But it had been—what?—fifteen, sixteen years since they'd even exchanged Christmas cards.

A burst of laughter exploded from the kitchen as Dhlamina, evidently responding to some sally on the radio, rattled the dishes with her mirth. In spite of herself, Magda smiled.

Dhlamina Mopede had arrived to replace the unspeakable Fiela, sweeping in to her first day at work in a purple and scarlet sarong, gold bracelets clattering on her wrists, braids clicking with hundreds of tiny coloured beads. The next day she wore a bright African print and the next, a sari tinkling with mirrored glass and charms. She wore high strappy sandals that showed off her strongly arched feet, gold flashed at her wrists and ears, her nails glistened with shiny paint and her skin had the lustrous sheen that only nightly applications of cocoa butter could achieve. She rubbed olive oil through the length of her hair, twisting dozens of braids into effulgent designs across her beautiful head. If Magda had thought to trouble her with the traditional uniform of the housebroken domestic, the matching overalls and doek, the apron and noiseless slippers, she was swiftly disabused.

Times had certainly changed, thought Magda, which was why she liked a little order to her mornings. A hot breakfast, a decent cup of coffee, and a crossword to solve.

Pursing her lips once more, Magda made the little popping sounds that indicated deep thought. *Po po po*. But the crossword puzzle before her remained dismayingly cryptic despite her best efforts to decipher seven down.

Aged breasts, she muttered. Cling to, part from.

Cleave, offered Dhlamina, her gold tooth flashing as she smoothed the linen tablecloth and placed a plate of steaming kippers before her.

Six letters. To cut apart, to carve. Also, to adhere, unite. From cleavage, hnh?

Magda nodded her thanks, distracted by wafts of salt fish and roasting coffee beans. Abandoning her crossword she gave herself over to the uncomplicated pleasures of breakfast. One thing at a time, and that thing well done, as her mother-in-law used to say. From the grounds of Wisteria Gardens she could hear the distant noise of dogs and scolding women. The apartment block had been hastily renamed after it was declared a heritage building. The former name, Tontina Towers, an amalgam, no doubt, of the names of some earlier landowner's children—Tony and Tina? Tonto and Ina?—had not, it was agreed by Council, taken advantage of the purple and white wisteria that frothed from the trellises and arboretum of the cloistered forecourt each spring. From the kitchen, accompanied by the sound of Kwela jiving on radio waves, Magda could hear the clatter of last night's supper dishes being agitated in the sink while Dhlamina chatted on the phone with the grocer at Thrupps. Although Magda had loved her mother-in-law, and more every day since her death she sometimes thought, the joyous ruckus within which Dhlamina moved and thrived unaffected, no positively en*vig*oured, by the lovely kippery tang of the everyday, was curiously comforting.

While calling out crossword solutions from the open kitchen door Dhlamina could toss a tolerably good luncheon salad, her enthusiastic hips twitching in time to the radio. This radio, perched precariously above the iridescent bubbles of washing-up liquid as they popped and plashed in the sink, played continuously from the moment she arrived early in the morning, cupping cold cheeks in her hands, to late afternoon when, Magda's light supper warming over in the oven, the dishcloth wrung out to dry over a gleaming kitchen sink, Dhlamina boomed her sonorous goodbyes and left with a final convulsive shudder of the front door. An abrupt and painful silence would descend in which Magda fancied she could hear her mother-in-law's delicately intrusive cough, Ah-a-*hem*.

As for her cooking, Magda had to admit that her culinary skills were progressing in delicious leaps and bounds. Last week's kingklip coated in spicy batter and served with malt vinegar had proven quite splendid. Yes, she had a savoury touch, that one, and a near perfect feeling for spices particularly the slightly tremulous sweetness of coriander and fennel that were so often added to ground lamb or beef. If she had a rather heavy hand with the starches—well what did you expect, the Africans all grew up on that indigestible pap and it *ruined* them for whole grains—and if she wouldn't or, Magda supposed, *couldn't* make a decent cup of tea to save her life, what of it? Her sauces were divine, her pastry was superb and even her pickled gherkins had acquired an incongruous air of subtlety. Magda could always make her own tea, couldn't she?

At this very moment Dhlamina was mashing three teabags against the side of a mug of hot milky water until the mixture ran deep red and the scent of tea billowed up into her face. She began to add teaspoons of sugar — three, four — stirred and sipped appreciatively. Then, dividing her time evenly between her steaming mug and *Mrs. Moffert's Inquire Within*, she began to page through the recipe book in search of inspiration. She had wedged a circular, courtesy of Thrupp's Meat Market, between Mrs. Moffert's "Perfect Pickles" and "Piquant Chutneys" and was allowing her mind to wander down the side streets and byways of gastronomy. Presently, with a pencil lazily scratching at the meandering paths of scalp between her braids, she began to compose her grocery list.

Rocket, stilton, (4) Bartlett pears, Dettol, she jotted, the tip of her tongue poking out.

Bottle fish oil, tin coconut milk, Prep H, good bunch kaffir leaves.

What would Beauty say if she could see the list that her stepdaughter was compiling? Dhlamina smiled. Beauty was a cross old thing and the years had only rendered her more grumpy than ever. Are you mad, my daughter, she would exclaim holding her hands to her head. Has the devil taken your brain! And what of the child in your belly, whoever heard of an African child growing strong on — what is this? — fish oil and kaffir leaves! Once again Dhlamina laughed out loud and her laughter was the sunlight that billowed through the room tugging the wind and the curtains and the sound of a jazz trumpet on the radio in its wake.

What now? thought Magda hearing her maid's noisy joy. Was she never to have any peace? She was distracted and a little nervous with the task she had set herself of contacting her old friend, Patrice Verhoeffen. Dhlamina appeared, buttoned carelessly into her red winter coat, a string shopping bag looped about the wrist of one tap-tapping hand, the other smoothing a recalcitrant braid.

Does Mrs. Magda want kingklip for supper again, hmm?

Only if it's fresh, my girl. You know how to check the eyes. And firm to the touch because—

—there's nothing worse than old fish, *yebo*! she finished for her, already turning to the unopened day that beckoned behind the locked front door.

Dhlamina, hold on a seccy, Magda interrupted and Dhlamina turned back obligingly.

Erm, say you haven't spoken to someone for oh, fourteen, fifteen years? Haven't even seen her, in fact. What do you say to her, uh, this lady, when she answers the telephone?

Dhlamina screwed up her eyes in an attempt to whoosh herself back past fifteen years to when she was, hmm, eleven? Who who *who* did she remember? But all she could come up with was the face but not the name of her Grade Two teacher at Sibisi School who had hit her on the head daily and called her fidget-Dhlamina and ants-in-her-pants because she wouldn't-couldn't-*didn't* sit still in class. Well, what would she say to old stink-face, old hyena-breath, that grinning *matekatsi*, that fool?

Ask her how much money she makes and if she still lives all alone because no one wants to marry a fishwife.

Dhlamina paused.

Yes, and you must ask if she enjoys being ninety years old and if she still has to stroke her own pussy every night, she suggested after some thought.

Unlike other children's dreams Givvie's dreams had had weight and heft, were filled with portent. What's more the child had been blessed with waking memory and so, most mornings, was able to report these bright splashes of colour to her mother.

What did you dream last night, *nunkula*? Beauty would inquire in those days when her child woke beside her with milky breath, her hair that Beauty had carefully oiled and plaited the night before a little disordered on the pillow they shared.

Sometimes Givvie dreamed of sharks, a goat, wild marogo growing in the veld or fish scales coming off on the knife. And sometimes she dreamed of the tokoloshe, that spiteful veld goblin who only revealed himself to children, rising up out of the darkness of her sleep to chase her all night with a fork and a soup spoon in his hands and the hunger for a fat brown girl in his heart. At such times her dreams were as cracked and opaque as a silvered hand mirror but more often they were clear as the glass that Beauty could easily see through to the lucky numbers that would take the kitty in the Chinaman's daily fahfee game.

The bottle of milk that the man from Nels dairy deposited at the front door each morning, its silver cap beaded with early morning dew, was number 10 winning eleven rand fifty-five cents off the Chinaman in successive games, and the colour red that resembled the thirsty earth around Hammanskraal was number 17 and had already earned Beauty forty-two rand sixty cents before Givvie was taken from her and buried in this very same earth of which she had so often dreamed.

After Givvie died Beauty's luck with the Chinaman ended but that didn't prevent her dicing fahfee whenever she could get away only now it was a game without joy or assurance, the slow attrition of money lost never quite balanced against the satisfaction of a portentous dream or a lucky flutter. But playing the Chinaman's game reminded Beauty of waking beside her long-legged girl, of early mornings hanging over the ironing board as she flipped through the dog-eared, porridge encrusted *Book of Lucky Numbers* that tumbled her daughter's dreams into the secret combinations that released good fortune from all the hidden places of the world.

Givvie: light as a dream, heavy as memory. From the moment of her conception she had lodged in Beauty as a weight that seemed to accumulate in density with every passing week. By the time she was born her mother was exhausted by the gravity of this pregnancy that seemed to require such solemnity of carriage, such weight of purpose. But the earth, it seemed, was Givvie's natural medium for the air roused her, the sun made her light-headed, the wind blew her clear and lifted her high. As another might be buoyed in water so Givvie became weightless in her mother's arms.

Then she died and Beauty was left, once again, struggling to carry her daughter. Cold cheeks, slack limbs, memory.

Goodnight my mother.

Stay safe, my child. Even in your dreams.

Unlike so many others who still searched for a son's bones, a daughter's last resting place, Beauty carried Givvie with her. Meanwhile the graveyards were full. Avalon Cemetery in Soweto and East Bank Cemetery in Alex Township were overcrowded yet still the lost children ran through the fields in the wake of that tokoloshe. Laughing and singing they beckoned to their mothers. Whistling, dancing, they waved goodbye. But Givvie, Givvie remained silent, hidden. She wouldn't dance with the other children nor would she return to Sugarbush Road to linger by the tire tree or the fish pond. It was as if when she died she had forever vacated the earth that had been her true home and if Beauty wished to imagine her soul in its heaven of blue acres gamboling amongst wooly clouds she was free to do so. Much comfort might it give her.

The trouble was, Beauty knew, ghosts only appeared if you believed them. Believed them and believed in them. Like God and the angels, Hosiah would have said, Hosiah Mopede, first preacher of the Church of Zion, who had once beheld a fallen angel in the veld only it had turned out to be just another dead body with a broken back instead of wings and the police had taken it away in a municipal body bag. Well, let Hosiah believe in his heavenly visitors, his patiently bleeding Son of God Who Died for Our Sins only such a lot of bleeding hadn't stopped thousands of other sons from dying. Yes, and daughters too.

Now, on her way to the Chinaman's game of a winter morning, the sun ashy on the horizon, Beauty once more turned her thoughts to milk, coaxing Givvie out of hiding and into her heart.

And did the child come? Come loping long-legged through the veld to her mother's side, did she balance with the blue crane at the edge of the spruit?

Not a chance, not a hope in hell. Not that girl.

Givvie had disappeared forever on the day that Beauty got the *come quickly* phone call from Sipho at the Post Office and not all the pleas and urging, not all the salt in a mother's heart would bring her back. Still, *Givvie!* Beauty called when an Egyptian goose passed swiftly overhead, and *Givvie?* she cried as a hadeda rattled from a clump of brush on the path before her.

Today, as she made her way through the veld to where the Chinaman waited with his handful of dice and his ivory teeth, Beauty distracted herself by calculating her weekly savings. Five rand fifty, a tip for taking Benjamin's suit to the Portuguese Dry Cleaning. Six rand forty for lying about the cost of laundering at the Portuguese Dry Cleaning. Ten rand fifty, each, for shortening two pairs of trousers for Mrs. Joubert, in advance. Eleven rand, about, maybe more, in parking change lifted from Benjamin's briefcase although surely he was beginning to tip her the sideways glance when he thought she wasn't looking but when wasn't she looking? Perhaps he was catching on at last, that one, and what a *mampara* to take so long about it too, but a pity also because now she must behave herself, keep her sticky fingers out of his pockets.

Seven hundred and fifty-four rand clear profit from the cash crop she'd started with Agremon from the first dagga plant he had established behind the compost heap. Fifteen rand straight to hem Mrs. de Beer's skirt by Friday which meant working late into Thursday night, Agremon's half day, but so be it. After all, what were a couple of roll-ups and a round of sour beers, the chance to sit still somewhere warm and smoky, against the promise of the little house that remained to be built but, ah *suka*, what a house it would be! What else? A two rand coin wedged in a storm gutter, eight rand twenty-two scraped together from the bread money she always forgot to return to Ouma but whose fault was it if the old woman couldn't count, didn't notice what was owed her and didn't seem to care?

This brought the grand total to Three Thousand Eight Hundred and Forty-Two Rand saved over a total of five years and three months painstakingly recorded in her dark green Building Society Savings

Booklet. Beauty carried the booklet everywhere with her: slipped into an apron pocket, settled under her brassiere when she went to town, folded beneath her pillow at night. Sometimes during an odd moment of the day while she waited for the kettle to boil or the iron to heat, she'd slide the booklet from her pocket and out of its plastic cover filmed with fingerprints and grease marks. And, sometimes, as she stood in the open air scullery blinking to prevent herself from remembering how she'd once hung rows of baby clothes on the washing carousel, Beauty would again slip the little booklet from its cover. Gazing down the steady column of deposits, she carefully averted her eyes from occasional but necessary withdrawals—Rothman's new radio, Mamma Thlali's burial plot deposit—items she didn't begrudge, of course not, but which always caught her off guard.

In the last column, directly under the word TOTAL printed in red ink, was the current balance and Beauty was always astonished, astonished and proud, to think that she, Beauty Mapule, had brought such a word into being: TOTAL. Not the petrol station, not the children's hairdresser down the road with its neon sign, *Total Kids*, blinking on and off, but a smart red exclamation at the end of a long column of figures. At such times Beauty felt herself swell with pride like a pigeon on a park bench although she always anticipated the moment when the shoe would come down from the sky and, *whoosh*, she'd be left panting and wingless.

In the harsh winter light slanting in through the kitchen windows she would begin, once more, to add and subtract. So much for a deposit on the building materials, so much for the contractor's down payment. A percentage to grease palms and so many itchy palms to grease! Building costs kept rising, Gideon Thandile of Thandile Construction complained, and what whites called the Standard of Living was the elevator travelling in the other direction, and seemed always to be going down down down. Huh, whatever this standard of living meant, Beauty was sure, sure as tapeworms settling in the gut, that *such* a standard and *such* a living would effect the little house she'd set her heart upon building.

The trouble was, of course, that Beauty did not altogether trust Mister Gideon Thandile to whom she had already entrusted a substantial deposit and so was obliged to invest her optimism if not the remainder of her savings. She had originally approached him because of the name of his company which was self-evident and not at all boastful unlike *Freedom Builders* or *Asigadli Contractors* which meant "We are not lying," an unnecessary reassurance that immediately conjured its opposite. Besides, apart from his non-refundable deposit, Thandile accepted a pay-as-you-build schedule that would allow her to bypass the township loan sharks, those extortionist and fly-by-night financing companies collectively known as *Mashonisa*, a name synonymous with high interest rates, unregulated business practices, and violent reprisals should repayment not be rendered in a timely fashion. Many of these companies were so new, Beauty had heard it joked, that they came in unopened boxes. One should not be surprised then, if one night they simply disappeared into their brand new boxes; goodbye and good luck.

As for Gideon Thandile, he was undoubtedly a handsome somebody and his hands, when he sketched out the dimensions of the house in the air before her, were broad and well-formed. But he was also a cocky one, arrogant even. A man—she knew the type—who, on being led to a dripping honeycomb, does not trouble to pay the honey bird his due. Instead he talked of *mabunu*, those whites whose right wing politics and left wing economics caused small businesses to teeter on the edge of bankruptcy.

But when Beauty reported these views to Mamma Thlali, the other woman chortled. What did it matter, she asked, whether her daughter-in-law's savings flew away on their left wings or their right?

No, Mamma, Beauty explained. These wings of which we speak are politics not feathers!

But Mamma Thlali, who remained nobody's fool, merely poked an eagle shaft through her earlobe and sucked air through the hole between her front teeth.

Now, crossing the veld that had been scorched and blackened from a grass fire earlier in the week, Beauty wondered if today would be her lucky day. The fire had been sudden and spontaneous, crackling up out of the drought, and the ground beneath her feet was still hot as if subterranean flames were banked beneath the blackened stubble. Thin streamers of smoke spiraled into the air. Ah luck!

Beauty believed in luck as a religious man—Hosiah Mopede, first preacher of the Church of Zion, say—believed in the face of God, averted the better to prove His love. Luck was the little bird fluttering inside her ribcage as the child had once fluttered against her breast-bone all those years ago. Luck was what she rubbed between her fingers like the occasional length of lush velvet that one of the madams brought for her to make into a skirt or a jacket, Beauty please, but careful with the cross-stitching, hey. Luck was the five rand coin she'd once found in Mejuffrou de Wet's winter skirt that she was letting out as she did every year because that one was as fat as she was mean. And luck was what Benjamin forgot to deduct from her wages in the way of broken crockery, spoiled fruit, and lamb chops that disap-peared at a prodigious rate because working outside all day depleted Agremon's blood and nothing short of fresh eggs and grade A butch-er's meat, nothing short of strong tea with four spoonfuls of sugar could transform Agremon from the stringy, tired man who limped home every evening—*ai kona*, I am ready for the glue factory today, my Beauty!—to the vigorous lover she desired.

But if it was to be her lucky day Beauty would never know it. As she passed the row of electricity pylons that bisected the veld she was just in time to see the Chinaman leaping over rocks like a fugitive as a police car cruised past on the road below. The officers with their T-bone holsters scrambled out to give chase, stopping only to man-handle Snuki, asleep in the long grass, before he could sound the alarm.

Danger! Gevaar! Ingozi! cautioned the municipal notice on each of the great striding pylons. And, *Humba!* shouted one cop, *Hierso!* yelled the other in hilarious contradiction but the thick rolls at the back of their necks, their rugby scrum-reddened ears, were identical.

Beauty turned home with a heavy heart, her pockets flapping like empty mouths. Just her luck, *tcha!* Once again she passed the pylons, each one flying its skull and crossbones warning. Once again she scrambled across the sluggish course of the spruit noticing that the water had become thick and heavy, could barely push itself through the roots of sedge and wire grass. Upstream the river had almost petered out and there were places where loose stones rattled at the bottom of the dry courses as if the river's spine had been exposed by the drought. But here, at the crossing, the slow-running spruit was crowded with three-day tadpoles, little black commas that further impeded the water's flow.

Pause-hop, pause-hop.

If the spring rains arrived this year the waters would bulge and swell as they did every year, as they'd done the year of the floods when Givvie and Benjamin had toed off their sandals to paddle in the roaring spruit under the careful eyes and outstretched arms of Beauty. All afternoon the children had burrowed about in the thick black river mud, splashing each other and chanting *dirty mud, juicy road, gush gush gush*.

But when they'd returned, all three of them, the children jubilantly tugging a suddenly sheepish and mutinous Beauty in their wake, Ilse had been aghast.

Water rats, spiders, river snakes, she'd scolded. *Bilharzias, malaria, God-forbid-polio!*

Drawing a bath, Ilse had stirred in half a bottle of Dettol, making the children soak in water layered with a scum of oily gold coins. They'd been too young to know the difference between boys and girls, too young to feel shame or the urge towards privacy and Beauty—suitably chastened but far from humbled—had ventured into the steam with fresh towels unable, for a moment, to tell one sleepy head from the other.

It was late by the time she got home and Beauty was tired and in the mood to take her spite out upon Benjamin who was on the phone to the hospital, a stack of jam-smeared bread tottering before him. She put on her apron and went to the sink, taking pains to clatter away at the dishes so that it would soon become impossible for him to hear.

Bite bite, jam on the chin swiped away by a hasty palm. Boom-bang, crash of vicious pot against malicious pan!

Presently, Beauty was rewarded by an indignant glance, a muttered imprecation, the phone slammed down, she hoped, long before the conclusion to any conversation could be reached. *Cheers*!

The sound of his footsteps thumping angrily against the hall stairs reduced her to the first belly laugh she'd enjoyed all week.

But, like Benjamin's conversation, her laughter was abbreviated. Cut short by the agitated gruffle of a dog. Outside, sheltered by the verandah, carefully tipped on its side, was the plum-coloured couch (no, *sofa*) with gold trim and tassels and plump, velvet-covered buttons that Ouma had promised was hers to dispose of only she'd better do it soon—before the rains, Beauty, but heaven knows *when* this terrible drought will break—and, just as she thought, there was that *brak*, that half-breed, lifting its crooked hind leg at one of the sturdy mahogany legs.

One, two steps and a heartbeat and Beauty had scooped up the dog by the ill-fitting skin at the back of its neck, flinging him with peremptory spite and the strength of a grip honed on thirty years of housework into the prickly winter scrub at the edge of the property line.

But when the dog had departed, yelping into the house, haunches quivering self-righteously, Beauty realized that the problem of what to do about the sofa had not, like that miserable excuse for a dog, disappeared. This sofa that she had carefully dusted and polished for years when it was so far from being her own, this sturdy familiar, a little frayed by the sun, true, but still deep, soft as the summer plums from which it took its colour, was hers to own. Hers to keep forever although it was clear that if forever was not to be soaked by spring rains and canine urine she must make chop-chop as Meneer himself would have said, find some means of transporting her sofa from the verandah of the house on Sugarbush Road, where it was precariously wedged, to the "nearly-there" house on the unnamed street in Hammanskraal.

Beauty sat down heavily on her habitual stump, tucked her hands into her apron and prepared to give the matter some consideration.

The House on Sugarbush Road

The sun was at its peak and drummed down on the earth. Beside her foot a contingent of ants were attacking a dead salamander, breaking up the flesh with their jaws and carrying it away a bit at a time. Soon there would be nothing but the dried up tail which no ant would touch. Beauty scowled in disgust, scuffed her toe at the mess of carcass then turned her thoughts to the problem at hand.

In the first place a sofa was not a stock pot or a frying pan. A sofa was not a set of four dessert plates or the last of the only slightly chipped teacups with matching saucers and roses blooming deep inside that Ilse had given her over the years and which she'd carefully wrapped, first in toilet paper then in newspaper and finally in plastic bags from the supermarket, tenderly carrying each dear parcel home to Mamma Thlali. A sofa was not the purple-veined glass vase that Ilse told Mrs. Magda had been accidentally broken—ag, such a *pity!*—but that had been pressed upon Beauty the next day with a take-it-away-quickly shake of the head and the caution not to let Mrs. Magda know.

And Beauty had taken it away quickly, why not? She thought it was beautiful and so did Mamma Thlali. Too beautiful for flowers and too beautiful for the shack where she lived so far but not for long. So the glass vase and the teacups, the clock in the shape of Africa beaten out of real copper, the ostrich egg painted with a View of Oudtshoorn, the calendars—one year birds, next year flowers—from Snelling Butchery, all these treasures languished in newsprint and brown paper until the time was ripe when they would be carefully unwrapped, dusted, bathed in soapy water then set to sparkle on this wall or that table.

Sometimes, before she fell asleep and in order to distract herself from the endless figures that added and divided all day in her head, over and over, to distract herself from these numbers and the distance they measured between her heart and what she most desired, Beauty would run her mind gently over her collection of hoarded treasures. Gently and with a soft touch like a hand stroking purple-veined glass or a finger tapping the lip of an only slightly chipped china teacup with a painted rose blowing deep in its ivory interior. And, in turn, each of these precious, hard-won objects reminded Beauty of what she was saving for, for what she schemed and dissembled and pined. Always in her imagination and daydreams, at the borders of waking and sleep, the house that she would build shimmered in the heat and dust like a mirage.

It had a front door of varnished wood that shone in the sun to welcome visitors but there were burglar bars on the windows and barbed wire on the walls to discourage tsotsis. In the back garden vegetables grew in orderly rows but the front yard was profuse with flowers so that the people would know that inside this house there dwelled women of leisure, women who did not have so much to do that they lacked the time to grow a bed of dahlias, a rosebush, or a marigold border. Consider the lilies for they neither spin nor toil, thundered the long ago voice of Hosiah Mopede in Beauty's head for this had always been one of his favourite texts and Beauty admired his passion and the words that drew piety from the hearts of his listeners just as bicarbonate of soda and hot water draw forth pus from a whitlow.

Yes, assuredly, in the front yard of her brand new house there would be place even for the inconsiderate lilies!

But the fact remained that a sofa was not a small and only slightly sun-fatigued area rug, a sofa was not a kettle or an electric sandwich-maker (for one day the little house would sing with electricity) or a set of Birds of Africa coasters. A sofa was much bigger than a pair of salt and pepper shakers in the shape of mielies. A sofa was bigger even than the kitchen table that Beauty had struggled home with one Christmas, wedging her charge sideways onto the train and then into the back of the dusty twice-a-week bus. Balancing it on her head for the last mile. A sofa was bigger than all of these things put together and how was she, Beauty, only one woman after all and not as strong as she once had been, how was she to drag the plum-coloured, stout-legged, three-seater with smart gold tassels home and where must she store it while the little house was being built?

The colour of the sofa reminded Beauty of the plums that grew on the tree overhanging the sandpit where Givvie and Benjamin had played once in a summer so abundant that the fruit fermented on the branch and all the birds for miles around were drunk by nightfall. That she couldn't leave her treasure wedged beneath the verandah was as plain as the bird droppings already crusting one arm and the melancholy sag of the double row of tassels gaping from a runner upon which that skelm dog was even now sharpening his teeth. Beauty entertained herself with visions of canine strangulation or poisoning but even apart from that brak, that four-legged piece of mongrel nonsense, there was still rain and birds and theft to consider. (Ah, but one day she must just kill that excuse for a dog, not for any good reason but simply for the pleasure of inflicting pain.)

Overhead the sun stung like a paper cut, like red ants rubbing their fierce muric acid into the tender skin behind the knees. The noon sun foreshortened Beauty's shadow across the dry grass. Usually her shadow rose tall and imperious, elongating itself across the garden, over the fence and into the neighbour's winter-green swimming pool. But today her shadow was small and growing smaller with each sad thought. For Beauty was heartsore at the solution to her predicament. What choice did she have but to store the sofa at a neighbour's until she could contrive to erect a house of her own?

And people, she knew from experience, were spiteful by inclination, destructive by nature.

They will be jealous, she thought, their hearts will prick with needles. Jealousy was a terrible thing, terrible, Hosiah would often remark, turning milk sour and the heart sour also. Now jealousy would enter the hearts of her neighbours, they would scorch the plush cushions with their cigarettes and kick at the legs of her sofa. But what choice did she have?

Pulling the ribbed collar of her cardigan close to her throat Beauty shook the pins and needles from her feet and stumbled into the house.

In her bright winter coat Dhlamina's pregnant body flared out like a bell as she laboured up the hill past the Zoo Lake where cinnamon-coloured laughing doves cooed in clumps of pampas grass. *Krull-Krull* she answered, opening her throat and lifting her face to the heavens. But she needed all her breath for the climb, the child moving like a pendulum in her belly, as she concentrated on achieving the rise of the hill.

It was a tight shiny day, a day on which the sun cast abrupt shadows. If she listened carefully Dhlamina could almost hear the light ringing like a tuning fork. At noon the Zoo Lake was thin and wrinkled as the skin of a very old person. Ducks and rowing boats trailed wakes like sudden scars that puckered briefly before smoothing out. All around, men and women dozed in the sun or dealt cards or kept themselves awake by smoking and arguing in the shade.

As Dhlamina walked, twining the string shopping bag through her fingers, she remembered breakfast fondly and with impartial fondness anticipated lunch. She would need ripe tomatoes and purple onions, hmm-hm. Crusty baguette from the bakery in the Mall and tender young mozzarella cheeses individually wrapped in salty paper from the Italian Grotto. In her fifth month of pregnancy she had regained her equanimity, her good nature, and her appetite. Nothing turned her stomach anymore and she was always hungry, these days, always.

Dhlamina was reflecting that keeping house for Mrs. Magda had many advantages, not least of which were the banknotes she pressed into Dhlamina's hand every morning. And although she always checked receipts, counting her change with a pursed mouth, Mrs. M. never huffed at the expensive delicacies that her maid brought home: imported oils and balsamic vinegars whose existence Dhlamina had only recently learned of, courtesy of the incomparable *Mrs. Moffert.*

Hmmm, smoked snoek and capers, Dhlamina would murmur as she wandered the grocery aisles, granadilla jam or rose-hip? Take both, why not, might be good for the heartburn.

Wild honey which was rich in flavour and luminous to look upon. Designer fruits and hydroponic vegetables, free-range eggs and the grain-fed chickens that produced them, all tumbled into her trolley. Dhlamina relished the covetous glances she garnered at the checkout till when she paid for her luxurious purchases but of course nobody— neither the woman who rang her through nor the packing boy—really believed that the groceries were for anyone other than the white madam who'd sent her maid out to do her shopping for her. After all, a maid was a maid; civvies and wads of cash didn't change a thing.

In her short but ebullient life Dhlamina had been employed at a number of retail outlets ranging from vetkoek and grilled meat stands near the taxi ranks in town to fancy clothing boutiques and designer shoe stores along the Pritchard Street Pedestrian Mall. She always quit because of love. Other people's love. By-standers, passersby, idling gawkers, men with chewing gum under their shoes, or the patrons who wandered into the various stores where she stood behind various counters and before she could recognize the look or the sigh and shout *humba wena*, flapping her beautifully carved nails at this one or that one, it was too late. Love swooped down like a house bat to hover in the air and, like a house bat, never failed to miss her with centimeters to spare.

But how was it possible—Dhlamina would sometimes wonder—that no man or boy seemed immune to her charms yet she remained unmoved except, occasionally, to pity? Did the fault lie in the gentleman's susceptibility or in her own hardness of heart? Might the answer be found in acquiescence or in denial? In short, what type of fellow or breed of gent did Dhlamina Mopede attract, she of the bright sandals and beads and the cocoa butter skin? What manner of man did she tug in the wake of her perfumed sarongs and flying tresses combed through with olive oil and patchouli?

Innumerable boys and of every kind! There were the township lads and the good time fellows, the skelms and skollies and tsotsis, the high-flying ma'gents, the businessmen, vagabonds, and dandies. There were the trendy guys who tried to look casual as they idly swung the keys to their sports cars in one hand and the crude boys who urinated at the side of the road fisting their things and offering to slip her the *nkauza*, the snot *sjambok*.

Sies! For shame!

Sometimes an elderly township gentleman would follow her, panting, or an *amaguduka*, a migrant labourer from across the border, would be smitten even though his infatuation might put him in grave danger with her homeboys. More than once a *kleinbaas* from one of the white suburbs would try to inveigle her to the Chelsea Hotel on the 'Brow and how many times had a policeman—yes, even a police-man!—followed her home, his truncheon dangling between his legs like a tail?

Indeed, Dhlamina sometimes thought that it was true, as the say-ing went, that men thrived as pumpkin plants under the harsh sun of neglect. As a schoolgirl, socks rolled to display her ankles, she'd served behind the counter of MaNduza's township spaze shop, selling tuck—cool drinks and beer, potato chips, bread, Nestlé chocolates, and sausages—from a low fridge beneath the counter. Later, after an unfortunate incident involving two men who'd once been the best of friends, MaNduza had whisked her away to work behind the scenes at one of her informal drinking establishments where little harm, it was felt, could be wreaked upon her customers, hardened drinkers to a man.

Ho, MaNduza had thought, no harm can be done because these men are always thirsty or drunk or hungover.

But Dhlamina was the equivalent of a she-jackal. By the time she'd been glimpsed from the corner of the eye the damage was already done! Fights broke out between the drunks whose eyes became tinged with a venal gleam whenever they spied her working behind the bead-ed curtain of MaNduza's shebeen and then it was as if the very beer had turned to gall in their mouths and the devil had entered their souls. For good, for ever.

Yoh, love! exclaimed MaNduza. For it was love that drove these men to such lengths; love that the older woman had once compared to a house bat. For such love approached but never alighted upon its object. And when these bats began to hover in the air above her, when the night grew plaintive with their cries Dhlamina knew that it was time to flee because if there was one thing she was certain of it was the durability of her charms. Not to mention the persistence of the vari-ous lovers urging their suit over the years with Black Magic chocolates

and threats, day-old roses and fists, and in one case, an apparently irre-
sistible urge to set her alight—petroleum-soaked rags and lit matches
tossed through MaNduza's window—so that it was only with considerable luck and mild burns on her forearms that she escaped.

She is a piper! MaNduza had chuckled all those years ago but that
was before the old woman was reduced to the indignity of scrambling
from her window in her nylon nightgown to escape the flames yap-
ping like a pack of dogs at her ankles.

After that Dhlamina took to plaiting her hair into dozens of skinny braids and wearing sunglasses whenever she ventured out, in an
effort to curb the energy that crackled from her pores, whisking the
air into a fine static around her. But, casual accusations of witchcraft
aside, Dhlamina's love magnetism had only grown stronger through
the years since the days she'd led a raggle-taggle contingent of small
barefoot boys through the veld behind her swaying haunches.

Hau, *that-one*! chuckled MaNduza who wore a collection of old
keys pulled through the wide lobes of her ears and whose putu was
legendary since she judged the consistency of her mieliemeal pap by
the texture of these very same pendulous lobes.

MaNduza was a woman of few words, very few, and those scattered like salt pinched between thumb and forefinger over the bubbling
expanse of a hot pan of putu taken fresh off the fire, but that day she
whisked her full skirts over to the house of Dhlamina's mother to tell
her that she must straight away go after her daughter and bring her
home in order to rescue the young herd boys that she was luring to
their death under the flat hard sky.

She is a piper, exclaimed MaNduza, to describe the effect Dhlamina
had on the herd boys which was as clear as a single high-pitched note
from a reed flute.

Her mother had possessed it too, a jagged electrical current that
jolted through her blood and into the bodies of others but she'd been
luckier than Dhlamina since in her case, in the case of Gcina Mopede,
the tall Shona from across the border, the love current frequently
returned to its source. For Gcina Mopede had loved many men, some

boys, and then more men; Dhlamina well remembered the men that her mother had loved. Or at least she recalled their broad backs, their busy haunches, their guttural cries, as she'd passed her mother's bed on the way to play five stones or knucklebones in the veld.

But in the end Gcina Mopede had died of all this love. Set alight one night by the man who believed he was Dhlamina's father returning home early in the month from his job at the mines. As for Dhlamina's real father, the travelling preacher, Hosiah Mopede, he too burned but in those days for God and not for love. Or perhaps for God because of love, the crazy love his wife inspired even in his stern heart and which it was unseemly for a man of the cloth to feel.

She was a matchstick, explained MaNduza who took Dhlamina in when her mother's house went up in flames.

Like her mother before her, who was a Shona of the traditional sort, Gcina Mopede had put her faith in the chameleon which the people believed could look in two directions at the same time, one bulging eye gazing into the past, the other staring at the future, but her daughter jeered at this tradition. Folktales, superstitions! And in the end Dhlamina had been proved right for her mother certainly hadn't seen the flames at the close of her life, nor the cunning use that her lover had made of the household *mbawula* coal stove. Indeed her mother had even failed to foresee the babies that she would conceive and then blithely miscarry with the help, some said, of MaNduza's midwifely skills and neither did she appear to gaze too deeply into the past in order to regret them.

It was in the month of her daughter's *first red moon,* as the old people say, that Gcina lost her life to her lover's jealousy and Dhlamina still remembered her mother's hilarity as she pronounced these words. As if the moon could reach deep into her daughter's body and pull forth the blood tides upon which she would ride for all of her childbearing days until — here her mother bent almost double with mirth — until one day the moon would wane forever.

But it was no laughing matter what the people called her behind her back and sometimes also to her face — Gcina Mopede, the tall

Shona from across the border. For how many ways were there to name a woman immoral, indecent, and prone to stray? As they said in Sepedi, she had the blood of *makwerekwere* running through her veins; as the Sotho exclaimed, that *skaberash*! But in the Cape she was a *jentoe*, a *goose*, a *toit*. If a woman was suspected of being unfaithful the Afrikaners called her a *lossie* which was just another word for *letekatse*, *prostitute*, *izifebe*, *whore*.

These, of course, were only some of the words that the people threw against Gcina Mopede like sticks and stones.

In those days women were stoned for less, set alight, burnt to death. As if the fire that had consumed Gcina in the end was merely desire made manifest, the flames of passion that had pursued her all her life ignited in her lover's final despairing action. Everyone was thankful that at least her innocent young daughter had been spared.

The first time the girl was rescued from fire she moved in with MaNduza, the second time and in order to escape MaNduza's wrath, she relocated to the city where township houses were harder (but not impossible) to burn down. There, in the breeze block house in Diepkloof that overlooked a dried-up stream where pariah dogs congregated in the coolest part of the evening, in the rooming house that she shared with six other shopgirls, she hoped to disappear in a warm jumble of arms and legs, conversation, bustle, and feminine enterprise. On Friday nights they would dance around the sitting room under the poster that read *Sisters we Sing! Sisters we Bleed!* or they would go down to the Funda Centre to attend lectures on art or politics harmonizing old songs by Miriam Makeba and Aretha Franklin on the way home.

But all this was far in the future when Dhlamina Mopede took shelter with MaNduza between the fires that bracketed her youth.

She was a matchstick, observed MaNduza of Dhlamina's mother to explain the ease with which Gcina Mopede had burst into flame but already Dhlamina was weary of analogy and merely shrugged her beautiful shoulders as she plotted her escape to the brick and mortar, fire-resistant city.

As for love and its sticky residue she, Dhlamina, resolved there and then not to fall for it.

When she came to work for Mrs. Magda, to her joy, Dhlamina realized that her electric current had no effect on the white Madam. It clicked off with one glance from those light blue eyes. Consequently Dhlamina felt free to indulge herself amongst the rich soups and sauces that *Mrs. Moffert* concocted out of the magical properties of hot butter, a little steamed milk, a sprinkling of flour. With each pinch of salt, each shake of pepper, each golden thread of saffron, Dhlamina was learning a new skill and her water baby was reaping the benefit.

Never before had an unborn child enjoyed such glorious flavours: olives and capers and sweet pickled peppers, the salt tang of kippers, the crisp bite-back of radishes. For someone whose ribs had grown strong and supple as wicker on mother's milk, mieliepap, and stewed meat, Dhlamina was developing a taste for the glossily illustrated food in Mrs. Magda's cookery books especially that plump *Mrs. Moffert* who presided over the kitchen, opening with helpless desire each time Dhlamina consulted her, to the double page spread of orange glazed duckling with wild rice ragout.

Dhlamina had reached the Portuguese Grocery by now which was full of nannies clutching string shopping bags and grocery lists. Their voices were sweet and their words of greeting were juicy as the fruits they squeezed and discarded before settling on bags of oranges and onions, a pale winter melon or a handful of walnuts. Today an early shipment had arrived from the coast and shelf after shelf displayed boxes of rosy apples each fruit wrapped in a crinkle of purple tissue paper, trays of cling peaches and out-of-season mangoes weeping a little in their imperfect ripeness. Swatting at flies, the women dumped their purchases in front of José da Silva who was drunk as a fiddler, drunk as a lord, drunk as *usual* but that was all the better in the way of choice produce and a light hand with the scales.

Sober, José was surly, his spectacles glinting impatiently, his fingers thrifty as he piled half-pound and quarter-pound weights on the scales. But ferment him a little in the Peach Brandy he purchased by the case and he was all smile and shrug, popping grapes and cherries into the mouths of the children that the nannies led into the store, lunging with unsteady hands at these same nannies who hooted derisively, calling out to one another from beyond his reach.

Hayyi-i-i, watch out for ubaba wethu! the women would mock. *Here he comes, i-chief-com-mander!*

Selecting fruit and vegetables with her sunglasses on wasn't easy but Dhlamina would as soon have walked into the path of an oncoming taxi as lower her shades, even for an instant.

Because of this habit of masking her eyes even in sunless rooms Dhlamina had acquired a reputation for haughtiness amongst the other women who gave her the three-cornered smile and a wide berth. Behind her back and their own splayed fingers they laughed at her and gossiped but Dhlamina hardly noticed most days, her mind preoccupied with compotes and marmalades, her fingers tapping at the waxy, open-pored rinds of grapefruit and Jaffa oranges.

In the blanched winter landscape a splash of green apple or tomato, red as heartbreak, was just the thing to keep a girl going, with or without her sunglasses. A favourite corner to congregate on days when the winter sun drained the sky of colour and the body of compulsion, the Portuguese Grocery provided a place to let the morning sag a little, to squander time like small change, to fill the day between the clatter of breakfast dishes and the afternoon orgy of dust-under-the-mat cleaning before various Madams returned from shopping, the hairdresser, the gym. God alone knew where!

The ear is a thief and the mouth is a beggar, MaNduza had often instructed Dhlamina upon the evils of gossip.

MaNduza was famous for her apt sayings which, some said, she merely invented willy-nilly to suit every occasion but her own contriving most of all. And it was true that the mamazala was at pains to prevent her girls from revealing the secrets of the shebeen. But, gazing now at the women spilling out onto the pavement, Dhlamina felt sadly excluded from their good fellowship, the laughter and stories they shared and that seemed to leap from mouth to ear.

Ehh... A considered pause, a sigh, then one would turn to another, beckoning her closer, and they were off, talking and gossiping as they walked, calling out to one another until distance swallowed their voices, laughter fading with the retreating footsteps of a friend. Or again they might stop, these women, for a moment, to chat on a street corner their conversation punctuated by the sound of burglar alarms and sirens and the sudden silences that followed them.

Laden now with produce, Dhlamina evaded José da Silva's drunkenly inaccurate hands and, following her belly, stalked into the busy main road leading to the Mall. In the sullen heat that always settled over the city around midday cars pulsed along the thoroughfare their drivers mouthing silent imperatives into cell phones as they wound between vendors pushing food carts, hawkers peddling stick giraffes and copper bracelets, wire candlestick holders, carved bowls and masks and beaded necklaces. At the east entrance to the Mall taxis huffed in their ranks, double parked. Engines revving they spilled across the road, screeching towards the commuters who waited patiently on the opposite sidewalk. Waiting in queues, shuffling in ranks, lining *up*—such was the lot of the average worker in this city. Hours, days, *weeks* could pass while a woman shifted from one foot to the other, waiting for a stamp, a government pension, a ride across town.

Although she'd come expressly to see him, exasperated by iBoyboy's message which Mhda had couched in the words of the old city poet—*the Madiba says he is still waiting and he will continue to wait* (consulting a filthy piece of paper, pointy tongue poking) *to wait until the rays of the sun that are like a pair of scissors, cut the blanket of dawn from the sky*—although she'd taken the long way home despite her five-month belly and the string shopping bag welting her wrist, Dhlamina started at her first glimpse. Madiba Mhda strutting around the taxi ranks, arms gyrating like train signals as he directed a capacious ousie with a nylon shopping bag balanced on her head and a child slung across her back.

Kwela-kwela!

He seemed intent on ushering the woman into the wrong minibus taxi or at least one to which she appeared reluctant to commit herself.

Orlando West and Dube, this side, mamazala!

Tcha. Humba, man.

Chiwelo, also Protea, *hekelemanzi.* Hurry, you slowpoke!

Mhda darted here and there like a terrier, harrying his customers into line, for time on its well-oiled wheels travelled in only one direction unlike his excellent taxis which traversed the city in all directions.

Mhda's taxis! How proud he was, how fervently he'd boasted to Dhlamina of their superior quality and safety standards. True, his taxi drivers travelled as swiftly as those of his competitors for how else were they to turn a profit, and his vehicles were as old—older, truth be told—and in as great a state of disrepair as theirs. And his drivers insisted on playing loud music, kwaito and hip hop, the hard rock that kept them awake on the long drives to Soweto and Alex and Bara, then back into Jozie. But Mhda's taxi drivers were forbidden to strong-arm their frightened customers or intimidate them with word or weapon. They must make change whenever possible—no slipping a twenty rand note into the pocket and telling the frightened passenger there wasn't any change, no hiking up fares in mid run, no drop-offs on deserted streets for the purposes of robbery or worse, no threats, fights, fists, or bets. Mhda ran a clean show, he had proudly informed Dhlamina, and if he was obliged to hand out graft to the police and bribe traffic cops so that he could buy licenses for those of his men who'd been unfairly suspended or who couldn't pass their driving tests, if he was forced to shell out good cash to the Department of Motor Vehicles and Licensing merely in order to ensure that his taxis were roadworthy then so bloody be it.

Now, Dhlamina watched as he continued to harry the ousie into the taxi that she seemed so reluctant to enter.

The driver of this taxi was well known to Dhlamina. One Zizi Molepe, he'd been ambushed by gunmen twice in the discharge of his duties, avoiding death by the simple expedient of rolling his reconstituted minibus off the road and into the veld, extricating himself intact both times although most of his passengers were not so lucky.

A veteran of the taxi wars, his vehicle, battered and pocked with bullet holes, more than somewhat inclined to shed its parts—a door, a wheel, a section of bumper or window—this taxi was widely considered to be inhabited by a devil and many were wary of trusting themselves to its driver even though he offered direct and remarkably swift service to Soweto at three-quarters the usual fare.

Taxi man, taxi man, have a care!
Think of the lives you hold in your hands,
went the song but Zizi Molepe was already half deaf from his misadventures in the taxi wars and besides—everyone agreed—the man couldn't carry a tune to save his life.

Presently, and with much supple exercise of what Dhlamina knew from experience to be Mhda's famous forked tongue—he could promise opposite things at once, both equally beguiling, offering his passengers alternate routes leading straight to hell but persuading them that the journey would be worth it in the end—presently, the woman clambered into the demon-taxi of Zizi Molepe and with a thump of the rear fender Mhda sent it on its way, watching approvingly as it reversed indignantly, hooted churlishly, and swung a wide swathe into oncoming traffic, scattering pedestrians and gesticulating hawkers. Soon even the vanity plates which were the only brand new component of Molepe's taxi because they were always replaced after each accident, even this shiny rectangle in its dusty waste of rattling metal, disappeared from view.

Now he turned and caught Dhlamina's eye and the water baby, as if recognizing its father, delivered a swift elbow to her ribs so that by the time Madiba Mhda crossed four lanes of traffic to stand grinning at her side she was breathless and irate.

So you came, my angel, my queen!
Even in the triumph of having his dearest wish granted Mhda was careful to sheath his words in extravagant but by no means insincere phrases that were as complimentary to Dhlamina as they were commendatory of his good sense in choosing her as the object of his

present and future devotions. Now he quickly relieved Dhlamina of her shopping bags, waving her to his "office," an empty upturned paint drum sheltered from the sun by a brolly and set well back from the wind. From this vantage point Mhda could survey his kingdom, direct traffic and pedestrians, and choreograph the peripatetic arrivals and departures of his vehicles en route to destinations as far afield as Soweto and Alex Township.

As soon as he saw her approaching Mhda had hastily begun stuffing papers into a cardboard suitcase, the sort that schoolchildren had once lugged to school. It was brown with triangular plastic reinforcements at each corner and was stuck all over with haphazard stickers: BUY SUNNY SHELL! GO BP PETROL! ENO FRUIT SALTS! DISPRIN DISSOLVES! When all his papers had been satisfactorily stored he latched the case with its flimsy metal clips then tried to wedge it under Dhlamina's feet so as to ensure her maximum comfort but his aboCherry, his aboBaby, his big-eyed, big-bellied bed-doll merely glared at him. It was at these times—crouched at her feet, gazing up at the face of his aboSweety, his aboLovey—that words failed Mhda. In fact only in the Sesotho language was there a word adequate to describe a woman of such radiant beauty. It was a bridal word: *seponono*. His own language having failed him, Mhda resolved to wear the other like a borrowed coat—*seponono!*

Lost in thought as he was, Mhda neglected to take account of Dhlamina who was angrily batting at the smoke from his cigarette which he hastily stubbed out against the sole of his shoe. Dhlamina waited for the air to clear before she began blowing her own smoke, huffing and puffing like the pressure cooker he knew her to be.

iBoyboy tells me that you're still waiting for the moon to rise in the morning and so I've come to tell you, Mhda, you must dispense with this nonsense, okay, you must stop bothering me with your messages and your poetry, hear?

Abo…aboBaby, my—

And no more aboBaby, aboHoney, aboThis and aboThat. No more sticky words and begging letters. No more greetings sent with this one and with that one. No more flowers, no more flattery, no more love. *Yebo*, no more *love*, do you understand, you foolish one?

Grudgingly, Dhlamina prepared to expand upon this startling concept because Mhda's mouth had fallen open and he looked like a man upon whom a plague had fallen but a sudden commotion broke out between an enraged customer and a bellowing taxi man and Mhda was obliged to gallop across the road with a "wait here" pat on the arm and a pleading glance from his eyes that seemed to turn the colour and softness of last season's winter suede whenever they looked upon her. Attempting to settle herself more comfortably on the upturned paint drum, Dhlamina reflected that the apparent humbleness of Mhda's working quarters was deceptive. Appearances to the contrary—and that one wasn't above manipulating the appearance of humility to his own inscrutable but by no means trivial ends—Mhda was a powerful man. A mover, a fixer, one who, in the ancestral phrase, carried his trunk as lightly as a bull elephant. Ah, but he was also a man in love and this detail diminished him to no small degree in Dhlamina's wide open albeit sun-shaded eyes.

The queue of passengers had tightened into a thick knot around the driver and his indignant passenger. *Hay-i suka wena!* broke from one group and *Hau voetsak! Fokof! Humba!* from another. So many ways to tell a person to get lost, mused Dhlamina, but no way to make it stick.

She'd first met Madiba Mhda, Taxi Man, in the old-fashioned Muti Shop into which she'd wandered in search of a cure for the love magnetism. In the dusty storefront, herbs and braided grasses jostled stoppered bottles of patent medicines and home remedies. Inside it was dim and shadowy and smelled of unwashed scalp, old skin, a musty staleness punctuated by sweet whiffs of something rotten, not yet cured, not quite dried.

Something tapped her shoulder, brushed at her hair. Dhlamina looked up.

Hanging down from hooks or tied to the rafters hovered hundreds of dead and drying animals: bats, roosters, snakes, owls, meerkats. It was too dark and the animals too closely jammed together to distinguish one from the other. Here Dhlamina made out a dangling claw, there a crusted coxcomb, a bat's crochet hook finger joints, rat's tails woven into a clumpy braid, and the sheathed skin of what looked to have been an enormous snake. A puffadder, perhaps, or a python. In the dim space with its smell of meat and decay the animal parts lost their separateness, became one monstrous beast that rose and fell, thrusting out claws and crooked wings, whiskers, teeth, a feather. Stumbling, Dhlamina would have fallen had a hand not caught and held her arm, angling her out the door where the sudden light sliced her mind into inside and outside, past and future, the sullen dusk of the Muti Shop and the skittering brightness of the street.

Madiba Mhda, stammered the man belonging to the (trembling, was it?) hand at her elbow.

Madiba Mhda, Taxi Man, at your service.

Dhlamina fumbled for her sunglasses but it was too late. Smitten, more than somewhat winged by Cupid's swift arrow, his hands (yes, trembling) still fumbling for her arm, Mhda was nevertheless able to use his golden tongue to good effect, persuading the only passingly reluctant Dhlamina that a little food, a cold beer, would put the heart back into her, would settle her racing pulse, her shimmering nerves.

In the Saturday afternoon heat the city was slowly running down, closing up for the weekend. Indian traders, enjoying a last smoke in the doorways of their stores, tossed their butts expertly into the gutters like underhand bowlers then rolled down their shutters with a tremendous clatter. Behind their backs coloured saris flashed amongst merchandise as wives and mothers, perhaps a visiting auntie from Bombay, gossiped in the barricaded stores. Mhda, whose humour acted upon others much like sandpaper—roughening up those with smooth surfaces and smoothing down those with rough edges—made haste to steer the beautiful woman away from the takeaway cafes and fast food vendors, the stalls selling giblets and chicken feet for soup stock, the pavement tailors, and the little sidewalk surgery where the old district dentist pulled teeth for ready cash and where customers could get a discount on three or more extractions.

The entrance to Captains was a low, awning-hooded doorway through which they had to stoop, picking their way over a gutter flowing with refuse. For the second time that day Dhlamina was blinded as she passed from dazzling sunlight into the dimness of a truncated staircase that led up to a dark room full of bright things: fuchsia tablecloths and beaded alcoves and out-of-season tinsel looped over bottles piled in haphazard displays.

So koud. The waitress was layered against the room's dank chill, an overall over her pinnie topped by a stretched-out cardigan and a gay chiffon scarf that was meant to be worn raffishly off-centre but instead was clutched and tucked against the inching cold. *Ag, never mind,* she comforted them, *the curry will warm you up.* The sound of her slippers padding across the floor, retreating towards the kitchen, was oddly consoling.

Left alone with Dhlamina, Madiba Mhda, Taxi Man, began to show off. He pointed to the wall where a letter, sent from Robben Island by the great Nelson Mandela, had been framed. Now it hung at a jaunty angle, prominently displayed above their table.

"I am so sorry to hear that your fine restaurant is about to close," he read raising his voice in imitation of the great leader, "I sometimes fear that by the time I am released from prison the whole world will have disappeared."

Huh, said Dhlamina, secretly impressed. Why does this restaurant want to hang letters from all its customers on the wall?

Not all the customers — only a letter sent by the great Madiba, he replied.

Well, perhaps when we leave they will hang up our bill, huh? After all another great Madiba *he* will have signed it?

Crestfallen, Madiba Mhda reflected that at least the comely one had taken note of his name but Dhlamina paid him no mind, enraged that even this passing insult had betrayed her interest, and instead immersed herself in the chicken biryani, the bubbling mutton stew, the fat brown bottles of Castle Lager that had been brought to their table in a bucket filled to the brim with kitchen ice.

And all that was how long ago? A year already, and here she sat in the meantime, wriggling to get comfortable on an upturned paint drum while Mhda (she refused to call him by his outrageous first name) gave the taxi drivers what-for before darting across the road to squat at her feet, studying her face with such intensity that Dhlamina experienced the not unpleasant sensation of being gently licked into life by a gaze as fervent and fastidious as a cat's tongue. Slowly and without conscious thought she lowered her sunglasses to half-mast, surveying him over their tortoiseshell frames. As always her eyes seemed to flash and then dim as if her retinas had just photo-copied his image. Mhda was careful to mask his satisfaction because no one was as contrary, as zigzag and criss-crossed as this beautiful Dhlamina, angel of his heart and mother of his child.

Overcome by his good fortune—for wasn't she sitting before him, his sway-hipped, his big-bellied queen?—Mhda tried to grasp one of her neatly turned ankles in order to remove a shoe and gently mas-sage her instep, a disarming manoeuvre that in the past and with any number of grateful, weary women had never failed to beguile. But Dhlamina was having none of it and merely used her unshod foot to kick him over.

Voetsak! she snapped, gold tooth flashing rhythmically with the hide-and-go-seek dimple that concealed itself in her cheek until lured by anger or hilarity to reveal itself. Taxis snarled past and the smell of diesel fumes and dagga, hot tar, dust, and tired bodies mingled. Dhlamina struggled to her feet, groping for her shoe.

All right, no hands. I promise.

He held them up in mock surrender although, truth to tell, the threat of her departure alarmed him considerably.

So now I've come, huh. What do you want, Mhda?

Dhlamina's tone was snap-finger weary. Although she'd never fallen into anything in her life, least of all love, and with a taxi man from the townships at that, she was too honest not to admit to herself that he tickled her disdainful fancy. It wasn't his looks that attracted her, wiry and seamed with scars, his nose a fish hook between eyes too close-set to see into the future with any accuracy, and besides Dhlamina had turned down any number of fine, well set-up young men. Men with broad shoulders and wide cheekbones, men with straight backs and buttocks as strong and thrusting as those she'd passed in her mother's bed on her way to play knucklebones in the veld. It wasn't his power either or the money he was rumoured to be making from his many lucrative commissions all over the city. It wasn't his passion or his pain or even his love for her; such things bored Dhlamina to tears, to eye-watering, jaw-aching *tears*, accustomed as she was to the love of good men and bad, not to mention all the various kinds in between. Why, even dogs followed her in the street, throwing themselves at her legs and whining inconsolably.

For Dhlamina was a piper for love, as MaNduza had observed all those years ago, and one skinny taxi man more or less wasn't going to entice her, even a hair's breadth, off course.

No, something quite different, altogether too strange to think about if she thought about it at all, which she seldom did, made her pause as he grasped her by the elbow and trembled, convinced her to nod when he offered (but with his eyes he begged) to take her to the best curry restaurant in all of Joburg, and everyone knew curry was strong on the stomach but gentle on the nerves. What excited Dhlamina, what drew her up the hill and onto the main road and out to the taxi ranks even on a day when she was planning to make grilled tomato compote for lunch, was Mhda's golden tongue which, in turn, evoked the object he'd fished from his pocket the moment he saw her, as if by reflex.

Compact and solid with a good heft to the hand, Mhda had consulted his gold pocket watch intently before snapping closed the cover with its engraving of entwined proteas, slipping the case casually into the pocket of his jacket. This jacket, worn, cracked by rain, bought cheap off the leather hawkers at Bruma Flea Market, contrasted oddly with that glinting, egg-shaped piece of gold. Without his pocket watch Mhda was importunate, a man—and of all men she was most scornful of *this* sort of man—on the verge of the fall. Into sin or sickness or love, one was as ignominious as the rest as far as Dhlamina was concerned.

Without his watch he was just a man who hustled her on the street, grabbing at the sleeve of her coat as she passed by as so many had done before and when she paused and turned—hmmm?—failed to distinguish himself save by shifting from foot to foot and stammering.

H-h-hau Sisi, what do they call such a b-beauty?

Tcha.

N-n-not even the great Miriam Makeba, not Brenda Fassie, not even Miss Africa South, n-none of these compare—

Tcha, what a storyteller!

T-tell me Sisi, are you a model, an actress, a beauty queen? Where have I seen you before, hmm? Or have you been conjured by the imbongi, just this minute, to break my heart?

As if she hadn't heard it all before, not precisely in those words, true—few homeboys or township men were as fulsome in their praise—but words that invariably ended with a request for the pleasure of her company in tones ranging from arrogance to pleading but that always met with the same stony resistance in her heart.

But with his watch, ah, with that subtle glimmer of gold caught between thumb and forefinger (yanked out to disprove her claim that she had to go, that she was *late*), Mhda was transformed into a magician, a hypnotist. A man whose tongue flashed words as golden and elaborately figured as his watch case, a man whose heart kept faith with the mechanical rotations of his timepiece. From that moment her own heart softened towards him, not much but enough that his words no longer fell fallow but sprouted tiny seedlings in the soil of her good regard.

Over lunch, the curry fanning her blood, she began to pay idle attention to his outrageous stories. With an unlit cigarette poking from behind one ear he talked and gesticulated, smoking another cigarette down to its filter, and barely even taking a moment to sample the delicious curry although his first words upon sitting down had been those of an old proverb: *Fepa mmele o ho sebeletsang!* Feed the body that works for you!

Rapidly and with barely a breath between sentences he told her about his plans and dreams, about his assets and business ventures and reputation for canny dealing, interspersing his spiel with various improvised endearments. *AboHoney*, he murmured trying to take the hand that she promptly snatched away, *aboSugar*, for he surely couldn't help himself.

As for Dhlamina, tossing her hair so that the gold beads clicked rapidly, the more she listened to his voice, his stories, the less attention she paid to her surroundings, to the restaurant and the food that she ate, to the waitress sitting and crocheting on a riempie stool near the kitchen door and to the cry of the hawkers on the street below. Idly—for he'd taken up her hand again—she scratched at his palm with her long nails, a gesture that in itself was far from ambiguous. A charge had been released like that between the positive and negative ions in metals and for once Dhlamina wasn't merely its conductor. When the waitress padded over to clear the dishes and offer her guests their choice of desserts-included—"vetkoek with cold syrup, ice-cream with hot syrup"—Dhlamina waved her away kindly.

Let's go, she said carefully not meeting her companion's gaze.

In the months that followed, the single-mindedness of the taxi man's ardour convinced her that love was less a fall from grace than a leap of faith, on his part at least. As for Dhlamina, Mhda assured her that she needn't leap at all. Needn't so much as bend her knees or tuck her skirt about her thighs because there was very little to lose and even something—here he plied her with expensive sandals, gold bracelets, bottom-heavy magnums of Veuve Cliquot—a little something to be gained.

A year ago almost, that was, and that little something turned out to be the water baby she was busy hatching and well worth the trouble, Dhlamina had decided. Ah, but here he was groveling at her feet again, his eyes lifted humbly to the prow of her curved belly.

How have you been, my queen?

As you see me, Mhda. I have no complaints.

Crimping her voice with a sternness she did not feel Dhlamina sketched a series of abbreviated half circles in the air to indicate that her time was not her own and that he must come to the point of his preamble if such indeed there was. Click-ck-ck-*lick*, her gold bracelets knocked together like the knucklebones she'd once thrown into the air and caught one by one, but Mhda heard only the sound of his time running out. He cleared his throat of gravel and the words he'd prepared in his head came out in a dismaying gush, not one after the other like soldiers on parade but disorderly, scattered, as if these same soldiers had already suffered their defeat and now were fleeing from the scene of battle in wild disarray.

You must come and live with me, aboBaby! One day I'll be a rich man, *one day*, but already I am building a house for you. For you and for the little one. And, in time, who knows for how many little ones? Meanwhile no more slaving for that fat Madam, do you hear? No more making food that no one but a fat Madam wants to eat!

Mhda cast a scornful glance at her shopping bag knobbly with tomatoes, crisp cellophane packets of Californian sun-dried peppers, balsamic vinegar, and pursed artichokes.

Dhlamina slapped her sunglasses onto the haughty bridge of her nose, hissing like the cobra that Mhda knew her to be. But what did it matter? Cobra that she was he was bound to her; she was his angel, his queen, the gravy on his mieliepap, the lucky charm on the dashboard of his minibus taxi. Ever since she'd stumbled into his waiting arms that day in the Muti Shop in a clatter of clicking heels and bracelets, ever since he'd grabbed her by the arm talking fast, too fast, but one glance at her scornful eyes told him that his time was running out! So he'd flashed his pocket watch because it was the only thing of value he owned and she was a woman who shone, *shone*, from her buckles and her rings and her beads to the dental gold twinkling in her left incisor.

As for Mhda, his eyes were too close-set, too focused, to see very far into the past but even an ugly man, a man *famous* for his ugliness, knew enough not to squint at any luck that might come his way in the future. And truly she remained lucky for him. In fact, the more Dhlamina scorned him the luckier Mhda got. Revenue from his taxi franchise, the shebeens and gambling dens, the peddler's carts along Diagonal Street and his share in a small but lucrative brothel in downtown Hillbrow, poured in. Weekdays he directed traffic and pedestrians at his taxi depot in the suburbs or collected protection money and lender's interest from the hawkers in town. Nights he rattled through the city on his cranky, much-patched motor scooter. Like a demented pinball he flew from shebeen to gambling house, and with every *ping* the board lit up. Jackpot! Another fifty free games to go!

The people said Madiba Mhda, Taxi Man, no longer needed to sleep. He was a tokoloshe in the body of a man, one who could sidestep Mister Death, that old pretender, as if he was a sleepy puffadder dozing on the path. Sure enough, Mhda had already survived the taxi wars, two gang clashes, the hostel raids, police cross-fire during a bank robbery, various township skirmishes, the long convulsive violence of the Emergency Years and the democratic but no less vicious violence of the months before the election. Not to mention countless rusty crashes on the scooter. And if he'd escaped it hadn't been unscathed. Many scars had been acquired, so many the people said he'd been unstitched and sewn together again like a fertility doll. But Mhda was of that fortunate breed of men who are like lizards drying in the sun; their tails grow back as you watch. In Mhda's case his fractured bones would knit together again within a matter of days and all the blood he'd lost was as so much sawdust.

The people said the reason for his luck was his ugliness. They whispered that the evil eye winked when it looked upon him, but Mhda knew better. He was lucky because of love and if it wasn't the kind of luck that attracted the heart of his beloved at least it was the kind that pulled money into his orbit, money and contacts and business transactions and deals and graft and propositions various, not to mention friends willing to overlook his famous ugliness for the favours he granted. For the opportunity to grasp the hand of a man, even for a moment, whose touch, it was rumoured, left gold fingerprints on the skin. Fingerprints like smudges of pollen and this pollen, in turn, attracted the bees of good fortune that buzzed through the city shaking wealth and providence from under their wings.

Crazily superstitious, his bony wrists encircled with copper bracelets to ward off rheumatism, Mhda was careful neither to confirm nor to deny these rumours. Instead he doggedly averted his gaze from the evidence of his prodigious good luck, concentrating instead on the task of beguiling his aboDarling, his aboDearest, his aboDhlamina, while trying to ignore the unwritten laws of good fortune which perversely dictated that winning her meant losing everything else.

Meanwhile, another rumour was beginning to circulate — Dhlamina had only just caught wind of it — that Mhda was considered to be so potent, such a powerful force for economic growth, he'd infiltrated the dream life of the city. Now, more and more women and even some men were dreaming of him and these dreams were considered to be lucky, portentous, *fortunate* dreams. When a woman woke in the morning having dreamt of Mhda she might very well convert the wishfulness of dreams into hard cash by placing a bet in the afternoon fahfee draw.

Number 26, one of the girls at the Portuguese Grocery had giggled. Which was the number for bees, naturally.

Exasperated, more than a little embarrassed, Dhlamina cursed the prickle of curiosity that had obliged her to obey Mhda's summons so that here she was again, a cat against a scratching post, arching her back and mewling to rid herself of the fleas that hopped from his mouth to her ears.

Eish, are you mad as well as ugly! Must I give up cooking for this Madam who showers me with cash for a man who expects me to cook for free? And how do I know you won't fill my belly with nothing but sorghum and babies for the rest of my life? No, no Mhda, you must do better than this, *tcha*.

So saying, Dhlamina struggled to her feet, pulling her coat about her and brushing at the shoulders to indicate that he, Mhda, was so much loose hair and dandruff to be dashed off with a wave of the hand.

In order not to lose face in front of his taxi men who might or might not be observing their altercation but it wasn't worth taking the chance because authority was the least of what might be lost by way of a thoughtless gesture, Mhda did not grab her wrist, her arm. Neither did he kiss the tips of her fingers or pat the murmuring belly with a proprietary air so that it was with a distinct sense of anti-climax that Dhlamina hefted her shopping bags and stalked off, heels, bracelets and yes, even the little coloured beads in her hair clicking indignantly and never once did she glance back, not once. At least not until she was passably certain that Mhda could no longer observe her. Then, pausing to adjust the weight of her load and the breadth of her stomach, Dhlamina turned to discover that Madiba Mhda, Taxi Man (Bee-Keeper, Dream-Merchant), without missing a beat, was already engaged in the next order of business. Through a fleeting gap in the traffic she saw him bending towards a thin curry boy she didn't recognize. Heads propped together over the brown suitcase the two were arguing furiously or agreeing emphatically, who could say?

At that moment the lights changed, cars and taxis, pedestrians and hawkers swerved into the street. Quick as a knife laid flat against the cheek and to the grate of ratcheting gears the two were hidden from her view.

4:02, time of death, Benjamin informed the nurse.

A hijacked taxi had rolled onto the highway and careened across three lanes before bursting into flame. The survivors, pried from the wreckage, together with the unlucky passengers of oncoming vehicles, were brought in early Sunday morning and from the moment Benjamin had bent over the blank, shock-eyed face of a child, her hair still smoking, he hadn't looked up again until well after sunrise when the relatives began arriving with their ashen faces, their dry, wrung-out hands.

Sweetheart, he'd murmured. *Honey, don't be afraid.*

The House on Sugarbush Road

He thought she heard him but in the escalating violence of cracking ribs and electric shocks by which they'd tried to massage her small red heart into life he lost her attention.

Anyway, he suspected, she'd no longer have believed she had nothing to fear from him.

4:02, time of death, Benjamin informed the attending nurse, already reaching for the next stretcher, the nearest scudding pulse. But all night as he and the others staunched blood, set ragged bones, alternately cutting flesh open and sewing it closed, the words beat like a pulse against his temple. *Past four, two minutes past.* It wasn't her death so much as what he'd done to that limp child's body as it lay draining away on its gurney and how everything he'd done hadn't been enough so that the bone-breaking effort of saving her life was, in the end, just another violence visited upon her as she died.

Later, and then later again, and then much later, the dead tagged and trundled off, the living gamely beeping beneath their consoles, Benjamin went in search of a reviving cup of something hot before the drive home. The staff room, lined with knocking pipes and clanking radiators, was empty except for Markham trying to take in the end of a one-day cricket test on the wavy, rabbit-eared television set. Hissing indignantly, the tea urn jolted out a thin stream of stewed black tea.

Hey chips, *chips* mate! Markham was yelling instructions to the captain of the South African team but shrugged in disgust when his directives went unheeded.

Big cricket wanker! offered Benjamin.

No, seriously fucked, *seriously*, said Markham not lifting his eyes from a showy, high-kicking, over-arm bowl.

The tarmac behind the Gen was swollen and blistered, split open at its seams; Benjamin teetered as he fumbled for his keys. The steering wheel was hot as the blazes and he had to drive with his thumbs for a couple of minutes, sucking air theatrically. As the Audi nosed back towards the suburbs, winter heat rolled through the car. Benjamin cranked windows, pulled down the sun visor, yanked the fan to full throttle but in no time at all he was coated with dust, his skin drawn

taut across irritable bones. A sudden lurch in the road brought the car
alongside a squatter camp patchworked in corrugated iron and sheet
metal lifted from building sites. Smoke puffed from a doorway and a
row of barefoot children turned their faces as the Audi sped by, tires
spinning off horsetails of dust. It was a relief to turn onto the easeful
Macadam of the highway.

In something of a daze, a dwaal, a dw-aaa-l, as Mus would say,
Benjamin drove on. Where was his lover at this very moment, he wondered, and with whom? He was probably still sleeping off a night at
the clubs where he went jolling with his friends—*just friends lovey,*
moenie worry nie—where he was a tireless drinker and dancer and
admirer of men. And where light glinted off the diamond studs and
nipple rings, the teeth of the young cannibals who stamped and gyrat-
ed to the pulse of beat and light, the night swirling in coloured rings
around them.

Ah, well.

But on off-call Sundays Benjamin would wake up beside Mustapha
in the little flat in Yeoville, the smell of marijuana and sex still trapped
in the sheets, dried cum in his chest hair, his balls achy.

Up on one elbow, staring at his lover's jutting collarbones or the
boy's cock caught in its tangle of hair or—

Boy wallah?

Mmm?

Stop perving at me, you hear!

What shall we do today, Mr. Fa?

But the question was rhetorical, they always did the same thing
on Sunday mornings; the *as per usual*, Mus would say rifling through
the bedside table in search of whatever was left of a halfway decent-
sized joint from the night before.

The little flat was Spartan and hopeful with its oak drop-leaf table
bought through the classifieds and surrounded by plastic garden chairs,
CDs carefully alphabetized on tomato crate bookshelves, and a tiny
bathroom retiled with cheap seconds. The kitchen rattled with cannisters and boxes and stoppered spice bottles bought wholesale from

the traders around the Oriental Plaza. Everywhere recipes torn out of *Bona* magazine or *Fair Lady* rustled amongst the open packets of licorice allsorts that Mus ate by the handful. A peculiarly rattling, rustling place, the kitchen was old and disorderly but spotless. Sunday mornings, Ben and Mus spent as much time in bed as they could stand what with wet spots and bagel crumbs, Vaseline, accumulating mounds of Kleenex, cooling cups of coffee, and newspapers smudging their ink and violence across the sheets. Then Mustapha, growing impatient with the stale air in the apartment, the sound of a family dispute wheeling above their heads, the smell of cheap cuts—shank and *sniff sniff* tripe?—simmering in a flat across the way, would harangue Benjamin out of bed.

Winter afternoons, the sun irritably bright but unconvincing in its warmth, Benjamin and Mustapha would drive out to one of the many parks in a city the colour of mange, a season so dry that people flocked to water as if by instinct. Then, carefully not touching, not talking much either, they'd join the families and the lovers wandering in overlapping circles around lakes and dams and ornamental ponds as the late afternoon sunlight moved slowly over the water.

Slouching along beside Benjamin, his beautiful neck bare, Mustapha would glance neither to the left nor the right and seldom noticed Benjamin's preoccupation. But at other times he'd grow oddly communicative, breaking into an excitable sort of chatter and rattling on about various had*dock* matters (does he mean *ad hoc*? Benjamin wondered) and what he proudly called his *vici*ous circle of friends and their Saturday night forays to various Hillbrow leather clubs. But although there were grounds for jealousy—there always were with Mus—Benjamin didn't begrudge the boy his pleasure.

Shame, he worked so hard all week long.

Once, on one of their walks around the Zoo Lake Mustapha heard his name called, twice, before wheeling reluctantly to greet Uncle Ismail, a 'Slamsie from way back, Mus later told Benjamin. The stout old paterfamilias had made it clear that he neither expected nor desired an introduction to the white man who was inexplicably accompanying his nephew but that didn't prevent him from keeping them standing there in the hot sun while he enquired with great gusto into the frequency of Mustapha's entirely imaginary devotions.

Five times a day on the prayer mat, yes that is all very well, my boy, but when will you be ready to make Hajj? That is the question, *that* is the question, surely?

Twenty minutes at least; Benjamin sweating and ignored, Mustapha shifting from foot to foot like a child but Uncle Ismail the very model of patient inquiry. Yes, *that* is the question, he finally allowed for the last time, shaking his head and stroking his chin and turning to wave at his nephew, his voice growing louder for some reason as he departed. The question, the *Question*, the QUESTION!

At other times Mustapha was greeted by various young men who hailed him raucously, cryptically.

Hey Kunju, I don't fucking believe it!

No-ja! Dis true, man.

Lekker joll, my china! Later.

From these coded exchanges Benjamin could never work out if the boys were lovers or friends, casual acquaintances or sworn enemies. It seems he'd lost the common touch.

Are you smiling at me or chewing a brick, bra Kunju?

Whaaa!

Cause either way you goan lose your front teeth, hey!

Ja, Farid, all the better to suck your big fat—

Here a burst of lewd laughter and catcalls would muffle the prurient content of Mustapha's rebuttal and Benjamin, his cheeks burning, would find himself pulled along in the wake of the boy's triumphant departure. Less frequently, when Mustapha was in a jovial mood, the boy might unbend a little; offer Benjamin a surreptitious but winning embrace. At such times he seemed gripped by a divine laughter that overflowed in raucous banter. *Ken jy vir Johannes?* he mimicked elaborating upon an old joke.

Mevrou van der Merwe, she's this old auntie and someone, her neighbour, asks, *Mevrou van der Merwe, ken jy vir Johannes? Hy naai vir mans innie hol!* And Mrs. van der Merwe who doesn't hear so good, you understand, she schemes, *Wat? Watse hall? Wie gaat trou?*

Ha ha *ha*. His laughter, so seldom heard, would suddenly gush forth. Ha *ha. Ag, lovey, the whole country's going to hell in a handbag!*

Benjamin turned off the highway onto Empire, the dense flatlands of Hillbrow and Joubert Park in the distance. On the western horizon smoke from the townships lassoed the city. How many Sunday evenings, having dropped Mustapha at his flat (quick kiss on the cheek), had he driven home through this same winter haze of smoke and stale desire? Home to the house on Sugarbush Road that was his house now, his inheritance. But the house was big, much too big, and there was only Ouma and himself to live in it.

Suddenly and with a keen longing, he wanted to be shot of it all: the weary stale-smelling city and the old house in the middle of it that he had almost escaped but been drawn back to at the end. And Ouma, even Ouma would be happier, wouldn't she, in a nursing home. But Beauty, most of all, Benjamin longed to be rid of Beauty. She'd loved him once, he was almost sure of it, but he could hardly remember when or why that had ended and the other had begun: the shit-eating grins, the quick-fingered pilfering, the *Master* this and the *Master* that. Oh Beauty, he mourned, you bloody-minded old bitch, why don't you love your boy?

The road grating beneath his wheels changed tone subtly as highway Macadam gave way to slightly granular tarmac. He wound through the sluggish suburban streets, past houses shuttered behind burglar bars and the odd face, likewise shuttered, closed in on itself, glimpsed in an adjacent car before the lights changed. But it was already past the hour, *past four*, when he finally turned into Sugarbush Road.

Ouma was sitting in the shade of the syringa once again, trying to warm her bones in the sunlight that slanted through the branches. The rubies above her knuckles glinted sullenly, old blood darkening with age or ill will. She was in a bad mood because she'd drunk too many cups of tepid tea and smoked too many cigarettes and had altogether too much time on her hands. Thoughts of death intruded as they often did at these times. Today she was impatient to be caught, to catch her death as others had so effortlessly caught their fevers and chills and cancers and apoplexies. Either that or the old boy must get off his lazy bones and catch *her*, already. Meanwhile the terrier had followed her outside and was yawning at her feet, shamelessly displaying the ribbed interior of his mouth.

Siestog, Ouma dug into the skin between his ears and the dog breathed deeply into her face, his eyes swarming with kindness made comical by the Harlequin patch over his eye. But when she returned to her cigarette, Eli set off at a trot to chase the fugitive scent of something rotten and desirable wafting from the stagnant water of the fish pond.

Ouma turned her head until she could see Agremon in his overalls washing her grandson's car in the driveway. Soap bubbles drenched the kikuyu border and briefly transformed the gravel into shiny facets of blue-veined stone. For moments at a time the dull winter earth shone like copper. In the distance Beauty turned a corner, one hand twisted into her apron. She was carrying a pan of mieliemeal pap to scrape into the dustbin in the yard and she called out to Agremon who turned his head but their words were lost in the wind.

Ouma lit another cigarette and inhaled. Today the whole world smelled of ashes like the morning after Guy Fawkes when the city reeked of the smoke from used-up fire crackers. From where she sat she could look out over the reef that in summer was covered with grass and scrub. But the winter landscape shed flesh, grew close to the bone. Until one day, suddenly, the earth's scalp poked through.

It had been eighteen months without rain and temperatures on the highveld began to rise early in the morning, climbing steadily until noon when all was crackle and glare. Eighteen straight months, the television newscaster had announced a couple of nights ago. Which sets a new record, he'd concluded, rustling the papers on his desk and looking proud.

Every night the news showed pictures of rural communities in the drought- stricken lands to the north and west. Farmers projected devastating crop failures while their workers lugged plastic buckets to rivers that had already turned themselves inside out. Then, in a dream-like procession, came the cattle with their wrung-out hearts gulping like mouths from between washboard ribs, the dirt-guzzling chickens, the silent stick children. One night, all the grass on the wide plains simply shrivelled up and blew away. Now the earth stretched tight as skin crisping in the sun. Rocks like charred bones poked through.

After the news there had been a short continuity program, a country-wide report on the drought and its consequences.

You know what this country is like! snapped a harried city councillor. We're completely unequipped to deal with anything except braaivleis and sunny skies. When the drought or the flood come we're all at a loss, *yebo*, we behave as if such events have never occurred before.

Hmm, said Benjamin who was watching the news with her, someone's going to have to make a public apology tomorrow.

But Ouma sympathized with the city councillor. Besides, perhaps he was right. This city had been built on the gold mines—surely dust and drought were the order of the day? Why act as if these terrible days were an outrage of nature? People had no memory, perhaps that was the problem. Now everything was panic and prediction: so many weeks before the dams emptied, so many days before the rivers dried up, so many hours before the end of the world.

Light flashed through the branches of the syringa and Ouma flinched, moving her head into the shade. From over the wall she glimpsed the churned-up tunnels of earth that marked how far the workers had progressed with the neighbour's retaining wall. Ouma stubbed her cigarette out impatiently and looked about her. Already the garden was a dustbowl, a handful of knucklebones, an empty shell. *Ag*, you could put the garden to your ear and hear only the endless rustle of insects picking their way through the long runners of dying kikuyu.

Near her foot the dog was digging something raw and tasty from the earth. His haunches were trembling with excitement and he kept glancing up at her from beneath one overturned ear. The drought had shrunk down the earth and now all around the garden, wherever she looked, Ouma could see Eli's discarded bones rising to the surface. Watching Eli tug the bone from the earth, Ouma sighed.

Eighteen months without rain and now a new calamity had befallen them. All over the country the earth was being dug over but for another and even more terrible reason than the drought. The people were searching for the remains of fathers and aunts, mothers and brothers; daughters pulled half-naked from their beds, sons who'd never returned from school, children who'd followed the sound of pipes or police whistles, the cries of their comrades or the false calls of their betrayers. Yes, all those who had disappeared, *pfft*, during the bloody years of the last Emergency.

A day didn't pass without a story rising from the earth.

And every evening these stories were delivered to Ouma's door, a little torn if the newspaper boy had thrown them into the razor wire again, or marked with terrier prints or streaked with dust but always freshly shocking. Communities huddled around anthills of earth as the skeleton of a teacher or a father was brought up in pieces. First the skull, whether bashed in or bullet-shattered, then the brief coil of spinal column and clenched ribcage. And finally the muddy shoes, the indistinguishable cloth with its spray of buttons, each button gathered, saved for reburial.

But these were the lucky families, Ouma knew. Those with something to bury, a shaft of bone, a handful of ash.

Tell me where my son, my daughter died, mothers begged the murderers, the amnesty seekers, the police informers, as they twitched and stuttered in various courts of various cities in a country that itself seemed to revolve in tight bright circles of shame.

Shame, exclaimed Magda. Imagine not knowing where your child is buried!

What a country, Ouma marvelled bitterly. Well, perhaps it was only right that gardens were dying to make room for the new graves that were yawning open all over the city. It had turned colder and Ouma thought she would go back indoors.

Eli, she called. Eli, Eli!

But the terrier, gripping the bone in his jaw, had trotted across the garden and was scooping out a new hole, all the while casting quick sly glances over his shoulder.

6

A LONG JOURNEY

The fault lay in the soil which was both chalk and clay. Then the first rains made the earth swell, like a woman near her time, Mamma Thlali would say, as she whisked her arms vigorously through the air to demonstrate how, when the second rains released the birth waters in a flood, Beauty's little shack would slide off its makeshift foundations and into the drainage ditches by the latrines. This had happened three times already. Three times! The only solution, as Gideon "The Bone" Thandile of Thandile Construction had informed her, was to dig a foundation deep into the earth, past the layers of chalk and clay. To imitate a tree, he explained, sketching this very tree in the air between them. A tree that must fasten itself to the land with roots.

Not that rain looked like so much of a problem this year. In fact, if the drought persisted, and there was every reason to believe it would, the shack appeared to be one hundred percent safe. But safe was more than she, Beauty, could say for the thirsty vegetable garden that Mamma Thlali scratched out of the earth every spring, hardly more than a patch of corn and beans and three good pumpkin plants. With no rains expected the older woman found it too arduous to hobble to the communal water pump three times a day, the corrugated iron basin she balanced on her head pressing more heavily with each splay-footed trek.

As for Rothman, he was nowhere to be found. Mamma Thlali hadn't heard from him for months now and for months now Beauty kept expecting him to turn up at Sugarbush Road, the latest wildfire scheme to make money kindling in his eyes but his wrists jerking and his nose dripping like a tap, shame. (Sometimes the boy reminded Beauty of herself, the eternal counting in his head; this much and that much and so much and such and such; two rand and five rand added to fifty cents and so on. But unlike his grandmother, Rothman never came up with the same number twice and if he didn't stay in school, Beauty was quick to warn, he never would.) Meanwhile, without wild spinach and sugar beets, without the green onions Mamma Thlali boiled to eke out her mieliemeal, there was nothing to thicken the blood. Beauty shuddered to think of her mother-in-law spending another thin-blooded winter in the lean-to.

Gideon "The Bone" Thandile was so called for his prowess on the trombone, the only instrument, he was wont to add with a fat wink, that went in and out all night long.

About Gideon it might well be said, in Mamma Thlali's favourite phrase, *o se bone thola borethe, teng ga yona go a baba*. For he was as smooth and shiny as the bitter apple whose pleasing exterior concealed the acrid taste of deceit. Besides, like everyone else in this memory-eater city, he suffered from chronic amnesia, forgetting to return Beauty's receipts, her telephone calls, her greetings even, when once she spotted his panel-beaten delivery van parked outside a neighbourhood house (it was well known that Gideon was tromboning the Jacobs' maid, Lindiwe). Beauty lay in wait for him but Gideon was too hasty for her, reversing wildly down the street, glancing neither to the left nor the right, and miserably failing to be calmed by the newly erected traffic-calming circle installed by the municipality at the bottom of Oleander Drive. Beauty wasn't at all certain that she trusted him but he already had two thousand three hundred rand of her money in his pocket, money borrowed from Benjamin with no small outlay of pride. Too late now to withdraw from their joint enterprise whose glorious consequence, as Gideon put it, was to see her living like a queen in her cinder block house come the new year.

But hold on a minute, *wag 'n bietjie*. It was "new year" at the beginning of winter, and then it was *after* new year when the worst of the rains had passed and the concrete could set hard as a good woman's heart, as Gideon put it. Only now it was just "soon" sometimes, more often "soon enough." Beauty was never able to ask Gideon when exactly soon was enough because as far as she was concerned, soon had come and gone long ago. Soon was the bus that had left the depot five minutes before she arrived, the freight train that no longer ran through the valley although the tracks stretched rustily into the distance to remind the people of Hammanskraal that while the way of the Lord was mysterious, the way of the white man was direct—the shortest distance between two points, the closest proximity between railway station and rural lay-by—but equally direct in its withdrawal of favour.

Tcha, clearly it was a case—wasn't it *always* the case? thought Beauty—that the fountain ahead could not be trusted, neither could the foot smell where it was going.

Now the question remained as to whether Gideon, smooth, apple-cheeked, bitter-toothed Gideon Thandile, would consent to transport the newly acquired sofa across the province by night, payment in cash and on delivery. At first he said yes, then he said soon. Almost two weeks later the sofa was still wedged beneath the verandah, golden tassels hanging sadly from gaping runners and Beauty knew, *knew*, she'd have to make haste to detach the shining, ropey braid before the bloody dog finished it off once and for all. She borrowed Ouma's nail scissors and snipped the few remaining stitches holding the looped lengths in place, carefully carding them onto the empty roll she'd saved from the paper towels. Then she took the business card from her apron pocket and went to phone the man called Madiba Mhda.

When was it—three weeks ago, a month?—that Beauty had caught a minibus taxi to the Rosebank Mall to pay a visit to Clicks where stock pots were being advertised, cut rate. "Real Aluminum," the flyer announced, "Genuine Bakelite Grips and Big Enough to Bath the Baby!" But when she arrived at aisle three—Household Appliances, Pots & Pans, Kettles, Mixers, Mincers—the shelves beneath the glorious illustration of the Big-Enough Stockpot were empty. Disgruntled and spoiling for a fight, Beauty joined the other ousies clustered around a harassed looking in-store manager.

Shipment was hijacked, he informed them moving uneasily on the balls of his feet. Truck carrying the lot got shoved off the road near Harrismith. Driver's dead. Be-*head*-ed.

He lunged closer on this last word as if to scatter the women with his vehemence but they only clucked and heckled him, refusing to part ranks so that eventually Mister "My Name is *Trevor* Can I Help You?" had to wedge his way through the thick heat of their bodies and flee to the calendar-bespattered haven of his customer-service cubicle.

Without her stock pot but passingly refreshed by this encounter as well as by the bottle of syrupy cream soda she was sipping through two straws, Beauty made her remaining purchases then tried to find somewhere to keep her money safe until she returned home. While a man might carry his change in his sock, a note folded into a cuff or pinned discretely inside his vest, it wasn't dignified for a woman to disarrange herself in this manner simply to outwit thieves. Yet the problem remained; a bag could be snatched, a purse lifted. It used to be safe for a shopper to tie her money in her headscarf, then it was no longer so. It had become commonplace for women to keep their money in their brassieres, a difficulty when it came time to pass the notes into a shopkeeper's hands and not entirely comfortable in the matter of small change. Now there was nowhere on the body, hidden or displayed, that was safe anymore.

Beauty wound the strap of her handbag three times around her wrist then tucked the bag under her arm beneath body and coat and took herself off to the taxi ranks where a wire-thin man with sparks in his eyes harried her into line.

Kwela kwela, huffed the big shot trying to hurry her along. He had doffed his cap and was slamming it irritatedly against his thigh. Beauty knew there to be three kinds of men in this world, three kinds: drunk, hungover. Thirsty. This last was the rarest but this last was what she divined in the taxi man, a thirst, moreover, that couldn't be satiated by Skokiaan or Marula or Amasi, couldn't be quenched in all the beer halls and bars, the shebeens, drink dens, and bottle stores of the city. Such a man was *marengenya*, worn out with alcohol, even if such a man (and he looked to be *just* such a man) never touched a drop save for a rinsing mouthful of traditional ale on feast days. Thirst without addiction was a rare condition so Beauty allowed him to usher her bossily across to the first available *kwela-kwela* taxi before collecting her fare and dispensing change along with the business card that she hooked under her bra strap because you never could tell what brought luck these days nor when you would require luck's execution.

Besides, everyone knew strangers had the advantage of angels when it came to lending a helping hand, a healing touch, or a cool Samaritan drink of water.

Well, looks like we're all set for a strike come December.

Beauty thumped Benjamin's dinner onto the table before him, the chicken thighs trembling a little before settling into the watery gravy. Benjamin, who had been reading the evening paper and trying to engage Beauty in conversation, glanced at his wobbling plateful. The thighs were wan and goose pimpled as if the chicken had succumbed to exposure.

Strike while the iron's hot, hey Beauty?

Beauty rolled her eyes and turned her back on him. The kitchen was damp and warm with the odour of chicken roasted in its juices, an odour that had beckoned Eli who'd snuffled like the tsotsi that he was, all afternoon, at the narrow length of fragrant light beneath the kitchen door. Beauty had cooked two chickens; far too much food for Benjamin. Even putting aside the tender breasts for Ouma's soup, there would be sufficient, *more* than enough, for Agremon, a generous helping piled high with fried onions and thick wedges of tomato to put strength in his heart and fat on his bones.

Too many skinny black men in this country, Beauty thought, spooning gravy on the crackling skins. In the servant's quarters behind the kitchen, where water snickered in the drains every night around suppertime, Beauty sensed Agremon slumped on the bed with its iron legs hoisted in buckets of water to deter the cockroaches that were

The House on Sugarbush Road

a plague in the city even in winter. Stomach growling sourly for the chicken that was always served first on other tables, to other men.

Wag 'n bietjie, my man, she murmured. *Just wait.*

Benjamin was still going on about the strike, Cosatu this and Cosatu that, and what did Beauty think? So she snapped on the tumble-dryer to shut him up. Now not only would his dinner be accompanied by the slurp of moistly resistant underclothes but Beauty would be free of having to talk to that spic and span, recently-showered Mister Highness seated at the kitchen table reading his paper and chewing with such regularity that he reminded her of the rust-coloured cows she would sometimes glimpse from the window of the train creaking its way towards the red dust of Hammanskraal.

That man with his comb-parted hair, his water-wrinkled fingertips, *tcha*! That a man should be so careless, so ignorant of his wealth that he allowed another to go through his briefcase every night and pocket the change—it astonished Beauty. Truly, Benjamin had the unmistakable serenity of one of those cows. Because nothing Beauty could do to rile him had the effect of disrupting, not even for a moment, the steady rhythm of his digestion.

Once Beauty had seen just such a cow upended in a field of lucerne, stomach bloated beneath four strangely thin legs all straining heavenwards. This was not a real cow, she realized almost immediately, but an impossible cow, a vision. After all, real cows did not turn themselves upside down for the passing interest of bored passengers, real cows did not low their surprise and grief to the heavens! It only remained for Beauty to understand what the visionary cow was trying to communicate and even this did not remain doubtful for long because when she arrived home she was met by Mamma Thlali who took her by the hand and led her to the mortuary and after that Beauty never again had the luxury of misunderstanding cows and what they represented.

Seated on her battered kitchen chair by the tumble-dryer, with clothes pegs pinned up and down the front of her overalls, Beauty suddenly felt exhausted, diminished by the years and the children and the various schemes; the radio she'd bought Rothman from Freedman

Electronics and the new school shoes that Givvie had set out in on that terrible day, Mamma Thlali said, but when her daughter was returned to her her feet were bare. Against the death of her daughter the loss of the shoes was as nothing. As nothing. Yet to Beauty's astonishment it seemed that these two things could yet exist beside each other — the terrible loss that blotted out her world and the small niggling mercenary cost of the shoes. How was this possible? It was one more way in which her life shamed her so that she welcomed the nights in which she woke with her feet as cold as if they'd been frozen in the earth all these years.

So many other things lost as well: so much money disappearing into the Chinaman's purse, the deep pockets of Gideon Thandile, so much pain vanishing nobody knew where, so much time and effort — what Meneer used to call elbow-grease — spent on this house. And the house itself rubbed into life each day, surfaces shining, but from where did the shine come if not from the palms of Beauty's own hands grown dull over the years because the healthy brown gloss of her skin had seeped into the furniture like so much good polish.

And this didn't even account for the men she'd lost. Isaac, whose lungs had turned to stone, who'd died without a voice to tell her what to do next, where to go, but only (and only just) how to name their son. Hosiah, who'd disappeared one day and some of his congregation said he was taken up to heaven in a fiery chariot with the chanting of angels in his ears. But even these stalwarts couldn't mistake the odour of frankincense and myrrh for the thick black smell of burning tires that had announced his death. And not to forget Agremon, of course, who was much too thin, who seemed to be whittling away to skin and wishbones before her eyes. And the son called Lucky who was, and the grandson called Rothman who wasn't, but both equally lost to her because when you gave birth to a son you surrendered him up to the world but when you gave birth to a daughter she was yours to keep.

With this thought Beauty closed her eyes to keep the memories safe because already they were trying to escape. That's what memories did; they turned to water so you couldn't hold them anymore. Only

she wouldn't cry this time, not least of all because Benjamin was folding his paper, sliding his plate across the table and Beauty would be
good and damned, dead, ripe, buried, the worms sliding in her gullet,
before she let him see her cry.

No let up in the drought yet, Benjamin announced as if this in
itself was news. He got up and poured himself a glass of water from
the tap and drank it straight down and then poured himself another.
Beauty couldn't blame him.

For weeks, months now, the drought had been an uninvited guest
that had arrived in time for dinner and decided to stay the night, the
next night, and all the nights after that. Every day the sky heated up
like corrugated iron, a tin roof that creaked and cracked over the
reef. Dust settled on everything: on the plaster of house fronts and
security fences, on privet hedges and shrubberies and rock gardens.
Dust drifted through threadbare willows, through windows and across
thresholds and over storefronts beneath their faded awnings where
the rows of dusty winter melon and spanspek and pawpaw slowly
grew indistinguishable.

Eish, thirst! thought Beauty, swallowing hard.

Because the people were always thirsty these days. They drank
rooibos tea or coffee, beer thumbed straight from the can and wine
necked from the bottle and brandy mixed with Coke to take the
sweetness from one and add it to the other. But whatever they drank
(whether fizzy water or clear, whether cold water from the fridge or
warm water from the outdoor tap), the liquid barely wet the dust at
the back of the throat before the drinker was thirsty again

Suddenly Beauty hawked deliberately and as loudly as she could
but Benjamin didn't even wince.

Ko Ko Ko.

Agremon was at the kitchen door come to call her not, as Beauty
had first thought, because he'd been lured by the smell of chicken and
his impatient hunger but because a visitor had arrived. Behind him
stood a man who was even thinner than Agremon but as full of life
as the other man was slack with overwork or exhaustion or whatever

you called one who slumped inside his skin as if it was a shapeless old jersey, buttons missing and holes in the elbows.

This man says I must call you, Agremon started to explain, rolling his eyes to indicate his companion who had already thrust himself forward, hand outstretched.

Mhda at your service, he snapped. Come to collect the auntie's sofa.

Ko Ko Ko.

Benjamin threw open a window to let in the cool night air. The kitchen exhaled in warm gusts of chicken. Already the windows were beaded with the mingling of steamy inside and raw outside. With the knock at the kitchen door and Beauty's hasty departure in the wake of the man whose name he hadn't been quick enough to catch when it was thrown at him but who crackled with purpose, Benjamin ran water and detergent into the sink. He'd offered to clear the table, stack dishes, and sweep up. Gladly.

And if — if Ouma calls you must tell her that Beauty had to go out just-now.

Her embarrassment at asking this favour was matched by Benjamin's willingness to roll up his sleeves and pitch in — yes, Beauty, of *course*, and I'll wash the dishes too — an eagerness, if only he knew it, that scratched at the surface of Beauty's composure like fingernails against chalkboard. Ah, but she must leave, regretfully she couldn't stay to give him what-for, so Beauty contented herself with banging out of the kitchen, slamming the door vengefully and cutting him the snake eye. Hmph.

When she'd gone Benjamin wondered, as he'd wondered so many times before, what to do about the damn woman. Her rudeness and apparent hatred of him. Her quick-fingered pilfering that in recent months had grown too obvious to ignore although, true to form, he was still managing to ignore it. A thief, Ouma would call her if he were to tell her about the pickpocketing. She's a thief, plain and simple. A thief can strike anywhere, anytime, his Ouma would often say, and what she takes from you remains stolen. Hidden. Here Ouma would hold up the inside of her wrist to demonstrate the hiddeness of what remained. Assuredly, Beauty Mapule was nothing more than a thief, common or garden.

Yes, but.

This yes-comma-but tended to stop Benjamin in his tracks.

Yes, *but* Beauty was old and poor and tired. Yes, *but* Beauty's hands were cracked with the difference between hot water and cold weather and they trembled slightly but noticeably at the end of the day. Yes, *but* once Benjamin had watched her walking through the veld at dusk and the small figure winding between vast pylons (their arms akimbo, heads splitting telephone lines) was inestimably dwarfed. Yes, *but* Beauty's handwriting was childlike and she misspelled most of the items on the grocery list. Yes, *but* Beauty washed his socks and cooked his dinner; Beauty took responsibility for the dirt he produced and failed to clean up, the mess he created (steamed bathroom, rumpled bed) on his abbreviated way to cure illness, save lives. Yes, but—this, most of all—*but* she had once been his very own, his big black Beauty who had loved him and protected him from his busy preoccupied parents and all the world with its sharp surfaces and unkind ways. And he had loved her too, he had loved her back.

Ah Beauty, he mourned, the sticky residue of that childish love stirring memory as he allowed his hands to drift in the warm rinse water. He was so lost in the past that he failed to hear the second knock at the kitchen door so that it was the cracked reed of an adolescent voice that jerked him back into the world.

After Mhda had backed the battered delivery truck down the driveway, Beauty, stout of heart and strong of arm, helped load the sofa into the pickup. They covered the sofa with tarpaulin and trussed it up securely as if it was a sheep on the way to market, then started out on the road to Hammanskraal.

Mhda hunched over the steering wheel, driving with three-cornered concentration. Every few minutes he glanced at the rearview mirror, at the wing mirror hanging at an awkward angle from the door and, with triangular emphasis, at the road unwinding before his crooked headlights. He was a driver who paid attention to the past, where he was coming from was as important as where he was going and he glanced compulsively into the rearview mirror from which dangled a couple of osprey feathers and a pair of furry green dice. At first Beauty thought they were being pursued. But no, it was just his way, she decided. This one was a jigsaw man, the pieces of his body, his mind, fitting together like crazy-paving. Where was the peace in that? Such a man, Beauty knew, would always feel pursued. For such a man dragged his persecutors behind him wherever he went in the world.

How long do you go by train? Mhda inquired.

By train is four, five hours. And then the bus. All in all you must plan for a day's travelling.

Tonight we will make the journey in two, three hours, hey? Tops.

In the flare of the match struck to light his Marlboro Beauty saw that Mhda's face was seamed with scars, the skin around the scars stretched tight over curved narrow bones.

Hungry face, she thought. Tokoloshe face.

To a sudden fury of barking from the neighbourhood dogs, Benjamin opened the door to a young boy in a voluminous khaki jacket. He wore dirty runners and grimy fingerless gloves and slouched deep within his jacket as the light from the kitchen trapped him in a tight rectangle of dark-edged brilliance. Eyes narrowed, the boy peered into the room, flicking the corners. It was clear that he was looking for someone.

Benjamin stepped backwards into the kitchen, a little disconcerted as the boy cleared his throat and it became evident that he hadn't attempted speech for some days. Cracking, splintering, his voice slipped between registers as if he'd suddenly lost control of his diaphragm. Benjamin saw that he wasn't so much slouched as hunched into his jacket, his body drawn around an obscure wound. The whites of his eyes had an oily sheen like the eyes of the jaundiced children he often saw at the Gen. The doctor in him stretched out a hand to the boy's pulse but the kid snatched his arm away.

I am here looking for Mama who works for the Madam in Parktown North.

Fourteen or fifteen, small for his age, Benjamin calculated, surprised. I didn't know Beauty had such a young son—

Grandson, the boy interrupted. Her grandson. I'm Rothman.

At first minibus taxis swished past them on the road out of town, all of them crowded, some travelling two and three abreast. One in particular, a wheelbarrow carelessly strapped to its roof, listed badly, and Mhda gave it a wide berth and a stiff finger. After a while they passed the industrial estates and the new housing schemes with their satellite squatter communities and then they were out on the open road.

The moon was a cheese-paring, a hangnail, and when they'd left the lights of the city behind, darkness came down like a handshake, abrupt and soundless. Mhda, hunching ever closer to the windshield, peered through the small cones his headlights threw upon the tilting road. The pickup wavered through the night, the wind and the noise of the wind seeming to rock it upon its chassis. Every now and then they'd pass an isolated farmhouse or a rusty windmill straddled above iron struts. But soon enough even these scattered landmarks became indistinguishable and Beauty and Mhda fell back upon the congenial mood of strangers who've been thrown together for an hour or two but who will soon part to go their separate ways. Everything conspired to lend intimacy to their journey: the darkness outside and the wind careening down off the mountains that seemed to want to claw the little truck off the road. Even the cold only made the two feel ever more companionable, safe in the snug cab of the pickup.

To the slosh and slide of the sea water that Mhda was transporting in sealed two-litre Coca-Cola bottles (a cure for assorted stomach ailments), various confidences flew between the travellers. Indeed, so hospitable was the mood, so companionable the darkness, that soon Mhda reached into his pocket to extract his box of Best Brand and in

Méira Cook

no time at all the two were as thick as the snuff they shared. Sneezing voluptuously, Beauty told him about her little house, the concrete foundations that would hold firm come the rains and the double bed she would purchase on lay-by from Morkels. Deftly she passed the shoe polish tin topped up with first-grade snuff to Mhda and, in turn, he told her of the woman he loved. His angel, his queen.

Mhda's skin was so tight he shone. The crimp of his knuckles on the steering wheel, the grip of his fingers as he expertly pinched the snuff, seemed to glow as if the taxi man had swallowed a sixty watt bulb and this strange light, Beauty recognized, was love.

So where is she, this girl who puts the rest of us to shame? Beauty teased.

Yoh, Mama, what can I say? Mhda looked stricken.

The truth is she's working for a rich Madam and she tells me she's making too much money to stop. This although I, Madiba Mhda, I too am making handsome money from my taxis, the shebeen, my—all my businesses. This although she's carrying my child in her belly, this although she wears my heart on a gold chain around her neck—

Words failed him. Mhda rolled down the window and spat vehemently into the night.

Atchoo! sneezed Beauty. Yes, girls these days are too independent. It wasn't always so. When I was young I wondered who my husband would be. I wished that he would be a handsome and good-humoured man. But in those days we had to consult other heads before our own hearts. Our mothers and fathers, uncles and aunts, grandparents, yes, even older brothers and sisters had to be appeased before any course of action could be undertaken. These days the young are like blackjacks, they grow on the side of the road and stick to anything that comes past.

Remembering her stepdaughter, Beauty sighed. She was just the sort of happy-go-lucky girl who would never dream of consulting anyone or anything but her own headstrong desires. And now she was pregnant, and if she knew who the father of her child was—*if* she knew—Beauty would be the last to find out. Once more, Beauty sighed. Sighed and sneezed and turned her attention back to Mhda who was still exclaiming upon his one and only.

But does she ask for advice? Oh no, not her. And will she take it? Quite the contrary. But that doesn't stop her from giving advice, *tcha*. Now I must get rid of this taxi man and that shebeen queen, she tells me. Doesn't like the look of this one, doesn't like the sound of that one. Now she wants me to open up a restaurant in town. Maybe *then* she'll come and cook for me, huh. *Maybe*. But how can you trust such a woman? Woman with an itchy heart and money in her pocket!

Give her what she wants she will only stop wanting it.

Yebo, I tell you, mamazala, one look at that one and I begin to rehearse the words of the psalms in my head because I know I will soon require them—*Lo though I walk through the valley of the shadow of death I am comforted for Thou art with me!*

Offer her the world and she will demand the moon! Yes, Beauty knew the sort, and how well.

No, my son, she continued, you must act the opposite of what you feel. You say you love her? Good, then you must pretend to hate her. You think she is beautiful? Imagine maggots crawling in cow dung when you look at her, imagine lemon juice poured into a fresh wound, silver paper caught between the teeth. You want to grovel at her feet? Then you must stand a little taller when you are beside her. Lift your chin and look over her head to the mountains beyond, to their peaks and valleys that are so much like a woman and remember all the women who have loved you.

Beauty sneezed three times in quick succession. Some people drank to forget, Beauty took snuff to remember. But seldom had she experienced such first-grade snuff. The sneezes began deep at the base of her skull amongst the roots and bulbs of memory. I also, I too was a beauty once, she told Mhda. Let me tell you a story.

The boy was ravenous. Hand over fist he shovelled thick slices of bread and jam into his mouth while Benjamin shuffled and cut until the loaf was half its size, the jam jar empty. He refused to surrender his coat and a sweet-musky odour rose from its folds as he warmed and expanded in the damp kitchen; an oddly chemical compound of unwashed skin, dagga smoke, pungent exhaustion.

Your Ouma had to go away this evening. She'll be back tomorrow.

It was the second time that Benjamin had reassured the boy and again he barely responded except for lifting his eyes briefly from the surface of the plate. But when he raised his mug his hands shook insistently. Benjamin recognized a glue-sniffer when he saw one, or worse, a Meths-drinker, a *blue train rider*. His nails were bitten to their bloody quicks, his wrists almost as chafed and ragged as the cuffs of the sweater unravelling beneath his coat. The boy, the *child*, looked shell-shocked by cold or hunger or something worse, perhaps, because less immediately solvable. Benjamin rubbed his eyes with the heel of his hand and tried to set the boy at ease with a steady stream of words like a rallying hand on the shoulder but Rothman remained silent except for the slurrup-slurrup of hot tea.

You can sleep in Beauty's room tonight, I'm sure your Ouma won't mind.

Interpreting this invitation as his dismissal, the boy shuffled to the door, eyes flicking, once more, from corner to corner.

As Benjamin locked the kitchen door he was stricken with two contradictory anxieties: that he hadn't done enough for the boy and that he'd done far too much, overstepping the bounds of decorum and inviting him into his house. But what else could he do? A child was wrenched from a car wreck only to die as he watched while all about him others winced and shuddered beyond the comfort of human touch. All he could do, thought Benjamin sadly, was to feed the one who showed up on his doorstep, hungry and cold. But sweet Jesus, he was tired.

The sudden quiet of the kitchen reminded Benjamin of earlier times. Sitting alone at the kitchen table, doing his homework, he'd hear Beauty come in and haul a piece of frozen meat from the fridge to thaw overnight. She'd already taken against him even in those days, he seemed to recall. And her daughter had died around that time too so who could blame her? Given, her name was, Givvie for short. She was Benjamin's great pal when they were kids.

Shaking himself slightly, Benjamin glanced around the neatened kitchen one last time before turning off the light.

Later, after he'd put Ouma to bed and watched the eleven o'clock news, Benjamin went back through the house on Sugarbush Road, locking up, battening down for the night. Eli, who had taken himself upstairs for the evening, needed to be let out one more time after which Benjamin set the alarm—be-eep be-eep, two short dashes followed by the steady red eye of the circuit beam above the panic button. In the hallway Grandfather stood with his hands cupped at midnight as if pronouncing a silent salaam.

It took him a long time to fall asleep and when at last he did he dreamed of the plums that fell all summer long in the garden of his childhood, thudding to the ground where they fermented in their own juices, intoxicating the birds that lit through the long summer evenings and paused only to settle momentarily on lower branches. Branches that were always, for some reason that was unclear to him, always a hand's width out of reach.

Although the night was dark and the wind cold, the company was congenial, the mood high-spirited. When Beauty had finished relating the story of her youthful good looks and her many admirers the two discussed the terrible drought (tcha), the exorbitant cost of living (hmph!), and the way this city forgot its own streets and stories and, yes, even its children, so that the people must always be counting their own, counting and praying, because how else to hold onto a pocketful of something at the end of a day's work (tcha, *tcha*).

Do you think this drought will break soon? asked Beauty.

But Mhda, who had inherited a feeling for weather from his maternal grandmother whether it was the anticipation of rain just five miles and half an hour distant or the dreadful knowledge of years locked in unrelieved drought, had no good news to relate on this score. There had been years when cattle lapped at the dust of dry river beds until their tongues came up in boils.

Not a chance, mamazala, Mhda replied mashing his cigarette into the saucer he kept balanced on the dashboard. Not a chance in hell.

And Mhda went on to relate what he'd heard about the maize crop; that farmers believed as little as four bags of corn would come to harvest that year rather than the usual eight or ten per hectare. But even though he was a city man, more at home with the roll of the dice than with the revolutions of the combine harvester, Mhda felt that such predictions were unduly optimistic. Few would be able to piece together even two bags per hectare, he confided to Beauty, and what would that do to the sharecroppers out in the rural areas, those unable to secure government loans and subsidies? Ah well, but that was life, was it not, there were always two queues at the bank; one for the rich and the other for the others. Mhda had long ago resolved never to stand in any such queue, his hat in his hand, his armpits prickling with shame.

To cheer themselves up after this sobering discussion Mhda offered to sing a couple of rousing struggle songs. Beauty added her own elaborations to these songs, stamping her feet and clapping her hands and drawing out long ululations as in the old days when people demonstrated their delight and pleasure in this manner. And since Mhda was without vocal talent, at the same time manoeuvring his vehicle swiftly rather than skillfully, the last half hour passed in a pleasant blur of jeers and near misses.

In this mood of raucous exuberance they approached the left turn into the service road that lead to the shantytown and Beauty began to pull her stockings straight and untwist her petticoat in preparation for disembarking.

But wait, what was this? A light loomed in the road ahead of them. Mhda jarred to a halt before the tail lights of a police van.

Gee pad, gee pad! Kom julle twee, wat gaan aan nou? The uniformed sergeant flashed his torch at the knobbly shape beneath the tarpaulin.

Both policemen looked remarkably alike, thought Beauty, brutish and dull, throwbacks to an earlier time as so often happened in these rural outposts. Both were muscle-bound with two thick rolls of flesh propping up the backs of their necks and hair cut so close to their skulls that it resembled khaki-coloured suede. By the light of the police van Beauty noticed that the tips of their ears were rubbed brick-red and raw, as if each man had spent the better part of his life stuck headfirst in a rugby scrum. A police Alsatian fretted, pulling at its leash.

Dis mos stolen, the second sergeant agreed. But when Beauty lifted the sailcloth to show them her second-hand sofa he shook his bullet-shaped head and demanded a sale's slip.

But my Madam gave me the sofa. For my own. How must I have a sale's slip?

Receipt? Bill of sale? Cheque stub?

I am telling you, my Madam, Mrs. du Plessis of Sugarbush Road—

Then you must get a letter from her. To say she gave it to you, this Mrs. du Plessis. She must write down today's date and a description of the article in question. And the date she gave it to you. And your name, your whole name, mind, and her own. She must write all this down in a letter addressed to Sergeant Viljoen. Then you must bring this letter to me, *jy weet,* at the police station.

But my Madam, Mrs. du Plessis, she lives in Johannesburg.

Then you must go back to Johannesburg.

The wind was blowing so hard that it seemed to pull the water, from their eyes. The first sergeant clucked under his breath and the second sergeant bullied Mhda into off-loading the sofa upon the dust road. All at once Beauty's heart failed her and she was unable to help lift the heavy brocade piece.

Be glad they haven't confiscated the truck, consoled Mhda because the brutes had emptied his bottles of sea water into the thirsty dust.

Be grateful they haven't thrown you into the back of the panda with that stupid dog, he comforted as they turned and made their way up the service road. But Beauty was looking back at her heart's desire, the deep plush sofa, colour of ripe plums, abandoned in the slip road at the turn-off to Hammanskraal.

Tick tick tick, the landscape clicked by again. The sun had risen when no one was looking and now swung off-centre in a bird-flecked sky. On the way to the highway they passed a woman in a dressing gown standing beside the dirt road. Her skin was lightly oiled by the early sun and her feet were bare and raw-looking. She seemed bewildered, astonished to find herself stalled on the side road out of town, and she clutched her washed-out, greyish dressing gown with hands wrung out by worry and the hard rusty water of the region.

The angle of the sun slanting through the grass reminded Beauty of dancing in the veld on Easter morning with the other Church of Zionists. To the sound of tambourines and a mouth organ, a couple of horns and a drum, she and the other women would hold their skirts above their ankles, careful not to tread in the fire-scorched veld, lift up their voices and sing unto the Lord—

He Who He Who He Who Sa-a-a-v-es!

Then, too, the wind would blow the swamp grass flat but she never felt cold because *He Who* had entered her body and moved her as the spirit moves upon the water. And always, in front of his congregants, stood Hosiah Mopede in his white surplus and ecclesiastical collar, Hosiah Mopede with his Moses frown and his Prophet's eyes, one hand lifted up to God but the other held out to his people. Yes, always Beauty saw him like this, the first rays of the rising sun touching his forehead and his shadow laid out so far across the veld that it reached the highway where passing motorists ran him over, again and again.

It took only two hours to get back to the city but then they had to wake Ouma so that she could write the letter to Sergeant Viljoen. Ouma's hands were clawed and her writing scrawled recklessly from one side of the page to the other. Like the woman on the side of the road she too looked bewildered, stranded in her bright pain, but Beauty had no time for words of comfort. Back soon, Mama, she snapped and was gone. By the time they were on the road again the morning rush hour was in full throttle and with the best will in the world (but no more stories, no snuff, no confidences and no freedom songs) it took Mhda, driving with one hand on the steering and one on the hooter, an additional four hours to get back to the police station.

As for the sergeant he did not apologize for his blunder, didn't even look ashamed. Just took the letter, scanned it with his dead fish eyes then waved Beauty away as if she was an annoying fly. As for Mhda's truck it was already covered with a fine red dust that would thicken over the course of the morning until they arrived back in the city where Agremon would have to rub it down with a dribbling hosepipe and rags dipped in soapy water, clicking his tongue as he scraped away to remove the dead insects from the windshield. As for the sofa it was damp through with early morning frost, already damp through.

They will cry, Beauty thought sorrowfully of the policemen. They will cry tears one day.

Then she climbed back into the truck with Mhda whom she would have to pay for the extra journey, and drove slowly down the dust road to the home of the Nongenes who had promised to look after her sofa until such time as she could build the little house that would one day shelter her old age.

7

DOG DAYS

It was spring and then summer in the city built upon gold mines. The November rains had arrived at last to break the drought and all but washed an entire country grown dry as stale bread into the Indian Ocean. The earth was exhausted by the prolonged winter, it had lost all resilience and the rains turned the land into a gasping, boiling river that floated all manner of flotsam and jetsam in its wake. Whole towns and villages in the Eastern Cape, in the rural homelands, slid into the waters, their residents forced to flee houses and farms, the flood lapping at their ankles. So many casualties had been reported amongst animals in the game reserves and cattle in the farmlands that it seemed as if a deluge of biblical proportions had come to agitate the land once more. Every night on the news the swollen bodies of cattle chugged past fallen trees and spinning cars, past dwellings reduced to rubble and their hand-wringing inhabitants, past wooden beams and tires, suitcases filled with photographs and love letters and handwritten recipes handed down from mothers to their daughters.

Yet the city held fast. The city built from the gold that flowed through its underground reefs was safely landlocked. Ouma was thinking these thoughts, and others, as she sat at her post beneath the syringa tree, looking out at the familiar skyline blowing greyly like dirty washing between the twin water towers of the reef. Suddenly the sun came out and the crickets were loud in the bushes. The rains had caused her arthritis to flare up and her joints ached horribly but with some difficulty Ouma straightened her fingers so that she could admire the wavering light of her rubies.

From the kitchen the clatter of a lawnmower rolling over slate tiles interrupted her thoughts.

Pick it *up*, Agremon, Ouma called but he pretended not to hear her.

It was still too wet to mow the lawn anyway. The rains that had fall-en all through November, first saturating the earth then welling to its surface, had only recently receded but the ground was logy with water.

With each step the garden rippled and brimmed.

Agremon was anxious. If she wouldn't allow him to mow the lawn how was he supposed to earn his wages? True, she'd never docked him before but this had been such a strange year, drought followed by floods and who knew what would happen next. Already the Ferreiras next door had told him not to come back until the waters slid back into the earth. *Way* down, said Mister Ferreira, showing him with one hand against the rotten scaffolding of the long-abandoned retaining wall exactly how far *down* had fallen. And now here she was press-ing her heels into the earth and shaking her head as the water flowed into her shoes.

Muddy-pawed, haunches sprung, Ouma's dog advanced upon Agremon, a fatuous expression upon his skelm face and the inten-tion to topple the gardener clearly visible to any fool with eyes to see.

That's right, muttered Agremon, *bendifunanje inyathele ekonsini.* Tread on my rows of corn.

He was in the mood, unusual for him, to take out his frustration on the animal. To this end he hoped to tempt the dog into wrongdo-ing so as to give vent to his anger. I want you to tread on my corn, as a farmer will say to a jackal, then I can pay you back for other griev-ances as well. But Eli, sensing retribution on the wind, veered sharply, trotting off on a fugitive scent and Agremon was left to cast anxious eyes about the garden searching for something to do.

Does Ouma want me to prune the tree? he offered, pointing.

She told him to go ahead as he'd hoped she would and Agremon continued with his train of thought as he went off to fetch the garden ladder. Dog love! Agremon would never understand it. Neither the fondness of an owner for his animal nor the love of a dog such as Eli who, smelling his mistress's arrival in his sleep, stirs and hurries to the window to wait for her. Such love was a mongrel thing, monstrous, a pariah dog haunting the shadows with tin cans tied to its tail, its ears running pus and the corners of its eyes encrusted with flies. Clicking softly, Agremon was glad that he'd found something to do in the garden although it was equally true that these days Ouma was agreeable to anything provided she was left alone.

She's tired these days, Beauty told him. Gettting old.

Already there, said Agremon. Old he meant. But Beauty didn't laugh as he'd meant her to.

Well okay, thought Agremon, okay. "Getting old," it turned out, was just this white Ouma beneath her tree and so far as Agremon was concerned, whatever left him free to putter in the garden was an A-1 okay deal. Besides, since Ouma never ate the plums from her tree, he and Beauty would benefit from a good pruning come the season of ripeness. By cutting away excess growth, by thinning the blossoms, Agremon would make room for the first plums to grow, cool and sweet, from their hard green buds. With the taste of last summer's fermented plum juice on his tongue Agremon raised the garden shears above his head.

The water that tipped into her insoles from the overflowing earth was cold. Gingerly Ouma toed off her shoes, tilting each one in turn so that the moisture ran out.

Rain clouds seemed to be gathering again, all the weight of weather taken up in the sky. Somewhere above her head she could hear the *hut*-ssnip *hut*-ssnip of Agremon's secateurs. *Gudden wek*, *gudden wek*, he seemed to be chanting, in time to the hazing of the branches, the brisk sun-crackle of sliced foliage. At the base of the plum tree Eli was harrying an exposed root and ducking for cover each time Agremon let fall a sheaf of shivering leaves.

Humba! Suka wena!

Beyond the garden the cicada chorus rasped along the edges of the veld. A vast communal throat clearing to which Eli lent his gruffle-bark.

Shaya! Shaya!

Ouma raised her head and listened. Happiness flared briefly just as, in past years, grief had opened out like an accordion in her chest. *Ag*, but she missed him, her Lourens, and more every day since his passing. What then? Perhaps something in the first rains had broken the drought in her, too. Lately she'd begun to worry that Mister Death had forgotten all about her, that she would live on forever, this sick old woman beneath her syringa tree. And every year grow older and sicker but not quite old enough or sick enough to die.

For shame! Ouma chastised herself now. Because with the coming of the rains it seemed quite certain that all would unfold as it must in this best of all possible worlds. And Death, her old friend, had surely not forgotten her. Closing her eyes she turned her face once more to the sun and, nodding every now and then as at the answer to a question, soon fell asleep.

Mustapha felt as if he was breathing through plastic. The heat clung like saran wrap as he dodged through traffic in the rusty Peugeot that his new friend, Mhda, had secured for him. The car was old, too old to have been stolen or at least recently stolen, and despite its rattles and unpredictable jerks, the rust that filigreed the bonnet, the scattered bullet holes in the rear upholstery (also a large uneven stain resembling a map of Africa) Mustapha, who'd never owned a car before, was buoyant. Exhilarated by the sound of his wheels unzipping the long black lengths of tarmac.

Still, it was hot. Even with the windows cracked and the wind drying the sweat off the back of his neck, Mustapha's skin felt swollen and tight at the same time, as if his organs were boiling and expanding. The hair at his nape and temples was permanently damp these days, always in danger of curling out of the sleek silhouette that he carefully finger-combed each morning, applying liberal lashings of Jolla Mousse after his shower and towel drying from the root.

In Commissioner Street traffic snarled along, the taxis darting at fast-as-reflex gaps. Mustapha was searching for Mhda, for his new friend and business partner, changing gears ineptly but with wild abandon as he scanned the taxi ranks, the vending stands and market stalls. He revved past tall pinstriped office buildings that broke the reflections of distressed tenement blocks against their mirrored facades, swerving along the one way streets and blind corners of the central business district where entrepreneurs had set up shop, laying out their wares on trestle tables and tomato boxes. Whatever came to hand. In the countdown before Christmas everything, it seemed, was for sale: ladies' blouses wrapped in thin plastic shrouds, cassette tapes and batteries and sunglasses, sweating toffees and melting chocolates and cheap perfume turning vinegary in the sun.

Like ghosts of their previous owners, pleated skirts and ruffled shirts swayed on fences, wire hangers twisted through gratings adorned with phony Rolex watches and phony Gucci handbags with flashy clasps that bounced the light off in all directions. Bras and stockings hung from the makeshift racks on Jeppe Street along with Bic lighters and pens, cartons of cigarettes, string bags lumpy with onions and potatoes, and jubilant posters of the Bafana Bafana Football Team. Women swayed by balanced between vast nylon bags stuffed with day-old produce. Along Kort Street, along Market and Diagonal and President, the gutters overflowed with fruit rinds and cigarette butts, Styrofoam containers and plastic bags, a river of debris bobbing in the wake of human hunger and thirst; the sudden appetite for a fried cake or a boerewors roll bought off a vendor's stand and devoured in the street, greasy papers falling from a hand rubbed briskly against a trouser leg. Weary hawkers tilted into the shade, counting change.

Mustapha passed the Post Office, Main Branch, where the queue was already winding into the street. Women with umbrellas hoisted against the sun were standing in line faintly fanning themselves with newspapers and bamboo fans.

Eina! Shoo!

The women dug in their heels preparing for the long, toe-tapping wait in the midday sun, the line moving forward on its centipede legs, a little bit at a time, *hmph*.

A little bit was better than nothing at all but by the time that dratted insect wriggled its way into the Post Office, Main Branch, so that
the women could get a whiff of the inky smell of old paper and dust,
the special antiquated dust that collects on the covers of ring-binders
containing applications and triplicate forms, dead and slightly decom-
posing letters, the gum-like odour of bureaucracy, these poor women
were drained of energy and good spirits, their faces wet as discarded
cabbage leaves. Through their legs children darted, undaunted by the
heat rising steeply between buildings, the tar already softening and
pooling in the street.

For a moment Mustapha thought he caught sight of a familiar cocky saunter disappearing down a side street. Swinging a violent left he rattled the Peugeot down a one-way coming to a boiling
halt on a pair of yellow lines. But by the time he'd darted down the
alley in pursuit of the man who always greeted him with a cheery,
Hey bra! as if to say, *Is ons nie manne saam nie?* — Are we not both
men of the world? — by the time he'd cleared the alley, Mhda, if it
was he, had disappeared. Instead Mustapha found himself becalmed
in a narrow byway where women sat in the sun having their hair
braided and oiled. Outside beauty salons that advertised Flow-and-
Glow Hair Calming Product and Pearl Girl Skin Lightening Cream
radio music blared from pavement speakers while wicked looking hair tongs and copper combs and curling irons swung from
pegged displays. A burst of raucous laughter coincided with his
faltering progress past International Skin & Hair and it seemed
to Mustapha that the stylist, her knuckles knocking professionally
against the braided scalp beneath her hands, was singling him out for
particular ridicule.

Eff off now, you hear? You mus' jus' eff off now! exploded
Mustapha with uncharacteristic phlegm.

Another burst of laughter accompanied him down the street followed by catcalls and whistles and various sexual exhortations. As
always, when agitated, Mustapha's recourse was indignation, gener-
alized and swift.

This country, he reflected, was going straight to hell. Shortest way possible. The people didn't care, the government were fuckwits, and the police only hung around long enough to pocket the bribes. Even the criminal classes, he reasoned enjoying the sound of this last portentous phrase, the crim-in-al cl-a-a-a-ses, were seriously fucked. Hell, look at the tsotsis these days. Lazy buggers! Preying on the old, the weak, the lame. Windfall, sitting ducks! Shame, but maybe it had always been so.

Banging his way into the Peugeot he relieved his feelings by revving savagely up Rissik Street. The midday heat had reached boiling point, a pan of ghee upon the stove over which a cook might flick a handful of water to test for steam. Mustapha had no doubt that each separate drop of water would skip like a stone across the day's taut surface.

There was no sign of Mhda near the Law Courts on Pritchard amongst the walking business suits and the lawyers with their mobile phones angled to their ears, the consulting attorneys stirring their words into cups of bitter black coffee at various outdoor cafés. But by the time he'd crossed town to Joubert Park, to the north entrance of the Art Gallery where the taxi ranks stretched out for a block and a half and the competing sounds of kwela jazz and township kwaito, hip-hop, rap, rock, and jive blared from a dozen speakers, Mustapha's good mood had been restored. He parked his car illegally and went in search of his new friend, Mhda, the man he'd known for a mere month or two but whose golden touch and silver words had already brought such unexpected riches into his life.

"The lemon alludes to minor catastrophes," the volunteer guide was saying when Mhda darted into the Art Gallery, joining the shuffle of art lovers semi-circled before a large, heavily-oiled canvas.

Cutting across Joubert Park he'd taken refuge in the Art Gallery on first spying the police cruiser approaching from one side, and Woza Alberton, henchman of his chief creditor, bearing down on him from the other. It wasn't so much the implied menace of either one of these events as their threatened collision that galvanized Mhda and motivated him to desert his post where he was directing pedestrian traffic into his taxis. With the presence of mind for which he was well-known and with the decisiveness that was so characteristic of him he had fled, hot-footing it through the midday park and disappearing into the dim, suddenly-cool rooms of the Art Gallery into which, until this day, Mhda had never set foot and where he was quickly regretting having just done so.

"Note the melons in the foreground," the guide pointed with an imperiously be-ringed finger. "*Melons*, you understand. To cure Melancholia."

The guide was a speckled, bespectacled woman with ill-fitting dentures. She'd clicked and clacked her way through the high-ceilinged rooms to shepherd her charges around a vast, fruit-filled platter of a painting: watermelon sliced into harsh pink spokes, overripe cling peaches, a plate of cut melons radiating from the centre and smack, in the middle, a half-peeled lemon, its curly twist of skin corkscrewed off to one side. The sight of so much fruit all at once gave Mhda a sharp bellyache which, if it was anything like this melon-cauliflower to which the guide referred would not, he knew, be eased by a dose of melons. No matter how sweet.

To take his mind off the pain draw-stringing his gut Mhda tried to focus on his other problems. The police cruiser that seemed to be heading straight for him was probably only his old friend and associate, Sonny-Boy Brixton, come to pick up his monthly packet but the coincidental appearance of the other man, as if he'd been conjured by the exhaust fumes of the police van, was infinitely more menacing. In a city of thin black men, men whittled to bone and dream, Woza Alberton looked as if he dined on a brace of his enemies nightly. He was the fattest black man Mhda knew and rumour had it that his boss, whom nobody had ever seen, the one the people called Umbulali, was even fatter.

Woza Alberton shook when he laughed, which was often. He prided himself on his geniality but his laughter sounded like buckshot sometimes, and sometimes like a door squeaking on its hinges, and at other times like drains gurgling deep in the earth, and his eyes when he laughed all these different types of laughter did not redden nor even did they water intemperately. No, the laughter, all three kinds, of Woza Alberton was not reassuring accompanied, as it was, by a hand on the arm; a thick meaty hand with cuffs of fat at the wrist, and fingers like breakfast sausages. There were only three and a half of these assorted fingers on each hand—thumb, index, ring finger, and half a pinkie on the right, the left composed of a different but no less ill-conceived arrangement—but their grip was strong enough to leave a permanent imprint on the arm of whomever he was detaining. And what with bracing himself against the triton grip of these fingers and watching Woza Alberton's pink polony tongue spreading with each *Ng Ng Ng* or *Sha-Sha* or *Tsi Tsi Tsitsitsi* Mhda knew enough not to mistake hilarity for menace.

Not that he and Woza Alberton's boss—Umbulali, they called him, short for Umbulalionequngu meaning one who kills through addiction—not that Mhda was on uncongenial terms with the sinister team. Far from it. Indeed it would be more accurate to call them business partners; Umbulali via Woza Alberton bankrolling Mhda's more ambitiously creative enterprises, agreeing to unusually accommodating terms on the understanding that his valued borrower contribute to a monthly interest plan remarkable for its compounding intricacies. For Woza Alberton and his boss had set up one of the infamous township *Mashonisa* business schemes and its product, Equality Financiers, was a model of extortion and usury. Up until now affairs had passed easy as jelly between Mhda and his business associates, Woza Alberton's thick-set appearance being greeted with the slide of banknotes from thin hand to meaty palm from where they disappeared into the capacious inner pockets of a series of grey sharkskin waistcoats. Then the two would settle down together (Woza Alberton creaking, grunting) on a pair of oil drums, share a joke or a tall tale, a hasty joint or a roll of tobacco or a couple of swallows of raw cane spirits passed between them in the cough mixture bottle that Mhda always carried to warm the cockles after one of his late night motorcycle jaunts.

May you have a ball when this life is over but you can have Bols now so why wait? Woza Alberton would sigh heavily, the air escaping, tsst-tsssst-*tst*, from between his back teeth like small sprays of fat off a hot grill.

Woza Alberton was a sharp dresser, it was true, but his eyeballs were yellowish giving an oily and unhealthy cast to his face. For some reason that Mhda could never understand he always carried about his person the free packets of condiments that came with takeout meals and in moments of contemplation Woza Alberton would fumble a greasy square of tomato sauce or pickles or vinegar from an inside pocket and palpate it slowly as he spoke or he would idly flick at the sachets of salt or sugar that must tumble forever in the deep pockets of his dress trousers. Mhda hated to think what would happen if one of these packets of sauce split open but so far as he knew disaster had been averted. Perhaps Woza Alberton simply needed to keep his hands busy, because only last week when the two had squatted together on the oil drums, sharing a takeaway meal from Nandos Chicken—this last being a business expense underwritten by Madiba Enterprises—the burly man had insisted on entertaining his client with his latest party trick.

Rattling a matchbox at his ear between ferocious bites of Chicken Piripiri he challenged Mhda to guess the number of matches remaining in the tray. Mhda was always wrong, off by more than ten matches at least, which set Woza Alberton to spraying the fat off the hot grill of his merriment once more.

Tsst-tsssssst-*tst*. Hey madoda! Is this one he is mad or what?

But when it was Woza Alberton's turn to make his guess the henchman suddenly tired of the game, pocketing the box carelessly and pulling closer Mhda's trusty cardboard suitcase on which the takeaway meal was spread—two half chickens reddened with the heat of rubbed spices and Portuguese pepper, slap chips doused in vinegar, and a couple of Lions to chase the chickens down the gullet, ha ha! Swiping beer foam from his upper lip, Woza Alberton roared with laughter.

Such a feast that was, hey monna Mhda! Yup yup, *yebo*.

Méira Cook

Mhda, you are a gentleman of the sidewalk! *Tsi Tsi Tsitsitsi.*

But next time remember, madoda, two chickens are better than one! *Ng ng ng.*

And on it went. No one besides Woza Alberton himself believed he was a humourist but equally surely no one was anxious to contradict him. Now, as Mhda wandered through the Art Gallery in the wake of Miss Lemon, the memory of his encounter with the wily thug remained vivid. He jingled the coins in his pocket and sighed.

Once again his gut twanged. All would be well if he could come up with this latest interest payment. Only the last week had been an ominous week for Mhda. His most lucrative shebeen, Dzimurai Moto, named for the raging fires of thirst and anger it was meant to assuage, had been raided by the township police and it had required a considerable amount of ready cash to post bail for his shebeen queens who were annoyed, to say the least, at the inconvenience not to mention the indignity of becoming charges of the state overnight. Especially since it was understood that a percentage of shebeen profits were regularly skimmed to augment the salaries of the township police. Why had the system failed him this time? Mhda had no idea why fortune was squinting in his direction these days. The four policemen who'd raided the shebeen were well known to him but they'd failed to catch his eye that night, neither did they respond to sundry polite but urgent requests for information sent by various intermediaries in the days that followed.

In addition, two of his swiftest taxi men had been slaughtered in a territorial dispute, the taxis themselves irredeemable except as scrap. Which was more than one could say for the bodies, riddled as they were with bullets and shrapnel, so that nothing remained but to stuff the corpses into garbage bags and return them to their families who immediately demanded burial money, death duties, cemetery tariffs and so forth. To the keen of women ululating their grief, Mhda was obliged to raid the township *stokvel* fund that he regularly managed before matters turned *really* ugly which, considering the homeliness of the situation so far, would take, Mhda imagined, some doing. But he had no doubt that with such considerate bad luck even this monumental pig-ugliness could be accomplished. Now he must find the funds to replace the *stokvel* and fast, before Christmas, with all its obligatory merry-making, forced a reckoning. The last thing he needed was for the township elders, who were responsible for the money and on whom he depended for a certain amount of goodwill, to peer into their coffers and catch their own greedy faces blinking back up.

And as if that wasn't all, payday had fallen out on a Friday this month which meant much drunkenness, many bad debts, bad drivers, bad accidents. Also a full moon and everyone knew that *such* a moon at *such* a time could effect the fahfee draws, especially the 7:30 evening draw for which Mhda employed his own runner who paid him a straight commission of ten percent on each punter, fifteen percent on pools and gaming houses.

Ah well, Mhda shrugged his thin shoulders to his ears, at once dislodging the pen he'd been using to scribble down calculations. Ah well. Perhaps these statistics existed merely to be broken like so much dry wood before the roaring fire of his good fortune, ha!

Yes, a particularly bad week. A week that spread out like an unlucky poker hand, a week charged with omens and portents, and not all the good luck in the world, Mhda reckoned, could redeem such a week.

Shrug, shrug.

Yebo, better just to fold in your hand and settle up.

But wait.

Already a new scheme was stirring in his brain, a business venture that required cunning and imagination, a persuasive tongue but scant capital. Like many others Mhda had been observing the rash of squatter camps that had sprung up wherever there was space and the makeshift homes and lean-tos that were scrambled together from the very detritus of the city itself. Now it suddenly occurred to him that a ready source of such materials — sheets of metal from bus shelters, unprimed plaster hoardings, even bricks and cinder blocks from building sites — might be provided directly to the householder, at cost. And while little could be procured from the squatters themselves, Mhda was well aware that others had a stake in the fortunes of these poor unfortunates. Politicians, rabble-rousers, troublemakers of various stripes whose various causes required this demonstration of the misery of others — these special interest groups might well pay for the convenient establishment and upkeep so necessary to the proper deployment of squalor. Besides, since his own expenses were practically non-existent — a couple of township boys to "collect" the materials and so on — anything he earned was profit, free and clear.

Grinning, licking his lips, Mhda could already anticipate an upswing in his fortunes.

Ha! scribbling away frantically at his figures again Mhda began to conduct hopeful feasibility studies from which he was only interrupted by the slight flurry of leave-taking in front of him. Pushing her spectacles high on the bridge of her nose, the guide clicked her dentures and dispensed, finally, with the rotten fruit painting.

"This way, this way, *this* way," she hectored her group over to an exhibition of Ndebele beadwork and traditional carved walking sticks.

"Imagine the mighty Zulu (click click) wandering for days through the mountains. When night falls he turns his walking stick over to pillow (clcl-lick) his head. Ah, but what does this wily warrior do (clack) so as not to lose his direction? Why, he points his stick towards home. Next morning (clickety-clickety-*clack*) he starts off again in the *opposite* direction."

The guide looked immensely proud of such enterprise and her charges clucked obligingly but Mhda was skeptical. Who ever heard of balancing your head on a stick or losing your way just because you went to sleep and woke up the next morning? No one, no *way*. Mhda had an unerring sense of direction, his pulse a compass needle ticking him towards the true north of his heart's desire. Never once through all the complexities of his taxi routes, the jagged map of his motorbike tracks through the city, had Mhda taken a wrong turn.

Left-right, up-down; a sense of direction was as necessary to a man like Mhda as gravity. Without it he would be at a loss, adrift, whirling through space, his hooked nose lodged in his arsehole to put it crudely but sometimes rough language was all that stood between truth and folly.

And just as his feeling for weather had been inherited from his grandmother so Mhda's sense of direction had been inherited from his uncle, his mother's brother, who had walked beneath the mountains rather than over them because he was a miner but who'd never lost his way — either in the earth or in his life above it as a hostel man stretched out on an iron bedstead beneath rough blankets with forty men or more, sleeping or not, dreaming or not, longing or not, until the smell of sheep's head and cooking tripe and melancholy grew too strong to bear. Who knew what crimes of habitation and hopelessness were committed in the hostels or on the mines but of one thing Mhda was certain — his uncle had never required a stick to direct him on his way.

Ha! Mhda seethed with sudden contempt for that stupid mountain man, that seedless pumpkin, fast asleep and snoring on his walking stick.

The guide motioned her charges forward: "As you can see the stick makes an effective weapon (click click) should the intrepid warrior encounter wild baboons or mountain snakes along his path."

sss-sss went the snake wriggling through Mhda's intestines or what felt like a snake, a couple of mating boomslangs. But despite the writhing pain, the miserly hiss of air leaking slowly from a punctured tire, Mhda began to smile because it had suddenly occurred to him that with the waning of his fortunes he had, at last, gained something more important. If his golden touch, his famous charm, had attracted all manner of business contacts and friendships, money, fame, fear masquerading as respect, assorted favours and various assurances, everything, in short, but the heart of the woman he loved, then this lightning streak of bad luck might very well accomplish what all the good luck in the world had failed to do.

Closing his eyes Mhda weighed the heft of his pocket watch in the palm of his hand, ran imaginary fingers over the cheekbones of his Dhlamina-Queen, over the swell and sway of his child.

Hmmm-hmm (tap tap tap).

Mustapha was waiting for the Barber to finish shaving his eleventh customer of the day. The Barber knew where everyone was, had been, or was going, and obliged his clients by passing on the messages people left at his stand under the stunted bluegum. His only requirement was quiet, strict silence during shave or haircut, conversation stubbed out like a cigarette when he lifted his cunning razor blade, the business of information all very well in its place but having no place at all when it came to the infinitely more serious business of styling hair.

The Barber would swathe his customers in newspaper, tilting them back into the sunlight that fell in jagged triangles from between the branches of the bluegum. Then he'd strop his razor on the length of sandpaper that hung from these same branches together with shards of mirror and combs hooked on nails and flick his stubble-sensitive fingers along the length of a jaw. Today, Mustapha noticed, the Barber had taken time to arrange his enviable collection of magazine photographs, football cards, and assorted posters. The grinning faces and carefully styled heads of various men torn out of newspaper advertisements and fashion magazines were tacked onto the tree trunk where they rustled in the breeze, tempting the passerby on his way to work or to lunch, promising him everything from a close shave or a crew cut to true happiness. For the Barber chose only the most joyful of the faces he collected to grace his display branches because happiness was his currency, the slick lifeblood of his vocation.

Nearby, an evangelical preacher had hauled himself up onto a box that had once contained Lux soap. He was exhorting the lunchtime passersby with their tin mugs and greasy newspaper wrappings, their paper plates puffing the fragrant steam of curried rice or stew.

Mwah-mwah, I love this book, he shouted, holding up his cracked Bible then offering it to hurrying strangers to be kissed. *Man, I love this book! This is the book of my heart and my soul, Ow!*

But the people shuffled past with barely a glance and only a mother who was pecking two-fingered bites of food into her child's mouth spared him a word.

You so ugly not even your book wants to kiss you back! she jeered.

Jumpy with nerves, palms slippery, Mustapha averted his eyes. He had already searched for Mhda along the taxi ranks, near the vendor stands on Diagonal, even on the edge of the squatter camp north of Joubert Park. But Mhda was nowhere to be found which was unusual enough for Mustapha to plump himself down with a sigh upon one of the tomato crates that the Barber provided for his customers, resigning himself to a delay that would last as long as it took the Barber to give this eleventh customer of the day one of his super-special shaves.

Long enough to knot the stomach and wring the hands dry. Long enough for heat to gather like a rash in all the crevices of the idle body. Long enough for Mustapha's thoughts to fly upward like so much steam forced from the valve of a pressure cooker, *ssst-t-t*, the sound of impatience escaping, the pressing need to be up and *doing*.

Since the fortuitous meeting with his new friend some two months ago, Mustapha had never been so busy. Busyness suited him, gave him something to do with his hands, somewhere to funnel the energy that otherwise hardened in the pit of his stomach like grape seeds, indigestible and dangerous. First came the business permit to expand, materializing magically from Mhda's side pocket where, Mustapha now firmly believed, all manner of good things proceeded, from a gold pocket watch to caffeine pills and amphetamines, vending licences and thick rolls of only slightly creased banknotes flipped across with an open hand and the instructions to buy four more custom-fitted vendor carts all smartly stencilled with the gold and brown Hurry-Curry logo. Under Mhda's direction Mustapha engaged five township youths to preside over the stands along with his original cart now stationed at a much sought-after corner on Diagonal Street, the Boerewors Bakkie that had once stood there disappearing mysteriously overnight, never again to be seen in the neighbourhood.

No longer required to parch and burn in the sun and wind in order to purvey his snacks, Mustapha often spent mornings at his preferred spice supplier, Mr. J. Malherbe on Fox Street, where great drums and barrels jostled for space and everywhere the pungent odour of cumin, so reminiscent of underarm sweat, was in evidence. In Mr. Malherbe's courtyard, amongst pots of bright turmeric and coloured cones of fennel and ginger and cayenne pepper, one could sometimes surprise little beetles drilling breathing holes. Ooh sis!

Then Mustapha would hurry home to his kitchen, to recipes torn from magazines or scribbled down from an auntie's patented Madras curry—"mustn't forget extra garlic, na,"—recipes that he'd almost perfected, techniques he never tired of testing. It was in this kitchen, breathless with enterprise, that he would fold his samosas into crisp triangles, mix up batches of spicy lentil dhal, experimenting with the strangely pungent, homemade mango chutney for which his franchise was justly famed. This joyous fruit chutney with its hint of cardamom, its aftertaste of "is that anise?" was his special pride, the hope of all future enterprise. Inside the early morning kitchen the light was subdued enough, being obliged to penetrate bottle glass and cracked panes, but the fragrance of assorted fruit curries seemed to emit their own glow. Pots boiled away on the little stove, the smell of lamb billowed out in heads of steam and gravy bubbled up, sloshing into the burners.

Ah, never mind, Mustapha would console himself, piling mixing bowls and thick handfuls of cutlery into his overflowing sink. One day, and not a moment too soon either, he would have his own dishwasher. Huh, *and* a maid.

Meanwhile, he entertained himself by imagining the reactions of his customers as the first jolt of Durban curry hit home, the slow throat-burn, the scalded tongue. (*Jislaaik!* they'd yell, clutching the top of their heads and grabbing for the paper cups of ice water with thick lemon slices that he'd provide complimentary to all customers.)

As his quick-wristed hands hovered over rows of samosas with their tight hospital corners, Mustapha would allow his mind to range over the peaks and summits of his ambition. At these times he dreamed of his name embossed in gold on the labels of slim-necked bottles perched on supermarket shelves and arranged in the windows of all the best delicatessens in the city. *Mustapha's Mango Chutney* the letters read, underneath a picture of his own—why not?—handsomely smiling face. After that, who knew? A range of atchars, hot sauces, spices, each bottle, each jar, stamped with his newly-minted image. The first of his family to succeed in business, bloody *hell* even to fail if it came to that, Mustapha occasionally suspected that he lacked proportion when it came to his hand-reared chutneys.

Which was more than he could say about his relationship with Doctor Bloody-Benjamin, a relationship that every day seemed more and more reminiscent of the one otherwise known as "the shit that hit the fan." Good thing that the fan was broken, as the saying went in this city, good thing that the fan was permanently on the fritz. Two nights ago he'd prepared dinner: a couple of indignant-looking stump-noses with olive oil and garlic, little potatoes in their jackets, brinjals and patty-pans in a tomato and onion gravy. Really tasty. Benjamin had arrived (late), bearing a bottle of Cape Shiraz (warm), and a grave expression on catching sight of the festively spread cloth, the glittering new wine glasses from which blue napkins sprouted like tail feathers.

All through the meal that followed Benjamin yakked (blah blah blah) and fidgeted (po po po) in an effort (vast and decorous and exhausting) to avert his eyes from Mustapha's recently acquired riches (dishes from Boardmans, dessert from Woolworths, tablecloth from African Prints in Sandton) in an effort *not* to inquire after his new friend, Mhda, about whom Mustapha was not, in any case, telling (smile). Ask me no questions and I'll tell you no lies, puffed the kettle or seemed to, and Benjamin, hastily declining an after-dinner coffee, a joint, or what*ever*, had pleaded the pressures of work and departed, his rubber-soled shoes squeaking like tiresomely hurt feelings all the way down the corridor.

And so far as Mustapha was concerned, good *rid*dance. The boy-wallah must just make himself scarce if he couldn't enjoy his lover's good fortune but he mustn't come into his flat and look disapproving. No, that he mustn't do.

The two were not, at present, on speaks. But that was all to the good since Mr. Fa, as Mhda playfully called him, was already far too busy. Christ, *much* too busy to chase after that one, that So-and-So, that Dr. Mind-Your-Own-Business! Afternoons he hurtled between his five Hurry-Curry boys, topping up chutney bottles and collecting money from the lunch trade, examining steam trays and gas stoves to ensure they'd been thoroughly scrubbed down the night before, exhorting greater efforts from his employees and distributing criticism where it was due. Which was often, apparently. Somewhere between mediocre and appalling was where Mustapha, who held no truck with loafers and laggards, situated the best efforts of his hirelings. If he came across one of his boys lounging in the shade chewing grass seeds or sipping a Coke, his cart unattended, Mustapha flew into a finely calibrated fury, shaking and hissing through thinly clenched teeth.

He'd already fired three boys just like that and looked to be on the verge of his fourth dismissal if Jubilee Muntu, who worked Sauer Street near the newspapers, if that Muntu-picannin didn't pull finger. But as many boys he dismissed so many Mhda replaced, without fuss or bother only warning Mustapha not to be quite so hasty in his rages since who knew what would set these boys off and besides there was always the problem of reprisals.

Fuck the bastards in the eye, Mustapha chortled gleefully. That way they won't see you coming.

Ah, but the city had acquired a reputation for small-mindedness, for grudgy acts of revenge. Avoiding death had become a national pastime and was neither so simple nor so invigorating as it appeared. Every day a taxi man was run off the road by machine-gunfire, a vendor was found with his pelvis minutely broken. Or one of the street angels was bottle-fucked, left for dead. Not dead, mind you, not quite, but left-for which was worse. Be careful, warned Mhda but without conviction because Mustapha, he'd come to realize, was a fanatic. A thin blue light like the halo around a flame thrown from a Bic lighter ringed each pupil whenever Mustapha discussed his business, his franchise, the jubilant harmony of his mango chutney. Still, Mhda continued to replace the boys that Mustapha snapped out of the air with his thin emphatic fingers.

Where did these boys come from? Mustapha occasionally wondered but had never worked up the temerity to ask Mhda who was in any case too busy to stop for questions, hurrying here and there with his brown suitcase and his pay packets and even a receipt book with its crinkly sheet of purple carbon paper sticking out of the side. Mhda with his pencil behind one ear and his cigarette burning down between two knuckles, his charm and his lies and his hustle; Mhda who seemed always to be swiping away at the ash that fell in drifts as he departed with the backward glance of an eternal sojourner directed over his shoulder. Well, they were friends now, reflected Mustapha, he and Mhda were friends.

Chommies for sure. For definite.

Now Mustapha lounged in the panting shade waiting for the Barber to pat his customer dry. Eleventh customer of the day and already a patient queue had begun to form behind Mustapha; men on lunch break yearning to take the weight off their feet, to sit with their hands loaded on their knees for the length of time it took the shade to swing six inches around the foot of the bluegum. While they waited the men thumbed through the day-old newspapers that the Barber had provided by the simple expedient of lifting them from the rubbish bins by the railway station. Or, greasy-fingered, perspiring, they chewed at the vinegar chips stuffed in hollow half loaves bought off the bunny-chow stand on the corner.

Dumela.
Dumela oogai.
Rustle. Humph.
Snip-snip-snip.

Méira Cook

The smell of hot vinegar rose steeply in the air sharpening the heat that pricked the back of his neck, his armpits, the creases of his groin. Mustapha shifted impatiently. The sun burnt away his appetite but the smell of vinegar chips restored it and the rapid shuttle from desirelessness to hunger rendered him dizzy.

Stay-at-home strike called next Thursday?

Heard about.

Rustle, rustle. Humph.

Suddenly, and for no discernable reason, the evangelical preacher who'd been revolving all this time on his soapbox stopped smooching the Good Book and instead began preaching a stirring sermon of Hellfire and Damnation in the hot noon sun while all around him elderly women arranged themselves, hoisting sunshades and nodding their heads. More passersby stopped, kindled, and caught fire until all had joined together in a rousing Zulu hymn. Swaying in time in the street, balanced between their shopping bags and their umbrellas, their stern notions of sin and redemption, the women raised their sweet soprano voices unto heaven—

Sigeza izono izono
Ngegazi
We wash the sins
With blood
Ayaya! Ayaya!
Ayaya! Ayaya!

In the distance Mustapha finally saw Mhda emerging from what looked like the Art Gallery only what was a street smart township-clever doing in that building full of unsaleable goods and recycled air? It didn't surprise Mustapha, however, to view his friend in the light of a connoisseur for assuredly Mhda was a magician, a shape-changer, a man who granted favours simply by reaching into his pocket. A man who plucked food licenses and vending rights and Hurry-Curry boys out of a clear blue sky; a piper. Yes, such a man distributed good luck as if he was handing out fat cakes, cheap and hot.

Ayaya! Ayaya!
Ayaya! Ayaya!

Away across the park Mhda too heard the familiar chorus but when he looked up he was dazzled, for a moment, by the afternoon glare. He was accustomed to acting without benefit of foresight, however, and so he merely put his head down and puffed his way onward, breaking into a run when he reached the old greenhouses. A couple of mongrels appeared at his heels from nowhere, stirring the afternoon with their tails but he kicked them away. Heat rippled and shimmered around him.

As if in slow motion Mhda swam forward through heat waves or the refraction of a tear caught between lashes. Mustapha, who never cried, never, hurried towards his friend, one hand fingering an envelope crackly with another month's loan repayment plus fifteen percent interest and another two percent for luck which, as Mhda had taken the trouble to explain, came more readily once it had been bought and paid for.

It was always hot in the kitchen, always much too hot, and the wild spinach and runner beans she tried to grow on the window sill were sparse and stunted and would stay that way, Beauty reckoned, while summer thickened in the hedges and fruit trees of the garden suburbs. So much for ripe green things, so much for peace and plenty and something tasty to mix in her mieliepap come Christmas day. Outside the dog let out a yelp closely followed by Rothman's *humba wena* but broken in half—*fucken hell!*—by the laughter of a boy who had finally and to his great satisfaction found something smaller, infinitely stupider, than himself to torment.

Up in the attic Beauty had grown irritable with the heat and the task at hand which today consisted of searching through the photo albums in the stinkwood chest because Ouma had gotten it into her head that Beauty must find the photographs from when they were all young; Meneer and Mrs. Magda and this one and that one—"Beauty you remember Mrs. Patrice, *nè?*"—only it hadn't proved an easy task.

Méira Cook

No, quite the opposite. For not only was the attic hot and dusty, the albums heavy and the light dim, but the photographs, when Beauty began to look at them, seemed indistinguishable; one group of merrymakers blending into another, one blandly smiling face taking on the features of all. And it was no use Ouma telling her to read the labels, because the writing beneath each faded rectangle was simply too small to make out in the attic light but Beauty wasn't going to drag the albums downstairs, was she? One misstep on the landing and it would be a broken leg for sure. Very least.

Yebo, Mama, and then we will all cry.

Reflecting on this disaster Beauty realized that the problem was that the photographs all looked the same to her because all white people had begun to look the same. The long ago sepia folk standing arm in arm in formal rooms and the ones that she saw whizzing down Kingsway in their speeding cars had begun to flow into one another but not in the way of the Spirit that Hosiah had taken pains to point out was colour-blind and would prevail forever, not in the way of this gently flowing Spirit that filled all with the glory of the Lord. No, the people she saw at the shops and on the television, in magazines and in cars and on their mobiles, were neither buoyed by the spirit nor crushed by its absence. They had simply begun to resemble one another, faces passing in a blur of faces, like soap bubbles blown on the wind.

Ko ko ko.

Tea, Mama, sang Beauty, once again imitating the sound of knuckles on wood, *Ko ko ko.*

New wine, hey Beauty, for the old bottle, offered Ouma in accordance with tradition, holding out cupped hands for her mug.

Because of the arthritis they'd had to stop using the bone china cups but Ouma still missed their lightness and delicacy and the roses that bloomed at the bottom of each cup when the tea was all gone. The ceramic mug Beauty handed her was heavy but easy enough to manoeuvre in hands that couldn't quite grasp their own limitations. The tea tasted slightly bitter as tea will that has been stewing for too long but that was how Beauty made tea, always had. Only tea poured scalding hot into real china had the properly bracing effect, everyone knew that. Still, the sugary substance that Beauty brewed was strong and full-bodied and succeeded in reviving Ouma which was something at least.

With patient hands Beauty helped Ouma to sit upright, easing pillows behind her back and drawing the little occasional table close. Beauty's hands were always cool, thought Ouma, soothing as menthol balm against a hot forehead. Mmm, she mumbled to herself now for she was tired out by the heat and all day had been on the verge of dozing off in her easy chair.

After your tea I will come and put Ouma to bed, said Beauty who was tired too but when had anyone ever paid attention to her weariness?

But Ouma, revived by the strong sweet tea, threw Beauty a "don't tell me" look, at the same time beckoning her close. So Beauty drew the riempie stool across the oak plank floor and made herself comfortable.

Who's that young boy staying with you, Beauty? asked Ouma. The one I see out by the yard sometimes.

That's my grandson, Mama. My Rothman.

Ah. Well you know the old saying, Beauty — *As jy kinders het, het jy altyd groen koring op jou land.* Not so?

Beauty shrugged, irritated.

Means, hmm, when you have children then you always have green corn on your land. Have to keep tending the crop, you see, the *children*, because they're a constant source of worry.

Ouma lifted her eyebrows as if to say, Tell me about your green corn, Beauty, tell me about this grandson of yours. But Beauty was tongue-tied when it came to Rothman and not only because of Hosiah's favourite caution about remaining silent if there was nothing good to say because the Lord was listening. He was always listening. His giant ear was pressed up against the world as if the world was nothing but a hollow sea shell. Truly, the ear of the Lord was a wondrous organ but Rothman just plain grieved Beauty. He was spineless, unkempt, always wrapped in the greatcoat that he wouldn't let her clean. And the vacancy in his eyes when he looked at her, at his Ouma who had raised him, his hands so big but what was the good of hands that were always empty?

But mostly what saddened Beauty was her grandson's greedy heart, how he peered into the corners of her room as if searching for treasure, his habit of running pick-pocket fingers through her discarded overalls, her apron. Searching for loose change and whatnot when he must just ask and she'd give him, gladly she'd give him pocket money for Chappies bubblegum and Simba crisps from the corner caffy.

On the wall above the thin foam mattress in the room he shared with Agremon, pictures had begun to appear, dark pencil sketches copied from photographs torn out of the newspaper. Burning houses, cars wrecked on the highway. Beauty, wringing her hands in her apron had decided to ignore these mad drawings, Rothman scratching his pain into the wall. Tortured animals, children melting in flames. But God in Heaven above, God with His ear cocked to the world's grief, what was wrong with the boy that he must lie in bed all day, twitching and leaking (nose, sores on the skin he wouldn't let her tend), why didn't he just ask for money as he'd once begged change to buy Banana Boys and Eskimo Pies?

Doesn't want money for sweets, baba, Agremon tried to explain. Too thin for sweets.

Mind your own business, she snapped at him, at Agremon, but Agremon said as long as the boy was sharing his room—well he couldn't share with his Ouma anymore, could he?—as long as the boy was snoring by the foot of his bed, Agremon said, it was also his business.

Ai kona but Beauty was sick and tired of these stick men in her life. Seemed nothing she cooked would fatten her lover or put one ounce of flesh on the washboard ribs of her grandson and it astonished her, truly it did, that a boy could possess such a hungry heart but no appetite.

And why now, she wondered, why now must Rothman come to burden her old age? If it was true about the green corn and the children who grew upon the land then when was the harvest time, the time of plenty and fulfillment?

But even as she harboured these disloyal thoughts Beauty reproached herself for, truly, the boy couldn't help himself. His mother had been a skaberash, plain and simple, a Jezebel, as Hosiah would have said, smacking his lips with disapproval but also relish at one of his favourite texts as who could not marvel at the story of that whore thrown from the balcony to the dogs and the dogs ate her up, all up, every last bite but the palms of the hands. And why, Beauty always wondered, were her palms exempted from the dog's feast?

The Mercy of the Lord! thundered Hosiah which answered but did not entirely explain the sudden pickiness of the dogs at least not to Beauty who prided herself on her powers of understanding. For Beauty could understand, yes and speak too, many languages: her mother tongue which was Sotho, and Tswana, English of course, a little Zulu, and she could even repeat some words in Xhosa — mostly derogatory, as was their way. By the time she came to work for the du Plessis she could understand quite a lot of Afrikaans but of this last she concealed her knowledge out of sheer perversity and accomplished this concealment so effectively that Mrs. Magda would always tut disapprovingly at her.

Ah, not bilingual, my girl. As is required of our citizens whether European or Native. Mmm?

Well, the next time Mrs. Magda came to visit perhaps Beauty must just surprise her. *As jy kinders het,* Beauty imagined herself nudging the old fool in the ribs, *het jy altyd groen koring op jou land.* Chuckling she tried to settle herself more comfortably on the hard weave of the riempie stool.

Beauty met Benjamin on the stairs, he was coming to see how his Ouma was doing.

Evening Beauty, he said but she just stared at him so that he'd know she was telling him to *voetsak*, go away. He must just *humba wena*.

Méira Cook

Is that you, my boy? Ouma's voice sounded as grey as the smoke Beauty could hear her exhaling in shallow breaths as that call-me-Ben, cool and clean from the shower but slippery as a bar of soap, side-stepped Beauty and disappeared into Ouma's room.

So that was that. Beauty went to let the dog out and she was glad, really glad, that she didn't have to spend the rest of the evening scuffing her shoes at Ouma's bedside. Let someone else have the fuss and the bother for a change. Eli cocked his head at her and the black patch over his eye that lent him the look of a villain, a tsotsi, enraged her for a moment so that it was all she could do not to kick him as he darted between her feet.

Helluva hot day, old girl, and what have you been up to? Benjamin bent to kiss his Ouma on the forehead and she put both her arms around him and held him fast. The two of them rocked together for a moment, Ouma breathing in the odour of his skin and the scent of the outdoors that accompanied him. Mmm, she mumbled, nothing much, my boy, nothing to speak of.

In the hall Grandfather let out a sudden baritone gong followed by the sound of a dog's claws rattling loosely over tile. Floorboards creaked, the roof ticked in the cooling spasms of nightfall.

How was the hospital? asked Ouma her voice hoarse with heat and cigarette smoke and the effort of inhaling one or the other.

Benjamin shrugged. December, what can I say? It's always the worst month of the year. The worst. And now we're trying to prepare for the strike. Everyone's being threatened, cleaning staff, orderlies, even the nurses. *Ag*, but what can you do?

What can you do? Ouma repeated. She agreed with her grandson, there was nothing to be done. Suddenly she thought of something. And how's your Mr. Wilson? she asked.

Benjamin thought of his patient, his Mr. Wilson. The man's body was a swamp drained by catheters yet his lips still moved reciting his endless silent rosary while his fingers, what was left of them, scrabbled at the thin hospital linen. *Salve Regina, Mater miseri...vita, vita...*

The House on Sugarbush Road

He suddenly remembered something and grinned with relief. It was a tidbit he'd been saving to amuse his Ouma, the latest hospital scandal. It seemed that Admin had recently uncovered a brisk trade in death certificates so that folks appeared to be dying two and three times over. S'truth they're a bunch of lazy good for nothings, Markham had exclaimed in admiration, not to say disbelief, at the ingenuity of such a scam. But you've got to admire the effort they put into fucking with our heads.

The problem seems to be that so many African names look alike, Benjamin explained to Ouma. At least to stupid whites like us. Mgabane, Mbagane, Mdabane. It's our own fault really if we can't tell the difference on paper but, man, are they driving Hospital Admin wild!

Ouma was tickled as he knew she'd be and laughed with great gusto at his account. Benjamin looked at her fondly. Well, she was a game old bird, wasn't she. She enjoyed nothing so much as a good story and a piece of nonsense at the end of the day. Love for her suddenly filled his heart and the feeling made him throw back his head and laugh with her.

Far away in the kitchen where she was waiting for the dog to finish its business Beauty heard their laughter like the faint susurration of water in a drain.

8

A GOOD RAIN

Nobody ever remembered how hot the city got in the days before Christmas.

Dhlamina was in her thirty-fourth week and counting. Every day, every hour, because the child was like a hot-water geyser in her belly, keeping her awake at night with its slow gurgle and chug. Some afternoons, caught in the sticky light of Mrs. Magda's flat like a fly trapped in honey, Dhlamina simply leaned up against the tumble-drier and cried. In the living room the potted plants languished while a dust that seemed to be composed of the heat itself fell all day, coating the ball and claw wingbacks, the broad mahogany dining table, the cabinets crammed with Wedgwood china and Victorian ostrich eggs, and a fleet of gravy boats stamped with the navy and white insignia of the Dutch East India Company.

Mrs. Magda never tired of telling Dhlamina of her terrible robbery, of what had been stolen from her, but looking about at the rows of photographs on the mantelpiece and the large oil painting over the bureau Dhlamina couldn't help thinking that the burglars had been too hasty. The painting, in particular, aggravated her sorely. It showed a mother clasping a baby in her arms and the baby was crying large perfectly shaped tears. Mrs. Magda loved her painting, not a day went by that she didn't gaze upon it fondly and fuss about whether it was hanging straight. But worst of all she wanted Dhlamina to admire it too and this Dhlamina could not do. In short she hated the painting, she just hated it. She was certain that it brought bad luck and she was certain that misfortune could not be waylaid for long and she wished that the burglars had been art lovers but, ah, what good would wishing do on such a hot day.

A protective scarf knotted about her braids, her eyes raw with swirling motes, Dhlamina tried to blow the dust from the silver cheeks of the tea urn but more dust fell, and more, and she was soon winded again and damp with tears. The walk to the taxi ranks, the long jolt home in an airless minibus soon proved impossible. The taxis were crowded with exhausted commuters, heat-sparked tempers, the jump of kwela and the thump of kwaito pumping from speakers, and even though Mhda bossily met her every day in order to escort her up the hill and into his choicest taxis, Dhlamina found his presence an agitation.

On the day that Mrs. Magda found her slumped on the outside stairs, sobbing at the thought of the long trek uphill, the embattled ride home, the Madam's kind heart shifted a little. Or maybe it was just her stomach, Dhlamina thought sourly, because certainly she didn't want to lose her maid's excellent hand with pastry crust.

Erm, uh, hmm, she began, holding out a hesitant hand. But Dhlamina's tears only increased. It wasn't in her nature to be comforted by ineptitude.

Mrs. Magda tutted. Uh, my dear, when is the due date?

What am I, a carton of milk two days past its sell-by? thought Dhlamina.

Mrs. Magda bent down to pat the girl's head. She recalled a line from a poem by Ingrid Jonker and wondered if it would comfort poor Dhlamina. *En my hart dat soos 'n cicada sing*—that was it—my heart that sings like a cicada! The poem was called "Pregnant Woman" but contemplating the sobbing girl she thought perhaps not. Gingerly, she hiked up her smart pantsuit at the knees and crouched awkwardly beside her.

Scared hey? Is that what?

Hnuh nh nh. Sniff.

Mustn't be scared, my girl. You're not the first to ah, and these days there's nothing to it. Doctors, hospitals, gas for the pain—they still have gas, don't they? Not to worry, *meisie*, we'll take care of you.

Scared, my foot, man! I am only hot. I am only hot but every day I am getting hotter in the transport from Soweto and one day, *one* day, I think it will not be possible anymore to show up here for work and what will you do then, Mrs. Magda, have you thought of that?

Magda fished a carefully squared handkerchief from her pocket and offered it to Dhlamina. Although she knew Dhlamina would leave her when the baby was born Magda had been putting the thought out of her mind with such firmness that it was a shock to confront it now. The truth was she couldn't do without her. She cleared her throat.

We must work together to solve your problem, my dear. Erm, I expect you have a driver's license?

From between every-which-way braids and a tangle of gold beads Dhlamina peered out at Mrs. Magda, dimpled. Sliced her a wide grin.

Actually it had been old Mrs. Moffert's automobile, an ancient but stately two-tone Anglia with a syncopated heartbeat in the region of the engine and sadly devoid of such indulgent luxuries as power-steering, brake pads or shock absorbers but Dhlamina who'd never driven so much as a macadamized inch in all her pedestrian life was grateful, more than, to accept the offer. The car was old but driving proved easy once she'd mastered the problem of packing her belly behind the wheel. A cursory glance in the rearview was all it took, another at the side mirror, then she must pump hard on the accelerator pedal and aim for the middle of the road where the long, unbroken white seam or the little yellow rows of stitches divided one side from the other.

VRrrrRRRmmm.

There were few other rules that Dhlamina could perceive. One mustn't travel too closely behind the taxis that stopped just like that. Mustn't make eye contact at traffic lights, shouldn't give lifts to strangers, never, for sure, give way. Parallel parking remained a deep mystery and the inscrutable ways of the traffic circle were a source of wonder but Dhlamina blithely utilized the pavement for all her parking needs and rolled gaily over the rumps of traffic circles blowing finger kisses to infuriated drivers forced to splutter in her dust.

She'd stopped listening to the radio because it only reported bad news, fatal accidents, and seven vehicle pile-ups on the M1 North, no survivors and emergency vehicles standing by but unable to approach because of the flames. Such news, reasoned Dhlamina, could only bring ill luck to the occupants—mother and child—of the indomitable little Anglia heading south, heading home. Instead, she'd slip a tape into the antiquated cassette player and the fat kwaito beat of Woza Africa's *iStokvel* would accompany her on her way back to Diepkloof. But at other times she preferred to listen to old-style African jazz, the *mbaqanga* that only Hugh Masekela knew how to blow clear out of the trumpet and Kippie Moeketsi out of the saxophone. Of course the water baby wasn't always amenable to the musical stylings of its mother's various addictions and would make its protests palpably known by jumping up and down in her belly until it was all Dhlamina could do not to swat the terrible child down. But this one must never do and so she would listen to Mr. Louis Armstrong instead and the tumult would quiet as if by magic.

Driving home to her room in the shared house of working girls and single mothers, the landscape rewinding as if on a giant spool, Dhlamina sometimes imagined the silence that would crash down on her were she to pull over onto the shoulder of the road where cosmos bobbed and startled bulbuls cried out. But she never stopped; the horizon seemed to urge her on as if to say, Make Haste, my girl, Put-Foot! Out there on the highway it was every driver for herself, cross your fingers and pray to the Lord for good fortune, it being luck and not skill, Dhlamina was certain, that protected her.

And she was—touch wood, hold thumbs—lucky. Nothing more serious than a couple of fender benders, assorted bumps and grinds, a rapidly descending muffler. And, while she'd witnessed many accidents in the last month—segmented mannequins strung out on the highway with blankets covering their faces—had starred in none of them and looked to be a reasonably good bet, she and the water baby both, to avoid inclusion in the higher-than-ever holiday death toll that the papers seemed so proud of this year. Mhda was pissed off, of course. No longer could he escort her up the hill, a proprietary hand under her elbow, his anxiety keen as the smell of mustard. Mhda was angry because she was in debt to the white bitch, as he put it, thumping at his ribcage.

Where will it end? Mhda shouted one day outside the Portuguese Grocery where he'd loitered, cleaning his nails with a pocket knife, until she emerged, her shopping bag full of aubergines and pickling spices in readiness for another stab at Mrs. Moffert's Canned Eggplant Supreme.

Where will it end? he hectored, flicking his cigarette butt into the gutter. *Do I have to shoot the bitch?*

The time will come, he yelled, *when you push me too far, Dhlamina-girl. You must learn who is the boss, hey!*

And he jangled the gold pocket watch in her face to emphasize that time was indeed passing. Was, in fact, running *out* and she would be wise to halt her headlong rush into whatever too late meant and pay him heed. He, Madiba Mhda, time-keeper. But for once the gold pocket watch failed to work its magic. Indeed, leaning up against the peeling wall with his ramshackle scooter, a Marlboro behind one ear, Mhda resembled nothing so much as a poster Dhlamina remembered from her youth. This poster (hanging in a corner of the Post Office, Rural Branch) displayed a snarling lion chasing a delivery boy on his bicycle. It was an advertisement for Raleigh bicycles ("faster than any wild animal") but the comical expression of fright on the face of the delivery boy, his popping eyes and rictus grin, remained with Dhlamina transferred like a bright decal upon the outraged face of her suitor.

Hmph, Dhlamina shrugged in disgust and, calibrating herself into the two-tone Anglia, she roared off, executing a neat three-point turn in double time.

Bark, bark, bark, she thought. Hmph.

So that disposed of Mhda for the time being, at least, and there was nothing else to concern her except for the heat pricking beneath her skin, the child that rose and set like a minor sun in her belly.

The weeks before the summer solstice were a steep staircase of days too hot to climb. The only antidote was water. Dhlamina drank glasses and bottles and litres of water, she smuggled herself into

Mrs. Magda's guest shower while she was taking her morning constitutional, her afternoon nap. Some days, enervated beyond bearing by the heat that hammered down on her all day, beating her flat, she simply shoved her whole head under the kitchen faucet, gold earrings, coloured beads and all.

A good rain would cool things down, the people said, but the clouds had dried up and blown away and the heavens were shut tight as a pair of praying hands. At night a plague of Christmas beetles would come, crashing and knocking their way into the light, dive-bombing the unwary and buzzing in the ears for days afterwards. At dawn, sparrows, too exhausted to fly, dropped by the score from telephone lines.

Water was strictly rationed but twice a week, in the affluent neighbourhoods of Rosebank and Parktown North and Houghton, home-owners turned on their sprinklers for a rigidly prescribed two hours. Then Dhlamina would hoist her sun shade and wander the streets, dazed in her bright floating cottons, listening to the *sssnick-ssn-snick* of sprinklers in hidden gardens. Inhaling, aa-aaah, the glorious smell of wet earth. Nothing disturbed her walks except for the occasional greeting of a woman propped on the sidewalk, rubbing her scalp or braiding her hair and sighing.

Dumela.

Dumela oogai.

Anything more was an effort.

Just the sight of water eased the mind. Which was why Dhlamina liked to drive down to the Zoo Lake on hot afternoons. Mrs. Magda had lately declared the city a war zone, a ferocious territory occupied by madmen and gangsters, con artists and murderers and deplorable motorists. Driving in this barbarous place set her hair on edge, as she put it, self-consciously smoothing the stiff waves of her weekly "set" over her high white forehead. It suited Dhlamina just fine. Tucking the *Fair Lady* summer cooking supplement under her arm, Dhlamina would jar the Anglia into second gear and barrel her way into the mid-week traffic. By the time she arrived at the Zoo Lake she'd be rumpled and hot, eager to lie beneath the willows that edged the lake, bending from their waists like long-haired river women.

Dhlamina made her way through the shimmering heat, fanning herself with her magazine. The food and cooldrink vendor parked at the rowboat concession was selling chili bites and curry snacks but there were no takers because who in hell wanted to heat up their insides on a day like this, Dhlamina thought. *Eish,* how stupid people could be! Fumbling for coins she bought a Fanta Orange—two straws, mister—and stumbled heavily to the shade of a willow where she made herself easy, leaning her head against the trunk and fervently pressing the can with its beads of cold sweat to her breasts and the clammy skin behind her neck. She lifted the strings of woven Ndebele beads she'd hung about her neck that morning and blew down the front of her sundress.

Aah…ah.

The sky was a rigging of clouds, vast sails filled with wind tacking across a choppy sea. Dhlamina closed her eyes and shaded her face with her magazine.

How long she'd been dozing she really couldn't say but it seemed as if no time at all had passed between wakefulness and sleep when she was rudely jerked awake by an insistent voice.

"Mrs. Ball's Chicken-Chutney Recipes. Potjiekos for the Suburban Kitchen. Sweet-Sweet Spanspek—Most Misunderstood of Melons."

Hnh?

Squinting, Dhlamina made out a shadow that was blocking her wedge of sunlight. From out of this shadow a thin voice continued to read aloud the cover of her magazine. Briefly, Dhlamina contemplated ignoring the voice and continuing her nap but the affront to her dignity was too acute to be dismissed. Besides, *tcha,* how rude the voice was in ignoring her indignant face on the other side of the magazine.

"Grow your own Kitchen Herbs," this voice advised. "Learn to Make Delicious Homemade Biltong."

En*ough.* Dhlamina snatched the curling pages from her face but the man—yes, it was a man—hovering over her blocked out the sun and all she could make out behind the red capillaries and flashes of light before her eyes was a flickering shadow and a voice that drove the sleep from her mind.

Voet-sak, she pronounced with cut-glass precision so that there would be no misunderstanding her intention, following this last with a decisive flap of the hand, a few tailgated *humba wenas* for good measure.

'*Skies,* sorry-sorry. The voice shoved around to the side of her head as the man lowered himself into the shade.

Only trying to be friendly, Sisi. Looks like a good read, hey?

It was the vendor from the curry wagon. The man who'd sold her the Fanta, handing over her change with a thin snap of his wrist, an even thinner smile. Strange that the smile should be thin when the lips were so full. So full that they split a little in the middle, ve-ry little, like an overripe plum. So full that Dhlamina wondered if the man, *tcha,* boy, he was a *boy,* was obliged to sleep with his mouth ajar. She felt desire slide through her belly, tautening the invisible triangle of lines between nipples and crotch. The water baby responded to its mother's excitement with a swift kick in the ribs, a series of butterfly ripples expanding outwards from her breastbone. *Eina,* in all this heat!

You enjoy cooking, Sisi?

The question was unexpected and irrelevant so Dhlamina ignored it. Instead she watched the mouth that formed these words, blowing them out one by one from lips that seemed ready to play the saxophone like Kippie Mocketsi even if their owner was a Hurry-Curry vendor with his pinfeathers on end. Pregnancy gave her the privilege of selective attention. As her companion chattered on she allowed herself to float upon the effulgence of his conversation, remaining awake solely to catch another glimpse of that hush-puppy tongue.

Effing hot, hey?

Hmmmm.

Bad day for curry, huh?

The people say when you heat up the inside you cool off the outside. Say a bowl of curry's as good as a cup of tea on a hot day. Want to try a nice bredie, Sisi? Good for you, a couple beef samosas? On the house, Ma'am, very nice, I promise.

But the voice didn't match the beautiful mouth at all. The voice was high-pitched and rang on her ears like wet fingers pulling at the rim of a wine glass. The voice called forth the heat prickling up inside Dhlamina's armpits and around the tilted equator of her belly.

Eina, eina! She waved him away with a hand made languorous by indifference. No mouth was worth the boredom.

But Mr. Curry in a Hurry wouldn't leave. Instead, *ftttzz-fttzzz*, he buzzed at the side of her head like an insect. Something must be done. Dhlamina snapped off her sunglasses and opened her eyes wide, in no mood to protect him from the magnetism. Let him fall in love, she thought.

With her eyes open Dhlamina saw at once that this was the kind of man, and there were few enough of his kind, for whom she held little attraction. But why — *why*, for crying in a bucket — come to buzz against her in the mid-afternoon glare, sunlight cutting the water at an agonizing angle, even the ducks rocking between water and sky too hot to swim away. Why must he crouch beside her, thick-skinned, blotting up the last of the cool air? Why must he snag his voice against her ear? Blah blah blah! Walla walla walla!

Gradually, through her lethargy, Dhlamina heard the vendor offer a name she recognized.

Mhda? he asked. Mhda the Taxi Man?

The question in his voice was a little bird that flew off with the end of the sentence on its back.

Madiba Mhda? he repeated.

But I saw you talking by the Rosebank Mall, he persisted.

Could be. Dhlamina roused herself.

So. You know him?

Seems like.

He a friend?

Could say that. *Could.*

Then we have a friend together, hey Sisi?

Dhlamina considered the question carefully, poking her tongue into the hide-and-go-seek dimple in her cheek. *Uh-uh.*

Relief, like the rainbow in an oil slick, surfaced in the boy's eyes. Dhlamina resolved to deflate him once and for all even if such an effort required telling the truth, an expedient she usually resisted on principle.

Not so much a friend.

Stroking her belly modestly Dhlamina pretended to consider the question of her relationship with Madiba Mhda, Taxi Man, he of the gold pocket watch and the incredible potency.

Not so much a stranger, either.

When she observed the ladyboy's gaze following the direction of her stroking hands Dhlamina slowed, waiting for his eyes to travel back over the globe of her belly, over the double scoop of her breasts and up to her playfully lowered lids. At the exact moment before *not* looking must defeat the purpose of such an elaborate pantomime Dhlamina raised her eyes, met his incredulous gaze and slowly nodded.

Uh-huh.

Agremon was squatting on a pile of newspapers in the causeway between the kitchen and the servant's quarters. He was polishing Baas Benjamin's hospital moccasins and whitening his running shoes, whistling through his teeth and making up riddles to wile away the time—

What ripples like a stone thrown into a lake?

A dog trembling after it has been beaten!

That was a good one; he must remember to tell Beauty. Then he recalled that the subject of dogs was a sore topic between them and he sighed heavily. These days, the smallest things sent her into a rage. This present one had begun trivially enough when he'd returned weary from the de Wets and their Rottweilers exclaiming, Even the dogs in this country are racists! Why else do they bark at the blacks, why else do they bare their teeth! It's as if, he reasoned building to his climax, as if the souls of Malan and Verwoerd and Strijdom have been reborn in the bodies of these ugly Rottweillers and Pitbulls and Alsatians.

But Beauty was in no mood for joking, she never was these days.

So, and if Malan is a Rottweiller then what is Dzlamani? Is he a cat or even worse a mouse that cringes at the first sign of teeth?

Truly, there was no pleasing her lately. Shaking his head, sighing, Agremon fell silent.

Silence had descended upon the two cement rooms with their adjoining bathroom that made up the servant's quarters at the back of the house on Sugarbush Road. In silence Beauty drew water from the washbasin in the bathroom to fill the aluminum kettle that she set to boil on the hot plate. In silence she scraped the last of the loose tea leaves out of the tin cannister and in silence she waited as the leaves steeped and rose to the surface of her cup. The buchu tea (good for the kidneys, the muti salesman had assured her, very good) tasted bitter as gall and was only palatable when sweetened with three or four heaped spoonfuls of sugar but Beauty gulped it eagerly on account of the ease it gave her in making water. An ease that, of late, had been sadly lacking. A pain, the size and shape of a lamb chop, was lodged in Beauty's side these days and the thick black tea seemed to dull the pain a little.

Gagging against the bitterness of the liquid, Beauty laid her sewing out on an empty suitcase selected from the battered trunks and cardboard cases piled beneath her bed. On the scarred surface of this suitcase she arranged two spools of thread, a pair of broken scissors (repaired with garden twine courtesy of Agremon), a length of measuring tape (bottom six inches missing), a wristband bristling pins, and a loose paper sheath of needles. As she matched her thread against the burgundy seams of Mevrou Terheyden's "letting it out *again*?" rapidly expanding waistband, Beauty contemplated the silence in which she worked. Biting off a length of thread, carefully knotting one end and easing the other through the eye of a needle, she reflected that the silence that had begun with the silencing of Rothman's radio and had continued through his speechless rage at her forgetting to buy new batteries, this silence was composed of heat and lethargy, the odour of vegetable peels from the dustbin in the yard, and the hot stink of dog shit softening in the midday sun.

When the batteries had finally been procured—Agremon unpocketing them one Friday afternoon along with his room key, Lotto ticket, a bag of loose tobacco—when these batteries, size double A, had been eagerly seized and fumbled into the plastic hollow at the base of the radio, a horrible *ftt-tt-zzzz-zzz* had resulted and the silence that followed was more dense, more concentrated, more full of pins dropping and angels passing than any that had gone before. Now Rothman's radio was for sure broken, at least if the smell of dust and hot electricity and exposed wires was anything to judge by.

So that was the end of the radio, broken for good this time, for ever. Rothman blamed Agremon, said the batteries were wrong but Agremon said Rothman was a fool, that he knew nothing about radios, that he'd foolishly put the batteries in upside down or the wrong way round and now this radio was well and truly broken, broken one hundred percent. Shame, the poor child, Beauty thought but Rothman cringed when she put her hand on the back of his neck. Winced, blew a thin jet of air through his teeth. Turned away.

So she slapped him. Don't cheek me, hey?

Sniffed.

Okay so now there was no radio and no jabbering voices, no advertisements for Lux Beauty Soap or Camel Smokes, no itchy-ear music or late night jazz or DJ with his promises of love love love. The radio had been a cheap object, a metal squawk box wrapped in a leather case punctured with rows of perforations for the sound to come through. Knobs and control buttons that confused Beauty but which had delighted Rothman poked through holes cut into the leather and there was a frequency band with a red dial that her grandson tuned in and out of various late night stations that played music she neither cared for nor understood but a radio was all she'd been able to afford or at least willing to pay for at the time, a fancy boom box being out of the question and Rothman had grown reluctantly accustomed to the old-fashioned machine whose plastic handle flipped back with such a satisfying snap.

But now Beauty knew that she would have to replace it with the latest costly stereo and so (what else could she do?) she promised to take the radio back to Freedman Electronics. Even though it was a year ago already since she'd bought this radio and even though the receipt, crumpled and torn though it was when she extracted it from behind the cistern, clearly read "No Exchanges on Sales Items" beneath the total which itself represented an unexpected triumph against the Chinaman together with the profits from one full week of alterations during the wedding season. Huh, fat chance.

But what else could she do?

The problem was her grandson who was so unhappy, this boy returned to her twice already as if he was himself a box of shop-soiled goods, a broken toaster or a burnt-out kettle. Poor Rothman, returned once when his mother disappeared into the night like the Xhosa that she was; returned twice when his father married that fishwife who swept him out of the house at the business end of her broom as if he was nothing more than a pile of rubbish. What could Beauty do but take him in after that? Truly, it was too much for any child to be thrown away twice. And even if such matters were at first a secret and then a scandal and finally all but forgotten, there was still the child to consider. Although not young anymore Mamma Thlali could at least catch the knife at the sharp end, as she herself said, before it cut her great-grandson. Rather he should stay with an old mother than that he should live as an orphan, learning customs from the tribal ward, Mamma Thlali had consoled her daughter-in-law.

Just make sure he eats his breakfast every day before he goes to school, Beauty told Mamma Thlali whose encroaching blindness was rapidly gaining her the reputation of a seer amongst her neighbours. Bearing gifts of maize meal, sugar, a handful of green onions, these neighbours had grown into the habit of dropping in to consult Mamma Thlali on matters of marital infidelity, bride's wealth, illness, and fertility. Always a shrewd one, Mamma Thlali contrived to align her advice to the course of action she perceived her listener was most inclined to follow and, being able to correctly foretell future events more or less better than half the time, her reputation was rapidly catching up to her self-regard so that, once or twice, Beauty had been obliged to quote her mother-in-law's words back to her: *Moipone ga a ipone selo mo tlhogong.* That which is upon her own head the seer does not recognize.

Ha! retorted Mamma Thlali, suddenly waspish, do you think I can't recognize the Angel of Death after all these years?

Indeed, the ghosts had begun to visit Mamma Thlali in earnest now and the very same neighbours whom she advised with such skill were often witness to these courtesy calls. Oh, Ma Mbagana, it's you! Mamma Thlali might beckon to one who'd been gone for ten years or she might howl with mirth at the remarks of an elderly Ntate whom even death hadn't robbed of his good humour. Inside her lean-to Mamma Thlali consulted with the neighbours and discoursed with the dead. But outside, the drought prevailed. All the pumpkins and marrows that had been planted that spring had deflated and now resembled leaking inner tubes dwindling in the earth.

Do you think I cannot recognize the Angel of Death? teased Mamma Thlali at such times.

Just make sure that Rothman eats his breakfast before school, Beauty instructed hastily.

So there was pap with margarine every day for breakfast but Beauty was willing to bet that the boy hadn't set foot in Limkile School for months before he ran away.

Years, more likely, Agremon said.

Long ago, *years* ago, Rothman had listened with an open heart to the stories that Mamma Thlali had told him of the mythical herd boy who roamed the veld catching flying ants and locusts to eat, roasting mopani worms and sucking at the juicy fruit of the marula tree when it was in season. His name was Cattlebest because he had a way with the cows and steers that were in his keeping. Each of these stories was different, for his great-Ouma exercised imagination and cunning in their execution but all ended in the same manner. After all sorts of adventures and initiation rites Cattlebest returned home, his step certain, his path assured. Each star was a herdsman, Mamma Thlali would always conclude, each star was a herdsman to call him back home.

These days it was clear to anyone with eyes to see, clear as the neat stitches she was tacking along the inside waistband of Mevrou Terhyden's church-going formal, that Beauty's grandson was rotting from the inside with his bad thoughts and idle ways. In her heart Beauty stood forever on a sand road, arms stretched out, eyes narrowed to the middle distance. In her heart she waited for her grandson to return to her along the jolts and bumps of the dusty corduroy road from where she watched as traffic surged past on the shiny highway, all metal and glare. In her heart she waited as the rains came, the river passing below overflowed its banks levelling the shantytown, once again, the lean-to in which Mamma Thlali lived sliding off its shallow foundations and into the mud.

Weighted with foreboding, her arms triangled towards the "going out again?" always retreating back of her grandson, Beauty waited, treading time like water. What else could she do? Rothman refused to return home to Mamma Thlali, refused to seek work or so much as hoist a bucket of soapy water to help his grandmother about the house. Instead he twiddled his thumbs on a pile of bricks beneath the washing carousel, occasionally lifting his head as Beauty whisked in and out with sheets and nighties, a row of pegs jamming her mouth like ill-fitting dentures.

The washing! The washing!

During the rainy season Beauty was kept ferociously busy throwing herself, again and again, like an ant at a vast pyramid of rice; scurrying outside, inside again, outside, heaps of damp laundry clutched to her chest first thing in the morning when the sun was thirsty for wet cotton. All day she polished her eye against the sky ready for the first abrupt drops that would announce the fury of mid-afternoon showers. Then, with that stupid dog weaving between her legs, she must run to gather the still clammy washing in her arms, scattering pegs and socks and safety pins in her headlong rush indoors. Winters were easier, the sun not so hot, of course, but at least no rain, no lightning, no shit to clean off the kitchen floor when that tsotsi-dog caught fright.

But summers like this the sun scalded the back of the neck. No sooner did she shake the sheets into neat folds, peg the towels and the bedding taut then it was time to gather them up again. All day Beauty dragged yards of cotton and linen and terrycloth indoors to be rubbed soft between her palms, laid flat on the board: iron and fold, iron and fold. Washing days Beauty felt as if she herself had been ironed flat, what with the heat outside, the steam inside. But some creases were too stiff to be patted away so easily, some wrinkles too enduring to be lifted with a sprinkle of water and a head of steam.

Every now and then as she bent over the ironing board, Beauty would glance outside. Yes, there he slouched, that Rothman, that lost son. With each twitch at the kitchen curtains a paper bag was snatched out of sight, disappearing into the folds of the sweat-streaked coat he wore every day despite the heat. Poking from one pocket was a grubby balaclava more suited to winter nights about a charcoal brazier but Beauty had seen her grandson pull this filthy cap, very same, over his brow when he slipped out at night.

Twitch. Sniff *sniff*.

Glue, Agremon told her, biting the word off at the root.

Just chips he gets from the caffy. Hey? Beauty offered.

Glue, Agremon insisted and Beauty was angry, at first, refusing to speak to her lover for two whole days but in the end she believed him because if it wasn't glue then it was something woroo. The boy's eyes were bloodshot and his nose dripped like an outdoor tap. All day, drip, drip.

On the third day she relented, taking a glass of water down to the bottom of the garden where Agremon was scrabbling at the roots of a clump of khakibos, nudging the dirt with his blunt earthworm fingers.

All right. Glue.

Mmph.

He's not a bad boy. Not so much. Just…otherwise.

Agremon cupped his palm round where the dense stems broke earth. In one swift, lightbulb-releasing movement he swivelled the weeds from their sockets, straightened.

Thwack.

Swatted the fistful of loamy roots against his thigh, scattering soil, thwack.

Uh-huh. Agremon nodded, swiped the sweat beading his hairline with a ropey forearm, nodded.

Hey hey, he shrugged, could be worse. Could be.

And that was that so far as Agremon was concerned, agreeable since birth and unlikely to make trouble at this late date. But, watching the gardener nod his head in emphatic agreement, Beauty was instantly certain that things were much worse.

For one thing, her grandson carried the rot of fermented liquor on his breath. She could smell it, every night, when she set his plate of meat stew and sourmilk pap before him. Not alcohol because where would he get the money, but something else. Something pungent, half-fermented. One day Beauty found a loaf of purple bread in the outdoor dustbin. Bright purple from the dye of the Methylated Spirits that had been drained through the spongy insides of the bread to funnel off the colour and a little of the harshness. What was left over, the colourless Meths, strained and purified, had long ago been gulped down.

That week the dustbin boys were late, too busy collecting Christmas ponsella from all the houses in the neighbourhood. *DUSTBIN! DUSTBIN!* they clamoured, clashing dustbin lids like cymbals and pretending to prostrate themselves before the master of the house as he flung open the front door in his boxer shorts: *uBabaWEThu! Ma-DEE-ba!*

Every time Beauty lifted the lid to pitch in the day's vegetable peelings and tea leaves, the dry curds of pap from the bottom of the pan, she caught a glimpse of the bright purple bread. Not even the maggots would touch it.

Ah, but it was the day that she discovered her grandson puffing from a packet of what she assumed must be stolen cigarettes that knocked Beauty sideways and into the middle of next week. The heat that had been building all day had dipped into the plateau of early evening. Hands drifting in warm water, Beauty stood before the open kitchen window trying to catch a breeze when she sniffed the acrid burn of cigarette smoke.

There he was, that Rothman, straddled on his throne of loose bricks, a cigarette clutched between gnawed-down fingers. An unlit cigarette angled from behind one ear and a familiar red and white box poked from the ripped pocket of his coat. That lucky red target concentrated Beauty's anger into a sudden spasm; she rushed outside. Yes, all at once she did what she'd never done in thirty years of working at the house on Sugarbush Road. She threw off her apron and tore outside.

Hai kona, smoking hey?

No answer.

Siestog! A young boy like you! Shame. Sha-aaa-me!

No answer. But he made an effort, at least, lifting his eyes wearily to meet her gaze. Incensed, Beauty rapped her grandson smartly on the side of the head with her knuckles. *Ko Ko Ko.*

No answer.

Count to ten.

No answer.

Beauty exploded: Wake up and go to work, you *skelm!* You come to live here but do you help your Ouma? Shame on you, *shame,* letting an old woman cook and clean while you lie in the sun like a—like a big fat *shongolulu!* What—are you going to let a woman work for you all your life? What—am I your slave? Someone you can steal from, someone you can lie to? One who has the misfortune of a soft heart so she doesn't throw you out? Yes, my son, a heart as soft as the inside of a loaf of bread!

And Beauty thumped her chest so hard that she rendered herself breathless, the rest of her sentence puffing out in short gasps of outrage.

Where? Where. You. Get. Themoney?

Shrug.

Skelm! she shrieked. Tsotsi! Thief!

Méira Cook

Ungrateful child! Serpent's tooth!

Mischief-maker, liar, *TOKOLOSHE!*

Beauty tried to talk to him, she really did.

Yebo, but she got nowhere that day. Rothman slouched before her, hangdog and surly, until her anger ran out of oxygen.

Why does he look into the corners of rooms? asked Agremon. Is he a stray dog? Is he a thief?

Beauty swatted him away but the thought ambushed her like a Christmas beetle, the thought buzzed against the brittle casing of her sleep so that, waking, she fumbled for the dark green Building Society Savings Book that, to her relief, showed that no withdrawals had been made in the last week.

With a wry face, as of someone biting into a sour guava, Beauty cut the last thread with her teeth. One by one she examined her seams (straight), her fingertips (pricked), the dusk outside her window gathering slowly, heavily. It was Agremon who told her he'd seen Benjamin offering Rothman the packet of smokes. So her grandson hadn't stolen the cigarettes and Beauty was sorry that she'd lost her temper but what was a mother to do? She tried to make it up to Rothman with extra helpings of stew and tomato and fried onion gravy for his mieliepap, but the boy hardly ate, he hardly ate at all. The only thing he put in his mouth these days, thought Beauty, were his fingernails, gnawed to the root. Shame.

Every time Beauty saw these fingers now, ten stubs smoked down past their filters, her heart contracted. Nunkula, she coaxed, reaching out to touch him as she passed, does my nunkula want a glass of milk, an orange? Remembering how he used to tug at her arm when he was a little boy, his puppy breath, his sticky fingers. But Rothman remained unresponsive—a grown-up boy hatching his pile of bricks, too-big hands stacked on his knees—without words of his own or any indication that he heard those his grandmother had fashioned to light his way home.

He hardly spoke to Agremon either. Every night, late, Rothman padded in from who knows where or why to squat in the yard until all the stars were out and the house bats fluttered and swooped from the eaves. Stretched on her bed, staring out at these same stars, Beauty distracted her waiting heart by repeating the words that Hosiah had printed out for her on the back of a church circular. Hosiah Mopede, first preacher of the Church of Zion in the Veld and educated by the missionaries to recognize daffodils and skylarks and nightingales, had once written Beauty a poem. Her one and only love letter. *To Beauty who walks in the night of climbing clouds and starry skies.*

The hot dry days of midsummer burned the sky free of clouds, climbing or otherwise, but the night skies remained abundant with the stars that Beauty scorned to count while she waited for her grandson to return.

Each star a herdsman to call him back home.

Eventually, when the darkness was so thick that it had swallowed her thoughts, when she could no longer see her hand in front of her nose, then Beauty would sense the apparition upon its little heap of bricks and rubble, stir and make its way into the servant's quarters where it would, once again, become her grandson. Shrugging his filthy coat, she imagined him bunking down on the makeshift mattress in the room he shared with Agremon where he would proceed to snore his way through what remained of the night and half the next day.

The only person he talked to, as far as Beauty could see, was Benjamin. Once, out of sight behind the washing carousel, a row of pegs stretching her mouth into the smile she most assuredly did not feel, Beauty overheard them chatting. Beauty didn't know why Benjamin was pissing his time away in the yard with the dustbins and the dog shit but there he was, *tcha*. At first she thought he was offering her grandson cigarettes again and her heart began to pound.

You've got an interesting name, he was saying. And then of course he must ask all about this so *in*teresting name and the boy was explaining—how did he put it? Well, no use pretending she didn't understand. Rothman said that he was being named for a cigarette.

Rothman for Rothman's Extra Special Lights, a high-class brand. Not like the Lucky Strikes that all the bras in the township smoked. Which his own father was named for. Lucky, for Lucky Strike, okay?

Méira Cook

When she heard this story Beauty wanted to cry.

After some days of brooding, she concluded that Benjamin was the cause of the sadness that collected at the back of her throat like the phlegm of which she couldn't rid herself, spit or swallow though she might. She began to despise the way his hair grew to a peak on his forehead, the crack-crack-rustle of the evening paper in his hands, the godless sound he made when, every paragraph or so, gutturally and without delicacy, he cleared his throat. Watching him in the evening through the kitchen window as he smoked a cigarette in the dusk she'd rattle the box of kitchen matches hard.

Tskah, tskah.

Half a box of matches, quarter full of used matchsticks. Because that lazy one couldn't be bothered to throw away even a used match. And why, *why?*

Her hatred was like the thin red line in Ouma's thermometer; it crawled slowly upwards but it kept Beauty upright at least and it concentrated her thoughts. One day she threw out half of Benjamin's socks instead of sorting them with their partners in the bureau. Another day she burned ironing tracks into his boxers then folded them neatly in his underwear drawer. She starched his sheets then neglected to rinse them thoroughly so that his sleep would be hard and uneasy, his dreams stiff with foreboding. Since Agremon and Rothman ate from the same pot she hesitated to tamper with his food but she made sure that he was always served the gristly piece of chicken, the fatty cut of lamb. In the privacy of her room Beauty carefully gathered the shaving stubble she'd shaken from his razor, the loose hairs she'd picked from his brush. There.

There.

Whistling through his teeth and squinting with concentration Agremon had begun to shine up the silver. Pausing every now and then to hawk satisfyingly into the outdoor drain he rubbed Silvo into the candlesticks. Yawned until his eyes ran clear. Watched as the shadow of the boy, Rothman, hunched off his pile of rubble and shuffled indoors to merge, silently, with the boy lying face down on the straw mattress.

Inside her room Beauty bit her thread in two. The silence of static electricity and stifled grief and broken radios (*tcha*, only five shopping days to go before Christmas) seemed to compress the walls. With careful fingers Beauty knotted her doek more firmly about her head. She peered out past the yard and the washing line, the spattered wall bracing the outdoor tap, past the dustbins and the dog shit and the barbed wire looped across the supporting wall.

Out in the veld she pictured herself striding away. A woman, bareheaded, sway-backed. Walking in beauty like the night.

When can we use the machine again? Sister demanded belligerently.

Josephus Nyatela, the one the nurses called Joe My Baby, had fought his way into a coma in the night, his face as grey as the ashes at the bottom of an all-night coal brazier. Although it was his day off, his *one* day off Benjamin reminded himself, he'd gone in early to check on a couple of his patients too unstable to trust to the ministrations of the new interns. In honour of the boy's failure to go gently into whatever approximation of darkness he now inhabited, Benjamin had lingered for a moment at Joe My Baby's bedside watching the fifteen-year-old heart monitor (one leg teetering, splinted together with duct tape) dot-dot-dash its way across the surface of the twenty-two-year-old's life. Someone had tied a rosary around one of the struts of the headboard and Benjamin bent to straighten the wooden cross.

A mistake. Sister cornered him. When can we use the machine again?

Boy isn't dead yet, he'd snapped, rubber soles squeaking against linoleum as if mimicking his irritation as he tried to outmanoeuvre her, quickstep his way out of Critical Care, past the dispensary and home free. But Sister wasn't interested in his huffy evasions for if the boy wasn't dead yet he would be, and soon, and others were dying and could perhaps benefit from the assistance of an extremely old, somewhat lopsided—but that's all she had to work with—heart monitor, doctor, so tell me, *ke a leboga*, when can we use the machine again?

It wasn't that she wanted him to pull the plug, Benjamin knew. She just wanted a timeline.

On his way out Benjamin heard Markham's characteristic bedside rumble—*Klaaring* out, hey? Going home soon, Mr. Notwani?

But the patient, an elderly man with corrugated iron hair, failed to be roused by his physician's enthusiasm. Which put him in the minority, Benjamin imagined, for few of Dr. Markham's patients could fail to be moved by the man's heartiness, his sure fingers on the pulse, his clap on the back, his rousing cry of *Moenie worry nie, my bra!* Sometimes Markham's enthusiasm got the better of him. Watching him bounce through the wards one couldn't help thinking that he might well be prepared to kill his patients the better to separate them from their diseases. But he was a good sort, old Markham, with his habit of striding into a room as if delivering the word of God Himself—*Dumelang, banna ba geso!* Greetings to you, my fellow men!

Markham, who wore Madiba shirts under his scrubs and tire sandals on his feet, had picked up a smattering of Sesotho and isiZulu in the course of his duties, township phrases and slang which he mixed into an odd patois, tsotsi-taaling away like the gangster that he so clearly was not. *Listen bafana-boys*, he'd say, striding briskly into a ward of post-operative old men, stopping off at each bed to scribble on a chart, rally a fading spirit or palpate a stomach, *Hem, hem, how goes the phalatsa—PHALATSA?*

Phalatsa was Markham's favourite word, he repeated it endlessly at bed after bed—*phalatsa,* to disgorge—and the attendant nurse would roll her eyes and translate for the patient's benefit, Have you gone pottie yet, Mr. Notwani?

Today, though, Mr. Notwani was unrousable.

Benjy, Howzit, *mfana!*

Markham was terribly pleased to catch Benjamin—and just in time too, *madoda!*—because he needed help in drafting a memo to the Health Minister in a last-ditch effort to save the hospital's essential services during the strike.

Won't do a bit of good, of course. Admin refuses to lift a finger but hell, man, we have to give it a shot and now they're warning us not to cross picket lines. I said to bloody Habib, thanks for the advice, hey, good thing it's free that way I know what to do with it. Fucking condoms!

Keeping up with Markham's rapidly diminishing footsteps being incompatible with extricating himself from this proposed project of civil reform, Benjamin soon found himself in the staff room. Markham was still going on about free advice that, like the free condoms the government supplied to all its citizens, tended to be neither valued nor utilized. The stopped clock on the staff room wall still read ten to two and the dredgy coffee with its sullen iridescent glaze was as tepid as it had ever been. Lord how he wished that just for bloody once someone would rinse the filter.

You all right, *jong*?

Markham had the grace to look chastened. He pushed a plate towards Benjamin. Someone had split open a packet of Eet Sum Mor biscuits and now they spilled over onto the thick hospital issue plate.

Ag, we must just *vasbyt*, man. Hang in there, as they say in the army. Used to, anyway. So, okay, Nurse Rita's volunteered to type out the memo and since I'm on call all day and this has to go out stat if it's to be any use, could you—man, would you *mind* running it downtown...

So his day off, his *one* day off as he kept reminding himself, had been frittered away in the end, sweating in stalled traffic, inching in serpentine queues through the intestines of sour-smelling city departments whose clerks seemed more than usually stunned by the heat and the stale, dusty air settling out of reach of the blunt rotation of various institutional ceiling fans. On the way home the air conditioning in his car packed up and he had to crank the windows which opened the way for every fruit vendor, flower seller, and trinket hawker to poke their heads in at every intersection along the entire length of Empire. Freelancers, freeloaders.

Kr-ee-sss-mus! cried the beggars or perhaps it was merely the cry of the city readying itself for the last fling of enterprise before the festive season got under way.

Kr-ee-sss-mus! And the stir of a breeze sour as the whiff of gingivitis.

Beauty was smearing shoe polish on the insides of Benjamin's shoes. Coldly and with malicious intent she was rubbing streaks of brown Nugget along the insides of his smart brogues. There. With a sudden burst of inspiration she began to pick at the plastic coating on one of his shoe laces until she'd succeeded in fraying it past the point where it could be threaded again. Ha!

Dumela, Beauty, too hot already this morning, hey? Benjamin had greeted her thumping down early to the kitchen where she was sitting in her kitchen chair, her doek untied. Mumbling something about a dream. With growing contempt Beauty realized that he was trying to give her his lucky dream so she could win the jackpot at fahfee. Ah *shaya*, you fool!

She'd spat in his early morning coffee, of course, but something in her had remained unsated. So she'd plugged in the iron, jiggling impatiently until it was ready to fold unsightly creases into his shirts, poke holes in his trouser pockets. And later? Hmm, perhaps a trip upstairs to mess up his books; slam those left open, crack spines, dog ear pages, encourage Eli to make a meal of the thick medical texts with their ghastly illustrations that she was certain he left open in order to frighten her. Huh, did that one think that skin and bone and blood had any power over her anymore?

Humming with anger Beauty thumped the iron onto the ironing board.

Again.

His heart pounding, Benjamin bent from the waist and gasped for a while. Quite a long while actually and when the world had stopped jumping about he straightened slowly and decided that was about it for his run, thank you very much, and perhaps he'd find a nice tree to sit under instead. But, once this tree had been found and he was beneath it, propped against it with his eyes closed, weariness overcame him, sour as a whiff of mud off the Zoo Lake. He'd only been round twice but he was already too damn tired to finish his run. It was the heat, he reasoned, the summer heat that, despite its impressive swell and girth, hadn't yet reached full term. It was the drought, the lake draining and gurgling before his eyes, a large muddy fish without gills. And it was the air that, even in the early morning, carried the taste of recycled tap water. The metallic landscape, the weary city with its violence and beggars, murderers and bureaucrats and con-artists and politicians. In the late afternoon the wind gave out a cry like the sound of over-stressed steel.

Benjamin couldn't remember a December like this one. Already the holiday death toll was exceeding records, the Gen was overrun with accident and trauma victims as well as patients suffering from all sorts of rancorous infections: tuberculosis and tetanus and meningitis and AIDS and hepatitis, even an odd strain of stubbornly resistant pneumonia. Malarias, fevers, and unexpected choleras ravaged the bodies waiting in the wards and corridors, actual beds being reserved, as Markham dryly put it, for the lucky dying. There were too few beds and no clean sheets (the laundry union had urged a pre-emptive strike) so the dispensary was hastily transformed into a makeshift triage station as the wait for a doctor lengthened into days. Family members, obliged to feed and clean their own, frequently fell ill themselves, crouched beside a sick child or a dying parent.

In the virulent heat (the air conditioning had packed up early in the month and there was no money for repairs since, it was latterly discovered, at least three and possibly *five* board members had been lining their pockets at the expense of Maintenance), in the thick air swarming with germs and wildly proliferating bacteria it wasn't safe to fall ill let alone give birth. (*Humba*, Benjamin heard Nurse Tsitsi turning away a woman in early labour. Squat rather in a field, she'd muttered under her breath). These days Benjamin smoothed on latex gloves in the parking lot then picked his way over those prone in hallways and makeshift wards, his surgical mask firmly affixed.

A plague, the newspapers announced periodically, smugly. But, in truth, the situation wasn't very different (strikes, corruption) than in previous years demonstrating, thought Benjamin when he had a moment to think about such things, that the human spirit, like water, found its own level. As for disease, death, disaster, they were so many lime stains and hard water scuffs on the inside of some vast, kettle-shaped world.

A good rain, everyone said and continued to say, would cure all. Would cool the fevers, flush out vice and virus alike, draw to a head some wholly original if nameless sin.

Meanwhile, in the suburbs a new menace had arisen. Amongst the kidney-shaped swimming pools and rock gardens and *braaivleis* pits of Triomf a white child had been bitten by a dog and died. Rabies! the newspapers insinuated then declared until dozens then scores of household pets had been shot by neighbourhood vigilante groups, their carcasses in the rank heat seeming to decay while watched as if filmed by the kind of time-lapse photography that had been devoted, in more temperate times, to documentaries on the fertilization of plants or the reproductive cycle of amphibians. A simple, cost-effective pro-phylactic injection was all that was needed, the vets pleaded. But in the baited heat canine bad temper was easy to mistake for some other, more malodorous, cause.

A spate of poisonings followed as suburban dogs were fed taint-ed meat by a variety of interested parties from incipient burglars to neighbours driven to insanity by the heat that was increased dispro-portionately by the root-canal of motiveless barking. And that wasn't all. During this, the second drought in as many years, the number of cats, of birds and squirrels and rough-pelted rodents killed by pellet guns reached epidemic proportions in the western suburbs, in Florida Park and Lenasia and Westdene, and in all the city not even one seed germinated from gardens planted in the spring. Not a shoot, not a bud, was able to lift itself from the exhausted soil.

A good rain, everyone said, voices rising on the inflection. And the hot winds that blew off the mountains caught the words, repeating them: *a good rain a good rain goodrain a good drain*, over and over like a communal sigh. Like the word amen at the end of a prayer.

Yet in other parts of the country opposite conditions prevailed. Unseasonable rains poured down through gurgling valleys and across water-leached farm lands. Flash floods and thunderstorms gathered over the Drakensberg, pounding down to the foothills and washing away topsoil and shacks and cattle, children and the fragile happiness of their parents. It was all there on the news every night; floods and drought in alternating montages of ruin.

Benjamin mopped his forehead on his sweatshirt and began to limp home. Not running, not exactly, but more than walking which was a considerable feat and one he wasn't willing to disown. A kind of calf-clenching, thigh-chafing hobble expressive of a full bladder or a swaying hard-on but unlikely to achieve the pleasure-in-release of either. Grunt-chug, grunt-chug, past a couple of jolla boys as they swaggered over to a girl-almost-woman fanning herself beneath a tree. She waved them away languidly, too hot, for once, to accept customers preferring instead to rest in the sullen late afternoon heat before the Saturday night rush hour. Salvaging their pride by shouting insults and poking rude holes in the air with their index fingers, the jolla boys swaggered off but the girl-almost-woman remained unoffended.

Hau, Benjamin thought he heard her sigh. *Uh*-huh.

Benjamin hobbled on. Past the rowing boats and the ticket sellers, past the concession stands and the parking lot and the loading bay behind the Tearoom where men were off-loading crates of beer in the dust, tossing the rattling bottles from the back of the van to their mates on the ground. Clink of glass on glass. Shouts of *hekelemanzi!* The sudden sharp smell of spilt beer from a broken bottle as Benjamin jolted past, swaying forward on the balls of his feet. At the main entrance to the Zoo Lake where the vendors and peddlers gathered and traffic roared up the hill, Babelas, the leather hawker, accosted him as he always did. Handbags and purses hung from his neck and his waist was looped with dozens of belts from which dangled a variety of sandals, wallets, holsters. Cowhide and snakeskin, pimpled warthog and imitation crocodile. The man had a large blob of Vaseline smeared over his nose and in long streaks across his cheeks and chin.

Asseblief Baas, he called, clapping cracked leather palms together.

Benjamin fished a couple of rand from the pocket of his jogging shorts.

Dankie Baas, dankie. Babelas clapped his hands again, bending his knees and whistling through his teeth then, this pantomime of gratitude concluded, he creaked away wafting the smell of hide and polish overlaid by the sour yeast of beer-distilled sweat.

In his wake Benjamin suddenly recognized one of the Hurry-Curry vendors bent over his mobile curry wagon. Beauty's grandson, it looked like. What was his name again? Named for a brand of cigarettes as he'd once informed Benjamin in return for a couple of fags. Returning late at night to the house on Sugarbush Road after long shifts at the hospital, Benjamin had grown accustomed to glimpsing Rothman silhouetted on his pedestal of rubble, waiting.

Now Benjamin waved but the boy seemed preoccupied although it was plain that there were no customers around.

'Lo, called Benjamin still breathing hard.

…'Mela.

Hot, hey?

The boy shook his head incredulously but whether at the heat or the depths of foolishness revealed in the question it was difficult to know. Cheers, Benjamin waved but Rothman had already turned away and was ostentatiously scouring his grill frame with a wire brush and a handful of stale bread.

Turning away, Benjamin felt anger and then almost immediately afterwards, pity. As always the pity cancelled out the anger. Any fool could see that the kid was sniffing and snorting his way to some needle-encrusted version of immolation. None of his business, *none.* Still, but. Once or twice (to salvage his conscience, naturally) Benjamin had tried to talk to him but Rothman was mutinously uncommunicative about everything except, on one occasion, his childish rage at the destruction of a—what was it now?—oh yes, his transistor radio.

Something about batteries, an explosion. That was when Benjamin had first noticed the grey burn marks smeared like ash on the boy's hands and held out his own to examine them. But Rothman had given him a "no one, no way" look before swivelling his hands into their cuffs.

On another occasion Benjamin, stooping in the driveway to check the Audi's tail lights, had caught a glimpse of Rothman reflected in the side mirror. The boy was eating a slice of overripe pawpaw, cutting into the burnt-orange flesh with a penknife, scraping seeds into a slimy mess at his feet. The rotten smell of ripe papaya wafted across.

A good rain, thought Benjamin.

But it looked as if Rothman had found a job at last. Marvelling at the coincidence that had united Beauty's grandson with Mustapha's business venture, Benjamin toiled up the knee-slamming incline of Kingsway. He jolted over split pavement flags, crushed windshield glass and scattered debris, his tardy endorphins finally kicking in so that the last sprint along Mebos was nothing less than a victory lap, sweat crowning his brow like a laurel wreath and all the neighbourhood dogs baying in admiration as he passed.

Home again, home again. Jiggedy-jig.

By the time he reached sight of the house on Sugarbush Road Benjamin had decided to reward Rothman's industry with a new radio or (why not?) an over-sized ghetto blaster with dual speakers. Something heavy to hoist on one shoulder, keep the kid grounded. It would cost him very little and mean so much to the boy, not to mention, a *minor* consideration, his splenetic grandmother. It might even reconcile said grandmother to his bony white self, mused Benjamin as he think-I-canned himself up the steep approach, past the alarm and the security gate and the fence. Home free.

9

DOG YEARS

This is a story without a head because while I am telling you this story its head is rolling down Lebowa Road in front of a taxi with defective brakes!

Mhda was trying to recruit workers for a new business venture he had in mind and as so often happened he began his pitch with bombast and a touch of the rhetoric for which he was so justly famed. But now, looking round at his youthful audience, he determined to lower the tone of his grandiloquence.

Those were the days (he began again) when the township smelled of burning petrol, of charred meat and human hair. In those days we picannins learned to run so fast that we'd burn holes in our shoes. But there was no money for new shoes—we'd have to patch the old ones with tire treads. When the police wanted to keep the kids from running away they came and confiscated our shoes. That way they thought we couldn't escape. *Ha!* not us, we just polished our feet with whitener and ran away again!

When the expected laughter failed to materialize, Mhda once more took stock of his audience. A couple of generations ago African children were taught to cast their eyes down as a sign of respect for their elders but that generation was long gone. Boldly, arrogantly, the young stared out at the world or, shifty-eyed, they glanced away with looks full of contempt.

But Mhda was not one to dwell in the past, far from it, and so rather than regretting the past he set about trying to solve the present. Now he stubbed his cigarette out on the side of the oil drum upon which he was sitting and beckoned the band of ten-and eleven-year-old street kids closer as if by this very gesture to invite them into his office, as if by this intimacy he was saying: Look ma'gents, I have a little problem which together and to our mutual benefit I think we might be able to solve.

Look ma'gents (he leaned closer) only think of the opportunity! A yellow duster, two cans of Nugget, a couple of bricks. Think of the tips, people! I provide the outlay—Madiba Mhda, at your service! You guys, my band of shoe polish boys—excuse me—Freedom Band Shoe Brothers, you my bras, you must learn to crack your dusters in the air, learn to open your eyes wide, learn to loosen purse strings with the wattage of your smiles. Go forth ma'gents, turn every shoe into a mirror, tell your customer that just by walking down the street he will be able to see every pair of legs, every pair of panties, every hot *ntepa* in the city—

Mhda faltered but the boys were leaning forward. It seemed he'd finally caught their attention. Whipping the pen from behind his ear he began jotting down names upon the employee contracts that he had extracted from the depths of his brown cardboard suitcase.

The city-wide stay-at-home strike had been called for the following day and Madiba Mhda, entrepreneur and investor, was worried. To say the least. As so often happened these days, Mhda's gut writhed as if a giant shongolulu was eating him up from the inside out, turning over the earth in his bowels, swallowing until his intestines curled tight, sizzling gently as these very same shongolulus curled and sizzled on hot summer pavements.

Astride his antiquated motorbike, his Chisa, Mhda swung a right through Rockey Street deciding to ignore the pain in his belly just as he ignored the blood in the toilet bowl, the steepening nausea that overcame him in the heat of the day so that he was often forced to duck down a side street and vomit quickly and efficiently into the gutter. *Yoh yoh yoh*, perhaps he was dying! After all he wouldn't be the first, far from it! But Mhda didn't think so, for death would have to be swift indeed to catch up with the Taxi Man. As for stomach cures, he'd already sampled his share: untreated sea water (transported from the coast and sold on the black market, ha-ha, a lucrative sideline so far as it went but otherwise ineffective), castor oil, Epsom Salts, milk of magnesia, cream of tartar, digestive tablets, and an assortment of stomach pills and potions from the Ngaka Surgery in town. Even that odd fellow, bra Mustapha, had pressed upon him a traditional Indian remedy for indigestion, *Sat-isab-gol*, which had come highly recommended by Auntie Whatever but which tasted like Eno's Fruit Salts and had the same dyspeptic effect. The free clinic doctor had prescribed a bottle of yellow capsules and a box of dubious powders, and through various sources, licit and less than, Mhda had partaken of liver pills, kidney balms, heart restoratives, a submarine-like suppository, and a wicked dose of chocolate-flavoured senna pods, natural but like so much else in nature, explosive.

Just last week, Portia, his favourite shebeen queen, a comely Bapedi lass from Limpopo Province, had introduced Mhda to the kiwi fruit with its legendary curative properties. Very good for the stomach, she assured him. But alas, the acidic fruit had no effect on Mhda save for the childlike glee he experienced when he first discovered the unexpected green flesh hidden inside its dreary husk.

In turn Mhda had run, clogged up and bogged down until, weary of allowing His Majesty the stomach to constrict his life, he'd divested himself of all the pills and ointments, capsules, powders, potions and tablets, flushing them down the toilet after a particularly protracted visit to that malodorous throne of dishonour.

E-nough. What would be would be.

Besides, the snuff helped a little, the unaccustomed cane spirits a great deal more, an occasional fat joint or something stronger taken in through the nose in deep, aching snorts. And perhaps Mhda's justly-celebrated high spirits helped most of all, despite the roving pains, to keep him buoyant if not honest. Meanwhile his luck remained elusive and this was an excellent sign, Mhda was certain, in matters of the heart.

As for Chisa, as Mhda jovially called his motor scooter, well, she was still burning up the heat as her name indicated. Like an old whore, sprightly but past her prime, her lipstick a bright slash of crimson confidence, she no longer attracted attention except in the misalliance between her ambition and her decrepitude. Might as well call her *Seraga-mabje*, laughed Portia, referring to the Sepedi phrase for stone-kicker and to the manner in which the scooter catapulted down the street in short, destructive bursts. Nevertheless—and this was why Mhda adored the old Chisa—patched though she was, headlights awry, tail lights and signals largely absent, front fender held together with duct tape, rear fender gone the inexplicable way of shock absorbers, mirror, muffler, and kickstand (the exhaust angled off like a dislocated limb and, as if to correct this imbalance, the right handlebar twisted up like a bull's horn); despite the fuel tank (pocked) and the cylinder head (popped), Mhda's trusty Chisa was possessed of a curious, fluttering self-assurance. Battered, buckled, the plucky survivor of miscellaneous crashes and misadventures, she was the one thing that still responded to his golden touch, coughing her way into obliging life whenever Mhda turned his key in her ignition.

Such singular allegiance lent Mhda confidence in the rest of his affairs. Soon, he reasoned, his Dhlamina-Queen, his aboLovey, would capitulate, turn to him with butter in her mouth and honey in her eyes. Soon he would be presented with a son and heir (if not this child then the next), a living piece of coal to bank up the fires of immortality. And when that time came, Mhda speculated, revving past the jazz clubs and beer halls on Rockey, past darkened stores crouching behind rolled metal shutters and iron grilles, past drunks puddling on corners, the night women in their heels stepping high, when that blissful time arrived he must be ready to strike.

Meanwhile Mhda couldn't ignore his creditors, the men he was obliged to reimburse for services rendered, the rollbacks and anticipatory costs, the bakshir and gratuities, the graft and cuts and tips and bribes, the security money, the ponsella, the goodwill, the blood-from-a-stone, skin-of-the-teeth pay-offs. And neither could he ignore anymore the empty *stokvel* fund and the township elders who seemed to have gotten wind of the situation and were, even now, sniffing for his blood. Hence this midnight run, this attempt to hold his creditors at bay before the strike began and his last chance to put things right disappeared entirely and forever like the reputation of a man who can neither control his woman nor subdue his ill fortune.

In truth, matters were growing desperate.

More than.

Mhda clapped a hasty hand to the inner pocket of his leather jacket where he'd arranged his envelopes, money he hoped to fling into the paths of the various furies that stalked him these days. Might slow them down, he thought, might give them pause.

Might.

Trouble with this city, grumbled Mhda swinging an illegal left into Louis Botha, trouble was that it had lost its memory. So much had changed in three or four short years that the people no longer remembered the time before, the terrible years of the Emergency and before; the years of passbooks and detentions and forced removals when the life of a black man must be measured in dog years, a mere twelve months trailing seven years worth of hardship and grief in its wake. Hah, in those days a boy of twelve was as bruised by experience as an old man or a windfall. But now, *hee banna*, might as well try to store water in a cracked pot, might as well throw beer in the fire as discover a man who could accurately recall the stench of the old days.

Forgive and forget, admonished Portia; that is the way to cure the stomach. Forgive but do not forget, advised old Mandela; that is the way to cure the heart. And Mhda, who suffered both from the stomach and from the heart, Mhda who suffered also from memory, took his ease where he could: speed, the feel of the wind on his skin, the companionable knock-cough of his engine, and the headlights of the approaching cars that dipped and blazed in the dark reminding him that memory, like right of way, is best yielded the moment before impact.

On the other hand, Mhda reminded himself, and one always had to take account of *both* hands in this game of life, on the other hand, the people still remembered certain matters. Election promises, for

instance, slogans, battle cries. A chicken in every pot, one party comrade had promised in the first spasms of democracy: a BMW in every
carport, a swimming pool in every backyard, a Jacuzzi in every bathroom and a bathroom—no, two, *three* bathrooms—in every mansion. Now the people wanted their BMWs, their swimming pools, their
Jacuzzis, their bathrooms and, oh yes, a couple of juicy chickens—that
would be good for a start. It was no wonder that the city was disas-
sembling itself through a series of rotating strikes and consumer boy-
cotts and go-slows and lock-outs and embargoes. No wonder that the
unions were growing so powerful that they were able to persuade the
people to arrive punctually, peacefully, one day, stay home the next;
work to rule some days, on others to go slow or lock up or down tools
entirely. On the *other* hand—how many hands was that now? surely
enough for a game of poker!—on the other hand, the unions were
unsubtle in their persuasions, employing gangs of roving thugs who
lay in wait for commuters at the train station, at the transport depot,
at every taxi rank and bus stop on the way into town. And woe betide
the anxious wage earner or family man, threatened by his employers
with dismissal, who turned up for work only to be humiliated, beat-
en, divested of his cash, his lunch packet, his dignity. His clothes torn
and his progeny cursed.

Uh-huh, sighed Mhda, pinching the filter of his last Marlboro
between two fingers and flinging the butt over his shoulder.

In his travels about the city Mhda had come across every sort
of prejudice and it no longer surprised him to consider the variety
and vigour of hatemongering that existed between people who had
only recently escaped the worst of oppressions. Everyone had their
own best worst enemy, and these enemies had theirs, and everywhere
there thrived the pleasure in others' downfall that Mhda didn't think
reflected well on his people. But who were his people? The Xhosas
hated the Zulus, the Zulus hated the Pedis, and everyone blamed the
Nigerians for the spread of AIDS, those foreigners, *makwerekwere*,
those nonsense-talkers whose speech was so much babble—*kwere
kwere, kwere kwere, kwere kwere.*

Méira Cook

The respectable women hated the *lekgosha*, the prostitutes who beguiled their men, and the street smart *lelaenara* jolla boys hated the new breed of trendy black businessmen who played squash at the Health and Racquet Club and flashed designer sunglasses and cell phones and the keys to imported sports cars.

Tcha, it was a mess, thought Mhda, revving vehemently. One must either think like a thief or run the risk of finding oneself stretched flat on the ground, the pavement pushed up against one's face. In other words, mugged! Those were the options; one was either *for* or *against* a person, a cause, a political party. In that case perhaps it was, after all, the fault of history. Not the whites or the blacks, not the politicians or the workers, not the people, but History itself, thought Mhda, upon which we must all choke as if on tiny, inedible chicken bones. And that's why this country sickens and convulses, this choking is our way of ridding ourselves of History. Mhda grinned suddenly, proud of his analogy. Yes, History was the breathless pause, the last gasp. History was the bone in the throat.

Retch, retch, he laughed as he gunned his way through a series of traffic lights all indicating Stop! but such was his hilarity that halting at the mere suggestion of civil obedience was about the very last thing he could have done.

At such times, despite the weightiness of his mission and the disrepair into which his life had so recently fallen, Mhda felt a sudden pride that was as unexpected as it was welcome. The feeling began with a pricking sensation in the region of his chest reminding him of how the city poet had described the old warrior chief Shaka Zulu, with nerves "as sharp as syringa thorns." Mtshale himself had once been a messenger on a scooter delivering office mail and parcels all over the city and Mhda astride his Chisa felt a kinship with the poet.

Nerves as sharp as syringa thorns, he repeated, banging himself heartily against his breastbone.

For it could not be denied that a man required nerve to succeed in this world. Before departing on this evening's undertaking Mhda had obtained news that yet another of his taxis had received a death blow, this one brought about by nothing more nor less than profound foolishness, the *mbongolo* in question never having owned an alarm clock or a wristwatch and so remaining ignorant of the significance of the clockwise hand motions required of the passenger seated at the window to the driver's left. It transpired that the deceased passenger, a migrant labourer from across the boarder, had merely been waving his arms about idly but unbeknown to him their movements had roused the ire of taxi drivers in competing lanes.

Fucken *amaguduka*! Bloody migrant! the driver had yelled, surveying the burnt-out wreck of his taxi which had been in pretty good condition for a ten-year-old minivan with no indicators and faulty brakes.

Now the driver had come to Mhda demanding insurance for his wrecked vehicle, calling him a stray dog and heaping indignities upon his head when it soon became apparent that he was drawing from a dry well. Strangely enough the other customers seemed to delight in Mhda's loss of face and even the queue marshals joined in with taunts and cries of *Phansi ngo Mhda, phansi!* Down with Mhda!

It was no wonder that after such a thuggish encounter, and one for which he was so ill prepared, Mhda felt the need to console himself with yet another business venture, a scheme by means of which he might recoup his losses, replace his depleted funds, and—who knows?—even return to that exalted state of flourishing prosperity it had once been his good fortune to inhabit. But what to do? With his mind occupied in this manner Mhda almost failed to see the gaping hole in the road until it was too late. But luck sharpened his eyes and quickened his reflexes at the last moment and he was able to swerve.

Hee monna, who was stealing all the manhole covers? he wondered angrily.

Grumbling, cursing under his breath, Mhda rode on until, presently, an idea formed and he began to smile.

Wola kawu, called Funny Galore in greeting. *Wola*, bra Mhda!

Hey, *madoda*, Mhda waved at his old comrade who'd acquired his nickname, Fanagalo, by mimicking the pidgin spoken by the mine boys. Old Funny Galore was a stiff-necked one, *untamo-lukhuni* as they said. A hard-head, a right-winger, even.

Mhda had come downtown to Fanagalo's Twist Street headquarters to find out more about the stay-at-home strike and its likely fallout because if anyone had an ear to the ground it was his childhood friend who was being paid by the unions to report instances of strike-breaking on the part of management. Fanagalo, like Mhda, had been born in Kumalo Street in Thokoza Township but at night they'd sneak into the Whites-only drive-in where, with the other township kids, they'd stare at the soundless, flickering screen and cheer for the bad guys. But Fanagalo couldn't divest himself of the images of those swaggering villains and, watching him, Mhda could see that his friend was in his element now. Striding down Twist Street in his vast, tractor-tread runners, drinking Castle Milk Stout from an old mayonnaise jar, a cell phone cocked to one ear, he'd broken step to heckle his old mate.

Hey hey, Mr. Taxi! Better hope COSATU call off the strike otherwise bang goes this month's profit, eh?

Tcha. Why you want to give me grief, bra? If the taxis run who is there to board them—if transport stops then how must I still pay my drivers? And for what? You think the union bosses care what happens if the workers eat, if they don't eat? Do you think *their* tables will be bare next week, you think *their* stomachs will be empty?

It was true. Mhda spoke for many, *too* many, workers who resented the threats and intimidation that would keep them from their jobs during the lucrative Christmas season when money flowed from an open faucet and the matter of year-end bonuses and ponsella and Christmas boxes hung in the balance. But Fanagalo, capering foolishly, oversized shoes flapping on the grimy pavement, was not to be deterred. To the tune of a popular song he caroled:

> *Egoli-goli-goli-e-e-goli!*
> *City of Gold*
> *Don't leave me*
> *Oo-ou-t in the cold, goli-goli-e-e-goli!*

Ai Kona. Mhda was angry at his friend for playing the fool, for gum-booting it in this undignified fashion. Eyeing the deep-cut treads of Fanagalo's expensive runners he said: Be careful, my friend, because one day you are certain to step in some fancy dog shit with your fancy shoes. *Pasop*!

In the old days such uncharacteristic ill will would have had a sobering effect on the object of his scorn but Fanagalo continued to caper and sing and Mhda had no choice but to register his disgust in the form of a glistening spitball, a classic pavement gobstopper.

Hey!

Mhda turned.

Don't blame me, china. At the meetings they're saying four, five days and we'll bring the restaurants and fast food chains down. Give us a week to close the supermarkets, then the malls. By the end of the month every caffy and coffee shop, it will be shut tighter than a whore's mouth. *Amandla*, we must bring them to their *knees*, my friend!

Mhda had to laugh. And he guffawed every time he thought of Fanagalo's words, imagining the jowly brokers at the stock exchange, the shopkeepers and restaurateurs in the suburbs, the wily "special price for you, madam" merchants who plied their wares around the Oriental Plaza, the Portuguese Greengrocers and the Greek Caffy owners all over the city. Each one pulling up their trouser legs and creakily, cartilage-crackingly, kneeling to the workers who, come tomorrow or the next day or the next, simply would not turn up to their jobs.

Meanwhile, the horizon was so sharp it cut the eye and the sky stretched thin over the bare bones of heaven and with each breath the people gasped and panted as if they were inhaling chalk but despite the drought and the heat and the dust the city was dreaming of a white Christmas. Of course it would take swathes of cottonwool, kilometres of tinsel, wild blizzards of paper snowflakes to achieve such a miracle in the freakish heat of this rogue season, and even then. Reindeers and elves leapt crazily across their harnesses and into the piped air of shopping malls while heavily robed Father Christmases of all creeds and colours, as the newspapers proclaimed, sweated themselves to precisely the same degree of enervation as they drooped in parking lots and at crossroads, wearily ringing their bells and palming donations.

In the coffee suburbs the wire-boys gaped forlornly on the sidewalks. Their feet dangling in the gutters, they twisted lengths of silver wire and copper thread between dexterous hands and strong white teeth, fashioning stars and angels and pyramid-shaped Christmas trees while the beggars at traffic lights held up their "No Job and Nothing to Eat" signs mumbling "God Bless" with each tinkle of change dropped into cap or tin can or outstretched palm. Throughout the Oriental Plaza, Christmas decorations were especially elaborate, the rustle of bunting and tinsel and trailing bows competing with the crackle and static of afternoon prayers relayed by loudspeaker from the roof of a nearby mosque. *Merry Xmas!* read the fringed gold and red banners in shop windows all over the city, and *Geseënde Kersfees!* and *Keresemose ee Monate Masego Nala!* and *o Bene Khisemose ee Monande!* but everyone knew that there would be an end to the merry-merry and the happy-happy as soon as the strike began, as soon as the toyi-toyi dancers lined up in the streets, a lead voice incanting: "u-Nelson Mande-e-ela!" (*uBabawethu*, the dancers would reply, *i-Chief commander!*). Or, perhaps, if vilification was the order of the day: "Gat-sha Buthele-e-ezi!" (*Voetsak! Humba!*).

Ah, but one mustn't pick at the scab of history, Mhda chided himself. For what would one discover but the raw and bloody knee underneath! Chuckling in appreciation of his wit, Mhda gunned down Twist Street and made his way back towards the taxi ranks abutting Joubert Park.

In truth, Mhda was heartily sick of Christmas and all that it promised year after year but failed to deliver: peace and goodwill, a day of rest, a quiet smoke, a tender bone to gnaw and a family to call his own. *Yebo*, fat chance. Besides, the glare of the sun careening off tinsel and glitter made his eyes water, the rooting of sirens and ambulances toting up the holiday death toll clashed oddly with the sugar-water carols blaring from speakers all over the city. On every street corner Salvation Army marching bands boomed their brassy hymns, pa-ram-pampa-ing and fa-la-la-ing their way through the season to the jeers and brickbats of those rendered less than festive by last minute shopping and the bulging heat.

As for saviours, Mhda hated to admit it but he much preferred the warrior-like Shaka Zulu whom History reported had torn his own son apart, than the milky white God-boy whose picture the missionaries had handed around at Lebowa School. The Christ looked like an undernourished bra with his pink-rimmed eyes and his skinny wrists nailed hard to the wooden cross. Thorns in his hair.

Nerves as sharp as syringa thorns.

No fine, well Mhda had seen plenty of corpses and assuredly they didn't look like that one did. Even long ago when he'd first been introduced to Comrade Christ in the school primer (a ring of angels blowing cool air on his temples), Mhda had known what a body turned into after it was beaten, strung up by the limbs. Arms wrenched from their sockets, sinews broken, the downward thrust of meat spinning on a hook.

No, Madiba Mhda, Taxi Man, had only ever anticipated one miracle birth.

This is a story without a head, began Mhda who had once again gathered his street boys around him. Members of the recently formed Freedom Band Shoe Brothers were there and others: the forgotten vagrants whose numbers remained more or less constant although their faces were often different, their bodies merely replacing the bodies of those of their companions who had disappeared, died, dried up and blown away for all anyone knew.

Listen ma'gents (Mhda began again) don't be like the bridegroom who wakes up the day after all the merrymaking and joy only to discover that he's dead! I say to you live your life to the full, I say to you—no, no come back, sit down! All right I'll get straight to the point, people. I, Madiba Mhda, I am willing to pay cash in hand, money down and no questions asked for all varieties of scrap metal wherever you find it and whatever it may be—hubcaps, ball bearings, fenders. Yes, even manhole covers, ma'gents, if you are strong enough and brave enough to lift them.

Mhda paused. He gazed about the impassive faces of the newly formed Democracy Scrap Metal Boys but it wasn't their faces he was seeing. The future opened up bright and abundant before him as he imagined his boys picking the streets clean of scrap metal: water main covers, wrought iron fencing, the numbers on a garden gate or the burglar bars off a factory warehouse.

Hee banna, ma'gents, Mhda sighed.

People, he continued, the world is yours for the taking. Only believe.

Magda lay awake, her heart pounding. She'd been dreaming about the dead cats again, and it seemed to her that the stink and the flies had entered her very sleep. She tried to calm herself down, breathing deeply and turning her thoughts to pleasant things and presently her heart stopped racing and her pulses slowed. But sleep still eluded her. *Ag, what* was the matter with her? Magda sighed. Perhaps it was that she was simply unused to sharing her home with a guest, any guest, let alone the one sleeping between lilac-scented sheets in her mother-in-law's old room. But with the strike looming it had become impossible to send Dhlamina home.

Since Dhlamina had taken to driving the old two-toned Anglia she no longer needed to rely on the peripatetic minibus taxis to transport her to and from the township but the newspapers were reporting widespread road blocks on routes into town. And it was clear that if Magda was to continue to enjoy the pleasure of her company, not to mention the slightly more profound pleasures of her malva brandy pudding, the orange glazed sauce and the candied friandise for which the imported mandarins, even now, were ripening on the kitchen window sills, then she must not be allowed to travel the perilous highway. Not this year.

These days Dhlamina spent all her spare time riffling through *Mrs. Moffert,* her charming dimple working busily and her gold tooth flashing, as she ran through cooking techniques and ingredients, occasionally pausing to cluck indignantly. *Blanch* you say, hmm? Glancing into the kitchen of an afternoon, Magda was startled at the felicitous picture Dhlamina made as she leaned against the sink, one finger running down a column of weights and measures, her forehead wrinkled around the perplexing problem of converting one pound of russet potatoes into how many kilos? The late afternoon sunlight seemed to turn up the glow beneath her skin and her body, under the tight harness of her bright African print, appeared charming and marsupial and not at all the hard bulge of belly that Magda had imagined it to be, always threatening to capsize ornaments or knock Wedgwood display plates from their easels.

Maybe not so safe to drive backwards and forwards, *meisie?* These days, hey? Magda hazarded.

Don't worry about the car, Mrs. Magda, I'll be careful.

Scalded, Magda hastened to reassure Dhlamina that she was the sole object of her Madam's concern and in the process was so solicitous that she somehow found herself pressing upon her a bed for the night, indeed as many nights as were required before the roads were again traversable by one in her delicate condition.

Yebo, Mrs. Magda. Dhlamina watched Magda's flailings from far away, too hot to try to rescue her from the shoal of agonized good manners upon which she was shipwrecked.

You must take out clean sheets and see if you can find the guest towels and the Lux soap and … gracious, whatever else you need.

Spluttering, gesticulating, Magda indicated with a wave of her hand that the apartment and all its contents were at her maid's disposal but, in truth, she had no very firm notion of how to make the other woman comfortable. And a black woman at that, a *pregnant* black woman. And now here was Dhlamina, asleep in the room that had once been her mother-in-law's and Magda couldn't imagine, she really couldn't imagine, what the old lady would have had to say about such a guest.

Presently the Ormolu clock on the mantelpiece struck twelve announcing in tripping semi-quavers the night's slow rotation on its fulcrum of worry and inertia.

Ah-a-*hem*.

Dhlamina was enjoying the old woman's bed. She had pulled off the blankets and the counterpane and was sitting cross-legged on the lilac-scented sheets, threading beads and making up outlandish phrases for the Zulu love letter she was composing.

Lalelani Rra-baki! Listen, Mr. Suit! The woman you love is not a shank bone so don't you dare show her your teeth!

Giggling, she pulled the last of the turquoise beads through the slipstitch of the pattern she was creating and cut the double-knotted thread with her teeth. There.

Dhlamina had recently run into Tuesday Dube who was still making love to the tourists. Indeed, so successful was she, she told Dhlamina, that she now required part-time seamstresses. Would Dhlamina consider becoming one of her shift workers, one of the merry band of women whose only qualifications were a sense of humour and a cunning needle? Dhlamina would. She liked the chance of extra cash what with the water baby's imminent arrival, she liked the opportunity for irreverence that the beaded messages provided, and she liked Tuesday who was both wicked and clever; Tuesday whom she'd known from her first rooming house when her friend had been weighed down with the responsibility of the children she was rearing and who were now "grown up you say?"

Tuesday had laughed. Yes, even the baby! So what do you say, Dhlamina, girl, you want to become one of *Tuesday's Children*?

Dhlamina had indeed become one of *Tuesday's Children* which was the hugely successful label that her enterprising friend had developed and the two had begun to spend afternoons together threading beads and inventing erotic or mischievous or comical Zulu love letters to fool the tourists and loosen their fists as Tuesday put it who wasn't Zulu or even Ndebele, had never been taught the craft of beading and neither did she hold any reverence for the ancient tribal art but *hee banna*, this was the New South Africa, was it not? Listening to Tuesday take down orders and talk to customers on her cell, Dhlamina had to laugh. For Tuesday was a terrible tease and a first-class business-woman and with these two qualities she'd transformed the desultory curio enterprise of "Zulu Love Beads" into an art form. Her first large mounted beadwork "installation," as she called it, was entitled *Rainbow Nation.*

"Red is for our blood and orange for the flames of our passion and indigo—indigo is for the bruises we suffered on our bodies and our souls." When Tuesday showed Dhlamina the interview she'd given the journalist from *The Citizen*, and that he'd included in his ecstatic review of her work at Jive Art Gallery in Newtown, the two women stuck their hands on their hips and roared with laughter.

And yellow is for the urine we let loose on the heads of our oppressors!

And green is for the grass that grows on the graves of our enemies!

Ha ha ha!

Ah, suka!

Dhlamina sighed and shifted on the bed. She plumped up the old woman's pillows to pack against her back so that she could stretch luxuriously and admire the length of her legs that even at this late stage of pregnancy had not begun to swell with water or ripple with veins. Her skin gleamed with cocoa butter.

The great thing about Tuesday was that she made Dhlamina laugh. Just yesterday the two women had been reduced to wet rags of merriment by her story of the tourist who'd tried to purchase a pendant from the *Mayibuye Afrika* range. "Come Back Africa" was a popular series of jewellery designs in Tuesday's trademark colours of carmine, turquoise, and deep earth browns. But the rich American's misunderstanding of the old struggle slogan which had resulted in her halting request—excuse me, ma'am, *May I buy Africa?*—had thrown the two friends into such a prolonged state of hysterical laughter that they'd grown weak and limp and been unable to finish threading the preliminary strands to a design that Tuesday now confided had been specially commissioned for an exhibition to celebrate the city's inaugural Bead Art Project.

But no rainbows, okay? Tuesday was still laughing as she outlined her idea to Dhlamina.

In the darkness of her own room Magda was still searching in vain for a cool place on the pillow. Lately she had begun to sense malevolence in the air, a crooked energy that seemed to gather in the corners of the flat. As if the sun had suddenly reversed its course and was shining through the wrong windows. Shadows fell awkwardly and aligned themselves in impossible formations. Light broke through windowpanes and glass shattered.

Overnight, practically over*night* Magda told herself, the old accustomed rooms seemed to itch with restlessness. There was an impatient tilt to the angle of the photographs on the mantelpiece and a positive fury in the hang of the drapes. It didn't take long to recognize her dear mother-in-law's presence but something seemed to be bothering the old lady these days for there was nothing gracious about the peremptory clatter of curtain rings on their brass rods or the ceiling fan that started up of its own accord and agitated the thin skin of dust that had collected all day under the cornice with its plaster festoons of cherubs.

Ah-a-*hem*.

Perhaps, thought Magda, it was simply the heat. Certainly it had become too hot to do much of anything except wake and sleep, drag oneself out of bed and sit stunned beneath the windless trees of Wisteria Gardens. And yet people were such fools! Why, only that morning she'd glanced outside to see that her neighbours, the Papenfus sisters, had apparently taken leave of their senses. The two old girls, dressed in ancient bathing suits, had spread themselves out in the sun. Already their milk-white shanks and freckled arms were reddening fiercely. Get inside, get inside! *Kom binne!* called kind Mrs. Ferreira, even sending her maid outside to collect the foolish women. But the maid, dazzled and distracted, had wandered off and the Papenfus sisters continued to crisp in the sun.

Rotating, thought Magda as she hurried out to remonstrate with the pair, like chickens on a rotisserie.

On her way inside she'd come across Dhlamina and her new friend. They were sitting on the outside steps and cackling as they tended to do more and more these days. The friend, the one with the large bottom and the beaded jewellery, was going on about people who wanted to change from one colour to another and Dhlamina was holding her stomach and guffawing.

White to brown is very fashionable, now, very sexy to turn into a *dudlu* girl! But in the old days just let them catch you in a Whites-only area. Oho, not so good then, Miss Coppertone Bronze, hey!

I beg yours? Trying to push past their outstretched legs Magda couldn't rid herself of the feeling that she was being baited. But the women shifted obligingly and she soon gained the safety of the corridor. Looking back she could see the Papenfus sisters still burning fiercely in the midday sun.

Ah, it was the heat, no question. In Wisteria Gardens, a decorous complex if ever there was one, internecine spats had already declared themselves. Rumour had it that floors four through six were lodged in an irreconcilable laundry war while Mrs. Khusaf and Mrs. Ferreira, once the best of friends, had fallen out over old Mrs. Ferreira's dog, a pug of irreproachable virtue but who was apparently unable to control his bowels in the unseasonable weather, and who had, for the past four days, as Mrs. Khusaf confided to Magda in the stifling intimacy of the elevator, made doggie do-do on her doorstep.

One, two, three, four. *Four* days! Her voice rising as she crossed off each desecrated day on her trembling fingers.

In truth the heat didn't bother Magda as much as all that for she was cold-blooded, as she liked to say. Every evening, when the heat had abated somewhat, she would take a turn about the gardens and it was on returning from one of these walks that she discovered the fierce, scarred man striking matches on her doorstep.

Where's Dhlamina? he'd glared in answer to Magda's murmured inquiry.

Throat closing with enmity, her armpits scorching, Magda had pushed past the devil on her doorstep to insert her key into the Art Nouveau trellis of the security grille and the fierce one, growing ever more belligerent with each tumble of the lock, had lowered his brows and looked like he was about to attack, yes, actually to at*tack* her.

Luckily, Dhlamina, who must have been listening out for Magda, suddenly swung open the door. Sliding past her bulk Magda sank gratefully into an armchair, her heart beating heavily. How in blazes had that vandal, that tsotsi, got into the complex anyway? she wondered. Meanwhile, Dhlamina, one hand holding the door closed, was scolding the stranger. The rise and fall of her voice, ragged, hoarse with dust and anger, seemed to spike like a fever. To Magda's surprise, the commotion had lasted only a few moments, Dhlamina's indignant anger levelling off with the receding tread of the stranger's footsteps. In quick succession the front door, then the kitchen door, had been knocked shut followed by a ferocious clatter of pots and pans.

Who was that? Magda asked later over her only slightly burnt omelet. Dhlamina bent over her awkwardly, wringing the neck of the pepper-mill with a certain residual hostility. She steadied herself with one hand against Magda's shoulder and Magda was suddenly disarmed by the intimacy of the gesture. Who was he, that tsotsi? But Dhlamina only pointed to her belly, clicked her tongue and tossed her braids. Soon after, she crooned herself off to bed, extracting a pair of lavender-scented guest towels from the old lady's hope chest and lugging off the much-bespattered *Mrs. Moffert*.

In the dark of her room Magda continued to turn sleeplessly. Her pulse seemed to be jumping about like a cricket. Not the slow, steady *tick-tick* of sprinklers in summer gardens or the imperious *tick* (pause) tock-k of the Ormolu on the mantle. Was it anxiety that kept her awake, *nerves*, or something else? The spirit of her dear mother-in-law who would *not*, Magda knew, approve of the addition to their household, her well-remembered pique pulsing through what remained of the night in heated wafts of tea rose and orange water.

Agitating the air like carpet beaters.

Dhlamina was tired.

She gathered up her beads, her thread, the stretched canvas on which she'd been working, and put them aside. For a few moments she turned the pages of *Mrs. Moffert's Inquire Within* but she soon grew listless. Closing the majestic volume she couldn't help noticing that the book looked a little the worse for wear. The dust jacket was folded over and torn, the colour illustrations were faded, and some of her favourite recipes were too smeared with sauce to be read anymore. Even the finger-holds that had been cut out on the sides of the pages and that made it easy to find one's place, felt sticky. A sudden gust of disapproval seemed to blow through the room.

Dhlamina shivered.

From outside came the sound of the municipal street cleaner's truck brushing at the road with its hard circular brushes, shovelling wastepaper and refuse into the gutters. Every few moments the nozzle in front squirted out a thin jet of greasy water to slick down the street. In the tail lights the macadam unspooled behind the municipal vehicle with its sleepy, disgruntled crew. From her window Dhlamina watched as the moon followed the truck, darting in and out of the pools of water, in fragments.

Somehow, Portia Ngubane, the voluptuous hostess of Marengenya Shebeen, managed to convince her boss that she needed cash chop-chop. The homebrew supply was low, she explained, waggling her dipped-in-blood fingernails at him, and the whiskey, the KWV, the ale and the spirits also needed to be topped up. Thus Mhda was obliged to part with his last skimpy wad of notes before revving at full tilt down the highway. A gurgle of incredulous laughter accompanied him because Portia wasn't used to getting the better of Madiba Mhda, the one who deposited a sprinkling of deceptive gold dust when he shook your hand.

Hoo-hoo-hoo! she guffawed, her head flung back. It seemed that the Taxi Man was losing his touch.

Keep out of the puddles, Mhda! Keep out! his old crony Fanagalo called after him, strutting up and down like a praise poet for Portia's benefit.

Phuza-faced mbongolo! yelled Mhda over his shoulder. *Drunken fool! Dustbin scavenger!*

And, after a moment's thought: DIKWATA!

This last was a model of effrontery and referred to the fact that Fanagalo was reputed to mix the Castle Milk Stout that he relished and drank by the bucketful into his mieliepap like a hostel dweller.

Ho, you lie! May ringworm and lice be your lot, crabs and rickets and lovelessness!

Fanagalo flung his words at Mhda but the tail lights of the trusty Chisa had long disappeared by this time and Fanagalo, who was as full of beer as a tick is tight with blood, remained capering on the pavement until Portia extracted a couple of coins from an impossibly small purse, so puckered and red and softly leather that Fanagalo, worn out by alcohol though he was—*babelas*, as they say—was visited by an unaccustomed stab of lust and retreated behind a trestle table jingling his coins in confusion.

Mhda pointed the scooter towards Hillbrow where night-clubbers and revellers flowed into the streets, their shadows lapping his headlights. Their laughter and jeers, the smoke from their cigarettes and the fumes from their liquor pursued him down side streets. From far away, his voice thinned by distance and longing, he seemed to hear Fanagalo call, Keep out of the puddles, Mhda. Keep out!

As he snaked through the alleys and byways of Hillbrow on the Chisa, Mhda's thoughts returned to what had happened earlier at Marengenya Shebeen before Portia had sent him on his way with empty pockets. The talk that night had been on the nature of faith. No-doubt Sithole had been in the midst of a story about an altercation he claimed to have witnessed between a pious old woman and a gang of street thugs. *You want to feel something hard between your legs, you horny old cunt?* they'd taunted her. Although the old woman hadn't understood their words the brutality behind them was unmistakable and her hands had begun to tremble. *Ah, my sons, may God bless you,* she'd managed to mumble before hobbling away on swollen legs to the sound of the young men's coarse laughter. *Hey, mamazala, how about you come sit on my lap?*

No-doubt Sithole had paused to let his audience drink in the spectacle of the old woman's humiliation.

People, what is the function of faith in a broken world? asked the drunken philosopher. There is no doubt in my mind—no doubt at all—that we are set upon this earth to suffer and to die. And does our suffering enrich the kingdom of heaven, does our faith move mountains?

A lively debate had ensued that was interrupted only by the entrance of the street angels who made their usual visit to Marengenya Shebeen at this time and the assembly soon broke up. But as he manoeuvered the Chisa, Mhda continued to ponder the question that No-doubt Sithole had raised like a glass of brown ale and then, in his usual manner, drained to the dregs.

Within the blind alleys and vacant lots of this city, another city, a concealed boneyard of a city, was laid out. Folded into doorways or dank crevices in the walls of abandoned warehouses, one across the other like dogs in a litter, entire families slept. During the day while their parents went begging, the children on their stilt legs lolloped about in ragged little gangs, rooting in garbage bins for food and snapping over the odd charitable bone. But at night they disappeared, packs of them, each child sucked into a child-shaped hole in the bottom of the world. Although children died (their little bodies rotting in storm water drains, in sewers) and more were born, the population of vagrant starvelings, it seemed to Mhda, remained constant. Because every week exactly the same number of children pursued his motorcycle through the alleys that had followed him, jeering, throwing insults and stones, on previous weeks. It remained a conundrum upon which Mhda, bracing himself at the head of a twitching body of children, was unwilling to dwell.

Night jerked slightly under sodium. Every half block or so Mhda passed a spluttering streetlight tapping out its Morse code of panic— Jo *h* burg, Jo *h* burg—the rhythm of the streetlights, the tires on the road, his heartbeat, all seemed to exhale this word, this sigh, and Mhda responded as he always did, with his paean to the city, the one that went:

> *Egoli! City of Gold, City of milk and honey*
> *City of blood and bile*
> *City of blood is thicker than water*
> *And water under the bridge*
> *And throw yourself off the bridge*
> *And drown!*
> *Egoli! City of—*

And on it went. It was an impromptu song in the manner of the old praise singers and in the tradition of the praise singers it sought to express the singer's immediate surroundings—the phlegm-coloured dog hawking into the gutter and the beggar whose hands appeared to be constructed of dirty grey skin stretched over gaunt knuckles:

> *Egoli! We have given you our hearts now you want our throats*
> *To tighten your hands around. Come city!*
> *Pour yourself into us as if you are 10 ngudus of beer*
> *And when we are full*
> *Keep pouring.*
> *Better that the beer drain into the dust*
> *Than not be poured!*

A cockroach in its shiny armour of brown mail scuttled sideways across his path as he navigated an alley burning with the ammoniac stink of urine. *Agee!* yelped Mhda. Behold, Sir Filth! and he skidded to avoid colliding with the miserable creature. Now and then his headlights picked out an oily yellow iris in the night's blank face—beggar? stray cat? tokoloshe?—and Mhda would turn and hawk over his shoulder, his anxiety, as always, collecting in phlegmatic lumps at the bottom of his throat. Good job tomorrow was payday which meant

income from his vendors of whom young Mustapha Hurry-Curry
was surely the most reliable, the most zealous, and certainly the most
ambitious. Yes, Mhda had set him up first-class with low interest rates,
comparatively speaking, and a formidable line of credit, and in return
Mr. Fa was prompt in his payments, devout in his gratitude. On the
other hand, and if ever a man needed two hands then it was in order to
conduct business with sharp so-and-so's, smart *lelaenaras* like young
Hurry-Curry, on the other hand, it seemed as if the boy had cooled
towards his benefactor in recent days. A frown line bisected the scar-
map of Mhda's forehead.

One hand, two hands. Clap clap clap.

Who knew what a boy like that was thinking? All pant and puppy looks in the beginning but now there was a new hardness in his
voice, as if he was speaking to a dog, as if he was warning this dog:
Stay away! *Pasop!* Accusation like an oil spill in his eyes. But what
had Mhda done to earn this contempt? Helped the boy to his feet and
set him up in business? Provided a steady stream of township boys to
preside over his fast food carts and curry wagons? Boys, Mhda was
reminded, that Mustapha took upon himself to *humba wena* whenever the spirit moved him. Yes, just snapped them out of the air with
his fingers and sent them on their way. Then, of course, it was up to
the good Father Mhda to seek out the next boy, and the next after that
one too was sent packing with a cuff on the head and a boot in the rear.

Meanwhile Mhda was losing hope in finding boys to suit his young
protégé. Perhaps our stories are important, Portia once speculated,
because we own very little else. It was at the end of the night and
men sat about the beer hall cradling their heads in their hands. Yes,
very little else, Portia blew these words out with the smoke from her
cheroot and, like the smoke, they seemed to hang in the blue air for
a moment before drifting away. But Mhda was weary of the stories,
the lies people offered him because otherwise their hands were empty.
Also Mustapha was much too intolerant. Only a couple of days ago
he'd decided to fire the cigarette boy. *Yebo*, to stub him out. Said the
bra was too busy with his music when he was supposed to be selling

samosas. And where did he get that smart ghetto blaster anyway, must have been stolen. Must have. Boy said some white guy scored him but Mustapha wasn't a fool, was he?

You like music, bra, you must become a DJ! Mhda teased the youth to placate him and in the hope of forestalling any number of vengeful acts, both minor and major, that doubtless were gathering in the wake of Mustapha's foolish rage.

A DJ, bra Rothman, think about it. Make hundreds in a day, maybe, *thousands* in a week. *Yebo*, millions and millions of rand every year. Raking it in with a pitchfork, no lie. Come Christmas these guys, they take off to Cape Town, the Wild Coast, Plett. They *own* the city, my china. Yup, yup, *yebo*! That's the way to go. Young man like you with promise, what's he doing wearing an apron anyway? You must go and be a DJ bra—

But Mhda's testament was rudely halted by an exclamation from Mr. Fa himself:

Jesus H. Christ, man, what are you talking such bloody nonsense for? Am I a, a *lizard*? Was I born under a *rock*? he demanded of Mhda with that oil and water glare. Do I not know a tsotsi to see one?

Besides, that skelm was frightening away customers with the loud fucken music, he reminded Mhda, and how was poor Mustapha supposed to make a profit if he had no customers?

It was hardly necessary for Mustapha to point out that no profit for Hurry-Curry Inc. meant no profit for anyone else. Viz-and-namely, no profit for Madiba Mhda who looked like he could use a bit of credit these days, *nè*? That was how Mustapha talked, *viz-and-namely* and *etcetingra* and so on and on and Mhda had no fucking idea *what* the boy was talking about but the part about credit, that was true. That was certainly bloody true.

Or perhaps our stories are as unimportant as we are, Portia had whispered later in the dark of the back room, her fingertips coaxing the small of his back.

Ai kona, but it was a hard life sometimes. Mhda sighed deeply because it had become clear to him that no one, not one solitary soul in this world or the next, looked out for Madiba Mhda as he was expected to shelter everyone under his protection. Whether it was Mustapha Hurry-Curry or the luminous light of his life and mother of his child who only that afternoon had sent him on his way with a scowl and a shrug and a flea in the ear when he only wished to escort her home. Because with the strike imminent who knew what dangers lay on the road ahead?

Humba, snapping her fingers at him.

As if he was one of Mustapha's curry boys.

Balanced on the rickety Chisa with the wind flying up over the dash, the road opening in lopsided cones before him, Mhda suddenly regained his sense of humour. As dawn slunk through the back streets and alleyways of Hillbrow, he threw back his head and laughed. And his laughter—louder, more raucous even than the laughter of Portia Ngubane, the voluptuous hostess of Marengenya Shebeen—was the serious laughter of a man kindled by a divine spark, the astonishment, the deep green joy of discovering within a rough brown husk, something ripe and sweet and delicious.

10

HAPPY AFRICA

Ouma was dozing when the tsotsis exploded into the room. Viciously they secured her ankles and wrists with nylon panty-hose, stuffed her underpants in her mouth and abandoned her on the bed while they systematically picked the house clean.

The tsotsis worked quickly but without panic evidently believing their victim to be unconscious, probably dead. Perhaps because on first seeing the two shadows lurch up at her, Ouma had obediently closed her eyes the better to stare death in the face.

Magda fingered the telephone receiver for a moment then thoughtfully replaced it on its cradle. Ouma hardly ever answered the phone any-more but where was Beauty? *Ag*, but it was so hot these days perhaps she was sitting in the garden and who could blame her? Magda herself wished that Dhlamina would go and find a nice cool garden to sit in instead of doing what she was currently doing which was balancing on her hands and knees as, with scant attention to the impropriety of her jutting derriere, she scoured the kitchen floor. All day she'd fussed and finicked, cooking and cleaning, hauling jam jars, sauce bottles, and chutneys out of the refrigerator, briskly wiping down shelves and racks, paying particular attention to the long-neglected egg pockets and the dried vegetable matter at the bottom of the crisper. Good Lord, she'd even defrosted the freezer and reorganized the spice cabinet, and now she was boiling pots in a mixture of vinegar and baking soda so that each vessel became a mirror that reflected her face. Suddenly the whole kitchen was full of bulging Dhlaminas, her gold tooth flashing.

By noon Dhlamina was cross-eyed with heat and exhaustion but still she worked on, her braids taken up in a silk kerchief, her bright trailing skirts hooked behind her in an arrangement from which Magda tried to avert her eyes. Indeed Magda wished, and how fervently, that the woman would get up off her knees and pull herself together, pull the skirt out from between her buttocks and act the Madonna. Yes, she wished that her maid would cease her scrubbing and boiling and for pity's sake was that the smell of tea scones baking?

A fly, fat as a pontiff, fretted the window pane. Magda yawned.

The afternoon heat spiked to a fever, broke. In a voice bolstered by prescience the newscaster on Springbok Radio announced the hourly headlines: death toll on the roads mounting, drought holding firm, the city-wide strike threatening to spread to Natal and the Cape. A fugitive breeze crept through the apartment rustling the palm fronds and puffing at the curtains before petering out.

Exhausted by the heat and the flurry of domestic activity, Magda picked up the telephone receiver once more but she was too enervated to talk to Ouma and, after a moment, merely replaced it.

The Gen was eerily quiet. None of the staff had turned up for work, none of the aides or paramedics, orderlies or cleaners or any of the nurses not already in residence. A mere handful, and those who did were shamefaced, defiant, and more than a little inclined to quarrel. Doctors, some, but most lived in town, drove their own luxury vehicles and so were immune to the intimidation faced by commuters trying to enter the city by way of train stations, Putco buses, and transport taxis. The polished corridors leading off from Emergency, the ranks of bolted-down seats near the dispensary, the stairwells and hallways and wards gaped emptily. Indeed it was the contrast between yesterday's booming chaos and today's echoing silences that unnerved Benjamin most. No longer distracted by the urgencies of trauma and triage he was confronted with drab walls the colour of cloudy urine, long dark corridors, and everywhere, the odour of sickness overlaid with disinfectant. The pre-stressed concrete walls seemed to press down on him swerving off into their several scattered vanishing points and leaving him, suddenly dwarfed, the lone remnant of a human scale clumsily grafted upon the institutional. Only the lino shone, rubbed to a dull liniment gleam by the passage of so many urgent feet.

Just in time Markham came swinging into view rumpled from his shift at the Department of Labour which was what the weary interns had taken to calling Obstetrics. He had a nurse in tow and was telling her the one about the two leprosy patients at Warmbaths.

So the one says to the other *'skies, Meneer, is hierdie been joune of myne?*

Nurse Tsitsi shrugged and cuffed him one. Her story, and the one she was sticking to, was that she didn't understand Afrikaans. Not a word of it. Eight years of Bantu Education notwithstanding, and Markham was always trying to trip her up, coax a chuckle from her just to prove his point. Now he called after her retreating back—*is hierdie joune of myne!* Excuse me, Sir, is this leg yours or mine? Ag, bloody woman, it's not so funny when you have to explain it and besides I saw you crack a smile!

Howzit china, he greeted Benjamin with a half wave. Come upstairs later, the cricket's on.

After his rounds Benjamin stopped in to visit Joe-my-Baby. Despite all predictions to the contrary, Joe-my-Baby had managed to survive his coma, the shock of awakening, successive outbreaks of infection, and a hospital diet of enriched milk and barley soup. Weaned off life support he was learning to prop himself upright using the parallel bars that an enterprising physiotherapist had rigged up over his bed.

Nurse Rita's not so bad, he told Benjamin, grinning broadly as Nurse Rita, who possessed the heart of a lion as everyone knew, beamed upon him fondly.

Oh, *you.*

She batted him playfully on the breastbone so that it was with the image of this sad little buoyant gesture that Benjamin left the ward. For some reason he recalled an afternoon during his residency when he'd emerged alone from a dark movie theatre and stretched suddenly into the light. He'd just come off one of those thirty-six hour shifts and was too wound up to go home and sleep although he'd apparently achieved oblivion sitting upright in the almost empty theatre. A double feature. The light of that crazy long ago afternoon had almost sliced him in two but—stretching, yawning—he'd felt winged, reborn.

Alone again in the office he shared with Markham and two other surgeons, a cubbyhole capsizing with out-of-date periodicals, leatherette copies of various well-thumbed Merck's Manuals, and a grimy coffee machine, Benjamin began leafing through a sheaf of long overdue reports. But, as so often happened whenever he had a moment to himself these days, thoughts of his lover kept intruding. Mustapha who remained, he couldn't help thinking fondly, very funny in his funny little way, was busy building his curry empire, he'd informed Benjamin haughtily, and couldn't be expected to drop everything and retire, say, to an exclusive guest cottage in the Eastern Transvaal for the weekend. And when Benjamin—himself no lover of guest cottages, claustrophobic weekend retreats, and so on—mildly remarked that he wouldn't dream of taking Mustapha away from his business, the boy had lost his temper with a perceptible whoosh followed by the punctuation of a thoroughly slammed receiver. They hadn't spoken since.

Ah, well.

Yawning, grimy with fatigue, Benjamin rearranged a drawer of free samples, discarded expired bottles and blister packs, set about unclogging the coffee machine, and watched part of a desultory test match on the TV set in the staff lounge where the hands of the wall clock still read ten to two and time had stopped forever. Lunch had been slim pickings because the canteen staff hadn't turned up for work, naturally, and soon he was jittery with bitter coffee, stale Chelsea buns, and whatever passed for small talk amongst the skeleton staff of knuckle-cracking doctors gathered in the common room.

It was ten to two again, time to go.

'*Skies, Meneer,* Markham mock-apologized as they collided at the Emergency Entrance where he'd taken himself off for a smoke break. *Is hierdie been joune of myne?*

The streets were largely empty of taxis and commuters, and driving was less like a high-powered video game than Benjamin had ever remembered it being at this time of year. But the shopping malls and pedestrian walkways were thronged with last minute shoppers, and Mercedes and BMWs snarled for space in parking lots gusting with exhaust fumes and bad temper. Wet shirt clutching at his back, hair plastered to his brow, Benjamin suddenly recalled the sad little tap with which Nurse Rita had rewarded Joe-my-Baby's struggle to sit upright.

Oh, *you*!

Suddenly he decided, why not? to take in a matinee. It was so long since he'd wasted an afternoon and besides the movies at the Mall were air-conditioned. Fingertips wincing against the steering wheel, Benjamin executed a cunning U-turn into oncoming traffic, accepting the crescendo of indignant hooting that followed as a well-deserved tribute to his daring.

Oh, you.

I want help I'll ask for it, *skattebol!* I got a tongue in my head, *nè*.

Mustapha was racing through the Oriental Plaza scattering scorn in his wake. The aunties whose polite enquiries had rained down this vitriol upon their heads were taken aback but after a moment they recovered themselves and tittered at his effrontery until even the tops of their arms jiggled in the short sleeves of their saris.

Moenie worry nie, Mustapha called over his shoulder, just don't upset yourselves. Mr. Fa can take care of himself.

Truth to tell, Mustapha was in a state. The encounter with Mhda's chippie had upset him no end—that *hoer-meisie* with her great big sit-upon and her twin suck-its! Mhda must have schemed he'd string him along for a while, thought Mustapha, churning. In the sticky Christmas heat he rushed from store to store buying clothes wildly, trinkets and gewgaws. Anything to rid himself of the interest that he must otherwise pay to Madiba Mhda, Taxi Man. *I Have What You Need!*

Blood money. Filthy lucre.

In the windows of Achmat's Discount Emporium Mustapha spotted a smart button-down shirt with an oxford collar that he thought might do for Benjamin.

Shame. Might suit him, *might*.

But a second glance revealed that the stock in the dusty windows was ancient and the mannequins they'd been pinned onto seemed to have suffered a terrible collision from which only the clothing had survived intact. Pants flapped from missing legs, sleeves rustled back from empty arms and everywhere joints gleamed cruelly.

Perfect.

Giggling, Mustapha skidded into Achmat's Discount Emporium and beckoned to the auntie behind the counter.

Ouma was dying. Her mouth was stuffed with underwear and her arms were twisted above her head, tied at the wrists with nylon stockings. She shut her eyes and tried to slow her breathing to a halt. Not to fool the tsotsis who appeared to have lost interest in her, but to welcome Mister Death who'd come, at last, in this violent but better-late-than-never fashion. Her wrists and ankles throbbed and the throbbing filled her whole body and then the room and then the world.

Time slowed down, panic brief as a sneezing fit rushed to fill the vacuum before it, too, subsided. Her head was a brimming cup of bright pain but as long as she remained still, quiet, the cup wouldn't overflow. But she could not be quiet, she could not lie still. The throbbing began again and seemed to pick her up and throw her about, first one way and then another. *No, not like this!* Ouma thought suddenly. For so long she'd wanted to die but no, she did not want to go like this.

The movie, or at least the half Benjamin had just seen, was a French *flic*, so full of gratuitous drollery and over-elegant slapstick that, by intermission when dial pads lit up all over the cinema as patrons feverishly tried to reconnect with their answering services, he'd had his fill. Now he was back in the car, reversing out of the parking garage and into the afternoon light.

The heat was ferocious; it seemed to loosen the flesh from the bone. But amongst the exhausted palm trees and dusty bougainvillea of the suburbs the effect of the strike was less evident. Benjamin passed a municipal garden with lunch hour picnickers strewn on the scorched grass. Some of the people slept, others talked and argued, sharing a bottle or a smoke. Further along, a road crew had downed tools. But, overalls stripped to their waists, most of the men were simply dozing peacefully in the meager shade of a grader. By the time he crossed the main intersection Benjamin noticed a line of taxis inching along one side of the Mall attended by a straggle of commuters.

Fingers tapping at the burning wheel Benjamin turned into Jan Smuts Avenue, the muffled boom that followed shortly after failing to register as anything more than the speechless, incommunicable voice of the heat.

She wasn't in trouble because the date that the doctor had given her, and which she'd carefully ringed on her calendar, was more than two weeks away. Still, the water baby was blowing bubbles and the bubbles burst against the inside of her belly and the small of her back, filling her up with incandescence as if she was a bottle of soda. Shaken *up*, shaken *hard*. Her stomach was tight with gas and she couldn't rid herself of any of it although she bore down heroically. By mid-afternoon the kitchen and everything in it was so shiny it cut her eyes to look at the gleaming counters, the polished parquet of the floor, the bright jars of preserves and jams. With an *oof-oof* and a gusty *huff*, Dhlamina got down on her hands and knees where the air was cooler. There she crouched, puffing every time a stream of bubbles tightened her belly. That fish-child, water baby, so-and-so! Didn't give her a moment's peace even in this bloody weather.

Just like Mrs. Magda, who also didn't give her any peace but instead pottered about the house like an old lady poking her nose into this and that. How Dhlamina wished that just for once she'd leave her alone with her thoughts and her soapsuds and her bubbles. Suddenly the water baby was ferociously hungry; a square-mouthed, bare-gum baby-hunger that forced Dhlamina to mix up a pan of hasty tea scones from a scribbled recipe on *Mrs. Moffert's* marbled end papers. But no sooner had she set the pan under the grill than the fragrance of heated butter and raisins boscocd Mrs. Magda into the kitchen. Galled, Dhlamina wriggled her haunches at her and she retreated as Dhlamina knew she would, and pretty soon, but not soon *enough*, she heard the front door slam.

An hour or so she had to herself while Mrs. Magda went upstairs to visit her friend, Mrs. Ferreira, as she often did these days or perhaps she'd merely gone for a stroll about Wisteria Gardens after which she'd sit beneath a tree fanning herself in her shiny pink skin. Dhlamina clucked with irritation and turned her attention, once more, to her scones.

But something mineral in her throat rejected the scones when, at last, they were ready. Dawdling at the kitchen window, absent-mindedly sucking at the wooden spoon she'd used to mix the tea biscuits and which, for no reason that she could understand, she promptly dipped in the salt cannister, Dhlamina noticed that the horizon seemed less sharp. Not the gentle bluntness that betokened rain, not quite, but slightly less taut as if the seam of earth and sky had been unpicked slightly by an impatient finger. What she desired most to eat was a bowl of umphothulo, the childhood maize porridge on which she had, so to speak, first cut her teeth.

But Mother, where am I to find sour milk or mielie flour in this house? Dhlamina asked silently, her mouth pressed like a hot flower against the window pane.

Two minutes, three minutes, perhaps thirty sped by (surely not so much!) and still the taste for umphothulo did not subside. Stir a dash of apple cider vinegar into a half pint warmish milk, advised *Mrs. Moffert* upon the matter of sour milk but, naturally, not even a handful of mielie flour was to be found amongst the whole grains and imported cereals of Mrs. Magda's pantry. In the course of her foraging Dhlamina was fortunate to discover a dusty tin of Eagle's condensed milk at the back of a shelf and she fell upon it eagerly, punching a hole in the metal and sucking with the undiluted joy of childhood. But the sickly sweet milk only seemed to increase her hunger for fermented maize meal. Eventually, her stomach growling like a terrier, Dhlamina unearthed an open packet of polenta, somewhat weevily, as she discovered when she peered inside, noting the breathing holes, the dash and scurry of burrowing insect life.

Hau, a little gogga never hurt anybody, she remembered her mother admonishing, long ago, in a room centered by an iron brazier its pan encrusted with the curling remains of cooked mielie meal.

How much can a little gogga eat? Coal smoke on the walls and on the ceiling.

In this room there was also a scuffed kitchen table, one leg askew but propped against a Shona bible that one of the missionaries had pressed upon Gcina Mopede who was, in any case, an original sinner, one who required neither the abominations of Leviticus nor the rantings of Paul to inspire her. Also in this room: twists of drying meat tied to a washing line strung between rafters, milk cartons fermenting home brew, a couple of hubcaps beaten flat to hold candles. Everything else hung from nails in the wall: tin cups and plates, an enamel basin for carrying water, plastic buckets for hauling clothes to the river. In this way, her mind's eye panning into the tight corners of her mother's kitchen, Dhlamina counted off the minutes while the milk soured and the polenta stiffened on Mrs. Magda's stove. Outside the shack was a scratching of dull red earth. When it rained the earth turned thick and bright and oozed between her little girl toes.

*Fin*ally the polenta was ready, the milk exhibiting the watery glaze to which *Mrs. Moffert* had alerted her reader. Spoon to mouth, spoon to mouth, swiftly Dhlamina devoured her way to the bottom of the bowl, gnawing a path back to childhood through the palate-clenching sourness of the milk, the bland cornsilk of polenta irritated by a little salt, a grinding of cracked pepper. Hmmm-hm.

Aaah.

Burp-URP.

Dhlamina doubled over the toilet, heaving, the climacteric of her childhood squarely upon her. Grunting, great drops of sweat sizzling into the water as if she was a candle burning down, guttering where she stood, Dhlamina deposited her helping of umphothulo with relief tempered by regret (itself an uneasy mixture) into the toilet bowl of Mrs. Magda's guest bathroom.

Joo-mma-wee! she gasped calling on her mother as, slowly, the room came back into focus.

Mauve wallpaper edged by forget-me-nots. Charcoal tiles above the sink. A bowl of, ugh, pine cones and mushrooms it looked like, dyed purple and smelling of sweet rottenness. Po-silent-"t"-pourri. Hmph. Three different-sized towels, *three*, descending order, hung from the rack. Dhlamina soaked the face cloth with cold water, wiped her mouth, forehead, back of the neck. Felt better. Patted her face dry with a hand towel. Good thing there were three.

Better still.

Could have sworn she saw the curtains twitch, heard the high, humourless chuckle of a woman's spite bounce back from the bathroom mirror.

Beneath the fine-needled spray of the shower head, the water washing her clean and cool again, Dhlamina remembered how her nights in the old woman's room had been disturbed by the stink of whatever old white women stuffed in their underwear to disguise their decay. And in the morning a heat rash had sprung up, bristling over her breasts, the stretched frame of her belly. Her fingertips were bloody with scratching. For the last few nights she'd slept restlessly, *Mrs. Moffert* abandoned on the floor beside the bed, and she herself turning from side to side as if she too was a book of tempting recipes thumbed this way and that by a wayward appetite. Around midnight, a plump woman in a mauve housecoat would enter the room. The rest of the night was given up to hijinks—handfuls of face powder scattered on the carpet, ground into the pile; pale pink lipstick smeared on the rim of the water glass; fingerprints smudged across the mirror. One night the cloth that draped the vanity in swathes of chintz was snatched undone and it had taken Dhlamina all the next morning to sew the flounces back into place. Another night the wall sconces were cracked and yellowed as if aged by ill will or the breath of some feverish but still powerful adversary. All night, it seemed, the plump pink woman kicked up her heels in spite. Next morning the residue of her malice was a fine webbing of dust over all the surfaces of the room.

No, assuredly, the old woman's lilac-sprigged room was not a healthy place for Dhlamina to spend the night. Full of half-sounds and sighs, something angry and restless that wanted her going-going-gone.

What shall I do, Mother? asked Dhlamina surprising herself with the question.

The answer seemed to fly straight from the mouth of the woman who had never given her a straight answer, not once in her life. But death altered things, perhaps, because from somewhere she heard her mother urge: *Be gone, child. Get going!*

Ouma struggled back into consciousness.

Soon she would be with Lourens again, with her son. And with Groot Oupa, of course, and all who'd gone before. In the distance she heard glass breaking, furniture being agitated across bare floor boards. For a moment, Ouma found herself admiring the efficiency of the tsotsis. They seemed to accomplish a great deal aided only by mumbled grunts and occasional directives in a language she didn't understand.

Beauty, she thought suddenly.

The name was a photographic flash going off before her eyes.

Beauty! But there was no sound of tea being made, no water boiling or the deliberation of the refrigerator clicking open. No hand knocking aside jars as it reached for the milk, no crik-crak of the sugar tin, and no bright *ting* of silver spoon against ceramic mug as the tea borne upon Beauty's tray glided through passage and hall and into Ouma's bedroom.

Had her absence conjured these two tsotsis? wondered Ouma. But, no, Beauty wouldn't have had anything to do with such wicked creatures, not the woman she'd known for three decades, more than three. Beauty would be back soon, police in tow. *Tcha*, Mama, what have they done to you! She'd untie Ouma's wrists, chafe her hands and smooth the damp hair from her forehead.

There, there.

But where had Beauty gone? Had Ouma forgotten that it was her day off? Or was Beauty tired of looking after a sick old woman who didn't even have the good sense to die? What if Beauty had finally saved enough money to build her house? Was she, even now, opening her new front door, a prayer of thanksgiving flying powerful as a raptor to the treetops of heaven?

Or this. This: Beauty in a pool of blood on the stairs, hands covering her face to ward off the blows of the tsotsis. *Take what you want but don't harm my Madam.* The words blooming on her lips as they struck her down softly, expertly. While Ouma died.

And died. Through the lengthening shadows and her creeping, oxygen-deprived lethargy, Ouma strained towards the staircase, to the breath that fluttered like a flag at half-mast on Beauty's lips. To the staggered heartbeat, the pulse skipping like a stone across water.

Beauty, she thought once, briefly, before falling into the black spaces between stars, the white spaces between words.

Nkosikas is crying
She doesn't like to tell
But now she feels quite certain
That she dropped them down the well!

The words to the silly little poem that Dhlamina had learned in Grade Two kept running through her head as she searched with trembling hands for the car keys that might just as well have been dropped into some fathomless well for all the good they were doing her. Sobbing with frustration, at first she wasn't certain that she could collect her scattered resources sufficiently to leave the flat, toil down the stairs (the elevator was stalled on fourth again) and stagger into the empty street.

Joo-mma-wee, she called. Oh my mother!

Behind burglar bars and trellised security grilles, doors and windows gaped ajar. But there was no wind to enter these rooms, to ruffle their curtains and puff out their sunfilters, or blow the dust bunnies that collected behind the sofas where the maids never swept, hither and yon. Her mother's warning had so invigorated her that in her headlong flight from Wisteria Gardens Dhlamina had taken nothing but a sunshade, her voluminous shoulder bag and, for no good reason except that it had been in her hands at the time, the sturdy bulk of *Mrs. Moffert's Inquire Within*. Stalled at the bottom of the hill Dhlamina was certain she wouldn't make it to the stomach-clenching summit, and then she was equally certain she didn't have it in her to drag herself to the awning-fronted shopping mall. But by the time she was dreading the traffic, the exhaust-filled, exhausting trek to the taxis, she'd already cleared the main road and was staggering across to the curiously empty stretch of tarmac where the taxis were usually ranked in the midday sun.

Breathing *one*-one-two between heavy footsteps, idling at every traffic light to let the water baby stretch and contract in her belly, Dhlamina shaded her eyes against the sun that was tight as a drum in the sky. Even behind dark glasses and the protective curve of her sun brolly it was excruciating to crank her eyes to the sunlight, to breach the glare that skimmed every surface, swarming off plate glass and windshield, the hard metallic surfaces of the cars that shot past as she hesitated on the corner. An Egyptian goose flapped by, its vast wingspan eclipsing the sun. Dhlamina shuddered. Baby, she whispered, *Baby*.

When she looked up again she saw that Mhda's taxi ranks were unusually depleted. In contrast to the double lanes of furiously revving transport taxis that habitually clogged the side streets spewing exhaust fumes and epithets, only four or five battered vehicles remained, edged by a scraggly line of pedestrians. A queue marshal was waving the nearest taxi onto the platform yet it seemed to Dhlamina that both the taxi men and their customers fervently wished themselves elsewhere. Only Mhda looked to be at home in the world; Madiba Mhda who was notorious for pressing his luck between the double clamps of avarice and hard-headed business dealing. You could be sure that if anyone's taxis were to run during the strike then Mhda was at the bottom of it, wiry, tough, loping this way and that, collecting fares and haranguing passengers into line.

Hee banna, man! a woman in the overalls and matching doek of a domestic servant admonished him. Whoever heard the people must queue in a strike?

Sisi, Mhda replied, in this country you must queue up even to die!

The woman's mocking laughter startled Dhlamina. The afternoon had the strained, stilted quality of newsprint, a black and white photograph clipped from an old file.

Dhlamina stooped under the narrow border of shade, leaning against a parking meter whose window suddenly swung round to display a crimson EXPIRED sign. With a start she turned her head towards the huddle of hawkers and vendors peddling their wares on blankets in front of the Mall. The smell of varnished wood wafted towards her, the faint blood-musk of animal skins and leather, masks rubbed in beeswax, curry paste, grilled meats, and the guttery stink of overripe mangos.

Dhlamina staggered under the onslaught. She had lost the key to her tranquility. *Nkosikas is crying, is crying!*

Baby, she called, clutching her stomach gone suddenly tight as the sun. BABY!

Befok, man. Good and fucked! Mhda crumpled the flip top packet from which he'd just extracted his last cigarette and flung it sideways into the gutter.

You reckon, *madoda?* Woza Alberton sighed.

The two had been discussing mullah, the strike, and certain pirate taxis that had recently made their unwelcome appearance on the scene. Since these taxis were both unregistered and illegal they couldn't be managed by businessmen such as Mhda nor could they be financed by Woza Alberton and the notorious *ngamola,* the businessman, Umbulali. But mostly, of course, and to Mhda's regret, they were discussing Woza Alberton's most absorbing topic of interest — mullah, money, cash. Mhda's sudden short supply, the urgent need of Woza Alberton's infamous boss to raise his interest rates — there must be no appearance of favourites, my bra! — these topics had taken on a new intensity in the days leading up to the strike.

Tcha. Now Woza Alberton clicked his tongue sorrowfully at the pass to which his poor friend had been brought for, assuredly, fifty percent interest was no laughing matter. With one hand he reached inside his natty pinstripe jacket to pass Mhda the flat bottle of cane spirits and with the other he took a little packet of mustard from his trouser pocket and began to palpate it as was his habit when thinking deeply.

Yup, yup, *yebo.*

Woza Alberton sighed.

But Mhda was agitated, unable, for once, to pretend to be convinced by Woza Alberton's shoulder-shrugging ways. For who, after all, would be paying this hefty fifty percent interest? Not Woza Alberton, assuredly! No, the fat man merely picked his teeth on the bones of his skinny debtors and went on his merry way, that one. Mhda shrugged irritably. The sun was hot on the back of his neck and seemed to be moving unusually swiftly across the sky today. It put him in mind of the poem by Mtshale in which the venerable old poet spun the sun like a coin across the sky. And then at sunset he clicked this sun into the slot of a parking meter and watched the neon lights of the city blink on. Mhda had been drawing so deeply on his cigarette in his agitation that he'd inhaled it down to the filter in double time. Now he pinched the burning tip between wet fingers. The unaccustomed alcohol had given his eyes a strange petroleum glaze yet still he sought to reassure the henchman of his good faith.

Moja, moja! he began, it's okay—

Suddenly the fat one leaned back on his commodious haunches and began to chuckle.

Ng ng ng! Tsi tsi tsi—I have heard, my friend, that there are compensations to your current financial crisis. Heh heh heh!

Incensed, Mhda waited for Woza Alberton to continue.

Sha sha sha! What is it that the old people say of the man who's strapped for cash but of other assets he possesses an abundance? It may be that your cattle are thin, my friend, but your women are *dudlu. Yebo,* fat and juicy!

And, once again, Woza Alberton began to hiss and fizz and buck with laughter, crying, That, *that* is honey indeed, my friend, *ho*—that is farm fresh butter!

Mhda was scalded. Angrily he snapped the brown cardboard suitcase shut and hurried across the road seemingly to remonstrate with one of his customers. But the dispute with the ousie who was unwilling to wait quietly in the taxi queue merely increased his irritation. For in the background it seemed he could still hear the sound of Woza Alberton's laughter hissing like fat off a grill.

From across the street Mhda saw Dhlamina step out from behind the entrance to the Mall. Or was it that he heard her call his name? In truth he couldn't say for sure, then or ever after. Dhlamina moved awkwardly from the shelter of the building and Mhda left off wrangling with his customer to run towards her.

The water baby bubbled up from beneath Dhlamina's breastbone and the sweat started out on her forehead.

"Mhda," she called out aloud; "Mother" in her head.

Dhlamina! he started towards her.

The landscape split apart.

One half, the narrow length of road by the taxi ranks, exploded into flame and hellfire and the other half, the side of the building where Mhda stood shielding Dhlamina with his body, quaked in the aftermath. With the sound of Velcro ripping, the earth pulled away from the sky. In the terrible silence the explosion had hollowed from the world Dhlamina looked up to see with her own eyes the coming of the Lord, for nothing less, surely, would cause such an inhuman commotion. But the heavens flickered and remained an impenetrable blue, the fraudulent reflection of white on white through which the face of God did not, alas, deign to shine through.

Assassin! yelled Mhda into the silence. Yet it was clear even to Dhlamina in her state of God-readiness that he was addressing no one. There was no one to address. Strangely, a half-smoked Marlboro poked from behind his right ear, the explosion having failed to dislodge it.

Méira Cook

ASSASSIN!

No answer.

Experimentally, shyly, Dhlamina reached her hand to the sky but the sky remained out of reach.

Then it began to rain.

Stones and rubble, masonry, exhaust pipes, falling glass and tubas and African masks rained down on vendors and peddlers, pedestrians and shoppers, the Father Christmases with their dark startled faces beneath curly white beards, and the Salvation Army Marching Band who, moments before, had begun a rather lacklustre rendition of The Little Drummer Boy.

Param-pam-pam-pa, a sheet of flame from the petrol tank of an upturned minibus taxi whooshed heavenward. Like the pillar of fire, an onlooker later told *The Sowetan* reporter, which had guided the Israelites by night.

With uncanny presentiment Dhlamina watched the almond-seller jump behind his cart his hands stretched out in a comical crucifix of astonishment. Rapidly, as if to cancel time, he stepped forward smartly and began to line up his paper spills. Into each cone he funnelled a precise measure of roasted almonds from the shallow pan in front of him. In and out, in and out, his hands moved faster and faster as the pan in which his almonds jumped and sizzled began to fill with a strange, dark, sticky liquid. All the taxis were burning now and the straggling row of pedestrians waiting to board them was dispersed to the winds.

Rampampam-pa, some hung upside down from the branches of a nearby bluegum, some were blown in pieces clear across the street by the force of the explosion. *Rampampam-pa rampampam-pa*, others had simply turned inside out so that secret organs were suddenly displayed for all to see.

An ousie, shucking her feet as easily as if they were bedroom slippers, crawled on bleeding hands and knees towards a parcel, still strangely intact, wrapped in reindeer and mistletoe paper. An elderly man with a comically bewildered expression tried to fumble his intestines back into his stomach. The woman who earlier had been hectoring Mhda tacked up and down across the road searching in the bushes for her child. Somebody was screaming; somebody was crying. In and out, in and out, the roasted nut vendor was still furiously spooning blood-soaked almonds into his paper spills, shaking his head as if to say, No time, No time! Too much to do today, by jingo!

Watching him Dhlamina began to keen. The sound she produced was an insect, a mosquito whine beneath the thunderous recoil of the explosion and its aftermath but Mhda heard her. With his left hand he cupped her damp nape, hid her face in his shoulder.

Moja, moja! he tried to calm her. My aboLovey! My sweety!

Voetsak! Dhlamina spat at him, spinning on one heel the better to launch her offensive: *Look* what you've done now, you *fool!*

Tula, woman. Quiet! What has Mhda to do with this…this—

Words failed him. To think that even in the middle of a bomb blast this impossible woman could still turn on him. Outrage struggled with admiration in his heart but won in the end. Truly, she was crazy if she thought that he'd destroy his own business in this preposterous manner. Not to mention the terrible waste of lives. Glancing over his shoulder Mhda suddenly spied Woza Alberton—or what was left of him. The body of the man who, moments before had been cracking wise, sharing a joint and an oil drum while discussing the feasibility of defying the agitators and running a couple of rogue taxis out to the townships, lay across the old brown cardboard suitcase with its stickers that read "Eno's Fruit Salts!" and "Dispirin Dissolves!"

No, excuse me, Mhda corrected himself, the *headless* body of Woza Alberton.

For, some yards away, balanced against an expired parking meter, the wretched man's head had come to rest. Eyes staring, jaw slack, Woza Alberton's tongue was lolling from its mouth like the filling in a sandwich.

Condiment packets everywhere, Mhda thought inconsequentially. Smears of mustard, seeping vinegar.

Méira Cook

Only a moment earlier, and the irony wasn't lost on him, Mhda had interrupted Woza Alberton's dagga-induced optimism to preach caution.

Use your head, man—Mhda had exhorted moments before the explosion. The words still rang in his ear but so far from proving effective they merely emphasized the hopelessness of the situation. Because Woza Alberton—poor soul—would never again be in danger of losing his head.

Three, four taxis were burning now with the oily black flame of exploding gasoline. Thought-bubbles of smoke floated above the wreckage as if exclaiming BAM! KEPOW! POOF! The intermittent grunt of gunfire started up again. For a moment Mhda saw his own shocked face imprinted like a decal upon the glistening platter of Woza Alberton's face. Then something hot and tight burst in his shoulder. He grabbed Dhlamina by the arm trying to shift her from the doorway.

Come, we must get out of here, woman. Put-foot! Mhda shouted above the hissing of flames, the groans of the dying, the screams and the sirens and the *fttt-ftt* of bullets flying by which was just like the noise, as his mother had once told him, of the soul fleeing the body.

But Dhlamina had problems of her own. For one thing the sun was exploding into splinters of light and heat and noise, making her dizzy and releasing a flood of water that gushed from between her thighs and into her shoes.

All this and wet feet too, it was too much. Bloody *hell!* Gingerly, she stepped out of her sandals shaking each foot in turn like a cat.

What the—Mhda glanced down. *Hai kona!*

Hekelemanzi—
Hunh-*hunh*. Hmph.

The sound of men lifting and straining in unison filtered into the room with the rose-flocked wallpaper where Ouma lay dying. A light entered her vision and this light, Ouma recognized, was her death. She strained towards it; nearly there. But the sound of the tsotsis who were knocking about downstairs kept interrupting her and the bright square window light of her death began to recede.

Kri kri kri.

Echo of a dog barking in a locked room. The afternoon ebbed, shadows lapping the floor in panting waves. With the approach of evening the roses on the walls seemed to glow like lamps inside their leaves.

Soon, thought Ouma, soon.

But time did not pass quickly there in the room with only the tick tock of Grandfather to remark its passing. Ouma shut her eyes tight and tried, once more, to summon the bright light of her death but all was pain and darkness and fear.

Not like this, she thought. No, not like this.

Half conscious, Ouma strained to hear the sound of a human voice but all she could summon were the rubies muttering moodily in the darkness.

Hello Ouma, Ouma? called her grandson a little later.

But she didn't hear him. Neither the rasp of his key in the front door nor his unexpected tread on the stairs nor the frenzied yap of the terrier at the indignity of being locked all afternoon in the airless pantry. And neither did she hear the unruly man-boy's voice responding to the terrier's outcry.

Eli! Eli! he yelled. Shuddup you fucken brak.

Mhda push-pull-heaved his shuddering Dhlamina into Zizi Molepe's skelm-taxi which, true to form, had survived the blast with minor injuries although its owner wasn't quite so lucky for once. Indeed the bluegums along the taxi ranks were blooming with a collection of Zizi bits and pieces and never again would the passengers of the demon taxi be obliged to shout out "Have mercy, *bafana!*" when the possessed taxi man locked his foot on the accelerator and narrowed his eye to the horizon, kicking up dust and grit in the faces of wayfarers who must then watch his vanity plates recede into the distance: ZIZI 666!

But Mhda had not a moment to mourn his intrepid friend and fellow taxi man. Covering his hands with grocery bags he raked at the shattered glass across the front seat then tried to load Dhlamina into the back. His aboBaby had lost her shoulder bag and brolly in the melee but not the heavy book with which, even now, she was battering him as if to say, Why are men such idiots, such impossible bloody fools?

Hee banna, be quiet woman! he roared or tried to, but Dhlamina swatted him once again with her book—sweet Jesus what was she doing with such a book?—as if to say, Do not you look down on me from such a vast height with your head tilted back so as to demonstrate the great distance between us! Do not you provoke me with your cigarette still intact behind your ear as if to say, So little do women distress me!

Aitsa, bloody woman! bellowed Mhda trying to ward off her blows with one arm and failing because his shoulder had clamped painfully shut. With the other hand he fumbled the ignition, succeeding finally in gunning the engine and stuttering into laborious second.

GGggroagh-gh-GH-GH. The devil taxi of Zizi Molepe jerked into gear.

Hnnh, groaned Dhlamina and then *Hhnnnh?* It had emerged that the explosion, while focused within the sun-drum centre of her belly, was not confined to this burning middle of the world but had radiated outwards encompassing sky and earth, the street with its rivulets of gutter blood, and the bluegums that now resembled grotesque Christmas trees strung with shattered glass and human remains.

GGggroach-gh-GH-GH...

Something was wrong with the transmission and the left rear tire had blown in the blast. This left three goodish tires, Mhda calculated, and one rim. Enough to get onto the highway, please-to-God. Picking his way through the traffic Mhda drove with his left arm swinging this way and that across the steering wheel because his right shoulder was cramped into hard spasms that radiated across his back until each tightening circle was grounded in the lightning rod of his spine. Blood was soaking through his shirt, oddly warm at first and intimate, like the sensation a child feels when he wets himself in the night.

For the first few miles black cooking smoke and sulphur, the familiar odour of burning tires, pursued them. Also, and this dawned on

Mhda slowly, one of Zizi Molepe's favourite jazz tapes that had been playing at the time of the explosion was jammed deep in the cassette player and all attempts to turn the bloody thing off had only resulted in snatching assorted knobs and volume controls from the plastic dial. Now the unnecessarily loud strains of Louis Armstrong trumpeting one of Zizi Molepe's choice medleys, a jaunty blast from the past called *Skokiaan*, accompanied them past the mine dumps and water-cooling towers that bordered the highway.

Happy-appy-Africa, satchmoed Louis gaily, *a-bingo bingo bingo bing-o!* beneath the insect-like formations of underpasses, past warehouses and corporate headquarters and indignant-looking pylons, arms akimbo in the blanched veld.

In the back seat Dhlamina began to rock backwards and forwards, rubbing her thighs and humming deep in her throat.

Baby, sounded like. *BabyBabyBaby.*

Happy-appy Africa, offered Louis. *A-bingo bingo bingo* BING-O—

Ten miles along the highway and the second tire blew, followed by Mhda's precarious calm. *Chrissakes!* he yelled beating the steering wheel with his fists in time to the *BabyBabyBaby* that hummed through the van like a swarm of bees caught in the dark flower of his lover's throat.

*A-bingo-bingo-bingo-*BING!

Nothing to do but abandon the skelm-taxi on the side of the road, themselves to the compassion of a passing motorist who might—had it ever happened before?—stop to assist this Madonna and her wounded Joseph. It being the day before Christmas and all.

Fat chance, thought Mhda. Fat fat *fat.*

Nothing else to do, for the skelm-taxi was behaving as if an old devil was lodged in its gut, smoke squeezing in sausage-link puffs from the bonnet. Mhda ran around, tried to coax Dhlamina from her sanctuary in the back seat. It wasn't easy.

Voetsak, she told him, briefly disengaging herself from the bee-call in her throat.

Fat! swore Mhda. Fatfatfat.

And *Hhnnh?* asked Dhlamina, answering her own question with the only reply possible: Baby-Aby-ABY.

Madiba Mhda, Taxi Man, had enough sense left, but only just, to know when he was being flipped between the frying pan and the fire, the devil and the deep blue, the rock and the hard place of the soul. The blood had stiffened the cotton of his shirt into outlandish peaks and troughs beneath which his wound pulsed unsteadily. Glass from the windshield still fell upon him making him glitter dangerously and while the ragged ache in his shoulder could be ignored for minutes at a time it would be foolish to expect a motorist to stop for such a case of blood and guts. Flinching, cursing, Mhda draped the Basuto blanket that he'd found sliding around in the back of Zizi Molepe's taxi over his shoulders.

Haw haw *haw,* cackled Dhlamina in a momentary lull. Mine boy!

Mhda snatched the half-smoked cigarette from behind his ear and jammed it between his teeth but his Bic was out of fluid and one after another of his emergency matches snapped in two between trembling fingers until, in anger born of despair, he flipped the whole box over the embankment. For the next two hours Mhda divided his time unevenly between the side of the road, thumb out in an effort to flag a passing Samaritan, and the airless back seat where his Dhlamina alternately fanned herself with the heavy book and clutched it as she heaved and swore. Already her palms had stained the cover leaving damp imprints on the maroon fabric and the spine was crooked, pulled out of alignment by her clutching hands.

Floom—floom—the sound of cars whizzing past on the highway, each motorist vacuum-sealed into his separate bubble of indifference, built up like a fever in Mhda. A silly-looking terrier barked into a cell phone on a giant billboard overhead. Please, begged Mhda, *please.* But the terrier, indifferent to his plight, barked on. Scalded, Mhda grew hot with shame for he was succeeding neither in attracting help nor in assisting the woman who, despite her terror and her temper, despite the hot white teeth she bared whenever he looked her way or the heavy book she bludgeoned him with, this woman was relying on his courage, his resourcefulness.

Two and a half hours later and Mhda had all but given up hope of surviving this ordeal let alone of saving his beloved Dhlamina from the indignity of giving birth to a highway baby or worse, when a rust-red Peugeot jarred to a halt on the shoulder beside him and the familiar sight of his crazy friend Mustapha Hurry-Curry greeted him like the answer to a prayer, like a reprieve from the Devil.

Like the hollow in the middle of the word God to which the true believer may put his mouth and breathe.

Breathe.

Go limp, thought Benjamin as the first bullet clipped his ear. Another had lodged in the ornate walnut casing of Grandfather in the hall. The clock seemed to shudder and sigh, the bullet must have glanced one of the hanging weights on its sideways cut across time because some inner mechanism gurgled deeply, brassily, and the pendulums swung wildly. Breaking step with time forever after.

The youth who'd risen from the shadows, gun cocked, was unknown to Benjamin but at the first clap of brass he looked up to catch the boy, Beauty's grandson, crouched halfway down the staircase. In his arms was a casual stack of Benjamin's shirts tamped down by a detached stereo speaker and a pile of CDs.

Hey! exclaimed Benjamin, and then, Hey?

In the background a dog imprisoned somewhere in the house stopped barking. As if in sympathy, the blood from Benjamin's nicked ear began to flow warmly down the side of his face, his neck, and over his collar bones.

Hey, said Rothman, hey.

In his voice the word was neither question nor answer, recognition nor its opposite.

Hey, he repeated, a dull thud, a three-fingered nudge. Hey man.

Then he motioned to his companion who was scratching his ear with his gun but who ceased this absorbing activity in order to hit Benjamin with it and then shove him into the next room. It was almost dark in there but Benjamin could make out a crumpled heap on the bed. Gingerly he moved closer, exclaimed, hit the light switch.

Ouma? he called uncertainly.

She was older than he remembered. Older, crumpled. They'd ripped off her underpants and stuffed them in her mouth.

Aghast, he looked again: the dilated pupils, the babble of pink nylon in her mouth, stood out grotesquely against her drained face. A pulse twitched at the side of her neck and with each heartbeat her whole body seemed to spasm upwards. Her nightie was twisted awry and the old body with its embarrassing hairs and sagging flesh lay bared to his gaze. He wanted to shut his eyes but he couldn't.

Ouma, he called again, Ouma—

He stooped over her body, called to Rothman he must fetch a knife from the kitchen, a blade. Something.

The other boy crowded into the bedroom. Benjamin called to him over his shoulder to fetch a knife from one of the kitchen drawers. A pair of scissors. Snip-snip, he sketched in the air, *hurry*. All the while his adrenaline-quickened fingers worked against the knots securing her ankles, loosening, releasing, almost…there.

Hurry, he urged, perhaps we can—

Both boys stared at him, neither moving.

The blood from his nicked ear was still pouring. The boys stared. Down his neck and over the front of his shirt. Either hypnotized or bored.

One Mississippi Two.

Then Rothman, lurching as if under water, took aim. Fired twice in rapid succession. Once more for good luck.

Hekelemanzi, panted Mhda as he and Mustapha worked together to ease Dhlamina into the back seat of the Peugeot. The back seat had been stuffed with rustling plastic bags from Achmat's Discount Emporium but to Mhda's surprise Mustapha had flung these parcels one by one and then in great armloads, out of the car and off the highway embankment, laughing like a maniac as he did so.

Mustapha, who almost didn't recognize Mhda in his absurd tribal blanket, had blanched with dismay when he first saw Dhlamina.

Where we goan take her? he asked, humid with disapproval.

But Mhda, in no mood to placate Mustapha Hurry-Curry, merely
indicated the turn-off to Soweto with a stern nod of the head and a
thin hiss of air from the lucky gap between his front teeth.

Road's closed, snapped Mustapha. Better make for the General,
and he jarred into emphatic if resentful gear. Besides, he added somewhat mollified by the thought, I know a doctor who works there.

Out of habit Mhda looked back once, only to see great billows of
clothing—shirts and pants and jackets—ballooning from their plastic bags and floating gracefully off the embankment.

But when they got to the hospital it was closed, or near as damn
it. No one was at the nurse's station or at reception, the passages were
empty of patients and staff, the polished linoleum clicking without res-
onance against his heels as Mhda skidded through a circuitry of inter-
connecting corridors, searching for help. Not an orderly or a cleaner,
not even the odd shift worker taking a clandestine smoke break in
the canteen or a lone mop-pushing janitor was to be found. Outside
a door marked Common Room Mhda came a cropper, clanging into
a ring of galvanized buckets left there like the denizens from some
lost, once populated world. From behind this door Mhda could hear
the mild, hiccupping *pock* of bat against ball followed by a TV-dulled
crowd-roar but he was too distracted to investigate. His shoulder was
by now a clenched fist of pain and shards of glass from the windshield
had worked their way into his skin so that he seemed to crackle with
every step. Yet, still, corridor after hospital corridor opened before
him, each one holding out the chimera of a doctor, a nurse, a soothing white-coated presence.

By the time Mhda had wound himself like a tapeworm through
the dark intestines of the hospital with its basement water pipes and
echoing stairwells and peristaltic grumblings and was pushed out by
this very same tapeworm into the flat glare of the parking lot, he was
purposeful with panic.

The earth must have shifted a little on its axis while Mhda was scouring the hospital because the light outside was sulphurous as if a storm was brewing, and the air was beer-coloured, the clouds tumbling about like a headful of foam on the day's sour thirst.

What kind music you want? Mustapha was repeating incredulously, *Who's* this bloody Skokiaan? and then *Jirre!* as, hopping from foot to foot beside the Peugeot, he clutched his head where Dhlamina had tried, once again, to brain him with her enormous book.

Bloody woman hit me, he gasped before taking a running-jump into the passenger seat because Mhda, unlit cigarette still clasped gamely between clenched teeth, was already reversing, revving off without him although *where* he thought he was going was a mystery to Mustapha but, *jirre* man, whose bloody car was it anyway?

Cutting through the parking lot, Mhda swerved into the main road that already had the windblown, tossed-about look of an approaching storm. Newspapers and leaves were rattling in the gutters but the wind hadn't yet risen beyond the ankles of scurrying pedestrians. Like a man tormented beyond endurance by terrible but ultimately vain choices — for everything he did, Mhda was convinced, would have the identical outcome — the taxi man cast about for a solution. Between the Hillbrow Tower at one end of the horizon and the Brixton Tower at the other the city stretched out like a line of dirty washing. In the distance the great hollow cylinder of Ponte loomed. It was the ugliest building in the city, no doubt about it, like a giant tampon rammed into the dirt. On the topmost storey the neon Coca-Cola sign had just begun to flash into the sky.

Fucking Ponte, grunted Mhda, obscurely gratified by the sight.

Far away, further even than Ponte, hoarse lightning rattled, followed by the dry heaves and wracking coughs of distant thunder. But no rain fell to break the fever, none at all.

With a sudden twist of the steering wheel that spun the pain in his shoulder to the balls of his feet so that even his Achilles tendons twanged in sympathy, Mhda turned in the direction of the northern suburbs. He would escort his Dhlamina-Queen back to the flat in Wisteria Gardens.

It was the only place he could think of and it was better than a stable.

The water baby was breaking out of its element, squeezing its way through the bony rock formations of its mother's pelvis. Dhlamina felt the dry knock of bone followed by the flip-flop of a fish out of water. Outside, the rain clattered down, a hard metallic fall, the sound of iron filings on a tin roof. Dhlamina screamed to remind herself that she was alive, screamed to give voice to the pain cropping her breath. Screamed. And Mhda, who was bending over where she lay on Mrs. Magda's chaise-lounge under the ceiling fan that pared the air into long breathable spirals, Mhda clasped his hands over his ears.

Stop, he begged. Please stop.

But the water baby ignored its father's pleas and Dhlamina spiraled with the ceiling fan down into the bottom of the afternoon where she lay panting. Mhda's face with its comically clasped ears was a milk jug, the handles chipped off. Now the water baby was grating against the stones at the bottom of Dhlamina's empty riverbed. The milk jug tilted forward, its mouth growing wider as pleas, a froth of entreaties, poured into the room. Mhda rocked backwards and forwards on his haunches.

Stop, he pleaded. *Please.*

A woman with the transparent skin of the long-ago dead knelt at Dhlamina's side. Dhlamina recognized the scent of orange water and old lady musk that always preceded some minor act of destruction or spite as when the drapes in the living room were snatched from their brass rings or the wire hangers in the guest room were set to clattering in empty cupboards.

Cross your legs, advised the transparent woman, and her voice was silk stockings with the seams awry.

Close your eyes, she hissed, and think of elsewhere.

Méira Cook

But her eyes were ardent with disapproval and Dhlamina caught the odour of betrayal in the air as it mingled with the orange water and old lady smell.

Hoof-hoof, she tried to push the old woman away but her hand went right through her and out the other side.

Whore! shrieked the transparent woman. How dare you birth your bastard on my Louis Quinze with brocade accents! And she spun on her heels, spun like a top, so that the room began to spin too. Naturally, the ceiling cherubs got into the spirit, huffing and puffing so that dust and dead insects tumbled down from above: stray hairs and spider webs and the long-forgotten carapaces of evil deeds. *Ffflflflttt*, the heavy grey living room drapes blew wide scrolling apart to display windows lashed with rain, pocked by the furor of wind, the wild, galloping waters. At two minute intervals long tearing scars of light ripped across the sky.

Something was trying to be born. But whether inside or out it was difficult to know. Something.

Dhlamina fixed her gaze on the slow-fast-slow ceiling fan, used the dot-dot-dash of shadow and light to corkscrew herself up and out of reach of the old woman's spite.

Joo-mma-wee! she called, either in her head or not, either loud or soft, either just once or half a dozen times. Oh, my mother!

Mhda rocked on his haunches at the feet of his Dhlamina-Queen. Propped against the wedge of her enormous book from which she had been tearing out recipes and illustrations, scattering torn pages with each violent contraction, Dhlamina strained upwards in order to watch the storm clouds race by. All at once the wind spun free of its axis, whirling off on its perverse and doom-laden trajectory as if, thought Mhda, even the wind knew enough to fly clear of the disastrous room. Clutching his lucky gold pocket watch he called on God or the devil, whoever was available. Rain spattered across the windows and his right shoulder jammed abruptly so that his arm curled into a useless, twitching claw at his side.

The House on Sugarbush Road

I'll be good, Mhda pledged hastily. I'll replace the funds in the *stokvel* and I'll subscribe to the township feeding schemes and never ever take another bribe, so help me. In addition, he bargained cannily, Madiba Mhda will bloody sober up and control his shebeen queens. He'll whip his homeboys into shape and contract out his taxis. You must just stop the room from spinning. You must just let Dhlamina and the water baby live.

And make her stop screaming, he finished hastily, scrambling from his knees and clutching at Mustapha Hurry-Curry who looked like he was plotting his escape.

Where you off to, man? he grabbed him back of the shirt and landed him like a carp. Mustapha had been lurking on the parquet margins of the living room ever since the pains had begun in earnest, paring his fingernails with one of Mrs. Magda's ivory-handled fruit knives. Now he was padding from the room on the balls of his feet, casting a *what the bloody hell?* backwards glance.

Going to get a doctor, man.

Mustapha shrugged him off but not roughly enough considering what he'd been forced to witness in the last few hours. Always resourceful, it had suddenly occurred to Mustapha that "the doctor" was only a couple of suburbs away. It took considerable effort to swallow the lump of *who d'you think you are* that arose in Mustapha's throat whenever he thought of Benjamin but what to do, what else to do? Besides, and by no means incidentally, such a mission would allow him to escape the revolving room with Mhda's whore and her hard round belly spinning like a globe at its centre. The bloodied show that was already staining the chaise was causing the saliva to fill Mustapha's mouth and the familiar uh-oh of an incipient let-go was upon him.

Hurry, urged Mhda, releasing him. *Hurry*, and he snatched the packet of smokes poking from Mustapha's pocket. Then, but not addressing his gratitude to Mustapha who certainly deserved it if anyone did, *thanks, man.*

Mustapha fled the room, the flat, the building, taking the steps two, three at a time and brushing against, all but toppling, some old woman teetering in the stairwell. *Nee, man*—the woman tutted, turned in a half-circle by the force of Mustapha's descent but Mustapha was out of the building and free at last by the time she'd caught her breath.

The water baby was well and truly landed, its head twisting through the successive locks and gauges of Dhlamina's underwater river. Cursing, Dhlamina tore at *Mrs. Moffert*, cracked open her spine, yanking the front and back boards out of alignment. Loosed from their bindings, pages spilled out onto the floor.

Joo-mma-wee!

Dhlamina focused on the crazy overlapping spirals that the ceiling fan was cutting then uncutting into the air and tried to breathe between the pains that split her in half.

An overripe melon bisected with one slice of a serrated knife.

An earthworm sheared by the lawnmower, both halves trying to wriggle their way back into the easeful dirt.

The word *cleave* from a long ago crossword puzzle, a word that was both itself and its opposite.

Happy-appy Africa, boomed the thunder. *A-bingo bingo bingo* BING-O!

Dhlamina cleaved to the thought of the water baby even as she was cloven by its passage through her. A woman neither treacherous nor transparent knelt at her side. She touched Dhlamina on the inside of her wrist to draw her attention.

Nearly, nearly, whispered the tall mountain woman, Dhlamina's mother. She wore copper earrings that swayed amiably as she rocked and her skin emitted the cordial glow of the peaceful dead.

Next pain comes you must begin to push, she murmured placing a cool palm on Dhlamina's brow. Letting her daughter suck at the tips of her frozen fingers.

At the sound of a key recognizing its lock Mhda whirled. Storm-bewildered and uncertain, Mrs. Magda wobbled in the doorway, her face beneath the stiff waves of her hairdo aghast yet curiously reassuring to Mhda whose first thought and the one after that and the one after *that*, was that someone had come, at last, to assist.

Magda teetered on the threshold, rain-lashed and troubled yet unwilling to commit herself to a version of events that refused coherency despite her best efforts to make sense of the spinning room, the billowing drapes, the dust motes whirling from the blades of the ceiling fan. Not to mention the scowling, blood-splattered tsotsi in the centre of the living room, one cigarette hitching up the corner of his mouth, one cupped in his palm, both lit. Striking matches on the baseboards and cracking his knuckles. She'd seen him once before but where? And who, in God's name, was that scissored on her chaise-lounge, legs splayed?

Loose pages blew about the room; a woman screamed.

Alternately wringing her dripping skirt and her hands, Magda ventured closer, peered over the edge of the sofa and gasped. With trembling hands she fumbled for the edge of something; a table, a chair. But there was nothing to hold onto anymore. Instead, she found herself plucking vacantly at the tsotsi's sleeve.

Get help, woman. Phone for help.

Mhda shook her off. But Magda continued to stare blindly at him.

Phone. For. Help. Mhda tried again, each word separate, plosive.

Magda, tottering back on her heels, only stared. *Shit*, thought Mhda. Shitshit*shit*. He grabbed the first thing that came to hand, a vase of wilting roses.

The shock of the slightly rotten water brought Magda to her senses. Perched on the side of her bed she tried to shake herself to attention but succeeded only in dislodging the loose petals that drifted from her shoulders onto the telephone. With increasing panic she hit first one number and then another. But her hands were trembling too violently, her fingers seemed to thicken as she watched, their tips were strangely distended and unable to land with accuracy. Even more troubling was her humiliating failure to line up the numbers in her mind or transfer even this rudimentary information to her fingers. Again and again she attempted first one Emergency Number then another—Fire, Police, Flying Squad. *Poison* Control, for Chrissakes.

Twice she got through to an answering machine informing her that the Hennemans were unable to take her call but would get back to her as soon as possible. She must just leave a message together with the time she called, thank you, *dankie, totsiens* and have a nice day. Four times she drew the unforgiving drawl of a busy signal and more times than she cared to count or remember disembodied and unrecognizable voices floated out at her, their owners shouting insults into faraway mouthpieces: *Hello...Hello?* and *Voetsak!* and Fucken *moron!*

Once, marshalling a supreme effort, she succeeded in getting through to a voice that crisply tried to extract her name and address in four of the eleven official languages but she was so flustered at the questions that she dropped the phone, disconnecting the voice, and reducing herself to large slippery tears that slid down her cheeks and her neck. Somehow the very wetness of the tears loosened even further her faltering grip on the receiver.

Inside the storm lashed, crashed into furniture. Outside a woman howled and cursed. In the increasingly short breaks between the thunder and the lightning that contracted the horizon to a keyhole, a woman seemed to be singing.

SKOK-I-AAN! SKOK-I-AAN! A-BINGO BINGO BINGO BING-O!

Hurry, Mhda screamed. Hurry, woman.

In despair Magda stabbed at the speed dial with fear-stiffened fingers.

And again.

Again.

Through the rooms of the house on Sugarbush Road a telephone rang and rang. The intruders had departed leaving lights flickering in the streaming dusk. From a distance the house glowed like a yellow lamp against the darkness and the rain.

11

BLOOD MONEY

Beauty hovered on the threshold balancing a tea tray in one hand. Morning, Madoo-oom! she called in her husky, early morning voice and the Madoo-oom who never slept much anymore, struggled to free herself from the drag of bed linen, the bars of sunlight falling across her counterpane. Ever since the burglary Beauty no longer called the other woman Mama to her face or Ouma in her head. She was Madoo-oom in both places, the elongated vowels a concession to the good blood that had once flowed so freely between them.

Ouma braced her shoulders against the shape of the day to come. Waking was a jerky shudder into awareness from the dreams that flickered before her eyes like images in a slide show. Ever since her hands had been amputated these dreams were full of paired things: mating geckos and footprints that disappeared into the distance, pale-eyed nesting weavers. The powdery, mirrored wings of moths as they flapped at the double row of burglar bars at her window.

These bars loomed large in her dreams, taunting her with their inefficacy since they had played no part at all, it seemed, in deterring the tsotsis. It had taken the buckled and belted Sergeant Visser only half an hour to work out exactly how the two assailants, as he called them, had entered the house, incapacitated the incumbent, and systematically stripped the interior of all valuables.

Through the ceiling vent, Madam. He pointed it out to Ouma, pale and ill and newly-released from hospital.

The assailants entered the domicile from a louvered window abutting the roof which they accessed via the servant's quarters.

And he'd lifted his tufted brows, nudging Ouma into the realization that it had been an inside job.

An inside job, she agreed in her head but her heart rebelled. True, there came to her moments of clarity, snaps of recognition in the drift of shadows across her bedroom ceiling, in the harsh echo of a voice crying *Eli, Eli!* But these moments were unreliable, fugitive. Who was Eli?

These'll have to come off, said the surgeon, prodding her broken finger joints, the purple-black fingers. But where do they go afterwards? Ouma wondered. Was there a cemetery for dead hands, little graves planted with Tickberry and Fever Tree? Grotesquely, embarrassingly, a couple of rings had been returned to her, *afterwards*, the nurse stuffing them, wrapped in tissue paper, down the front of the bed jacket that the woman called Magda had brought her. The knitted jacket was an unsuitable shade of pink, the kind of garment that newly-delivered mothers had once worn but its lacy scallops and pompom tie discomforted Ouma although she was no longer certain why. As for the rings they said were hers, these rings were dull and dreary-looking. The diamonds had lost their sparkle, the rubies their colour, as if exhausted, diminished by circumstance. The woman named Magda brought her a thin gold chain and she threaded the unfamiliar bands around her neck where they rattled like knucklebones.

An inside job, Ouma muttered to herself but the words were a dog barking in the night. Sound without sense, thought unleavened by meaning or memory. They told her Eli was the dog she'd once loved, he used to sleep on her bed, didn't she remember? Where is he now, where is Eli the dog? she asked. He ran away, they replied. When the police came they broke open the pantry and the terrier jumped out and ran into the street. Who called the police? asked Ouma carefully, for the words no longer formed easily, in her mind or on her lips.

I myself, I called them, Beauty told her. When I came home the security gate was open so I ran to ask the next door Madam she must telephone to the police. (Ask her where she was all day, hissed the Magda woman, your precious Beauty. But that was later.) In truth the shock of the attack had shaken loose all the little pleats and tucks in memory. Of the burglary, the assault, Ouma retained almost nothing, even less of the years that had preceded it. All that remained was a kind of thin emotional residue like the coating left in a glass after the fruit juice has been drained.

Only Beauty lives here, Ouma told the Sergeant, and she's sturdy, an ousie. Couldn't climb through a vent. Couldn't possibly.

Could of hired someone, said the Sergeant. Could of. A relative, perhaps. Happens all the time. Madam, you wouldn't believe how often.

Did Beauty have relatives? Ouma contracted her mind to the tiny dot in the centre of the television that Magda had brought her, the tsotsis having picked the house clean of everything except heavy furniture, the bookshelves with their freight of old books many of which had been trashed (spite, explained Sergeant Visser), the rings that, they told her, had actually been on her fingers at the time. This tiny dot in the centre of the television screen when Beauty switched it on as she did more and more frequently these days, propping her in front of the set, had begun to preoccupy Ouma with vague yet insistent associations. But memory couldn't be summoned by the click of a button.

I don't think so, she ventured. A, a daughter, perhaps?

The Sergeant remained unconvinced. She knew this from the minute and brutal interrogation he exacted upon Beauty. *Where were you?* he demanded, arriving early one morning fresh from toothpaste and mouthwash, his double-ply curls wetly slicked down. *Where were you?* fingering one of Agremon's abandoned overalls, for the gardener, smelling danger on the wind, had long since fled and was staying with his cousin's brother-in-law in Observatory where grass grew prodigiously and swimming pools were as often in need of skimming, gardens of tending, as in Sugarbush Road. *Where were you?* demanded the Sergeant, over and over, until Ouma felt obliged to intervene. After all Beauty was the one who looked after her now, who fed her and turned her towards the sun in the morning and bundled her up when the wind dipped off the Drakensberg. *Damned,* if she was going to let Sergeant Visser chase her away with his agitation and his loud, stabbing finger.

Piss *off*, Visser, she told him, giggling.

You'll be hearing from us, Ma'am, he replied stiffly. We'll be in touch.

But she could tell by the way he rolled his eyes with that "don't tell me" look, snapping his notebook shut and stamping from the room that she would never hear from him again. So that was that. *Voetstoets* and *voetsak*, as Beauty exclaimed in the silence that followed the slammed door.

No, but don't you want to find the tsotsis? demanded Magda aghast. What about poor Benjamin, what they did to him? Magda began to cry.

Who was Benjamin, wondered Ouma, and what had happened to him? She no longer asked these questions aloud although one question stuck in her throat like a dry crust until she finally asked Beauty this question to clear her throat once and for all. To clear her head.

Beauty stared glass-eyed, unblinking.

But Madoom knows I must go to the eye doctor, she said. Madoom knows because Beauty asked her. Twice. And both times she said, Of course, Beauty. If your eyes make *eina* then of course you must go. Madoom gave me bus money and the afternoon off. Dr. Jacobs, in town. Why doesn't the Madoom telephone him?

If she had an appointment with the optometrist why the whole morning, most of the afternoon, did it take her to get back? hissed Magda standing over her mother's hospital bed in the private clinic that resembled a luxury hotel. There were fountains in the foyer and a restaurant with waiters who served hot meals on china plates. But such opulence didn't deflect Magda whose bewilderment at Ouma's failure to recognize her swiftly resolved into a pugilist's belligerence.

Because she's a liar, that's why, Magda continued, fists on her hips, breath heavy with outrage and bitter pear drops.

Because she's like all the rest of them, a liar and a thief! A cat-killer at heart! An assassin! What about poor Benjamin, you think she gives a damn what happened to him, *die arme man*? Mark my words, she'll be gone when you get out of here. Gone like a scone, thank you very much. *Ag*, why does that one even *need* to work when she has all that money now? Money from stolen goods, *sies*. Blood money!

Hsst hsst went the IV tubes threading into Ouma's veins. Magda cleared her throat and began to read from the story she'd cut out of the evening *Star*. Thirty-three-year-old Benjamin du Plessis, only son of the late popular leader, Lourens du Plessis, had been killed while attempting to save his grandmother who was attacked by home invaders last Thursday night. In the process he'd lost his life, been "summarily slaughtered," the papers reported but had not died in vain for the eighty-five-year-old woman was in serious but stable condition at the Rosebank Clinic.

That's good, said Ouma drowsily.

Beep, beep-beep BEEP went the heart monitor and presently a nurse bustled in to ask Magda to leave so that her patient could rest.

Blood money.

Ouma's blood had a wayward quality these days, the scrabbled veins in her forearms and the crooks of her elbows looked as if a child had tried to plain-purl the sleeves of an itchy winter cardigan around her own stump-ended arms. But when she returned to the house on Sugarbush Road where they said she lived, her wrists bandaged, her tattered skin hurriedly darned, Beauty was there to welcome her home.

Kettle's on, Madoo-oom, she called, helping Ouma into bed, plumping pillows then running to fetch the tea tray, holding a saucer to her lips so that she could sip at the strong rooibos with its aftertaste of river mud.

New wine, muttered Ouma, gumming the words against her palate, these words that seemed to come from far away. *New, new, new* ... until she gradually subsided.

Drink the tea, Madoom, Beauty admonished, before it gets cold, hnh?

That was the first cup of many more to come that Beauty poured down her throat in solicitous, breath-cooled mouthfuls while Ouma, who was still learning to control her bandaged stumps, helplessly allowed the tears to seep from her eyes and drip into the saucer.

But yes, Beauty was there when Ouma first came home from the hospital which meant, surely, that she was innocent of any participation in the burglary and its aftermath. So ha-ha to you, Sergeant Pisser, thought Ouma breaking into inconsequential giggles, an event that seemed to occur quite frequently; tears and laughter mere ripples that broke up the even surface of her days.

Ha-ha to *you*, thought Ouma watching innocent Beauty in her white doek with its bandage folds, her perfectly controlled hands that eased her Madoom into the shuddering world of convalescence and muffled pain. Those hands that flitted through Ouma's dreams like a pair of house bats judging distance by sound, those hands that bathed and washed and brushed and wiped, that coaxed, soothed, massaged. That tilted saucers of tea into a reluctant mouth, that scratched at hidden and embarrassing itches, that cupped themselves to catch falling objects: food and spoons, medicine and bedpans, an old woman pitched humiliatingly, unforgivably, off-centre by loss.

Yes, Beauty was there when Ouma first came home from the hospital, and Beauty was there still. Mornings after the gurgle of tea and ablutions had been accomplished and the complicated business of dressing had been achieved, Beauty would shoehorn Ouma out of her room and into the shaded sunlight beneath the syringa. Some days she'd sit with her, reading the newspaper aloud in a halting voice. Following the words with one slow finger as if picking out an unfamiliar tune.

The newspapers were full of stories about the Truth Hearings that were taking place all over the country. Re-con-cil-i-a-tion, read Beauty slowly, thinking that perhaps the country was waking up from its long years of amnesia at last. And just at the moment that Ouma had given up chasing memory in the same way that a dog, weary of stalking its tail, sighs once then settles down to the consolations of forgetfulness. Some days Beauty held a lit cigarette to Ouma's mouth, watching the other woman suck at the filter as her eyes wrinkled against the smoke. Strangely, at these times, Ouma reminded Beauty of one of her own babies and the unaccustomed tenderness helped to control the foot-tapping impatience she so often felt.

Tula-tula, Beauty cautioned as if she was herself the grizzling baby. *Tula-tula*, for as Mamma Thlali would have been the first to remind her, *Lefoku ga le boe go boa monoana.* Only the finger returns, not the word. Although, hmph, and here Beauty had to chuckle, in this case not even the finger would return. Poor Ouma.

One day Beauty's stepdaughter, Dhlamina, came to visit with her new baby and Beauty took her outside to where Ouma was sitting under her tree thinking to cheer up the old woman with the child. But the child was restless and Ouma was irritable although Dhlamina was always good humoured and didn't mind how many times she had to explain the origin of her son's name.

"Happy Africa" because he was born on Christmas day, she told Ouma kindly even going so far as to take out the newspaper clipping she carried with her everywhere. "Miracle Baby Born on Xmas Day," read the headline and underneath in two fat columns told about a domestic who'd given birth to the very first Christmas baby of the season, slapbang in her employer's flat. The part Dhlamina liked best, and this Beauty knew from much repetition, was how the new mother had courageously bitten through the cord with her teeth, *awah!* Meanwhile, the child's father had fainted from loss of blood—a bullet wound, the paper said but didn't bother to explain how a man could get shot in the middle of his child's birth.

Tcha, men! thought Beauty in disgust.

Dhlamina was still chattering away. Now she was telling Ouma about the beads that she and her good friend, Tuesday Dube, were stringing for the first ever Bead Art Project. No longer jewellery, no longer love letters for the stupid tourists but Art, hah, and what did Ouma think of that? The theme was to be—and here Dhlamina always raised her voice to a joyous shout—*Food, Yebo!* The Food of Our Ancestors, the Food of Our Freedom! Of course Tuesday Dube had herself decided upon the title and the idea and the political implications of such an idea but Dhlamina, who knew so very much about the preparation and enjoyment of actual food—but was she not well-suited to this extraordinary new Art?

So, Ouma, Dhlamina continued as the child reached up and twined his fingers in her braids, in one brief year, no even less, have I not become so many different things? A mother and a very excellent cook and now, *yoh weh*, even an artist. Wonders.

And indeed, she did, she shook her head in wonder, in innocent admiration at her manifold achievements but Ouma was no longer listening. Her eyes were unfocused and her bandaged wrists jerked spasmodically in her lap. Tilting her face into the sunlight she cocked her head as if she was listening for something else. But what was she listening for, Beauty wondered with some agitation.

What was Ouma listening for? The garden shifted and rustled under the feet of millions of insects. Crickets and grasshoppers agitated the wind, drawing stray breezes between their musical thighs and blowing them out again in a crescendo of chirps. The sound the crickets made was like a string of light bulbs going on and off all through the afternoon, *pop-pop-pop*, and towards sundown faster and louder, *popPopPOP*. This was the signal for the sun to dip west flooding the French windows with light, their golden surfaces swarming with reflected foliage.

But did Ouma stir, did she notice the mountain winds that blew into the city, cooling the garden in small mouthfuls as Beauty herself cooled the saucers of tea she held up to Ouma's lips? Did she notice the birds fleeing north with the jet planes or the krik-krak of the ghostly tire swing that sometimes started up again on quiet afternoons? When Beauty bustled out of the house carrying the old angora shawl to wrap around her shoulders it was clear that the angle of her head hadn't altered. One ear pressed against her shoulder as if cradling an imaginary phone, the other cocked to the blue bowl of heaven, she strained forward, listening.

Rothman was gone and that was for the best. Two days before the burglary he'd disappeared leaving no trace of his presence except for a small mound of pawpaw rinds on the ground near his pile of bricks. It was clear that Ouma didn't even remember his visit in the first place and this, too, was for the best. Certainly so far as the police were concerned and so far as they were concerned also, she, Beauty, was a loyal servant who remained to take care of Ouma in her sickness and old age. Only a skelm would leave now, a skelm, moreover, with the means to do so, Beauty reasoned. If that Sergeant Visser came around again he would see what such a one as Beauty was worth and he would be sorry, truly, for his ugly thoughts.

But Agremon was gone too, and this grieved Beauty.

Sala kahle, baba. He barely had time to say goodbye. Now all that was left of her lover was a pair of his old tennis shoes, laceless and down at heel, and Beauty had grown weary of throwing away the shoes of the men who'd once inhabited this house. Benjamin's old runners and his hospital moccasins, Rothman's fancy, brand new Nikes with their flashy trim and their thick soles. For some reason, Rothman had left these behind when he'd cleared out and Beauty had been swift to dispose of them before the police descended with their "what have we here?" and their "where is he now?," their questions and their threats.

Dawdling, half-dreaming, Beauty spent her evenings sketching on the wall above her bed, planning the layout of her house. Optimism unfurled in her. She was certain that come winter her little house would be standing foursquare and sturdy, Gideon "The Bone" Thandile of Thandile Construction proving, suddenly, more than obliging.

Soon, soon, she told Mamma Thlali. Mamma Thlali, who'd grown thin as a shank bone with fever that summer, merely nodded. Her skin was shiny with the effort of being pulled so tightly across bone and the bones themselves seemed sharper where they pressed against the surface of her skin, at the cheekbones and temples, at wrist and knuckle and ankle. At all these places—yes, and at the shiny rim of her pelvis too—the skin puckered and pulled like brown butcher's paper wrapped around a loose parcel of bone and gristle.

The kind of parcel that had once been delivered every Friday afternoon to the house on Sugarbush Road.

Dog meat.

Soon, soon, she told Mamma Thlali who didn't have to be a prophet to know what came next. For both women knew that whenever soon came wouldn't be soon enough. It was all too clear that Mamma Thlali wouldn't survive another season in the shanty. She was just too scrawny to withstand the cold come winter and there was no one now to draw water or carry paraffin, sugar, and maize meal from the village store. Worst of all her little patch of corn, melon, beans, and three good pumpkin plants that she had tended assiduously for so many years had fallen fallow at last. True, the neighbours lent a hand, a bucket of fresh water, but everyone had their own troubles and it wasn't in Mamma Thlali's nature to ask for assistance nor was it in Beauty's to rely on the good nature of others. *Tsie e fofa ka moswang*, Mamma Thlali tried to console the younger woman but Beauty knew that, unlike the wily locust, her frail mother-in-law couldn't keep flying forever. With or without a full stomach.

But, if Mamma Thlali's spirit was growing silent, her body railed on. Each hair on her head seemed to cry out *white!* and the bones in her back and shoulders urged *bend, bend!* Ah, poor Mamma Thlali whose voice was faltering but whose body continued, so eloquently, to speak. The lobes in her ears were empty now, no jaunty feathers or clinking keys adorned the stretched lobes and her fingertips moved constantly, squeezing and pinching as they had once mumbled together the tea leaves from the dented old tea cannister. Now those thin fingertips endlessly worked at gathering stray tea leaves into a little heap, twitching at her sides even in her sleep. Wordlessly Beauty took out a folded square of toilet paper to wipe away the water that seeped from Mamma Thlali's closed lids.

Soon, Mamma Thlali. Soon, she promised.

Sometimes Beauty felt as if she was going crazy. Sometimes the kidney-shaped pain at her side throbbed like a bad omen. Here she was trying to keep one old woman comfortable, coaxing life mouthful by mouthful down her indifferent throat while all the time the one to whom she was blood-knotted was crumbling to a handful of bone and dust. The last time Beauty visited she'd found her mother-in-law curled on her pallet, feverish with black-water sickness. Mamma Thlali was turned on her side in a sickle curve. Thin as a fruit paring, as the quarter moon, as a nail clipping. As the half smile on Ouma's listening face.

Soon, Beauty promised Mamma Thlali. Very soon.

Ouma was going to live forever. That rarest of creatures—sick, old, heart-broken—she was incapable of dying. Death had raided her life again and again, thieving all that was dearest, but her own flesh he would not touch. Some nights Ouma dreamed that she was a piece of tainted meat glowing in the dark with the phosphorescence of bacteria. So rife with swimming schools of trichinosis that not even a dog would touch her.

Some nights she was a corpse waking beside an unknown corpse. Unknown though he was, he flowered and died all through the night and in the morning the grotesque smell of roses confirmed that she herself, she Ouma du Plessis as she now knew herself to be called, was alive and indestructible.

Some nights Ouma heard a determined knocking at her front door:
Knock Knock!
Who's there?
Mister.
Mister Who? (Pulling open the door.)
Sorry, wrong number.
No matter how quickly she unlocked the door, trying to yank her reluctant caller over the threshold, he always evaporated in her hands—or at least the hands she'd once possessed and in her dreams, possessed still—and she was left clutching a button, a glove, a finger bone. It didn't surprise her that her dreams had turned into the kind of jokes that schoolchildren recited to one another.

She remembered nothing of the hours she'd spent crumpled on her bed although, little by little, glimmers of noise and light—the sound of a dog barking, a clock chiming, the cruel bite of nylon—flashed through her mind. But of her grandson—Benjamin was his name—she couldn't remember anything at all. Look, Magda would try, her eyes red-rimmed and her hands shaking as she showed her mother photo-graph after photograph.

Benjamin, your grandson, she'd begin—. Then she would be over-come by weeping.

Benjamin, your grandson, your grandson Benjamin...

Once or twice Ouma thought she recalled his face. But this face seemed to emerge luridly out of the past reminding her of the colour transparencies of muscle groups and blood flow that had fallen from a set of medical books as she looked on while Beauty packed her grand-son's remaining possessions into sturdy cardboard boxes. But once Beauty had accomplished her task she didn't seem to know what to do with the boxes and they remained piled up in his room at the top of the house.

Benjamin, your grandson, your grandson Benjamin...

Ouma thought, briefly, of offering the books and the boxes to the nice Indian fellow whose name she'd forgotten but who had turned up at the house shortly after the police arrived. A friend of Dr. Benjamin's, he'd said, said repeatedly, but the police hadn't believed him and took him in for questioning and the next time Ouma saw him (a police line-up at the Brixton Murder and Robbery Squad) he had the empty bal-loon face of a man who'd had the answers slowly leaked out of him. Ouma didn't think he took an interest in books anymore.

The remainder of the time Ouma listened.

She listened to the noise-mutter of the old house, to the legions of ghosts who seemed to throng through the rooms dancing and gossip-ing and clinking glasses and making toasts. She listened for the low-pitched rumble of the French windows and the clink of china, which meant that Beauty, bearing her tea tray, was approaching. She listened for the pick-rattle-tock of the shovels wielded by the workers who'd returned to do battle with the neighbour's retaining wall. She listened for the sound of summer retreating in the swallows flying north. She listened to Magda's ferocious accusations—that assassin! that ingrate! she maligned Beauty—between harassed preparations to move her mother into a Nursing Home because she mustn't stay with Beauty for one minute longer than was necessary. No, not a minute more. And yes, she sometimes listened for the guilt that would be audible, Ouma felt certain, like the rasp of a key in a locked door, behind the words that Beauty used to soothe and coax her.

Sometimes Ouma thought that her daughter's mistrust, as she'd sat by her mother's bed, had infected everything. Blood money! Magda had shrieked and Ouma tried in vain to remember if Beauty had ever before deserted her post. Eye-doctor or no eye-doctor, the fact remained that she'd left the house on Sugarbush Road early in the morning and returned only when everything of value had been carted off the premises or shot dead. Only what was unsalvageable, damaged, obsolete, remained. And Ouma.

Ouma remained.

But what could she do? Ouma needed Beauty, now more than ever. Without Beauty she was helpless, the bandaged stumps at the ends of her arms twitching and burning miserably. There would be no one to scratch phantom itches and real ones too, no one to polish her rings—the diamond solitaire, the spray of blood-rubies—that the tsotsis hadn't been able to wrench from her fingers. Once Groot Oupa had given Ouma these rings but to commemorate what occasion, what exalted state of love or approbation, she could no longer remember. Inside the house that, every night, swallowed its inhabitants down with a stern gulp of the burglar alarm, inside the room that overlooked the stoep and the veld beyond and the next door house where the fruit bats still swooped in the eaves, Ouma lay on her bed and listened.

Mostly, Ouma listened for the telephone. Not the everyday "is the madam in?" butcher's voice or grocery service. Not the daily "anybody out there?" inquiries that had once connected her to an ordered universe in the form of surveys, charitable solicitations, and political polls. Nor the more particular rasp of Magda's voice over the telephone lines that looped through the neighbourhood soothing the sparrows and starlings as they swung themselves to sleep between conversations. What she listened for was the sound of the dial tone clicking in her ear like a man swallowing his tongue. Like an automatic revolver choking on air.

Click-click.

Mister Death remembering his obligations.

Méira Cook

12

GOODNIGHT MOTHER

Click. It was summer and then it was autumn.

Deep blue veins pulsed through the sky and the wind burnished surfaces to a high gloss. Falling leaves clotted the drains and gutters of the northern suburbs in the months that followed. More leaves than anyone had ever seen before.

Leaves fell like hands in the garden of the house on Sugarbush Road. *New wine, old battles,* thought Ouma, the words forming and dispersing in her mind as if they were clouds in the brisk autumn winds. The syringa unclasped its waxy berries and released its glossy leaves and the ground beneath turned rotten. It was the last day of the season when she could reasonably expect to linger outside and already the chill had entered her bones.

Pick-rattle-tock, pick-rattle-tock, went the wind as the next door workers downed their shovels and blew into their palms.

Slitting her eyes against the wind Ouma watched the garden tilt, blow sideways, until it was connected to the house only by the little row of stitches fencing it in. On the property line where the neighbour's garden gate creaked, a little boy swung a latch between earth and sky. One blink and he was gone. One blink and he had returned, hand-in-hand with another child. Gingerbread children, they played together all through the afternoon, the white boy, the long-legged black girl, squatting at the outdoor tap or reaching with sticky fingers into the plum-darkness of fruit trees. Dusk fell slowly but with time to ripen. Leaves fell and then dusk.

Leaves fell like hands in the garden of the house on Sugarbush Road. At five, Beauty hurried out with the tea tray, flustered because she'd been held up on the telephone with an old friend of Mrs. Magda's.

Just returned from abroad, heard the old lady was attacked! Att*ack*ed?

She doesn't want to talk to anyone today, Beauty told her, deliberately snappish. But the phone continued to ring, setting her on edge with its empty jangle.

Ag, just tell her it's Mrs. Patrice. She'll remember me, *meisie.*

Yes, thought Beauty slamming down the receiver and pulling her doek into a tight indignant knot. For certain she will remember you, *tcha.*

Time for tea, Ouma, she called shuffling across the lawn.

The woman in the deck chair under the syringa had slumped to one side. She had leaves in her hair, upon her shoulders, and piled in runnels on her lap. Although she was already cold to the touch Beauty poured the first saucer and put it to Ouma's lips waiting, in vain, for the other woman to blow across the thin wrinkled surface.

Méira Cook

Acknowledgements

Grateful thanks to Chana Cook, Mark Libin, Maurice Mierau, Carolyn Swayze, and Joan Thomas. Thanks to the Canada Council, the Manitoba Arts Council and the Winnipeg Arts Council for generous funding that has allowed me to write this book.

The poem "This is our teacher" is by Ellen K. Kuzwayo in her beautiful book, *African Wisdom* (1998, Kwela Books). My gratitude also for her insights into Setswana proverbs. The city poet that I refer to is Oswald Joseph Mtshali and the poems I quote from are collected in *Sounds of a Cowhide Drum* (1971, Renoster Books). Finally, "Pregnant Woman" by Ingrid Jonker is included in her *Selected Poems* (1988, Human & Rousseau).

The city I describe, like all fictional cities, is both real and imagined. There exists, for example, a real Sugarbush Road in Johannesburg but it is situated in the southern rather than the northern suburbs where I have chosen to transplant it.